her boyfriend and an.......... g. You can contact
Andrea at her website: www.andrealaurence.com

New York Times and *USA TODAY* bestselling author
Barbara Dunlop has written more than forty novels for
Mills & Boon, including the acclaimed Chicago Sons
series for Mills & Boon Desire. Her sexy, lighthearted
stories regularly hit bestseller lists. Barbara is a three-
time finalist for the Romance Writers of America's
RITA® Award.

9112 0000 422011

Also by Andrea Laurence

Millionaires of Manhattan
What Lies Beneath
More Than He Expected
His Lover's Little Secret
The CEO's Unexpected Child
Little Secrets: Secretly Pregnant
Rags to Riches Baby
One Unforgettable Weekend
The Boyfriend Arrangement

Switched!
From Mistake to Millions

Also by Barbara Dunlop

Sex, Lies and the CEO
Seduced by the CEO
A Bargain with the Boss
His Stolen Bride
From Temptation to Twins
Twelve Nights of Temptation
His Temptation, Her Secret

Discover more at millsandboon.co.uk

FROM SEDUCTION TO SECRETS

ANDREA LAURENCE

THE TWIN SWITCH

BARBARA DUNLOP

MILLS & BOON

All rights reserved including the right of reproduction in whole or in part in any form. This edition is published by arrangement with Harlequin Books S.A.

This is a work of fiction. Names, characters, places, locations and incidents are purely fictional and bear no relationship to any real life individuals, living or dead, or to any actual places, business establishments, locations, events or incidents. Any resemblance is entirely coincidental.

This book is sold subject to the condition that it shall not, by way of trade or otherwise, be lent, resold, hired out or otherwise circulated without the prior consent of the publisher in any form of binding or cover other than that in which it is published and without a similar condition including this condition being imposed on the subsequent purchaser.

® and ™ are trademarks owned and used by the trademark owner and/ or its licensee. Trademarks marked with ® are registered with the United Kingdom Patent Office and/or the Office for Harmonisation in the Internal Market and in other countries.

First Published in Great Britain 2020
by Mills & Boon, an imprint of HarperCollinsPublishers,
1 London Bridge Street, London, SE1 9GF

From Seduction to Secrets © 2020 Andrea Laurence
The Twin Switch © 2020 Barbara Dunlop

ISBN: 978-0-263-27911-5

0120

MIX
Paper from
responsible sources
FSC™ C007454

This book is produced from independently certified FSC™ paper to ensure responsible forest management.

For more information visit: www.harpercollins.co.uk/green

Printed and bound in Spain
by CPI, Barcelona

FROM SEDUCTION
TO SECRETS

ANDREA LAURENCE

BRENT LIBRARIES	
91120000422011	
Askews & Holts	11-Dec-2019
AF ROM	£5.99

One

As weddings go, it was a nice enough one. Sawyer Steele hadn't been to many, but knowing his parents, it was probably an extravagant and expensive affair. Perhaps the greatest wedding ever held in Charleston. He wouldn't know the difference. It wasn't exactly Sawyer's thing. But his baby sister, Morgan, was celebrating her big day, so of course he was there to smile for pictures and eat cake. Not everyone could get shipped off to work a deal in China and miss it like Finn did.

It was probably strategy on Trevor Steele's part to have his most troublesome son out of the country for the event. Sawyer's twin was the one most likely to cause the bulk of their father's headaches. He could count on Sawyer and Tom, the oldest son, to attend and behave. As such, Sawyer had had his tuxedo dry-cleaned, his dark blond curls cut short and found a suitable date to bring with him. That was all that was really required of him tonight. Behave. Don't make a scene. Make sure Morgan is happy. Easy enough.

Now the event was starting to wind down. They'd eaten, said a million toasts, had all the requisite dances and cut into the towering ivory-and-gold confection his sister had chosen for her cake. A few more dances and they should be waving sparklers and seeing his sister and her new husband off to start their lives together. He was good with that. The bow tie he was wearing felt like it was getting tighter around his throat with each passing hour.

Glancing over, he noticed his date, Serena—a woman he'd met a few weeks earlier at a conference— eyeballing the people on the dance floor. He decided it was time to take her for a spin at last. Sawyer wasn't a dancer by any stretch, but he could manage a simple waltz for formal occasions. All the Steele children had been forced through junior cotillion to pick up some basic skills like that. They lived in the South, after all, and etiquette was paramount in the social circles he was forced into as one of the Steeles.

"Would you like to dance?" he asked Serena. The buxom blonde had chosen a low-cut, pale blue sheath dress that gave off some Cinderella vibes with her golden hair pulled up into a bun. She looked very pretty. At the same time, he just couldn't muster up much enthusiasm for her. She didn't have a very memorable personality. She actually reminded him of one of his mother's beautiful, priceless antiques. Lovely to look at, but mostly decorative.

His brother Finn preferred a sports car type girlfriend. Sexy, high performance and exciting to drive, so to speak. Those women were as high maintenance as the cars and likely to get Finn in trouble before too long.

Sawyer's ex, Mira, had been a Ferrari if ever he saw one. After that, he'd decided that maybe a roomy, luxury SUV was more his speed. Beautiful, adventurous, flexible, and if you took good care of it, it would reward your efforts for years to come.

But Serena looked so much like Mira that he instinctively wanted to call her by his ex's name, and had to stop himself each time. They looked so similar that his feelings about how things had ended with Mira may have been souring how he felt about Serena. Or maybe Serena just wasn't as much fun on the road as she appeared in the dealership.

"Sure, I'd love to dance," she said with a smile.

Oh well. There was nothing he would or could do about it tonight. He took her hand and led her to the illuminated dance floor, where at least twenty other couples were gliding along to a romantic old Sinatra song. He wrapped his arm around her waist and they started to sway slowly to the music.

It was then, with her pressed close against him, that he realized taking a woman to a wedding on a third date was way too soon. He had to bring a plus one, but it made things feel more serious than they were. They'd had drinks and dinner so far, and if this wedding hadn't come up, they might've gone to a movie. Maybe not even that, so he certainly didn't need her getting overly romantic notions when he didn't plan on a fourth date.

His gaze fell on a woman entering the ballroom. Even from this distance, she instantly captured his attention with fair skin that stood out against her black cocktail dress and bright auburn hair. She looked around the room, searching for someone. And then their eyes met. In an instant, it was like Sawyer had been hit directly in the gut. He'd never felt anything like that before. It was powerful. It made him forget all about the woman in his arms. At least for a moment.

Then he noticed the angry look on the newcomer's face and wondered if it wasn't attraction he was feeling so much as a woman's fury.

She moved quickly through the crowd toward him. Sawyer was frozen in place on the dance floor—unable to pull away from the hold the redhead had on him even though his brain was telling him to escape.

Then, at last, she arrived. "You skeevy little prick!"

The angry shout cut through the sounds in the ballroom like a knife. The dancers paused, and even the orchestra was startled into an awkward silence. Everyone turned to see the stunning redhead standing at the edge of the dance floor. Now she was only a few feet away from Sawyer, with her eyes still focused directly on him.

He'd thought for a moment that maybe he was in someone else's line of fire. He looked over his shoulder, but no one was there. Was she really talking to *him*? Shouting at him? That wasn't possible.

"Who is that woman, Sawyer?" his date asked.

That was a really good question. He'd never seen her before in his life. He certainly would've remembered a woman with hair like waves of fire and skin as flawless and pale as a porcelain doll. Even as angry as she was, he wanted to know more about her. Sawyer shook his head. "I have no idea. Can I help you, miss?"

"Can you help me?" she repeated bitterly. "Yes. You can hold still." The angry woman walked up to him and slapped him hard across the face.

He was too stunned to respond for a moment. He'd never been slapped before. Somehow, being hit by a stranger made it that much worse. She hadn't hurt him, not really. It just stung, but he could feel the emotion behind the slap. She'd wanted to hurt him, and for good reason. He just didn't know what that was.

There was a collective gasp as the whole ballroom seemed equally aghast, then a murmur as everyone started discussing what was going on. Out of the corner of his eye, Sawyer could see a couple brawny security guards his father had hired for the party making their way across the room to deal with the situation. Given that the last two events at the house had ended in a kidnapping and a bombing, respectively, it was a good move to have a little extra help in that regard.

"I'm going to have to ask you to come with us, ma'am," one of the guards, wearing a black suit and an earpiece, said.

The redhead hesitated for only a moment before she

spun on her heel and marched out of the ballroom with the two guards right behind her. She'd done what she'd come here to do, apparently.

Although he knew he shouldn't abandon his date to chase down the stranger, he had to go after the woman and figure out what was going on. "I'll be right back."

Serena nodded, and he jogged out of the ballroom and into the entry hall to see if he could find where security had taken the woman. Sawyer glanced around, catching a blur of movement out of the corner of his eye as the men escorted the woman out the front door.

He chased her across the marble entry and pushed past the guards as they came back inside without her. At the top of the front stairs, he looked down and saw the woman waiting for a parking attendant to bring her car.

"I told you to keep it close!" she shouted at one of the men his parents had hired to manage all the cars at the wedding. "This wasn't going to take long. Especially with those goons seeing me out after less than a minute." She nervously glanced over her shoulder, and that was when she spied Sawyer standing at the top of the stairs.

"Do you normally wear black to weddings?" he asked. Asking why she'd slapped him seemed like jumping ahead in a conversation he wasn't ready to wrap up so quickly. "Isn't that against the rules or something?"

She sighed and crossed her hands over her chest. "It was the only nice dress I had that still fit. No offense to your sister. Anyway, don't mind me," she said.

"Security has made it clear I'm not welcome, so I'm leaving. Go on back to your hot blonde. You've obviously moved on."

Sawyer took a few steps down the stairs to get closer, but out of arm's reach of the woman. He wasn't getting hit twice in one night. "I'm sorry, there's been some kind of mistake, I think. Do I know you?" The stinging welt on his cheek suggested that he did, but he was certain he'd never laid eyes on her before. She was stunning, even in the plain strapless black dress and simple makeup she was wearing. Her red hair shimmered in the moonlight, and fat curls cascaded over her bare shoulders.

No, he would remember meeting her.

"Are you serious?" She rolled her eyes, which were a dark shade of green like antique emeralds, and shook her head. "You ignored me for weeks after we got together, then when I finally track you down, you act like you have no idea what I'm even talking about. What? Are you going to tell me your evil doppelgänger slept with me, not you?"

Sawyer opened his mouth to argue, then stopped cold. Now it all started to make sense. Why hadn't he realized this sooner? Women slapped his brother all the time. Or at least they should. It might help things. "I think you're actually looking for my twin brother, not me."

"That's an even better excuse," she said.

"It's not an excuse. Ask anyone in the party and they'll tell you I have an identical twin brother. Most people can't tell us apart."

She narrowed her gaze at him for a moment. "So you're saying you're not Sawyer Steele?"

Sawyer stopped as he opened his mouth to answer. It was one thing for her to confuse him with his brother, but this was different. "No, I *am* Sawyer Steele. But I think you're looking for my twin, Finn Steele."

The woman turned to him with her hands curled up in fists at her sides. "Are you implying that I'm some kind of slut?"

His eyes grew large with surprise. Sawyer was usually pretty good with people, very diplomatic at handling bad situations, but he couldn't say the right thing to this woman for some reason. Her hair was as fiery as her temper, it seemed. "What? No, of course not."

"You just told me I don't know the name of a man I had sex with," she said, pointing at him accusingly.

"That's not what I meant." He held out his hands in surrender and slowly came down the stairs to stand on the brick patio where she was waiting. He hoped that she would take a minute to breathe and calm down. "People get my brother and me mixed up all the time, is all. I'm telling you I've never seen you in my life, so that's the only explanation that makes sense. What is your name?"

"Katherine McIntyre." She said it with an insulted tone, as though he should know her name. "I go by Kat, if that helps jog your memory."

Sawyer frowned. To be honest, the name did sound familiar, but he was certain he'd never seen her before, much less had sex with her. He glanced down over the tightly fitting black dress, which clung to her curves and stopped just above the knee to highlight her shapely legs. He was decidedly disappointed that she'd spent the night with his brother and not him. He wasn't entirely sure that he had a type, but Kat set off all the right bells and whistles. She was a bright red Lamborghini if he'd ever seen one.

When his face didn't light up with recognition, she continued speaking. "We met at the Charleston's Best awards at the aquarium about three months ago. We had a lot of champagne, we talked, and when we got tired of looking at fish, we got a hotel room and got... better acquainted." Kat looked at him with a pointed expression.

Sawyer didn't remember going to an event at the aquarium. Actually, he was certain he hadn't, although he remembered something was being held there a while back. That was it—he hadn't been feeling great that day. He'd gotten a stomach bug, but he was supposed to attend as the Steele family representative to accept their award while his parents were wrapped up in finalizing wedding details. He hadn't gone. In fact, he'd bribed his twin brother to go to the event in his place. Finn hadn't wanted to attend, either. Sawyer had been forced to give him his new Jet Ski in exchange for going to the party.

Damn it to hell.

The realization of what really happened washed over him like a wave. Sawyer brought a hand to his face and rubbed furiously at it in frustration. It had been years since Finn had done something like this. Maybe even since college. Back then, he'd liked to meet girls at bars and give them Sawyer's name instead of his own. He was never sure if his brother just did it for a laugh, or to keep the girls from tracking him down, but Sawyer had earned quite a reputation on campus without doing a single thing to get it. But now they were in their thirties. Thirty-three, to be exact. Way too old for this kind of childish bullshit.

"I think I know what the problem is."

"The sex was so amazing you blocked it from your memory because you knew you'd never experience anything that good again?"

His jaw dropped open for a moment, then he shook his head. He'd never been so jealous of Finn in his whole life. "Uh, no. I was supposed to attend that event, but my brother went in my place. Apparently he didn't bother to tell anyone he wasn't me."

"He was wearing a name tag that said Sawyer Steele," she argued.

Sawyer wasn't surprised. "Yeah. Knowing Finn, he just went with it and pretended to be me so our father wouldn't know I bailed on the party."

Kat stopped for a moment, her mind visibly racing to process what he was telling her. "And when he kissed me? When he got a hotel room? Wouldn't that have been a good time to mention that he wasn't really you?"

"A perfect time, and I have no idea why he didn't. Listen, I'm really sorry about all this. My brother is… the trickster of the family. If he were here right now, I'd drag him outside and make him apologize for lying, but he's actually in Beijing for business. He'll be there a few weeks more, but I'll be sure to pass along your message, slap included, when he gets back."

The redhead's bravado seemed to deflate as she listened to him talk. With her anger no longer aimed at Sawyer, she seemed smaller somehow. Almost petite compared to a moment ago. "So you're saying that the man I met was actually *Finn* Steele? I can't believe, after everything that happened, that he wouldn't tell me his real name."

Sawyer could believe it. Masquerading as his brother gave Finn free license to do what he wanted without consequence. "If you don't mind me asking, was it just a one-night thing between the two of you?"

She looked at him with conflict in her eyes. "Yes. That was the plan, at least."

That was his brother's style. Love 'em and leave 'em, regardless of what name he used. "Then I doubt he would bother to correct you if you thought he was me. In the end, what would it matter? It's just a one-night stand."

Kat's expression softened for a moment as she glanced down at the ground, her eyes hidden beneath her thick auburn lashes. "It does matter, Sawyer. That's why I've crashed this party even though it's obvious he doesn't want to see me again. It matters because I'm pregnant with his child."

Katherine McIntyre had never seen a man's face blanch to a ghostly white so quickly. Even at night, with the patio light behind him, she could see the blood drain from his face and his attractive tan fade. If he hadn't seemed so steady on his feet until now, she might worry that he was about to pass out.

She wasn't sure why he was so upset about the news. He wasn't the father. He wasn't pregnant. He hadn't just found out he'd slept with a lying cheat. She was the one having a terrible night. Sure, he'd been slapped by mistake and would have a lot of explaining to do when he saw his date again, but this was hardly his problem.

The valet brought her car around at last. "I'm sorry. It took a few times for it to turn over," he said.

Kat glanced to where the valet was waiting and then back at the dumbstruck Steele heir. "I'd better go."

He reached out to her, almost appearing to surprise himself as he did it. "Wait. Come back inside and we can talk some more."

She was tempted to say yes. There was a kindness in his eyes that beckoned her to climb the steps and chat with him. It was different than what she'd seen in those familiar eyes before, so his story seemed to hold up. While identical in appearance, the Steele twins were very different men. But talking made no sense when Sawyer wasn't the one she needed to talk to. At least about the baby.

A white Rolls Royce started up the driveway and the front doors of the house opened. People started pouring out onto the stairs. It must be time for the bride and groom to make their exit. Kat wasn't going to stay around for that. Even if her old Jeep wasn't in the way.

"I can't," she said. "But Saw—I mean *Finn*—should know how to reach me when he gets back to the States. Please have him call me." She reached into her purse and pulled out a business card. She'd given Finn one before, but it had likely ended up in the trash the next morning.

Sawyer glanced over his shoulder at all the people coming toward them and his jaw flexed with what looked like irritation as he reached to take the card from her hand. He sighed and nodded as he glanced down at it. "I'll make sure he calls you *before* he gets back. I'm actually going to phone and wake him up right now. He deserves it."

Kat nodded and walked around her Jeep to get inside. She told herself not to look in the rearview mirror as she pulled away, but she did it anyway. She watched Sawyer Steele as his gaze followed her into the distance. He was still watching as she turned out of the driveway and the big house disappeared from sight.

With a groan, she wrapped her fingers tightly around the steering wheel and pressed down the gas pedal. This was not how she had envisioned this night playing out. She'd just wanted to pin Sawyer—*Finn*—down to talk, the same as that first night. Pregnancy was not what she had been going for back then. Far from it. But now that it was done, she wanted to do the right thing and tell the father. If he wasn't going to return her calls, she had to find another way to reach him.

The idea was to locate him, pull him aside to talk, and take things from there. Slapping the father of her child hadn't been a part of her plan, but when she saw him dancing with that beautiful blonde, she couldn't help it. Between morning sickness and pure exhaustion, she'd been uncomfortable for the last few weeks. He could be uncomfortable for a moment or two himself.

Then she'd found out she'd hit the wrong guy and everything just unraveled. China. Her baby's father was in China and that was the least of her troubles. Her baby's father was also a "trickster" in his own brother's words, one who had no problem seducing a woman using his brother's name. That was not the kind of man she wanted in her child's life, but it was too late now. It was done and she would have to find a way to deal with the aftermath.

Kat slowly pulled into her narrow driveway and turned off the Jeep's engine. She looked over at the historic Charleston-style house she called home. Located in the heart of the Peninsula, it had always been enough for her. The twelve-hundred-square-foot structure was the perfect space for a free-spirited artist. It had plenty of light, the traditional piazza patio allowed her to work outside sometimes and, best of all…the place was paid for.

She climbed from her Jeep and went inside. Her little abode was no Steele mansion, but what was? To be honest, she really hadn't understood what kind of family she'd gotten involved with until she pulled into that driveway and got her first view of the house. The Corinthian columns, the whitewashed stone, the lane of old live oak trees dripping Spanish moss on the long drive to the house…it was like something out of a Southern gothic novel. In this day and age it was the kind of place that was usually a museum, or rented out for weddings and events. But no, the Steeles actually lived there.

Kat wasn't a stranger to money. Both her parents had been successful, her father a famous mystery writer and her mother a celebrated painter. They'd done well for themselves, and when they were both killed in a car accident, their estates and life insurance policies had supported Kat through art school and allowed her to be an artist herself without worrying about starving or working a day job. Yes, she needed a new car. And yes, the house probably needed a new coat of paint, but she didn't want for much.

She tossed her purse onto the couch beside a box of woodworking tools and wood scraps. It would go with her Monday morning when she went down to the District to work. The old warehouse-turned-artist-community was where she spent most of her days. She rented a studio in the building even though she had room at the house to work. Woodworking was messy, but being there was more about community and exposure than anything else. If she wasn't working there or selling pieces to folks strolling by, she was hanging out with the other artists, who had become her family since her parents died.

Honestly, losing that place would be like losing her parents all over again. And that was what she was facing. That was why she'd gotten all dressed up and gone downtown to that stupid awards ceremony the night she'd met Finn. Because she was going to lose it all to the wheels of progress and commerce.

Four months ago, the owner of the District passed

away and his children sold the building to a developer. The place would be gutted and renovated. It would remain an artist community—at least that's what the letters they all received said—but it would be more about selling than creating, by necessity. The rent would be tripling to cover the costs of the renovations and bring the place more in line with the new owner's vision.

Kat had the money to pay the rent at the new building, but most artists weren't so lucky. When the District reopened as a fancy, funky downtown venue for people to shop and be seen, most of the people she knew and loved would be long gone.

Walking up the stairs to her bedroom, she unzipped her dress and let it slip to the floor on the landing. Kat stepped out of it and turned sideways to admire her slightly rounding tummy in the hallway mirror. She'd just started to show in the last week or so. Her normally flat belly had begun to curve out, making her favorite jeans uncomfortably tight at the waistband. She'd told Sawyer the truth when she said this was the only dress she had that fit. Most formals weren't made of particularly forgiving fabrics.

Life didn't always turn out the way she expected it to. This baby was evidence enough of that. Kat had gone to that award ceremony to try and talk some sense into the District's new owner, Sawyer Steele. Instead, she was having his brother's baby.

Two

"You're a real piece of work, you know that?"

"What?"

As always, Finn's voice didn't betray even the slightest bit of guilt for what he might have done. There was only an edge of sleepiness, which was to be expected given the hour in China. At least where Finn was concerned. The average Beijing citizen was likely preparing to eat lunch by now, but his brother had still been asleep after a late Saturday night of high jinks that probably involved beautiful Chinese women and too much *baiju* to drink.

"Sawyer, you know I'm half asleep and half hungover. Why don't you just tell me what you think I've done wrong instead of making me guess. Then we can move straight on to you yelling, and I can take some ibuprofen and go back to sleep."

"You're not going back to sleep, Finn. And I don't *think* I know what you did, I'm certain of it. And it's a big one this time."

"I doubt that. You're prone to overreaction, like Father."

Sawyer swallowed an insult. He wasn't going to let his brother bait him. Finn knew how much he hated being compared to their father. Yes, they shared an affinity for keeping the peace and avoiding drama, but that was about it. "You know, when I gave you that Jet Ski for going in my place to the Charleston's Best awards, it was because I wanted the night to go smoothly."

"As I recall it did go smoothly," Finn replied. "I picked up a nice plaque for the company awards case, Dad didn't figure out you skipped, and I got a new Jet Ski. Win-win."

"Yes, well, that was because everyone at the party thought you were me. I thought we were past the childish identical-twin games, Finn."

There was a moment of silence on the line, but Sawyer knew it wasn't out of guilt. Knowing Finn, he was trying to figure out how to weasel out of getting into trouble.

"Okay, who told on me? There's no way you could know that I let everyone think I was you," he said at last. "It's been months since that party and there hasn't been a peep about it since then."

"Well, that's not entirely true. Apparently the red-head you seduced that night while you were pretending to be me has been trying to get in touch with you. Me. *Us*."

Finn groaned and audibly flopped back against the pillows. "The redhead. Yeah. That was a hell of a night, but I wasn't really interested in seeing her again. She's gorgeous, don't get me wrong, but she's not my usual type. She's too artsy and academic. She's more your type, I think."

That was true enough, but Sawyer wasn't interested in walking into the hot mess his brother had left behind. "Well, to be honest, I don't think she was wanting to see you again, either, but she doesn't have a choice."

Finn chuckled. "And why is that? She can't get enough of me? She wouldn't be the first."

"No, because she's having your baby, you thoughtless idiot. How could you not take precautions for a one-night stand? You know better than that."

"Whoa, whoa, whoa," Finn said, suddenly sounding very awake on the other end of the call. "My baby? The redhead is pregnant? Well, it can't be mine."

"Her name is Kat," Sawyer corrected with an irritated tone. For some reason it grated on him that Finn was starting a family with a woman whose name he couldn't remember. "And she says it's yours. Actually, she thought it was mine until I figured out what you did and got her straightened out."

"No, it's not my baby," Finn insisted. "Listen, you may think I'm stupid, but that is one area where I don't take chances. In all these years, I've never even had a scare. Nothing was different about my night with her. She's mistaken. It's someone else's baby."

Sawyer would've liked to believe that his brother took anything seriously, especially something like this. But he'd seen the pained look in those big green eyes. She believed her story, and he wanted to believe her. But belief and trust were two different things. "Are you sure? There were no rips, no slipups?"

"No, I'm telling you, I know how to use one properly."

"Fine." There had to be another explanation for why it failed. "Did you bring the condoms or did she?"

There was a pause as Finn lay in bed, likely sorting through his romantic memory bank. "Usually I do, but I remember I didn't have any on me that night. It was supposed to be a boring party, which is why I pretended to be you, to spice things up. She had the condoms."

That made Sawyer's stomach ache with worry. If Finn wasn't in control of them at all times, anything could happen. "That means she could've sabotaged them if she wanted to. Maybe poked holes in one."

"You think she got pregnant on purpose?"

Sawyer sighed and sat back in the leather wingback chair of the family library. He didn't know. Their father had raised them to be suspicious of women's motives. Getting pregnant was an easy way to weasel into the family, and more importantly, into their fortune. "I don't know. You know her better than I do."

"Hardly," Finn scoffed. "We flirted and looked at fish in the aquarium. I don't really know anything about…"

"Kat," Sawyer repeated. "Please remember the name of the woman who's carrying your child."

"*Might* be carrying my child," Finn corrected. "I'm not as convinced as you are."

"Yeah, well, until we know otherwise, you need to handle this situation as though it were true."

"Handle it how, Sawyer? I'm in Beijing. I couldn't even come back for Morgan's wedding. I can't just fly home in the middle of constructing the new manufacturing plant and deal with… *Kat*. Dad placed a lot of trust in me when he gave me this project. I can't screw it up or I won't get a second chance."

"And if Dad finds out that you've knocked up some stranger and walked away from the situation, it will be even worse."

Finn groaned aloud. "Please don't tell him until I have some time to think on this."

"You'd better think fast. He'll find out soon. She made quite a scene at the wedding tonight. Everyone will want to know what it was about."

"A scene?"

"Yeah." Sawyer's cheek still stung from the slap Kat had given him. "When you get back to Charleston, I'll pass her message along." He intended to hit his brother harder than Kat ever could.

"Does anyone else know?" Finn asked.

"No. I thought I'd tell you first, since she's been unsuccessful in telling you personally."

"Okay, good. Can we keep it that way for a while until I can figure out what I'm going to do?"

"I'll hold out as long as I can, but I'm not going to lie for you, Finn."

"That's fair enough. I'll give my attorney a call

and see what he recommends, then take it from there. Knowing him, he'll tell me to make a big opening offer, something she can't refuse, then she'll be happy and hopefully things won't escalate. I'll keep you posted."

"Fine. But one last thing before you go, Finn."

"What's that?"

Sawyer considered his words before he said them, speaking with slow, deliberate intention. "If you ever, *ever* pretend to be me again, I'm going to mess up your face so badly no one will be able to confuse us. Am I clear?"

There was a long silence before Finn answered. "Crystal."

The line disconnected and Sawyer slipped his phone into his coat pocket. By the time he stepped out of the library and into the grand foyer, he was surprised to find that the wedding appeared to be over. Once the happy couple left, things must have wrapped up. The guests were gone, the orchestra was breaking down and the caterers were bussing the tables. He glanced around for a blonde in a pale blue gown, but Serena was nowhere to be found.

Looking at his watch, he winced when he realized how late it was. So much for telling Serena he'd be right back. She'd probably given up on him long ago. And for good. For all she knew, he'd abandoned her on the dance floor and run off with some redhead. Serena deserved someone who couldn't get thoughts of her out of his mind.

Kind of like the feisty and mysterious Kat was on Sawyer's mind right now.

He strolled into the abandoned ballroom, heading

toward the wedding cake, or what was left of it. A few pieces were still sitting on china plates, waiting to be eaten, even as the caterers worked to disassemble and pack up the remaining tiers. He picked up a slice and carried it with him into the kitchen. After brewing a cup of coffee and slowly savoring his prize, he remembered the business card he'd thoughtlessly tucked into his breast coat pocket.

When he fished it out and looked down at it at last, a piece of the fluffy white cake caught in his throat. Sawyer coughed for a moment, fighting to breathe again. Then he picked up the card and reread the words that had surprised him so much the first time.

Katherine McIntyre, Artist.
The District, Floor 2, Studio 210

Suddenly he remembered why her name had sounded familiar. He hadn't lied when he said they hadn't met. He'd never laid eyes on her before. But she had emailed him, written him and called his office so many times in the last four months that his assistant had asked for a raise.

Kat was the voice of the District's resistance group. They were not happy about his plans for the building he'd purchased, and no amount of talking was budging either side of the argument. So far.

It was then that Sawyer was absolutely certain Kat's appearance at that party three months ago, and possibly in his brother's bed, was no coincidence.

Kat frowned at the misshaped hunk of wood in front of her. This was not her best work. Far from it. Honestly, it was crap. All she'd managed to produce was crap since the day she'd taken that pregnancy test and got a positive result. The creative zone had eluded her ever since then. She understood now why her parents had each been so protective of their work time and space. It was a fragile ecosystem, susceptible to imbalance when a sticky-fingered child was introduced to the situation.

That didn't bode well for her future work, but she refused to worry about it now. She would figure it out. And not the way her parents had. Locked office doors and nannies were effective, but not particularly warm and loving for a child who wanted nothing more than her family's love.

"So…" A familiar voice sounded from the entryway of her studio. "How'd last night go?"

Setting down her chisel, Kat turned to find one of her fellow artists and friends standing there in old overalls, fireproof gloves and a welding helmet. Hilda Levy rented the studio across from Kat, and despite the constant sounds of metal banging and sparks flying, she couldn't ask for a better friend to work nearby. That said, she also kept a fire extinguisher on hand in case her wood shavings and Hilda's blazing hot sparks collided.

"It went terribly," Kat confessed.

Hilda pushed her helmet up, exposing the laugh lines and quirky black cat-eye glasses she was known for. "Well, shit. What happened?"

Kat plopped down onto an old futon she kept in the corner of her studio, and Hilda followed suit. "Well, for one thing, I had the wrong guy."

Few things seemed to faze Hilda, but this caused her brow to knit in confusion. "What's that, now?"

"I didn't have sex with Sawyer Steele."

The older woman looked over the top of her glasses at Kat. "Then who the hell was it?"

"His twin brother, Finn. He just let me think he was Sawyer, for kicks or something."

"The plot thickens," Hilda said, as she leaned in with interest. "So did you talk to Finn?"

"Uh, no. After crashing the wedding and slapping Sawyer, I hightailed it out of there, after I found out the truth. I was so embarrassed by the whole thing, I wouldn't stay a moment longer. But I did find out that Finn is half a world away at the moment. So that complicates matters."

"Does it? I know I'm old, but I have heard tell of this fancy internet thing that lets people communicate around the world."

Kat rolled her eyes at her friend's deadpan commentary. "You're not old. And I'll talk to him. Eventually. Right now I'm still trying to wrap my head around the whole thing. I mean, I slept with the wrong guy. The whole reason I went to that stupid award ceremony was to talk to Sawyer. To try and convince him that his plans for the District would be detrimental to the whole art community."

"Not sleep with him," Hilda added.

"No, not sleep with him," Kat agreed. "That was... accidental. I went down in person to put him on the spot, because he wasn't returning any of my calls and I couldn't get past his stupid secretary. And it got us nowhere in the end, because not only did we never discuss his plans for the District that night, the man I met wasn't even the one who bought it."

"You didn't bring it up that night?"

Kat thought back to the dark aquarium, the blue tank lights and the dimpled smile that had lulled her into doing something stupid. "I tried. But whenever I did, he'd change the subject. Probably so I wouldn't figure out he wasn't Sawyer and had no idea what I was talking about." She groaned and dropped her face into her hand. "I'm such an idiot."

"You're not an idiot. You were swept away by a charming billionaire after drinking too much champagne. That's no crime. Personally, I'd love to make a mistake like that. It's been a long time."

Kat couldn't help smiling at her friend. Hilda always had an outlook on life that could pull her out of the dumps when she was wallowing there. She honestly wasn't sure how she would've gotten on after her parents died without Hilda. Without everyone here at the District, actually. Hilda was like her surrogate mother now. Except she gave advice like a girlfriend, not a mom. Since Hilda had never married or had kids of her own, maternal advice wasn't her strong suit. Or so she said.

"We need to get you some," Kat said. She was a little relieved to shift the topic off herself, even for a short time.

"Oh, Lordy," Hilda exclaimed. "That shop has been closed down for so long it would take more than a good dusting to get it up and operational again."

"I'm pretty sure it all still works. There's someone out there for you. And when you meet him, you won't be able to dust off that equipment fast enough."

"I'm not so sure," Hilda replied. This time when she spoke the smile in her eyes dimmed slightly. She was lonely. Kat knew it. Her smile and attitude tried to hide the fact, but Kat knew better.

"I've seen Zeke watching you work with more than a little appreciation in his gaze."

Hilda rolled her eyes and shook her head. "Zeke? You've got to be kidding me. He just likes my work."

"Are you sure?" Kat wagged her eyebrows suggestively. The older man was a sculptor with a studio on the other side of their floor. With Kat and Hilda at the back of the building, opposite the stairs and the restrooms, there was no reason for Zeke to be over on their side. But for some reason, he always seemed to be hanging around Hilda's studio. It couldn't be just because of her metalwork.

"No," she argued. "But even if there was more to it, I'm not interested."

"Why?" Kat challenged. Hilda had spent more than a few working hours over by Zeke's studio herself.

"Because he's a widower. His wife has been gone for a year now. Men his age don't date for love. They date because they can't function without a woman to cook and clean for them. I've avoided being someone's maid for fifty-eight years and I have no interest in starting now."

"You don't know what he wants until you ask."

Hilda sputtered for a moment before turning to Kat

with a disgruntled expression on her face. "Why are we talking about my love life? You're the one in the midst of a crisis."

"Thanks for the reminder." Kat pushed herself up from the couch and walked over to the table, where she'd left a bottle of water earlier. She took a sip and shook her head. "His brother said he'd get in touch with Finn, and hopefully, I'll hear something soon."

"And when you do hear from him, what exactly are you going to say? Have you decided what you want to do about the whole situation yet?"

Kat frowned. "Yes and no. My baby is my baby, end of story there. But as far as Finn and his role in our lives… I don't know. I just… My whole life I've had this vision of my future and my family. It includes marriage. It always has."

"From what you've said so far, this Finn guy doesn't really sound like marriage material."

"He's not. Absolutely not. But the more I think about it, the more I've come to realize that it doesn't change how I want things to be. I refuse to have my child born a bastard like I was. Regardless of the circumstances."

"Your parents were together for twenty-five years," Hilda argued.

"And never married," Kat added. For whatever reason, they'd never felt it was important to do so. She got the feeling they'd actually avoided it deliberately because of the stickiness of comingling their artistic property and intellectual rights. It was such a silly reason in her eyes.

"So what? It's not the 1950s anymore. Most of those

Karwashians aren't married and they're having kids left and right."

"It's Kardashian," Kat corrected, wishing she didn't know enough about them to notice Hilda mangling their name. "And some of them are married. But it's not the point."

"Then tell me what is the point, honey."

"I want my child to have a family."

"You hardly know this guy."

"Maybe it's better I don't. Maybe we should just jump in with both feet and see what happens. It's possible we only stay married a year. Or we barely make it past the baby's birthday before we call it quits. I can't tell you how it will end up. But I can't help but think it's the right thing to do for my baby."

"I'm not sure the Steele family is going to be as receptive as you're wanting them to be. They have more money than the state of South Carolina. Even if Finn agrees to marry you, there's going to be lawyers involved at every step. Prenuptial agreements. Custody arrangements. It's not going to be the least bit romantic."

"I don't care about romance and I don't care about the money. I have enough of that. I only want my baby to have what's his or hers. I don't need anything other than a father for my child. I want better for my baby than I had."

"Okay." Hilda gave a heavy sigh. "If you're determined, then I wish you the best of luck marrying into that family. As for me," she said, pushing up from the low futon with a groan, "I've got to get some work done. The clock is ticking on our time here and it's going to be a nightmare hauling all my scrap metal away."

Kat looked around her own studio, feeling guilty that she could afford to stay when others couldn't. She'd still have to pack up and move out for a few months while they renovated, but she could come back. "You're not moving out for good, Hilda. I promise. No matter what happened between Finn and myself, I still intend to pin down that jerk Sawyer Steele, and get him to change his mind about the District. Of course, now he probably thinks I'm just some gold-digging slut and won't take me seriously."

Hilda's gaze shifted over Kat's shoulder as her eyes widened behind her thick black glasses. She bit at her lip and gently shook her head.

Kat realized she was standing with her back to the entrance of her studio. "He's right behind me, isn't he?"

Hilda nodded and Kat groaned aloud.

"I might be a jerk, but if it's any consolation," a man's voice said from over her shoulder, "I don't think you're just a gold-digging slut."

Three

Kat turned slowly to look at him and he couldn't wipe the smug grin from his face. Sawyer's timing couldn't have been better if he'd tried. He'd caught her in the middle of a tirade about him, and that was fine, because he had a few choice words for her, too.

Most of those words dissipated from his mind when she was facing him. He thought she had looked beautiful at the wedding, but it didn't hold a candle to how she looked today. Her copper hair was twisted into a messy bun, with two pencils holding it in place and sawdust, like glitter, sprinkled over the top. Her face was devoid of makeup, unless you could count the smear of white paint on her cheek and a splatter of yellow paint dots across her forehead. She was wearing a tank top and a pair of denim cutoff shorts that fell at the perfect length to highlight her firm, smooth thighs.

He expected her to say something, but she stood motionless, obviously in shock at his timely appearance. Before he could say anything else, the older woman standing nearby opted to excuse herself.

"I'll let you two talk. I've got a piece to finish and five years of crap to pack up." She looked pointedly at Sawyer as she went by.

He was used to that by now. He was the big, bad real estate developer out to destroy all they held dear. At least, that was what most of the voice mail and phone messages seemed to say. Sawyer wished he could convince them that he was trying to help, but they would never see it from his point of view. They either didn't know or didn't care that the building was crumbling around them. The electrical was old and not up to code. The plumbing was putting out rust-colored water and the pressure was almost useless. The freight elevator barely passed inspection. Before long, the District was going to be condemned and they would all lose their precious studio community.

Sawyer intended to fix things. Making those fixes required a few big concessions on the tenants' parts: one, that they move out temporarily for the work to be done, and two, that their rent increase to cover the costs. When it was all said and done, he wasn't renovating this place out of the goodness of his heart. He was a businessman. He saw the potential of the District. With some improvements, it could be not only a studio community, but a place where people wanted to come. Customers. Those people would spend money.

It was a win-win in his eyes. He wished he wasn't the only one who saw that his plan was necessary to save the institution as a whole. Yes, some people might not be able to afford the rent at the new location, even with increased sales. But he'd learned a long time ago that he couldn't make everyone happy, so he'd stopped trying.

He watched the older woman leave, then turned back to where Kat was standing, red-faced, in front of him. "You know, when we first met, your name sounded familiar, but I didn't connect the dots. It wasn't until I looked at your business card." He fished it from his pocket and held it up. "Then all the pieces came together."

"What are you doing here, Sawyer?" She wiped self-consciously at her face, but the paint stayed stubbornly in place. "Have your lawyers put together some payoff package to make me go away?"

Sawyer smiled and turned toward the collection of works in progress she had scattered around her studio space. "I'm not sure what the lawyers have in mind. Or if anyone has told them yet. I told Finn he had to deal with all that." He stuffed his hands into his pockets and strolled over to admire an intricate carving of an owl on a nearby table. It was the size of a large watermelon, with big, lifelike eyes and feathers etched so delicately it seemed he could reach out and they would feel real. She was a very talented artist.

"So you've told Finn?"

He pulled away from the owl and turned to see Kat biting anxiously at her lower lip. He wanted to run his thumb across that same lip to protect it from her abuses. Instead, he kept his hands deep in his trouser pockets where they belonged. "The minute you left. I couldn't wake him up fast enough with the good news."

"He hasn't reached out to me."

Sawyer wasn't surprised. "I wouldn't let that worry you. I'm sure he wants to get his ducks in a row before he calls. And he has very unruly ducks. They're basically squirrels on a sugar high. It may take some time."

"I'm kinda on a set time line here," Kat said, with one hand protectively covering the slight curve of her belly. "I hope he doesn't take too long, because like it or not, his baby is going to be here come winter."

"I'm sure he'll be in touch. Once the shock wears off. He really wasn't expecting to hear from you again."

"Well, considering he didn't give me the right name, I'm not surprised."

"Yes. I think that's the last time he'll play that game, though. He's far too fond of his good looks to risk them by pretending to be me again. I do have to wonder, though."

"Wonder what?"

Sawyer turned and looked at Kat, who was standing a few feet away. He could easily imagine her in some slinky dress, all dolled up to go to the party and hunt down Sawyer Steele. She intended to get her way, no matter what it took. "It made me wonder how the night would've ended if it had been me there and not Finn."

To be honest, the thought had haunted him the last few days. She had come to the party to see him. To talk to him. Perhaps to seduce him. And somehow the spoils went to Finn instead. Just like usual.

"I'm sure it would've ended very differently," Kat said.

"Would it?" he asked with an arched eyebrow.

"I think so. For one thing, you probably wouldn't have dodged my questions about the District and we could've had a real dialogue about it. And for another, you don't have Finn's...*charisma*."

"Is that what you call it?" Sawyer chuckled. "I typically describe that skill set a little differently. I'm sure that played right into your hands, though."

Kat narrowed her gaze at him, her nose wrinkling in thought and a line creasing between her auburn eyebrows. "What's that supposed to mean?"

"I mean, if you went to that party with the intention of doing whatever it took to get your way... Finn made it easier. I would've been a more difficult mark."

"Wait a minute," Kat said, her hands held out defensively. "Are you suggesting that I deliberately went to the party to seduce you? As though I could be so good in bed that you would just change your mind about the District renovations and do whatever I asked?"

Sawyer shrugged. "I don't know what you were thinking. It does seem pretty convenient, though, the more I think about it. Nothing you were doing was yielding any results. If angry calls and letters didn't work, sympathetic news articles didn't work, protests didn't work…why not try a little honey instead of vinegar?"

"I did not go to that party with the intention of giving you any…*honey*! I went to that event to talk to you, because you wouldn't return any of my calls. It was the only way I could think of to pin you on the spot and make you listen to my side of the situation."

"And yet somehow you ended up sleeping with the man who claimed to be me. Sounds like you're quite the overachiever."

The steam was practically coming out of Kat's ears, and he found he quite liked her when she was angry. The flushed cheeks, the bright eyes, pursed lips…he imagined it wouldn't be much different from how she'd look in the throes of passion. He could just envision her auburn hair across the pillowcase, her sharp nails digging into the flesh of his back…

"Of all the arrogant, insulting things you could say!" Kat sputtered for a moment, at a loss for words before she shook her head. "I was a damned fool to go down there that night. A fool to think that you could be reasoned with. All you rich people care about is your bottom line. The people here are just walking, talking rent payments to you. You don't give a damn about what this place means to the tenants here. You don't care about the community that's grown here over the years, or how you're going to destroy it to make a buck!"

Her anger suddenly wasn't so attractive anymore and she was starting to rub Sawyer the wrong way. She wanted to know why he was doing what he was doing? Well, he was going to tell her. He closed the gap between them and spoke with cold, quiet anger, mere inches from her face. "And you don't seem to care that the rent I'm currently collecting barely covers the utilities for this place. There certainly isn't enough left over to do any repairs and it's falling down around you."

Sawyer pointed to the peeling plaster overhead. "That's going to come crashing down on you sooner or later. The sewer lines are going to fail and flood the ground floor. That wood lathe of yours could overtax the electrical circuits at any moment and set the building on fire. Who is going to fix that? Who is going to pay for all that? The previous owner just ignored the place and cashed the checks. Sure, rent was cheap, but there's a cost, and the building has paid the price for all of you. It's your turn to pay up, and no amount of sweet-talking or seduction is going to change that."

Kat was at a loss for words. It didn't happen very often, but Sawyer seemed to be able to render her mute. Especially when he stood this close to her. Yes, his words were icy cold with restrained anger and frustration, but she could feel the heat radiating off his body. His words were just static noise in the background, with her pounding heart drowning out everything but its sensual rhythm. She knew she should take a step back, reclaim her personal space and counter his argument with more pointed words, but she couldn't make herself do it. Her body wanted to move nearer and close the gap between them.

It was ridiculous. Foolish. But she couldn't help but be confused whenever she was around Sawyer. She was haunted by memories of a night in a downtown hotel room…memories of a man who looked like Sawyer. A man she'd thought *was* Sawyer. Somehow it felt like the most natural thing in the world to reach out and touch him like she had before. Her libido couldn't tell the difference between the two identical men.

But her brain knew. And it knew that was all a lie. Those memories, that man… It wasn't Sawyer she remembered. And no matter how familiar those dark eyes or that dimpled smile, it wasn't the same person. This man was a stranger. A stranger who intended to take away everything she held dear to make a buck. Sure, he wanted to make necessary improvements, but the fancy, downtown art scene he had in mind was a far cry from what the tenants truly needed. The necessary repairs weren't the changes driving the rent out of the realm of possibility for most of the artists. It was the coffee shop, the concert venue, the paved parking lot and the high-end landscaping with dancing fountains.

It was a great response, exactly what she wanted to say, but the argument eluded her when Sawyer gazed at her this way. It wasn't how Finn had looked at her. And yet it was the way she'd always wanted a man to look at her. Like he wanted to consume her, body and soul.

Even in his anger, Sawyer seemed almost as though he was on the verge of kissing her. A part of her wished he would, even if just to end this fight.

Okay, not *just* to end the fight.

Kat's gaze met Sawyer's. In the quiet stillness between them, they seemed to be even closer now. She could feel his breath softly brushing over her skin. Something had changed in the silence and it seemed that he noticed it, as well. It was almost an electricity.

"Aren't you going to say anything?" he asked.

"What do you want me to—"

That's when his lips pressed into hers and a warm tingle shot down her spine. His heat spread quickly through her veins, making her aware of every feverish beat of her heart. Kat didn't pull away from Sawyer. She couldn't even if she wanted to. Her body leaned into him instead, craving more even though it was the last thing she needed right now.

His arms slipped around her waist and pulled her tight against the hard wall of his body. It was then, with every inch of her curves molded against his hard angles, that Kat knew for certain appearances were deceiving. For one thing, Sawyer might look like Finn, but he certainly didn't kiss like him. His twin might have the reputation of being a playboy, but Sawyer had obviously gone for quality over quantity where women were concerned. As he deepened the kiss, his tongue slid leisurely along her bottom lip as though he had all the time in the world to study every inch of her. It elicited a groan of pleasure deep in Kat's throat— a sound she didn't even know she could make until that moment.

This buttoned-up businessman was hiding a skilled lover beneath that boring exterior. And the longer he touched her, the more she wished that it really had been Sawyer Steele in her bed that night three months ago.

But it wasn't.

The thought that was like a lightning bolt of reality. What the hell was she doing? Kissing Sawyer Steele when she wanted to marry his brother?

It took every ounce of determination she had, but she pulled away from his embrace and stepped back out of Sawyer's sphere of influence. Once she got some distance between them again, it was easier to control her impulses and regain what little composure she had left.

This was the wrong Steele twin. They looked alike, but they acted very differently, and like it or not, Sawyer was not the one she needed in her life. Finn was her baby's father. Kissing his brother did nothing but muddy the waters and make an already complicated situation even more so.

Kat covered her lips with her hand, hoping she could somehow wipe away the tingle that lingered there from Sawyer's kiss. It didn't work.

"Did I do something wrong?" Sawyer asked, seeming almost startled by her sudden retreat.

No. Somehow he'd done everything right. Yes, Finn was charming, but Sawyer had different powers that Kat couldn't resist. "No, you didn't. I just… I think that was probably a mistake."

She watched Sawyer's jaw flex and tighten as if he was holding something in. She wished he would just say it, but he didn't seem like that kind of man. He knew when to use restraint, unlike his twin, who did or said whatever he wanted whenever he liked.

His gaze followed her hand as it dropped protectively to her belly on reflex. Then his eyes squeezed shut for a moment and he nodded. "You're right. I overstepped."

"You didn't. We both—"

"No." He held up his palm to halt any further argument from her. "It's my fault. You're having my brother's child. There's no excuse for my behavior."

"And *my* behavior is okay?" she asked. It had been only a moment since they kissed, and her memory still served her pretty well. Whether or not she should've been an active and enthusiastic participant, she was.

"It's not your fault. You were attracted to my brother, obviously. I look exactly like him. I can imagine it's confusing. It's an easy mistake for you to make in the moment, feeling like you're attracted to me when you're not." Sawyer stuffed his hands in his pockets and took a step backward.

"I'm not so blinded by desire as to not know who I was kissing. You two don't look exactly alike," Kat argued.

Sawyer hesitated a moment and shook his head. "We're identical twins."

Kat shook her head in turn. "Maybe genetically, but there are subtle differences. You're mirror images of each other. Your dimple is on the opposite cheek from Finn's. And your eyes..." Her voice drifted off. "There's something there that I didn't see in him."

She wasn't sure what it was yet. He was the more serious, responsible brother, but that wasn't it. Beneath all that there was a kindness in Sawyer's eyes. A softness when he looked at her that faded when he looked at anyone else. Finn's eyes had reflected only desire. At the time, that had been enough. Now that she was hoping for a future and a family with Finn, she wished she would see more when she looked in his eyes.

More like she saw in Sawyer.

That was a dangerous thought. There was no way to go back in time and choose a different brother. No way to go back and stop this whole pregnancy from happening to begin with. She had made her bed, as her mother used to say. Now she had to lie in it. With Finn.

"I'd better go," Sawyer said, as though he'd heard the thoughts in her head.

Before Kat could say another word, Sawyer Steele turned on his heel and vanished from her shop, leaving her more confused than she'd been when he arrived.

Well, that hadn't gone the way he'd intended. It had started out well enough, but kissing Kat was one of the dumbest things he'd ever done. This woman was his nemesis at the District. She was having his brother's baby through potentially nefarious means. She couldn't be trusted.

And yet, he'd done it anyway.

Sawyer walked quickly out of the building, trying to ignore the disgusted looks from the tenants as he went by. They knew exactly who he was with his expensive suit and his dark sunglasses. He was the one who was ruining everything.

As he stepped outside into the summer sun, he could finally breathe again. As hot as it was in the parking lot, the old building was stifling without air condition-ing and only a few old windows for a cross breeze. He didn't know how anyone could work here in the sum-mer. That was number one on his list of things to fix, and if he was a tenant here, he'd be happy to pay more not to sweat to death.

As he climbed into his Audi, his cell phone rang and his brother's number came up on the screen. "Finn," he said as he answered.

"Twin," Finn responded. "How are things going at home?"

"Hmm…let's see… Our parents are badgering me relentlessly about the mystery woman at the wedding. Grandma Ingrid is home from Europe for good. Oh, and it turns out the mother of your child is the one try-ing to shut down my District renovations."

"Really? That must've been why she kept asking me about it that night. I dodged the questions because I didn't know the answers."

It would've been nice if his brother had bothered to mention the inquisitive woman from the party three months ago. "Yes, apparently she came there looking for me to talk about changing my plans. Sleeping with you was just a…"

"Bonus?" Finn suggested.

"I was going to say *mistake*, but use whatever word you like."

"I've been talking to my lawyers. They recommend coming in with a high offer to keep things quiet, so they're working on a package now."

Sawyer was surprised his brother was moving

so quickly with his attorneys. He'd asked his future brother-in-law, Harley Dalton, to run a background check on her, but the report wasn't back yet. "This seems awfully premature. Are you sure you want to do that before you know if the baby is yours?"

"Well, actually, that's why I'm calling. I could use your help. They can do a prenatal paternity test with a blood sample from the mother and the father. But to speed things along, it would help if you could pop by the lab and do that for me."

Sawyer shook his head in the empty cab of his SUV. "Are you serious?"

"Come on, for a standard paternity test, we share all the same markers as identical twins. It's not a murder case, it's a baby, so unless you've slept with her, too, your DNA would be enough to determine if I'm the father. Doing the testing in China and trying to send the sample to the States would be a hassle and would take forever. This can't wait until I get back either."

"Finn…"

"Please. I've got an appointment all set up if you can swing by. I'll text you the lab address. Just donate some blood and I'll handle the rest. I just need to know for certain before I tell Mom and Dad."

Somehow Sawyer doubted that Finn would be handling much of anything. "When is the appointment?"

"This afternoon at three."

Sawyer glanced at the console of his car. It was almost two, so Finn expected him to drop everything for him, per usual. "You have no idea how much you owe me for this, Finn."

"If it's a boy, we'll name him after you," Finn offered brightly.

In irritation, Sawyer hit the button to hang up the phone. "You're welcome," he snapped as he drove the car out of the District parking lot and headed for the lab.

Four

Kat came home to find a FedEx package on her door-step. She hadn't ordered anything, so when she picked up the envelope, she eyed the return address with curiosity.

Carson, Turner and Leeds. Attorneys at Law.

Lovely. She'd been expecting this package since someone from the lawyer's office called and asked her to take a paternity test. She'd complied but thought perhaps she might actually *speak* to Finn before she received anything else from them. Guess not.

With a sigh, she carried it in and let the hand-carved wooden door to the piazza swing shut behind her. Dumping her things onto the nearest patio chair, she sat down on the chaise and looked at the envelope again. Taking a deep breath, she pulled the tab to open it and removed the contents.

A thick pouch of paperwork slid out, clamped together with a heavy-duty binder clip. Her eyes scanned the cover letter, but it was what she expected. Finn's first volley in the legal battle ahead. She could've saved him a lot of time if he'd just called her instead of running to his attorneys at the first word of a child.

Flipping through, she eyed the paragraph about the paternity test results—surprise, it was Finn's baby. Then she moved on to the topics of shared custody arrangements, monthly financial support, a trust fund for the baby, and even an offer to purchase and maintain a residence for them both. To say that Finn was being generous was an understatement. She was stunned by the numbers she was seeing. He wasn't a man to walk away from his responsibility, but was the kind willing to pay enough to keep everyone quiet and happy. This was more than she ever expected. And absolutely nothing she wanted.

Maybe she was stupid and naive to hope for more, but she did. Not just a weekend daddy and a big check for her child. She wanted a family. A real, legitimate family. If she had to choose her future husband from a catalog, no, Finn wouldn't be the one she would pick, but she had to play the hand Fate had dealt her.

Hearing her cell phone ringing inside her purse, Kat tossed aside the paperwork with disgust and reached for it. It wasn't a number she recognized, or even a local number, but she answered, figuring a telemarketer might be a welcome distraction.

"Hello?" she answered with a heavy sigh.

"Um, Katherine?" a man's voice asked with uncertainty. "Kat?"

"Yes?" It wasn't a telemarketer. They never called her Kat. Only her friends and family called her by that name. She pulled the phone away from her ear to look at the number again. It wasn't local. It wasn't even a US number, from the looks of it.

"This is Finn Steele," she heard, as she pressed the phone back against her ear.

"Oh."

That wasn't what she expected to say. Or what she'd planned to say once she finally got in touch with the father of her child, but that was what came out. "I got the love letter you sent."

"The *what*?"

"The offer from your attorneys."

"Oh." Finn chuckled nervously. "I was hoping it hadn't arrived yet. I wanted to talk to you first and let you know it was coming, but my lawyer is more efficient than I expected for someone paid by the hour."

"I'm sure he has a standard template he uses for all his rich clients and their pregnant mistresses." Kat couldn't help the bitter tone from leeching into her voice. She even winced at the sound of it, compared to Finn's friendly, conversational tone. No matter what, being ugly to him wouldn't help matters. Slapping Sawyer certainly hadn't. "I'm sorry," she stated, when he didn't respond. "It's the pregnancy hormones. And calling me just as I was reading the legal paperwork didn't tip things in your favor."

"What's wrong with it? Patrick said he was going to put together a very generous offer."

"It was. Very generous. Maybe too generous, under the circumstances. I can't help but feel like you're trying to sweep us under the rug. You can't write a check and make this all go away, Finn. This isn't a fender bender. It's a child. Our child. And it deserves a family."

There was a long silence on the line. Kat was tempted to keep talking, but stopped herself. It was the truth and he needed to hear it, understand it, and respond accordingly. So she waited for him to answer.

"I'm sorry. You're right. You're not a dirty secret. You're carrying a Steele grandchild. It's not an ideal situation, but it's not the end of the world, either. I just wish I wasn't in China right now. There's only so much I can do from here. But I'm going to talk to my parents. I'll tell them everything tonight and I'm sure they'll be eager to meet you as soon as they can."

"You want me to meet your parents? Without you?"

"Yeah, sure. You'll be fine. You'll get to know everyone and by the time I get back stateside, I'm sure you'll feel better about having a family that accepts our child as one of their own."

That was nice, but that wasn't exactly what she had in mind. "I was actually thinking of something a little bit more legally binding on the family front, Finn."

"I can assure you that the offer my attorneys sent you is the best for everyone, Kat."

"Not for me, Finn. I want to get—"

"You don't want to marry me," he interrupted.

Kat was stunned into momentary silence by his abrupt response. She was expecting him to give her a reason why he couldn't or wouldn't marry her, not the other way around. "I don't?"

"No. Listen, you've spoken to my brother. I'm sure he was all too eager to tell you about all my flaws. He revels in them."

"I'm not concerned with your flaws," Kat argued.

"You should be. There's a lot of them. I know that in your head getting married and raising this family together is the practical, responsible thing to do. But I am neither practical nor responsible. Ask anyone who has ever met me. Marrying me would…not be the fantasy you have in your mind."

She could hear Finn sigh on the other end of the line before he continued. "This isn't the old days where we have to marry to cover up the fact that we sinned together. I doubt many happy marriages resulted from that practice back then, and it wouldn't result in a happy marriage now. If I thought that I would be a good husband and father, I would get down on one knee the moment I saw you again. But I can't offer what I don't have. What I can offer you is support, and my last name for our child. He or she will be a Steele, and will be raised as such. You can meet my family and be as involved with them as you'd like. But believe me when I say you don't want to compound this mistake with marriage."

It was a good argument. And Finn sold it well. And if marriage hadn't been such a firm fixture in Kat's mind since she was a small child, she might even be swayed by his words. But what Finn didn't understand, what none of them understood, was what it was like to grow up with parents who weren't married. It wasn't the fifties then, and it still made her feel different. As though she wasn't good enough. Kat never wanted her child to feel like that. Especially just because the father was being selfish.

"Are you sure you're not just saying all this because you don't want to get married?" she countered.

"Of course I don't want to get married!" he shouted over the line. "That's one of the reasons I'll be so terrible at being a husband. Kat, I am not the marrying kind of guy. I've never even considered the possibility. I love the ladies too much to pick one for the rest of my life. I've always known this about myself, and that's why I've always tried to be very careful where contraception was concerned. I never wanted to put myself or a woman in this position, and until now I've been successful. I don't know why it happened this time, but I can't change it, or me. I'm saying this for your sake, for our child's sake and for my own sake. None of us will be happy if we get married."

"Let's table that discussion for now," Kat said. "What about being a father? Let's set aside talk of child support and trust funds and discuss what being a father really means to you. Do you intend to be involved?"

"Absolutely. I believe my lawyer submitted a request for visitation every other weekend, alternate holidays and a week during the summer. That seemed to be pretty standard."

Kat sighed. "And what about the rest of the time?

What about school plays and ball games? Recitals, science projects? Playing in the park? Sitting up with him or her all night when our child has a fever and can't get comfortable?"

"To be honest, I didn't expect you to want me to be that involved. I'm willing to do as much or as little as is needed. I work long hours, and travel a lot, too. I may not be able to make every after-school game and class party. But if you really need me to be there, I will do what I can."

At this point, his words felt like a win to Kat. It wasn't all that she wanted, but it was a big step for their first talk. Maybe once he returned home from China, they could spend more time together. There was still a chance he might change his mind and want to be more involved in not only their child's life, but hers, too. She wouldn't give up hope yet.

"Look over the paperwork, Kat. It doesn't cover everything, but it does cover a lot. We can talk about it more in a few days. In the meantime, I'm going to talk to my parents. Keep an eye out for a mushroom cloud over Mount Pleasant. I'll talk to you soon."

Kat hung up the phone and leaned her head against the back of the seat. After everything that had happened the last few days with Sawyer and now with Finn, she was emotionally and physically exhausted. It didn't take much lately. The tiny human inside her seemed to sap her of any energy she might have. She wasn't sure how she was going to handle it when the baby got bigger, or worse, after it was born and mobile.

The idea of having a child alone was terrifying. It

was a thought she hadn't really allowed herself to entertain. Every time the scary what-ifs crept into her mind, she would tell herself that Finn would marry her and they would be one big, happy family. But was she just lying to herself? If she accepted the fact that she was doing this on her own, would she be better prepared to face the eventuality?

Kat glanced down at the legal papers she'd set aside. Finn's attorneys had promised her a great deal of security. As much as money could buy. That was something. But Finn's money wouldn't hold her at night or get up and change the baby at 2:00 a.m. when she was too exhausted to get out of bed.

She tried to picture Finn doing just that. She could see him in a pair of boxer shorts, clutching a small baby to his chest. Both he and the infant had the same golden-blond curls as he bent to kiss the baby on the top of the head. It was a touching image. One that nearly made her tear up at the thought. But as she let the fantasy play out in her mind, she knew one thing was different in this scenario.

It wasn't Finn holding her baby in her mind.

It was Sawyer.

Sawyer stood awkwardly on Kat's doorstep, holding a large box with a bow on it. He'd gotten the address from Finn's attorneys, but it felt weird to stand here on the piazza steps of her home with a gift. Unannounced. Like he was asking her to the prom or something. He suppressed that comparison lest the image of her in a slinky beaded dress completely derail why he was here today.

This visit wasn't about his brother. Or the District. Or his undeniable urge to see her again. And kiss her again. No. It was about his family.

He rang the doorbell, stopping to admire the intricate engravings on the front door. The edges were done in a Celtic knot design that ran all the way around, with leaves, acorns, chipmunks and other woodland creatures carved into the dark wood. It was incredible, and no doubt one of her pieces.

Kat opened the door, a look of confusion wrinkling her nose as she eyed him and the box in his arms. "Sawyer? What are you doing here?"

Considering he hadn't seen her since they kissed in her workshop and now he was at her home without prior warning, that was a valid question. To be honest, he hadn't called ahead because he thought she might tell him not to come. That was the smart thing to do. Let the lawyers handle the situation and stay far from the temptation of Kat McIntyre. And yet here he was, on a mission he'd volunteered for.

"I'm here today on official Steele family business," he said. At least that might ease any concerns she could have about him being here for less than altruistic reasons. He wasn't at her home to kiss her again. Although he'd have a hard time turning her down if she wanted him to. Kat was apparently the Achilles' heel he never knew he had until their lips touched that afternoon at the District. Since then, he'd thought of little else.

"What official business is that?" She crossed her arms over her chest and leaned against the door frame.

"Well, news of you and the baby has spread to the immediate family." Sawyer hadn't been at the house the night Finn called, so had heard the tale secondhand from Lena, their housekeeper. Apparently, they'd had to call the doctor, because his father had turned bright red as his blood pressure went through the roof. Sawyer wouldn't tell Kat that, though.

"Everyone is very excited to meet you and they don't want to wait until Finn gets home, so my parents have asked me to invite you to a little thing they're putting on this weekend at the house."

"A little thing?"

Sawyer knew well enough that nothing his parents ever did could be described as little. Perhaps in their mind a garden party for a hundred of their closest friends was an intimate get-together, but normal people knew better. "My grandmother is coming home. She's spent the last three years traveling around Europe after my grandfather passed away. I guess she finally got tired of Paris and has decided to come back to Charleston. They're throwing a welcome-home party for her Saturday afternoon and they'd like you to come."

He could tell by the look on Kat's face that she wasn't excited by the invitation. Some people dreamed of being invited to a Steele party. But some people weren't carrying the illegitimate child of the family's problem son. He imagined that, for someone in her position, a party like that would be akin to being dropped in a shark tank wearing a chum bikini. This might take some convincing.

"Can I come in?"

Kat nodded and stepped back to allow him up the stairs and inside the piazza. He followed her into the house, and as she shut the door and turned to face him, he held out the large box to her. "This is for you."

"What is it?" she asked cautiously.

Sawyer shrugged. "I think it's a dress. It's from my sister Jade, so I'm not entirely certain. She just told me to give it to you."

Kat accepted the box, but the line between her brows deepened with thought as she eyed the sizable package. "Why would she give me a dress? Or anything at all for that matter? We've never even met before."

"Well, that's true, but Jade is technically new to the family, too. I don't know if you follow the news, but she and my sister Morgan were switched at birth as part of some kidnapping and ransom scheme. Jade is my biological sister, but no one knew it until recently. When she heard about your situation, she told me she wanted to help out. She knows what it's like to walk into a room of Steeles as a stranger."

Kat carried the box over to the coffee table. "That's sweet of her. But why a dress? I have clothes. Is she worried I'm going to show up to this thing in cutoffs and flip-flops?"

"No, of course not. But she knows you're expecting. And I mentioned how you'd complained about your nice clothes not fitting at Morgan's wedding. Really, I don't know why. I didn't ask. She just gave me a box. It's her way of welcoming you to the family, I guess."

"I suppose I should be happy that someone is welcoming me," Kat muttered, as she opened the lid to expose the tissue-wrapped outfit inside.

It was coral-colored lace, and when she held it up, Sawyer could see why his sister had chosen it. It would flatter Kat's new curves nicely with its high waist, plunging V-neckline, and hem that would fall just above her knee. Her shapely calves would be on display all afternoon, and he couldn't complain about that. He was undoubtedly a leg man.

"This is beautiful," she said. "And just the right size. How did she know?"

He shrugged. He wouldn't even begin to guess what size a woman wore. It was a losing game for a man anyway, so he chose not to play. "She saw you hit me at the wedding reception and took a guess. She has an eye for clothes."

"I'll have to tell her thank-you when I see her at the party." Kat folded the dress and placed it neatly back inside the box.

"So you're coming?"

Kat sighed and sat back on her sofa. "I don't suppose I can say no or I'll be starting off on the wrong foot with Finn's family. Your family," she added, with a wistful look in her eye he didn't understand. "I wish it wasn't such a big, public spectacle, though."

"That's better, really." Sawyer sat on the sofa beside her. "There will be a lot of people there and the focus won't be on you. It will be on Grandma Ingrid. You'll be able to mingle and meet people, but you won't be trapped in the dining room with the immediate family grilling you over dinner."

Sawyer had been witness to one such family dinner in recent memory. His older brother, Tom, had brought home a woman to meet the family. He'd seriously been considering proposing to her. But watching her melt to a puddle under the scrutiny had changed his brother's mind. If she couldn't handle dinner, she couldn't handle being a Steele.

"Okay, I guess. What time?"

"Three o'clock at the house."

Kat nodded and picked up her phone to put the information into her digital calendar. "Is there anything else I should know?" she asked.

"I'd recommend wearing shoes that won't sink into the lawn. And wear some good sunscreen and insect repellant. My parents have the yard sprayed, but it's still summer in Charleston."

Kat smiled and shook her head. "Thanks, but that's not exactly what I meant."

He was afraid of that. "What do you want to know?" he asked. "I'll answer you as honestly as I'm able to."

"Your parents… Finn told me he was going to tell them. Are they okay with this? I can't imagine they took the news well."

Sawyer sighed. "They didn't. At least at first. My family has always been very focused on their public image. They're getting better, though. I think my father has finally come to terms with the fact that we are all adults now, and the more he meddles in our lives, the worse it can make things."

Kat's lower lip trembled just slightly as she turned away and looked at the dress on the table. "So they hate me," she said matter-of-factly.

Sawyer wanted to reach out to her. To brush his thumb across her lip and kiss her until she forgot about his parents and what they might think. In the end, that mattered very little. Not as much as seeing her smile again. He compromised with himself and instead reached out to place a comforting hand on her denim-clad knee. "No. They don't hate you, Kat. They don't know you. But they want to get to know you and see what kind of person you are."

"They may not hate me, but they blame me for this. They think I'm just after their money and their name."

"Again, they don't know you. I'm sure they have their concerns, but they're polite enough not to confront you with them. Their future grandchild is at stake. They want to like you, I promise. Honestly, in this situation they blame Finn. I'm sure they're surprised it's taken this long for something like this to happen."

The frown line returned between her brows. It seemed to whenever he spoke about his brother. He understood her concern. She hadn't said anything to him about Finn, but he could tell that his twin's reputation bothered her. One night together wasn't enough time to decide if someone is going to be a good parent or partner.

"Just be yourself, Kat. Come and meet everyone. It

will be fine. You'll get through Saturday and I'm sure it will be easier after that. My family isn't that scary."

"You're pretty scary." Kat gave him a shady bit of side eye and a knowing smirk as she said the words. It was enough to make him pull away his hand.

"I am. As you will soon learn, Morgan is the princess, Tom's the golden boy, Finn's the fuck-up and I'm the hard-ass." Sawyer stood and shoved his hands into his pockets. "Welcome to the family, Kat."

Five

The second time Kat drove up to the Steele mansion, the circumstances were very different. It had been only a few weeks and the live oak–lined drive with its dripping Spanish moss was just the same, but this time she had been invited. And hopefully, she wouldn't cause a scene.

There were already a lot of cars parked in the field when she pulled up and handed the keys of her Jeep to the valet. Another man directed her down a path along the side of the house to the backyard. She could hear a string quartet playing and the melody of voices and laughter in the distance.

But it wasn't until she rounded the corner of the house and caught a glimpse of the party that the wave of nerves hit her. She wasn't sure how many people she was expecting, but this was hardly a *little thing* Sawyer had invited her to. The event sprawled across the manicured lawn behind the house. A huge, white tent covered a portion of the tables and she could see a large buffet laid out in the shade.

There were more than a hundred people milling around in their garden party finery and flashy hats, with almost as many staff in white tuxedos catering to their every need.

As she stood at the edge of the crowd, trying to force herself to officially enter, one of the staff approached her with a tray of crystal flutes. "Would you care for some champagne, miss?"

Kat stopped herself from reaching out on impulse and dropped her hand to her stomach instead. Her baby belly was still little more than a bump, but the gown Jade had bought her for the party highlighted what she did have. "I'm not drinking."

"Of course, miss." The man snapped his fingers and another waiter appeared with a different tray of drinks. "The elder Mrs. Steele doesn't drink, so we also have sparkling cider and sparkling fruit waters available for guests."

Kat was surprised, but pleased. Alcohol was what she probably needed to calm her nerves, but at least she could have a crystal flute to hold, and feel like she belonged. She reached out and selected a glass of faintly pink bubbling water with a plump red strawberry wedged on the rim. "Thank you."

The waiters nodded and left, leaving Kat no choice but to finally move on. She slowly followed the trail toward the crowd, ignoring the drag of her feet, which felt almost as heavy as concrete. She knew it wasn't the shoes. If she allowed herself to turn and leave, she could probably sprint. She just didn't want to go to this party.

"Katherine?"

Kat wasn't used to people using her full name. Her mother was really the only one who ever called her Katherine. She stopped and turned her head toward the voice, seeing a stunning young blonde heading her direction. She immediately tensed. She didn't know who this woman was, but could tell in an instant that this was perhaps the most beautiful woman she'd ever seen in person.

Her hair was platinum blond, and she had big doe eyes and a wide grin, her fuchsia-colored lipstick matching her dress. She was tall, thin and elegant, moving with a swift grace in Kat's direction despite the four-inch heels she was wearing.

"You *are* Kat, aren't you?"

Kat took a breath and did her best to return the smile. "I am."

"I'm Jade, Finn's sister. I recognized you in the dress I sent over with Sawyer for the party."

With a sigh of relief, Kat felt the muscles in her shoulders start to unwind. At least she had one friendly face in the sea of strangers. "Oh! Thank you so much for sending this. You didn't have to, but it's lovely."

"Yes, I did have to. It fits you perfectly, I'm so glad. Asking Sawyer about your measurements was like asking a tiger how to prepare a five-course vegetarian meal."

Kat looked down to admire the coral lace and smiled. "I appreciate you thinking of me. Honestly, I'm not sure if I would've come today if you hadn't sent the dress over with Sawyer. I'm so nervous."

"I understand. The first time I met the Steeles, I was almost thirty years old. I was their biological daughter, and yet I'd never laid eyes on any of them, or them me. Seeing them face-to-face and finally learning the truth about our family and what happened was so stressful. But I don't regret it. Now I have two amazing families, four brothers and a sister of sorts that I adore."

"It's different for me," Kat replied, feeling her smile fade ever so slightly. "You were taken from them, but you belonged here. I'm an outsider who could be using their grandchild as a means of shoehorning her way into the family fortune."

Jade narrowed her gaze at Kat for a moment. "Is that what you're doing?"

Kat shook her head. "No, but I wouldn't believe me if I were in their shoes. Sawyer is certainly suspicious enough of my motives."

"Sawyer is suspicious of everyone. That's just the way he is. Ignore him."

Kat bit her tongue, but she wanted to say that was easier said than done. The serious Steele twin had gotten under her skin. Whether he was accusing her of something terrible or looking at her with blatant desire in his eyes, Kat couldn't help but want to be nearer to him. She'd never had that happen with a man before.

Being aggravated by and attracted to a man at the same time was infuriating and confusing. Never mind having all those thoughts about the wrong person.

"Have you met Grandmother yet?"

"I haven't met anyone. I just got here."

"Well then." Jade grinned. "Let's go find ourselves some Steeles." She reached out and took Kat's hand, leading her across the lawn to the tent.

It was probably just as well that Jade was virtually dragging her through the party, because Kat wasn't certain she could do it herself. The farther into the crowd they went, the more curious gazes she could feel upon her. No one knew who she was or why she was at such an exclusive event, she guessed. She wasn't really sure why she was there, either.

"Mother Patricia? Guess who I found loitering near the car lot."

Another pale blonde turned toward them and Kat would swear she was the spitting image of what Jade would look like in twenty-five years. They actually could've been confused as sisters. The woman took a moment to study Kat, and after her gaze fell on the slight curve of her stomach her dark eyes immediately shot back up to her face. "You must be Katherine," she said, with a smile that was warmer than expected, yet a little formal and stiff at the same time.

"Please call me Kat," she said, reaching out to shake the woman's hand.

"Kat, this is Patricia Steele, our mother."

Kat could've guessed that much without being told. "It's nice to meet you, Mrs. Steele."

Patricia looked around the crowd and frowned. "I think Trevor just slipped away into the house to talk business. He hates these dull affairs. Until he shows up again, I can introduce you to his mother, Ingrid. This party is in her honor. She's just returned to Charleston after several years in Europe."

Kat nodded blankly and let herself be carried along to meet someone else. She didn't expect what she found, however. Sitting in a chair near the stage was an older woman with the carriage of the queen of England. She was wearing a light pink suit dress with a matching blazer, white gloves and sensible white flats. There was a single strand of pearls around her throat and teardrop-shaped ones hanging from her ears. Her white hair was elegantly curled and coiffed, missing only a tiara to complete the look.

When the woman turned to look her way, Kat felt a surge of nerves worse than anything she'd felt before. This was the family matriarch, the guest of honor, and likely the one whose opinion would weigh the heaviest where Kat was concerned. Making a good impression was paramount.

"Mrs. Steele," the younger Mrs. Steele said. "I'd like to introduce you to Katherine McIntyre. This is Finn's lady friend."

The woman narrowed her dark brown eyes at Kat and smirked. "Judging by that little tummy, she's more than just his lady friend, Patricia." She turned away from her daughter-in-law to focus her full attention on Kat. "Come closer, dear. Have a seat beside me."

She patted the empty chair beside her with a gloved

hand and Kat knew better than to decline. The older woman was no cookie-baking granny—she was sharp-tongued and quick-witted. Kat needed to stay on her toes with Finn and Sawyer's grandmother, she could tell.

"It's lovely to meet you, Mrs. Steele. I've been told you just returned from Europe? That sounds amazing. I've always wanted to travel more."

The older woman shrugged nonchalantly, as though she hadn't been globe-trotting for the last few years. "Sometimes you need to run away from home to get some perspective. Though most people don't wait until they're eighty to do it. Katherine, is it? Or Kate, perhaps?"

"Kat."

"Kat. I like it. I'm Ingrid. There's too many Mrs. and Miss Steeles around here. It gets confusing. So just call me Ingrid to keep things simple."

Kat nodded, noticing Patricia stiffen beside her. It made her wonder if she was allowed to call her mother-in-law by her first name.

"Why don't you run along, Patricia. I'm sure you have guests to tend to. I want to get to know this young lady better."

Patricia looked at Jade with a bit of concern, then pasted a smile on her face. "Of course. We will have plenty of time to spend with Kat. Call me if you need anything, ladies." She took Jade's arm and led her daughter to the other side of the tent, where some ladies in decorative hats were chatting.

Ingrid turned to Kat and placed a gentle hand on

her knee. "Relax, dear. I know it's stressful, but I'm not going to bite. It's never easy being the wife of one of the Steele men. It's been over sixty years and I still remember the night Edward—that's Trevor's father—introduced me to his parents. It was nerve-racking to say the least, but I held my own. And so did Patricia. And so will you. Becoming Mrs. Steele is like taking on a new identity."

Her words were kind and reassuring, but Kat wondered why Ingrid was telling her this. Yes, she wanted to do the right thing and marry Finn, but she hadn't said as much to anyone aside from Finn himself. Then again, the family probably assumed that was what Kat would want: a diamond ring and a piece of the Steele pie for herself. That wasn't exactly the way she envisioned it.

"When my husband died three years ago," Ingrid continued, "I realized I didn't know who I was any longer. Who was Mrs. Steele without Mr. Steele? I was just some grandmother shuffling around the house having tea and waiting to die myself. That's why I left. I went to Europe to mourn Edward and find out who Ingrid was now. I went to London, to Barcelona, to Florence and finally to Paris. I sat on my balcony on the Île Saint-Louis overlooking the Seine and listened to the bells of Notre Dame cathedral ring every day. I sipped café crème, ate whatever I liked, and took long strolls down streets without knowing where I was headed. I found Ingrid again in Paris. And the night the cathedral burned, I decided it was time to come home."

Kat couldn't imagine living a life like that, but it

sounded like the kind of thing that would feed an artist's soul. She wondered if Ingrid had some artistic
talents, as well.

"It was time to come back to my family. And now I
know why. I needed to come back here for you."

At that, Kat perked up in her chair. "For me?"

The older woman smiled and nodded. "Yes. As I
said, it isn't an easy road to becoming Mrs. Steele, especially in your situation. People will talk, as though
they have any room to judge someone else. You need
someone on your side. The minute I laid eyes on you,
I decided I was that person."

Kat's nose wrinkled and she took a nervous sip of
her drink. "Shouldn't you be on your family's side?"
she asked, when she worked up the nerve.

"I am," Ingrid said with a curt nod. "They just don't
know it yet."

Sawyer wasn't sure how Kat did it. He'd seen people nearly pass out from anxiety when meeting his
grandmother. She didn't mince words, always speaking her mind whether she should or not. She also had
an uncanny ability to see through people's bullshit. Her
words, not his. Anyone approaching her with an ounce
of haughtiness would be quickly cut down to size, his
own mother included.

And yet, there Kat was at his grandmother's side.
She'd been there almost all afternoon. The party was
to welcome his grandmother home from Europe, and
he was certain there were people anxious to speak with

her, but Ingrid Steele simply didn't care. She seemed to be entranced by the young Miss McIntyre.

Sawyer knew exactly how she felt.

Leaning against one of the aluminum posts that held up the gigantic tent, Sawyer had watched over the two of them—Kat in particular—for quite a while. He'd argued with himself about why he was keeping such close tabs on his brother's lover. Of course, he told himself that he was waiting for the truth to come out about her and her motives. If anyone could get to the bottom of Kat and what she was after, it would be Grandmother. And yet the two of them were chatting, laughing and nibbling on tea cakes like old friends.

In that case, Kat was either an incredibly skilled con artist or she was telling him the truth. Despite his suspicious nature, he hadn't found out anything about Kat that would raise a red flag. Jade's fiancé, Harley Dalton, owned a security and investigations firm and had personally done a background check on her. She came back squeaky clean. Probably even cleaner than Sawyer would.

She'd been orphaned in her late teens when her parents were killed in a car accident. She'd inherited a tidy sum from her parents' estates and insurance policies. From what he could tell, she'd left most of it invested and lived on the interest after buying her house. No police record. No bad debts. They couldn't even find an off-color social media post that could come back to haunt her.

Unless she'd suddenly decided to better her position by seducing and getting impregnated by the richest guy she could find, it was probably truly an accident, as she'd said. He hated to admit it, but all the evidence pointed to that outcome. Even Finn had mentioned that Kat was reluctant to accept any of the things his lawyers had offered her. If she was a scam artist, she was either terrible at it or positively diabolical.

Deep down, Sawyer knew she was innocent of the things he'd accused her of. Of course, once he stopped looking at her with suspicion, he couldn't help but look at her in a way that could only cause trouble for everyone involved.

"If I didn't know better, I'd say you were checking out that hot redhead with Grandmother."

Sawyer turned at the sound of his sister's voice. "That's just what Morgan would say if she were here, instead of on her honeymoon, gallivanting about."

Jade laughed. "Today, the role of the Steele daughter will be played by the understudy, Jade Nolan."

Sawyer wrapped his arm around her and tugged her close. "You're not an understudy. You originated the part for a short run before leaving the production for a gritty indie role."

"Cute. But don't change the subject." Jade tilted her chin in the direction of Ingrid and Kat. "Why are you over in a corner leering at Finn's baby mama?"

"I am not leering." Sawyer pulled away and crossed his arms over his chest. "I told Finn I would handle things for him and keep an eye on her until he got back from China."

"I don't think he intended for you to keep *that* good a watch on her. I suppose you can't help it, though. If you built a woman in a computer to your precise specifications it would come out Kat McIntyre."

Sawyer turned toward his sister with an irritated scowl. "You don't know what you're talking about."

Jade arched an eyebrow and nodded. "If you say so."

"Besides," he argued, "she's not available even if she was my type. She's with Finn."

"Do you really think so?" Jade looked over at Kat and narrowed her gaze in intense study. "I never pegged him for the settling-down type. Even with a baby in the mix. I don't imagine those two are going to ride off into the sunset together when he gets back from China."

Finn *wasn't* the settling-down type. But in this family people didn't always get to do what they wanted to. If they did, Morgan wouldn't have had to marry her husband, River, twice. "You never know what will happen. Something brought them together once, so it could happen again. And even if they just end up as co-parents or whatever…that doesn't mean there's a blank space in her life ready for me to occupy."

"Why don't you let her be the one to make that decision?" Jade asked. "I've seen her look at you a few times this afternoon when you were distracted."

"What does that mean? I look exactly like Finn. She was probably just glancing at me and thinking about him. Or wondering if their baby will look like her or Finn. Even if she was staring me in the face, it'd be like she was looking at him."

"But she *wasn't* looking at him. She was looking at

you. And appearances and birthdays aside, there's very little in common between the two of you."

Sawyer sighed heavily. "What's your point, baby sister?"

"*My point* is that if Kat had to choose between the two of you to be her husband and father to her child, the rebellious, irresponsible playboy probably wouldn't be her first choice. That's all." Jade gave Sawyer a pointed look and slowly strolled off in the direction of her fiancé.

Sawyer watched her head over to where Harley was standing and slip comfortably into his strong embrace. The man was huge, ex-navy, and intimidating enough to get a confession out of the toughest insurgent. And yet with Jade, he was like a big teddy bear. If she could turn a bad boy like that into marriage material, there might be hope for Finn and Kat.

That's what he should want, right? For things to work out between them? That was what Kat seemed to want. And it was best for the child to be with its father, after all.

But that wasn't what Sawyer wanted when he looked at Kat. When he saw her, all he could think about was kissing her again. That afternoon in her studio had haunted him. Her soft mouth against his, the curves of her body pressed into him, the taste of her lingering on his lips long after he'd left the District... He'd lived the moment over and over in his mind.

She'd pulled away, but he wasn't sure she'd really wanted to. Maybe Jade was right and Kat was interested in him, but she had a guilty conscience. Or the desire to do the right thing for her child outweighed everything else.

Sawyer knew about trying to do the right thing. Sometimes he thought he was the only one in his family who even attempted to do what was right. For all the good it did him. It didn't garner him any additional praise from his parents. No additional promotions or important assignments at work. It was almost like it was taken for granted that Sawyer would do the right thing, and he was ignored because of it.

Glancing back at Kat and his grandmother, he found Kat looking at him. Jade had been right about that, at least. When she realized she was caught, she smiled softly and wiggled her fingers at him in greeting.

No, kissing Kat hadn't been the right thing to do. But it had certainly felt right. Right enough that he wanted to do it again the moment he got her alone.

For once in his responsible life, Sawyer wanted to do the wrong thing.

Six

"Come on, you stupid Jeep!"

The valet had returned a few minutes ago, after attempting to bring her car around, and given her the bad news—her Jeep wouldn't start. With a groan of resignation, she'd taken the keys from him and trekked across the yard to where the vehicle was parked. Now she was sitting in it, hoping she had some sort of magic mojo the valet didn't, and the car would start.

So far, no luck.

This was an eventuality she'd been avoiding. The Jeep had been a present from her parents for her high school graduation. Even as she got older, there wasn't really any reason to replace the car. It was old and didn't have all the fancy features of newer ones, but it got her from A to B.

Since she found out she was pregnant, she'd been thinking more seriously about getting a new ride. One with doors, perhaps. It seemed as though her old Jeep was making the decision for her.

"Please. Just get me home tonight and I'll promise to sell you to an outdoorsy guy that will fix you up and drive you through all the mud puddles." Kat tried to turn the engine over again and found her attempts to negotiate had fallen on deaf ears. Because her Jeep didn't have ears.

With a whimper, she dropped her head onto the steering wheel in defeat. Why did it have to happen today? And here? Now the family she was trying to impress would have to see her junky old car get towed away from their multi-million-dollar estate. As though she wasn't already having enough trouble fitting in. She and Grandma Ingrid had hit it off, but most of the other people at the party had just regarded her from a distance.

When she went to fix a plate, all the ladies near the buffet had hushed until she was gone. It was quite juvenile for grown-ups, really. Kat wasn't used to being the subject of hot new gossip. And now they could be confident in believing her a gold digger. She didn't even have a functioning car—of course she was after Finn's money.

"Need some help?"

Kat shot to attention and turned to find Sawyer had silently crept up beside her car. "Did you go to ninja school or something?" she asked, pressing her hand to her rapidly beating heart.

"Morgan says I'd make a terrible spy. She insists I couldn't sneak up on her with a marching band going by. I didn't even try to slip out of the house when we were teenagers because I knew I'd get caught. So I'd say you were distracted."

"That's a word for it," she said. Turning away from him, she reached for her purse and rummaged around for her cell phone. She needed to call a wrecker. Most of the other guests were gone by now, so hopefully only the family would still be around when it showed up.

"It's awfully late," Sawyer said. "They're going to charge you extra to drive all the way out here on a weekend after eight. Why don't I give you a ride home? Then you can call someone to get the car in the morning, or on Monday."

Kat turned to him with a sigh. She certainly didn't want to sit out here in the humid summer air and get eaten by mosquitos while she waited. Then again, accepting a ride home from Sawyer seemed equally perilous. "I can call an Uber."

"Don't be silly. I can give you a ride. No one is going to want to come way out here to get you. Besides, I pass near your neighborhood on my way home, anyway."

She regarded him suspiciously for a moment, but when he offered his hand and stood there with an expectant look on his face, she finally gave in. "Okay."

He helped her out and only released her hand when he pointed to his car a couple yards away. "Don't act so put out. Most people would love to be chauffeured around in a brand-new car like mine. It still has the new-car smell."

Kat looked in that direction and spied a silver Audi SUV parked beside a bright yellow Porsche Boxster. She held her breath for a moment to see which one lit up when he pulled out his key fob. The lights on the Audi blinked on and off. She should've known better than to think that Sawyer would drive the flashier car. If she had learned more about him before that night at the aquarium, she would've realized she was with Finn, not Sawyer, when they left for a hotel and got into his bright red Ferrari.

Sawyer opened the passenger door and held it for her until she was inside. She sat patiently waiting as he came around to his side and started the car. It did have the new-car smell. It also looked as though it was fresh from the dealership. No travel mug in the cup holder, no crumbled-up receipts on the floor. It was immaculate.

"How long have you had this car?" she asked as they drove off the property.

"Two months, I think?"

"Oh," Kat said with surprise. "I was thinking more like a few days. This thing looks like it's hardly been driven."

"It's been driven. I just keep it pretty tidy."

"Is your place really tidy, too?"

She watched Sawyer frown at the windshield for a moment before he responded. "Maybe. But I have a cleaning service that comes in twice a week."

That sounded nice. She'd love to have one come in twice a month. Kat shook her head. "I bet they hardly do anything. I bet your underwear drawer is organized like a museum exhibit."

"My underwear is hardly museum quality," Sawyer said with a chuckle. "But I do have them rolled and stood on end as Marie Kondo suggests."

Kat rolled her eyes and relaxed back into the plush leather seat. "You need a little messy in your life."

"How's that?" he asked.

"You just seem very…straightlaced. Maybe you're trying to compensate for your brother or something, but you never seem to make a misstep. You need to loosen up. Even your grandmother agrees."

Sawyer turned to her with a confused arch of his brow. "You were talking about me with my grandmother?"

"Yes. She had a lot of nice things to say about you, actually. I think you're her favorite."

"What makes you say that?"

"Just the way she talks about you. It seems like she really wants you to find someone and settle down. She wants you to find someone who makes you happy, not just someone you think the family will approve of, like your last few girls."

Kat watched Sawyer's knuckles tighten and grow white as he gripped the steering wheel. "I thought this afternoon was about my family getting to know you, not about Grandmother spilling all the family gossip to you."

She shrugged and turned back to the road. "We talked about me a lot, too. And about Finn. About Jade and Morgan's situation. Ingrid really seemed to take a liking to me for some reason. I don't know why."

"Really?"

"What do you mean, really?" Kat turned toward Sawyer as he slowed to a stop in front of her house.

He turned off his engine and looked at her. "My grandmother enjoys the company of interesting people. I don't know why you would think you aren't interesting enough to keep her attention. You're smart, you're easy to talk to, you're an artist. There's a lot of layers to you that I'm sure she would find fascinating. I certainly enjoy talking to you."

Kat noticed he said the last part a little more quietly than the rest. It was a curious admittance from a man who had at one time seemed adamant that she was some kind of crook out to fleece his family. "I enjoy talking to you, too," she admitted.

An awkward silence followed. With any other man in any other situation, Kat would've expected Sawyer to lean in and kiss her good-night. That was the natural progression of a conversation like that. She could sense the statically charged energy inside the car. Even with the air-conditioning on, she could feel the heat of his body nearby and smell the lingering scent of his cologne.

It was enough to make her want to slip off her seat belt and scoot closer to him. Judging by the blood racing hotly through her veins and the tingle that sizzled down her spine when he looked her way, it was clear that Kat wanted him to kiss her. And yet he hesitated. And she understood why.

Their attraction to each other was nothing more than mistaken identity combined with a cruel trick of chemistry. She needed to just thank him, get out of his car and go into her house. She needed to look at her finances and start thinking about buying a new car, not about Sawyer and the way his blazer clung to his broad shoulders. Or the way the deep brown of his eyes reminded her of decadent dark chocolate.

Yes, that was what she needed to do. With a surge of self-control, she reached for the door handle and turned to say goodbye. "Would you like to come in for some coffee or something?" she said, instead of good-night or thanks for the ride.

The words slipped from her lips before she could stop herself. Why would she invite Sawyer into her house? The last time they'd spent any real time alone, they'd ended up kissing, and that was in public at her studio. What would happen late on a Saturday night at her house? With no one there to interrupt or know what was happening inside?

Her belly clenched as she awaited his answer.

"I'd like that."

A surge of excitement and a good dose of worry washed over her. Kat was about to find out exactly what would happen if they were alone again. And deep inside, she couldn't wait.

What are you doing? What are you doing?

Every step Sawyer took up the path to Kat's piazza raised a chorus of doubts in his mind. He followed her inside, knowing full well that he was heading into dangerous territory.

It's just coffee, he told himself, but he knew that was a lie even as the thought entered his mind. If he crossed that threshold into Kat's home, it was like the point of no return. He already ached to kiss her. It had taken everything he had on the ride back not to reach over and cup her bare knee with his hand. He wanted to stroke the smooth skin he'd been eyeing all afternoon.

It was stupid. It was reckless. It was everything Sawyer typically looked upon with disapproval. And yet he couldn't help himself. He felt a bit like Finn, doing what he wanted without thinking about what others thought.

Inside her house, he watched Kat set down her things and kick off her heels with a sigh of relief. "That's the best thing to happen to me all day," she said with a soft smile. "Make yourself at home. I'm going to make some coffee."

He watched her disappear into the kitchen as he happily shrugged out of his blazer and tossed it over the back of a chair. Then he set about checking out more of Kat's place. He had been here before, when he'd delivered the dress from Jade, but he'd been too stressed out to pay much attention to his surroundings then. Now, with her in the other room, he was able to walk around and take in the place Kat called home.

The first thing he noticed was the collection of wood carvings around the living room. He recognized them as similar in style to some of her projects at her studio. There was a tall, narrow carving of a mermaid reaching toward the surface of the water, a couple embracing as the wind twirled her hair around them, and Kat's coffee table was an oval sheet of glass resting on the back of a green sea turtle. She really was a talented artist.

The piece that didn't seem to fit in was a large canvas painting above the sofa. It was a chaotic mash of colors that up close seemed like a mess, but from far away, you could see a little girl in a yellow slicker splashing in a rain puddle. He looked at the signature and recognized the name from Kat's background check. It was by her mother, Astrid Elliott. When he'd first read the name, it had sounded familiar, but now that he saw one of her pieces in front of him, he made the connection. Astrid had been a successful artist when she was alive, with the price of her works skyrocketing after her death. He'd even seen one of her pieces in the museum downtown.

On the fireplace mantel, he saw a framed family portrait that had to have been taken not long before the accident that killed both Astrid and Brent McIntyre, Kat's father. Kat looked like a younger, happier version of the woman he knew, surrounded by the parents who loved her.

He noticed it was the only picture around the house. There was nothing more recent. He supposed that was because she didn't want to have pictures taken of herself alone. It seemed like a depressing thing to do, although the idea had never occurred to him until now. He'd always had more family than he knew what to do with. Lately, he'd gained a sister and two new brothers-in-law. He didn't know what it would be like to be alone in the world the way Kat was.

"How do you take your coffee?" Kat asked, as she came into the room with two mugs on a small tray.

"Black, normally, but it's too late for that. Cream, no sugar, or I'll be up all night."

Kat looked at him curiously for a moment, the curve of her mouth inching upward in an amused expression before she nodded and set the tray down on the coffee table. Thinking over his words in the current context of being alone in her house late at night, he could see why. Coffee or not, he might very well be up all night. *God*, he wanted to be up all night.

He was about to sit down on the sofa when he noticed her fidgeting in her lace dress. "Would you like to change out of your party clothes? You seem uncomfortable."

"Yes," she said with a relieved sigh, as she poured cream into his coffee and then straightened. "This lace has gotten itchier as the night goes on. I just hope I can get ahold of the zipper."

"I can get that for you," Sawyer offered.

Kat's gaze fixed on his for a moment. It seemed as though neither of them took a breath the entire time as she thought over his helpful suggestion and what could come of it. "Okay," she said at last.

Kat swooped her long red hair up off her neck to expose the zipper, and turned her back to him.

Sawyer's hands were almost trembling as he reached out to grasp the tab and hold the fabric taut. He tugged down, separating the teeth and exposing more and more of Kat's bare skin as he went. His fingertips brushed over the clasp of her pale pink bra before they continued down to the curve of her back. The zipper stopped there, just where the top of her panties would be visible. But they weren't.

"Did you go commando to my grandmother's garden party?" Sawyer managed to ask, his mouth suddenly as dry as sand.

Kat chuckled and swept her hair over her shoulder as she turned to him. "I had to. This dress showed panty lines pretty badly and I've never really been a fan of thongs."

The smile faded slowly from her face when she looked him in the eye. He wasn't sure what she saw there, but he was certain every feeling he was trying to hide was visible if she peered hard enough. He was usually good at disguising his feelings, but that was because he rarely had any. Now, standing here with her dress about to slip from her shoulders, he was overwhelmed with feelings like never before.

Without saying a word, Sawyer reached out and caught the neckline of her dress where it rested across her skin. He heard Kat's breath catch in her throat as he pulled at the coral fabric. It slipped off her shoulder, the weight of the dress pulling it from her other shoulder, as well. Kat didn't try to stop it as it slid down her body and pooled at her bare feet.

Sawyer swallowed hard as his gaze raked across Kat's virtually naked body. When she finally did move, it wasn't to grab her dress or cover herself. She reached behind her back and unfastened her bra. In a moment, it fell to the floor with her dress, leaving nothing but the red waves of her hair to cover any of her body from him.

He let out a ragged breath as he studied her pale, creamy skin. He was drawn to her full breasts and the hardened peach nipples that seemed to reach out to him, begging him to touch them. He wanted to. It was wrong, but he wanted to. He was conflicted enough that he was frozen on the spot, unable to leave and unable to pursue her.

Instead, Kat closed the gap between them. She stepped gingerly out of her dress and stopped just short of having her nipples graze the cotton of his dress shirt. "Don't you want to touch me, Sawyer?" she asked.

Hearing her specifically say his name, not his brother's, lit a fire deep inside his belly. This wasn't just a case of mistaken identity. She wanted *him*. In this moment, naked and vulnerable in front of him, she wanted Sawyer to touch her, and he was desperate to give her what she needed.

"More than anything," he admitted, and he meant it. He couldn't remember another woman in his life who had gotten under his skin, or taken over his thoughts, the way Kat had.

"Then touch me. Please. I want you to."

She wanted this. He wanted this. In that moment, Sawyer decided that nothing else mattered. He had to have Kat or he was going to make himself crazy with unfulfilled desire. He would regret not taking the chance, just as he would probably regret sleeping with her, so he might as well do what he wanted to in the heat of the moment.

Reaching out, he cupped one breast in his hand. Kat's head tipped back and her eyes closed as she savored the sensation. Her skin was soft as silk as his thumb traced over it and then teased the taut peak that pressed insistently into his palm.

With his other hand, Sawyer reached around the back of her neck, weaving his fingers through her hair and pulling her mouth up to meet his. She opened herself to him, moaning softly with pleasure as his tongue grazed hers. He drank her in, enjoying the lingering taste of strawberries on her lips from the flavored seltzers she'd sipped all afternoon.

He felt her fingers at his throat and pulled away from her mouth long enough for Kat to tug his tie loose and throw it onto the floor. She unfastened the top button of his shirt, which was always his favorite moment of the day. He supposed it was like Kat kicking off her uncomfortable shoes. He sighed in relief, and was about to dip his head down to taste her breasts when Kat pressed insistently on his chest, forcing him backward until his calves met with the couch behind him.

She pushed him back onto the sofa and crawled onto his lap to sit astride him. Her fingers worked feverishly to unbutton his dress shirt and push the fabric out of her way. Sawyer's hands gripped the flesh of her hips as she dragged her nails through his chest hair to his belly, then unfastened his belt.

Kat rose up on her knees long enough to let him slide his pants down his thighs, then she slowly, deliberately, lowered herself onto him.

Sawyer groaned against her breasts as he wrapped his arms around her and pulled her close to him. He held her still for a moment once she was fully seated, and squeezed his eyes tightly shut. He wanted to savor every moment, every feeling, because this probably wouldn't ever happen again. Soon they would come to their senses and realize how stupid they were, but right now, right this very second, he was going to enjoy every delicious sensation.

After a moment of stillness, Kat ran her fingers through the curls on the top of his head and gripped a fistful. Gently, she pulled back, until Sawyer had no choice but to look into her bewitching green eyes. Then she eased up and sank down on him a second time. Moving slowly at first, Sawyer leaned back and enjoyed the view of his redheaded hellcat taking control. This was the woman who'd slapped him hard across the face at his sister's wedding. The one who had called him daily and tried to track him down to get her way over the artist community. She was feisty. Sexy as hell. Kat was unlike any woman he'd ever been with before.

The slow burn she was building was teetering on the edge of torture. He wanted more and he decided it was time to turn the intensity up a notch. Sawyer reached out and cupped her hips to hold her steady. She braced her arms on his shoulders, letting her breasts sway tantalizingly just out of his mouth's reach. Then he planted his feet firmly on the floor and thrust up into her.

Sawyer watched Kat's expression as he moved hard and fast inside her. Her emotions shifted from surprise to delight, then the tense, almost pained look of a woman on the verge of undoing. He slowed temporarily, reaching between them to allow his fingers to stroke her center. Kat's mouth fell open, her eyes closing as she rocked with him to her climax. And then, once her first cry escaped her throat, he gripped her hips and thrust hard into her again until they were both satisfied and spent.

Kat collapsed against him in exhaustion and he was happy to catch her as she melted into him. She buried her face in his neck, with her hair cascading over his chest and shoulders. He was content to wrap his arms around her and hold her close as their heartbeats and breaths slowed back to normal.

So this is what it was like to do what you wanted to do. Sawyer had to admit it was exhilarating to take a page from his twin's book, damn the consequences. True, he might rot in hell for sleeping with the woman having his brother's child, but he just didn't care. Tonight was worth it.

And he couldn't wait to have her again.

Seven

Kat woke up late. Later than she'd let herself sleep in a long time. Of course, she had been up late with Sawyer. After their encounter on the couch, they'd finally had their cooling coffee, then moved to the bedroom to make love again.

And again.

Now, she was afraid to open her eyes to the light of morning and face reality. As long as she stayed right where she was, she could revel in last night without pondering the consequences.

It had been amazing. She wasn't ashamed to admit it. While Finn and Sawyer might look alike, they were day and night when it came to the bedroom. Finn had the playboy reputation and an adventurous spirit, but she preferred Sawyer's style. He was more serious, but also more thoughtful. She'd never had a man focus so much on her needs in bed. Kat had lost count of how many times she'd come undone under his expert touch. It seemed like anything less would've been a failure on his part.

Things with Finn had been…fine. He was a little wilder than what she was used to. She'd had a good time. But somehow it didn't compare when it came to intimacy, which was what she found she really craved.

It made her wish more than anything that it had really been Sawyer, not Finn, who she'd met that night at the award ceremony. Somehow it seemed like having his baby would be easier. She could envision them actually having a future together where they might be happy. With Finn, she got the feeling she and the baby were just going to be a stone around his neck.

Kat ran her hand across the mattress, and when she found it empty and cold, she pried one eye open. Sawyer was gone. Long gone, by the feel of it.

It was a stark reminder that she wasn't having his child. And she wasn't living some fairy tale.

With a groan, Kat pushed herself up out of bed and clutched the sheets to her chest. She almost felt hungover despite not having a drop to drink. She supposed she was love drunk and still feeling the aftereffects.

"A fine punishment, and duly deserved," she said aloud as she swung her legs out of bed. She really needed to get her priorities in line. There wasn't much sense in sleeping with one twin while wanting to marry the other. At the very least, it didn't help matters. Finn wasn't a model of monogamy, of that she was sure, but she didn't think he'd take kindly to knowing that she and his brother were having sex while she waited for him to return from China.

That was why no one would ever know. Kat would never speak of it. And it certainly wouldn't happen again. It had been an amazing night. One that was hard to regret. But she couldn't let her desires compromise her child's future.

She reached for her floral silk robe from the hook in her closet and wrapped it around herself before stumbling down the stairs to the kitchen. She half expected to see Sawyer sitting there, smugly drinking a cup of coffee, but the house was silent and still.

Which was why the loud beeping of a tow truck outside caught her attention so easily. Realizing that Sawyer must've had her Jeep towed to the house, she slipped into a pair of flip-flops and went out to the piazza to see what was happening.

There, a tow truck was unloading what looked like some kind of luxury SUV into her driveway. The cherry-red vehicle was beautiful, but definitely not hers.

Great. They'd gotten the cars mixed up. Her Jeep was probably getting dropped at some rich guy's yard in Mount Pleasant, where they were about to throw a fit.

With a groan of irritation, Kat tightened the belt on her robe and pushed through the heavy wooden door to flag down the tow truck driver. "Hey!" she shouted, waving her arms at the guy in the cab.

Finally the man noticed her and stopped what he was doing. "Yeah?"

"What are you doing? This isn't my car. You've got the wrong car or the wrong house."

The man turned from the window and picked up a clipboard to read the pages there. "Are you Katherine McIntyre?"

"Yes."

"Then I've got the right house and the right person." He went to hit the lever to continue lowering the SUV off the truck.

"No, this isn't right. This isn't my car. I drive a Jeep. A broken-down, dark green, rusty Jeep Wrangler." She turned to the car halfway in her driveway. She could see now that it was a brand-new Lexus SUV. It wasn't even close to the right car. In her dreams.

"Listen, lady. I don't know anything about an old Jeep. All I know is that I was supposed to bring this vehicle from the dealership to this address and give the keys to you."

"On whose authority?"

The man rolled his eyes. He'd probably never had someone fight so hard against receiving a car. He looked down at the paper again. "Looks like a Mr. Steele had it sent. If you don't want the car, take it up with him. But I've got to deliver it. That's my job."

Before Kat could open her mouth to ask which Mr. Steele had sent it, he flipped the switch again and the cable lowered the SUV the rest of the way to the ground. The man finally climbed down from the cab and busied himself unhooking things and getting everything set up so he could leave. Then he raised the flatbed back into position and walked over to where she was waiting.

"Sign here," he said.

She was too tired to fight with him. She signed the paperwork, which drew an audible sigh of relief from the driver. Then he handed over a pair of key fobs.

"There are worse things than waking up to a new Lexus," he pointed out. "Have a nice day," he added, before crawling back into his cab and disappearing down the street.

Kat looked at the keys in her hand in disbelief, then slowly made her way over to the SUV. It was beautiful, with sporty lines and elegant chrome details. It had to be the latest model, with top-of-the-line trim features. The interior had red-and-black leather seats and a shiny polished wood-and-leather dashboard. It made her old Jeep look like it was made from papier-mâché or Tinkertoys or something.

It was exactly the kind of car she would have chosen for herself if she could've had any car in the whole world. Each detail, from the sunroof to the wheels, was perfect.

But she couldn't accept a gift like this. Not from Finn and certainly not from Sawyer.

Kat reluctantly walked back into her house and hunted down her phone from where she'd left it the night before. There, on her screen, was a text from Sawyer, answering her question at last.

Do you like it?

Kat rolled her eyes and shook her head before texting back. Of course I like it, she responded. But I can't accept it.

Her phone rang precisely five seconds later, with Sawyer's number coming up on the screen. "Come get your car," she answered without saying hello.

"Good morning to you, too," he said in an irritatingly chipper voice. He knew full well how she would react to a gift like that and he seemed to be reveling in it.

"Good morning, Sawyer. Now will you please tell me why there's a brand-new Lexus in my driveway? Where is my Jeep?"

"Your Jeep is at the repair shop. I had it towed there early this morning. The guy took a look at it and said it's on its last legs. The starter has gone out, which is why it won't turn over, but he didn't feel right charging you to fix that because the whole engine would need to be rebuilt before too long, anyway. I can't have you stranded on the side of the road, pregnant and at the mercy of random bystanders."

Kat had been afraid that the news about her Jeep wouldn't be good, but this was even worse than she'd expected. "And so naturally, you bought me a new car instead?"

"Naturally." She could almost hear his smug grin in his voice.

"Sawyer..." Kat said in a stern tone.

"Hear me out," Sawyer argued. "You need a new car."

"That may be true, but it doesn't mean that you need to sweep in and buy one for me. If the Jeep is

DOA, then I'll go get something else. You buying it after last night makes it feel like some sort of thank-you-for-the-sex gift."

Sawyer laughed over the phone line. It was one of the first times she'd ever heard him really, truly laugh. She liked the sound of it and wished she was with him in person to see if his eyes lit up or his dimple was on display. Finally, the laughter faded. "Do you really think I give cars to all the women I sleep with?"

"Well, no…"

"That would be an expensive habit, even for me, Kat. The truth is that yours isn't safe for you to drive and it certainly won't be safe to take my new niece or nephew around town, either. My brother asked me to keep an eye on things until he can get back, and in my opinion, the best thing I could do is get you a safe vehicle to drive."

While Kat was relieved it wasn't a morning-after gift, she still couldn't take something like that from him. Or from anyone. Even from Finn and his team of bribing attorneys, although they'd offered her everything but a car in their settlement package. "I can't accept this, Sawyer."

"That's a shame, since you currently have nothing else to drive. I can tell the mechanic to try and get your Jeep running, but it won't be a quick fix. I hope you don't have anything you need to do the next few days."

Kat sighed. "I actually have a doctor's appointment on Tuesday. Not to mention going to the District to work."

"Well, there's no way your car will be ready that

soon. The guy only took it in today as a favor to me. How about this? Since you need a car to get around, drive the Lexus for a couple of days. I'll see what he can do with your Jeep. If he can get it running, I will take the Lexus off your hands. Maybe I'll give it to Morgan for her birthday."

Kat was more suspicious of this than anything. He'd backed down quicker than she expected. "Are you serious?"

"Absolutely. Red isn't really Morgan's color, but I think she'll like it."

"Why not just return it to the dealership, and I'll get a rental car?"

"I got too good a deal on it. If you don't want it, fine, but someone is getting a new Lexus. There's no sense paying for a rental car, too, when it's sitting there in your driveway."

"Okay," Kat said reluctantly. "Is this why you crept out of my bed at dawn?"

"I hardly crept out at dawn. It was eight thirty and you were out like a light. I hated to wake you up, so I let you sleep."

That made Kat feel a little better, although as she looked down at the key fobs in her hand, she couldn't help but think that Sawyer would get his way where the car was concerned. Where everything was concerned, actually. No matter how much time they spent together, she never seemed to be able to pin him down to talk about the District. There were parties and family members and new cars to distract her, and she was running out of time.

"I'm going to talk to the guy about your Jeep and I'll give you a call back later, okay?"

"All right."

"Oh, and before I forget, do you have plans for the Fourth of July?"

Kat didn't need to look at her calendar to know she didn't. She figured she'd be working at the District, like she always was. They got higher than average foot traffic on holidays. Still, she liked the idea of seeing Sawyer again that soon. "I don't think so."

"Oh, good. Grandmother wanted me to invite you to the family Fourth of July party."

Kat tried to swallow her disappointment that it was Ingrid, not Sawyer, who wanted to see her again. At least she hadn't embarrassed herself too badly with the family if they'd invited her to another gathering. "Another party?" Kat asked. Her toes still hurt from the last one.

"This one is different. Just the immediate family cruising the harbor to watch fireworks from our yacht."

Kat cringed at the way Sawyer could talk about the family yacht as though that's what everyone did on a summer holiday. "I'll think about it," she said.

"I'll tell Grandmother Ingrid you said yes, then."

Before Kat could argue, the call ended and she found herself staring at her phone, dumbfounded. She certainly hadn't intended to get this involved with the Steele family, but now that she was, they were turning into a handful.

It was a nice change of pace from being alone.

* * *

"Come on back, Mr. Steele. Ms. McIntyre is already in the exam room, but the doctor is still with another patient."

Sawyer smiled and nodded to the nurse as she knocked gently on the door and then opened it to let him inside.

"Guess who's here?" the nurse said brightly. "Daddy was able to make the appointment, after all!"

Sawyer saw Kat whip her head around to where he was standing in the doorway. Her jaw clenched, but she didn't bother to argue with the nurse, or have him tossed and cause a scene.

"Great," she said flatly.

Once the nurse slipped back out the door, Kat's smile faded. "What exactly do you think you're doing, crashing my prenatal appointment?"

Sawyer shrugged and settled into the guest chair. "My brother told me to keep an eye on things. I'm sure he would want to be at this appointment if he were here, so I thought I'd pop in and pass any news along to him."

"So you just told them you were the father and they let you in?"

"Yes and no," he admitted. "I was waiting patiently in the lobby for you to finish. They approached and asked if I was the father and if I wanted to come back to see the ultrasound and get the lab results, so I said yes. It's not like they'll ever know me from Finn, anyway."

"I'll know." Kat fidgeted with her uncomfortable-looking paper gown.

"It's a little late to act shy around me," Sawyer said. "I've seen all this, and recently."

"This is different." Kat crossed her arms over her chest and twisted her lips in irritation.

Sawyer sat back in his seat and looked around. He'd never been in a gynecologist's office before. There were big posters on the walls with drawings that reminded him of fifth grade health class, and the exam table had handles coming out the ends like a motorcycle. "What are these?" he asked.

Kat rolled her eyes. "Stirrups."

"Like for a horse?"

"Not exactly, but my feet do go in them. It's for the…exam."

Oh. Yeah, he'd definitely never been in one of these offices before. Or given much thought to what actually happened in them.

He was second-guessing his decision to crash the appointment when a quick rap at the door disrupted their conversation, and a shorter man in a white lab coat rushed in. "Hey, everyone, how's it going today?"

"Hey, Dr. Wheeler."

He shook Kat's hand and turned around to face Sawyer. "Dad? Friend? Moral support?"

"All of the above," he said.

"Okay, great," Dr. Wheeler said without missing a beat. He sat down on his little rolling stool and flipped open the medical file he'd come in with. "So the results on all the tests from your initial appointment look normal. No concerns there. Are you taking your prenatal vitamins?"

"Yes."

"Good. Any problems so far? Nausea? Tenderness? Spotting?" The doctor stood up and guided Kat back onto the table. Sawyer heard her respond, but at that point he checked out. He hadn't fully comprehended what he was walking into today and realized now that he didn't want to see the man behind the curtain, so to speak.

He let his gaze drop to his lap and tried not to think about what that man was doing to Kat. The next thing he knew the lights were dimming in the room and the doctor was spraying gel across Kat's bare stomach.

"We're going to take some pictures and I'm going to try to get a heartbeat on the Doppler. Hopefully we can get a good look at the little guy today."

"It's a boy?" Sawyer asked, perking up from his stupor.

The doctor smiled and shook his head. "We actually haven't talked about that yet. I do have a preliminary result from the NIPT test, if you would like to know. It's 90 percent accurate, but I wouldn't go painting any rooms until after we do the gender confirmation ultrasound at twenty weeks. Maybe we can see something today, but that depends on the baby and how cooperative she or he is feeling."

"I would like to know the test results," Kat said.

"Sure thing." The doctor picked up the folder and flipped to a page filled with lab results numbers. "Well, it looks to me like you guys *should* be expecting a little girl."

Kat brought her hand up to her mouth to stifle a soft

cry. Sawyer wanted to rush to her side and share in the excitement, but it felt like intruding on someone else's moment. It wasn't his baby or his news, despite what he'd told them in the lobby earlier.

"My sisters are going to be thrilled," he said instead, with a reassuring nod to Kat. "And Mom and Grandma Ingrid, too. Once you know for certain you're going to be smothered in a sea of ruffled, pink baby clothes."

Kat laughed and he saw a shimmer of happy tears in her green eyes. He reached out and took her hand, squeezing it gently. He might not be the father, but until Finn got home, he would do what he could to support her through this.

Her gaze met his and she smiled. "Thank you for being here," she said. "I didn't realize I didn't want to be alone for this moment until right now."

He squeezed her hand again and they both turned their attention to the grainy image on the monitor. Dr. Wheeler moved the wand back and forth across her stomach while he searched the darkness for the tiny baby inside.

"Here we go. Hello, precious one."

Sawyer narrowed his gaze at the monitor, trying to make sense of what he was seeing. Then suddenly the profile of the baby came into focus and he felt the emotion of the moment hit him like a punch to his midsection.

He could see every little detail of her face, her little nose and mouth, and her hands balled up in front of her. He could see the curve of her spine and her legs drawn up to her tummy. The beating of her heart was visible, although they couldn't quite hear it over the static.

The doctor hit the keyboard repeatedly, capturing shot after shot of the baby, and then moving the wand to a different location for a new angle. At one point, he pointed out something completely indiscernible and said, "I'd say this is a girl for sure." He typed it on the screen, pointing out some blurry spots, and printed out another image. "You can go ahead and paint."

Then the doctor focused on the tiny fluttering heart on the screen and suddenly the room was filled with the rapid *wub-wub* sound of the baby's heartbeat.

Through it all, Sawyer held Kat's hand, fully enthralled in the moment as though this was his little girl on the screen, whose heartbeat he was hearing for the first time. His brother had screwed up a lot in his life, but Sawyer couldn't help but feel this wasn't just Finn's latest mistake. This might be the first thing Finn had gotten right.

He also felt an incredible sense of jealousy. He had no right to, really. I wasn't as though he'd been pining for a family of his own—far from it, actually. But somehow knowing that a simple twist of fate had put this woman in Finn's path instead of his own bothered him.

Kat. This baby girl. It was supposed to be his. Kat had come to that party looking for him, not Finn. If he hadn't been feeling poorly that night he would've been the one to meet her. Maybe he wouldn't have whisked her off to a hotel the way Finn did, but he couldn't help but think he would've asked her to dinner. And then more. And in time, maybe they would've been sharing this moment together over their child.

Finn hadn't just taken his Jet Ski and played pretend that night. It was as though his twin had stolen his whole future when he put on that name tag.

Eight

"Can I take you to lunch?"

Kat seemed surprised by his offer as they walked out of her doctor's building. "Don't you need to work or something?"

Sawyer frowned. "You sound like my dad. Come on, I'll take you wherever you want to go. Have you started having any weird food cravings yet?"

"I don't know, Sawyer." She seemed uncharacteristically uncomfortable with him. It felt odd to him after the moment they'd just shared. "I probably shouldn't."

Sawyer stopped and shoved his hands into his pockets. "Is something wrong?"

Kat squirmed beneath his gaze, adjusting her purse on her shoulder. His feisty hellcat seemed very out of her element at the moment. "I guess I'm just... I'm just thinking that maybe we shouldn't spend so much time together."

He wasn't sure why, but the words seemed to strike him in a tender spot. Maybe he was reading things wrong, but he thought they were having a good time together. Some could say too good of a time if they took Saturday night into consideration. And he'd bought her an expensive car that would raise eyebrows with his family if they knew about it. But he didn't care about any of that.

He'd done it because it felt like the right thing to do. Finn certainly wasn't going to show up and take care of her the way she deserved to be cared for. He wasn't going to go to doctor's checkups and worry about whether she had a safe vehicle to get around town. Being thousands of miles away was a convenient excuse, but if Finn were in Charleston this very moment, he still wouldn't be standing on this sidewalk beside Kat.

He'd asked Sawyer to handle things while he was gone, and Sawyer had gone over and above the call of duty. But Kat deserved someone who would do that for her. Being the go-between put Sawyer in a position he didn't expect to be in: one where he was starting to have feelings for the last woman and child on Earth that he should. They weren't serious feelings. But it was the closest thing to affection he'd felt for anyone since his breakup with Mira, and Kat's rebuff stung a little more than he expected it to.

"It's just lunch," he said. "I recommend keeping

your clothes on for that, if you're concerned about us crossing the line again."

Kat bit at her lip and tucked a stray strand of auburn hair behind her ear. She had it in a messy bun today, but the breeze had liberated just enough to curve along the edge of her face. It softened the look, in his opinion, but it seemed to be irritating Kat. As did Sawyer's mere presence at the moment.

"Lunch. Just lunch," she finally agreed. "I guess we need to talk, anyway."

Sawyer ignored her ominous addition and instead pointed out a restaurant across the street touting modern Southern fare. The Charleston foodie scene was booming with little spots like this in the last few years. "How do you feel about that place?" he asked.

"That's fine."

They crossed the road together and went inside the restaurant, which was pretty busy considering it was on the late side for lunch. The hostess took them to a booth near the window and they settled in. The waiter brought them glasses of water and a basket of fried corn fritters with a spicy honey dipping sauce, before stepping away to let them look over the menu.

Sawyer decided on a burger with bacon, pimento cheese and a fried green tomato on it. Kat chose a salad with diced fried chicken, candied pecans and dried cranberries.

"Sawyer, before I say anything else, I want to thank you for being there today. It was unexpected, but at the same time, it was nice to have someone to share that moment."

"You're welcome." He got the feeling this was going to be the nicest part of this conversation. She had that worry line between her brows and that was never good.

"That said, I feel like we need to talk about the other night," she said, once the waiter disappeared.

Here it comes, Sawyer thought. He'd insisted on this lunch and now he was about to be dumped by a woman he wasn't even dating. "What about it?" he said, playing coy. He reached for a fritter and shoved it nonchalantly into his mouth. If she wanted to backpedal on everything they'd shared, he certainly wasn't going to act like it was one of the greatest nights of his life and be at a disadvantage with her.

When he stripped the encounter down to the core, it was just sex. Great sex, but only sex. No promises, no emotional entanglements. They shouldn't need to talk about it unless one of them saw it as more than that. It piqued Sawyer's attention that Kat seemed to think it meant something.

"Well, it's just you left so early and then the stuff happened with the car and we just never... I don't know. Never *acknowledged* what we did and that it was probably a mistake that shouldn't ever happen again."

"I didn't really think it was a mistake." He shrugged. "It was fun. I had a good time, didn't you?"

"Yes, of course I did," she said, with a flush coming to her cheeks as she looked away from his gaze and focused on her place setting instead. "I meant that it probably shouldn't have happened, considering what's going on with your brother and me. Or what I hope to happen once he gets back."

Sawyer wanted to tell Kat not to hold her breath where Finn was concerned, but he wasn't sure if that was being helpful or being bitter. If she wanted to try things with Finn, she'd find out soon enough without him telling her.

"It might not have been the smartest thing I ever did, but I don't regret it, Kat. It was what it was. And if it never happens again, that's fine." Even as he said the words he knew they weren't really true, but it was what she needed to hear to feel better, so he'd say them.

Kat's gaze met his again. She studied his face, trying to see into his thoughts or something. She would fail. He wasn't even sure how he felt about all this. He understood her concerns about what was developing between them, even as he fought his own urges to spend as much time with her as he could.

"No one ever needs to know about it," he added. "If you and Finn end up one big, happy family, then great for the two of you. I'm not going to stand up and object at the wedding, if that's what you're thinking."

Now it was Kat who looked a little put out. Perhaps he'd been too aloof about their encounter, but he wasn't sure what else to say. Was she expecting him to slam his fist on the table and demand they be together? For him to tell her all the reasons why he was the better choice? What good would that do? She seemed to want his brother even though they both knew Finn wasn't the ideal candidate for dad and husband.

"Oh, okay," she said after a moment. "Well, then, I guess we just need to put it behind us and there isn't anything more to say about it."

"Very well."

"Speaking of Finn, I heard from him yesterday."

"Oh, really?" Sawyer hadn't spoken to his brother in a while. Finn had been lying low since the news about Kat and the baby had hit the family gossip circuit.

"He says he's coming home next week."

That was news to him. Sawyer had thought he had another couple weeks at least before Finn came back from Beijing. Ideally, he wanted to spend those weeks with Kat in his bed, but since that wasn't going to happen, he supposed it didn't matter when Finn returned.

"That's good to hear," he said, trying not to betray how he really felt. "That means things went well at the new Steele manufacturing facility. There was a bonus for him to open ahead of schedule, as I recall. That should be good for you."

"Why? I don't want any of Finn's money."

"You say that, I know, but you'll end up with something. A trust fund for your daughter, at least?"

Kat reached out anxiously for a corn fritter. "I suppose. He didn't mention anything about work when we spoke. Just that he would be back by next Wednesday afternoon."

"I'm glad to hear it. Then he can be the one here with you instead of me, and I can get back to work. The District closes down in two weeks and I'm going to be up to my neck in blueprints and contractors, getting that place remodeled in my proposed time line. I want it reopened and bustling by the Christmas shopping season. Things went so well in China, maybe I should have Finn handle it," he laughed.

Kat straightened in her seat at the mention of the District, as he'd anticipated. "Yes, I've taken some things home, but I've still got to get all my heavy equipment out. I'll have to hire someone, I suppose, but I've been procrastinating about moving. I guess I was hoping…" Her voice trailed off and she looked at him with her big, optimistic eyes.

"Hoping what? That you'd manage to change my mind and not have to leave?"

They hadn't really lit on this topic since that day at her studio. Other topics, like the baby and getting naked, had taken priority. Sawyer had hoped his argument had been convincing enough to silence her protests, but apparently neither of them had backed down. They'd just been distracted. If Kat was going to give him the cold shoulder and they weren't going to have sex anymore, they might as well return to arguing. That added a little excitement to his day, if nothing else.

"Well, yes," she admitted.

Maybe he had been distracted, but it was possible Kat had been working her side of the argument the whole time. "Is that why you slept with me?" he asked.

The red flush returned to her cheeks. "I would appreciate it if you would stop accusing me of sleeping with you for favors. I told you that wasn't true the first time, after my encounter with Finn, and the answer is the same now. I have not, nor would I ever, use sex as a tool to get my way."

"And yet you admit that you were hoping I would change my mind after the time we've spent together. Was it your stunning argument that you expected to sway me, or did you think you could take advantage of our closeness to get me to change my mind? Tell the truth."

Kat's jaw flexed tightly as she considered her words. "I had hoped that once you got to know me, you would understand where I was coming from. Or that you would be more interested in the plight of the people you're putting out on the street."

"I'm not putting them out on the street. They don't live there. And stop trying to turn me into the bad guy, when you very well could've been manipulating me this whole time."

"Yes, I'm so devious, spending all my time trying to seduce my way through the Steele family! And even if I did sleep with you to save the District, would it have even worked?"

Sawyer sat back in his chair. If he was honest with himself, she *had* worn away at his defenses. He had listened to her argument. Sunday morning as he'd lain in Kat's bed, he'd considered making changes to his plans just because he thought it might make her smile. But with Finn coming home, there was no sense in admitting that. Perhaps it was better to put an end to whatever was building between them, once and for all. Kat was trying to be polite about distancing herself, but he knew that rarely worked. Anger was like a wrecking ball to anything they'd built.

"Probably not," he said. "Like I told you, it was fun. But sex is sex, and business is business. I never mix the two. It doesn't matter what happened between us or how one of us might feel about the other. The District closes in two weeks for renovations. No reasoned argument or even a heartfelt declaration of love would change that."

Kat looked at him for a moment and then nodded stoically. "I see." She wadded up the cloth napkin in her lap and tossed it onto the table. "I think I'm going to go."

"We haven't eaten yet."

"The baby and I have lost our appetite." Kat scooped up her purse and got to her feet, then brushed past the confused waiter, who held their food in his hands.

They both watched her dart out the door. Sawyer wasn't surprised. He'd said what he'd said on purpose. Her leaving was the inevitable result, as much as it pained him to see her go. Better now than to go through this while he had to watch her with Finn.

"I'll take the burger," he said to the confused man standing with a plate in each hand. "Box up the salad to go. I'll have it for dinner."

Besides, he thought, knowing Kat, this argument was far from over.

"Nice Lexus."

Kat looked up from the box of tools she was packing up and saw Hilda in the doorway. "Hey there."

"I can't help but notice that your attempts to save the District seem to be backfiring spectacularly. Hot sex, billionaire babies, luxury cars, and yet we're still closing in a few weeks."

If those words had come from anyone else, Kat would've been insulted. But she knew Hilda better than that. "I've screwed it all up," she admitted. "Now every time I try to talk to Sawyer, there's family around who want to chat with me and discuss the baby. Pinning him down on the subject is impossible."

"Well, maybe the protest will make a difference. A little negative news coverage for the Steele family might be just what we need to get Sawyer's attention and keep it."

Protest? Oh, no.

Kat dropped her face into her hand. She'd completely forgotten about the protest *she* had organized outside the Steele corporate offices on July Fourth. It was intended to be the artists' way of reclaiming their independence from the new owner. She'd planned it weeks ago as a last-ditch effort to keep the place open if all her other plans failed. Before the wedding. Before she knew about the baby. Before Sawyer was in her bed.

And well before she'd agreed to go out with the same Steele family to celebrate July Fourth on their yacht.

"You forgot, didn't you?"

Kat turned around to face her dearest friend and shook her head in dismay. "How could I have forgotten? I planned the whole thing."

Hilda wrapped her arm around Kat's shoulder. "You haven't missed it yet. No worries. You've had a lot on your plate, hon. You've got pregnancy brain, so do what I do and put everything in your cell phone. If it isn't in my calendar it isn't happening."

"Right. My phone."

Hilda gave her a squeeze and stepped away. "What is it?"

"I… They've invited me to spend the holiday with them."

The older woman looked at her for a moment and then nodded. "Well, you should go."

"I can't! I'm supposed to be the one fighting to save this place. I can't go out on their yacht while I know you guys are out there sweating to death with picket signs and bullhorns. I would feel so hypocritical. I can't. I just can't."

"You're not the only one fighting for the District. You've been our most vocal member, but there are plenty of others here that need to do their part, too. Let them paint their picket signs and march their afternoon away. Maybe it's even better if you aren't there for that. It could cause you some unnecessary angst with your family."

"But *you're* my family. You're all I've got. All that matters."

"Not anymore. You've got new family now. And they're excited to include you in their lives. That's great. I'm very happy for you. It's what you've always wanted."

"But I don't want a new family. I want you and Zeke and everyone else."

Hilda wrapped her in a supportive hug. It was exactly what she needed in that moment, but it wasn't enough to stop the tears from overflowing down her cheeks and wetting her friend's T-shirt.

"We're not going anywhere, Kitty Kat. Family can

change, but they never really go away. Whether we're here at the District, or it closes and we scatter to the winds, you'll always be able to find us when you need us. I promise."

It was just like Hilda to say that and refuse to let her feel guilty. "You'll always be there for me, but I'm not going to be there for all of you. I ruined everything. I've lost focus."

"You did nothing of the sort. You've put your focus and your priorities where they belong—on your daughter. Tomorrow, you are going to put on a nice dress and a ton of sunscreen and go enjoy the holiday with your new family. We will carry the torch and things will be just fine. No matter what happens."

Kat opened her mouth to argue, but Hilda held up a finger to silence her. "No matter what happens."

Kat took a deep breath and made herself get out of the Lexus at the marina. There still hadn't been any word on her Jeep, which made her think that Sawyer was just humoring her and had no intention of taking back the Lexus. Of course, after the way their lunch had ended the other day, she might step outside some morning and find the Lexus had been towed off to the Steele compound out of pure spite.

Still, for now she had it, and it was allowing her to get around town, which she needed to do. If Finn's attorneys forced some kind of cash settlement on her, the first thing she'd do was pay Sawyer back for the car. She didn't want to feel like she owed him anything, especially after the ugly things he'd said.

She'd just been trying to get a little space to breathe and to think. It was necessary, especially after that moment they'd shared in the doctor's office. Sitting there, holding his hand and looking at the baby together had felt special. It felt right in a way that it shouldn't have. She didn't need those kinds of thoughts and feelings clouding the situation with Finn. Sawyer had reacted with anger, only proving that she was correct. They'd gotten too close and it could jeopardize everything.

Kat hadn't seen or heard from Sawyer since she'd left the restaurant and that was okay with her. She'd even planned on sitting out the holiday invitation in favor of protesting with her fellow artists, but Jade had called her and insisted she come. Morgan and her husband, River, were back from their honeymoon and wanted to meet her. No excuse seemed to stick with Jade, so now Kat was about to spend several hours on a small boat with Sawyer and his family in the middle of the harbor. Space was not an option.

She eyed the boats docked at the marina and her gaze caught the name of the biggest one: *License to Drill*. No doubt that belonged to the tool magnate Steele family. It looked like it had to be nearly two hundred feet in length, towering over the other boats, with four decks reaching to the sky. Maybe she would be able to avoid Sawyer after all.

As she headed that way, she noticed two women standing on the lowest deck. They were like day and night, blond and brunette. As she got closer, she recognized the blonde as Jade. That meant there would be at least one smiling face there to welcome her today and counteract Sawyer's grumpy countenance.

"Kat! You made it!" Jade was looking her direction and waving.

She waved back and walked up the pier to the stairs, where she could come aboard. The two women were there to meet her. "Kat, this is Morgan. She's finally back from her honeymoon."

"Hey, my first honeymoon was such a mess, we decided this one was going to be extra special. I highly recommend Fiji." The dark-haired woman with the golden tan smiled and stuck out her hand. "I'm Morgan Atkinson. I'm still getting used to saying that."

"I'm Kat," she responded, shaking her hand. "I'm sorry if I caused a problem at your wedding."

Morgan waved away her concerns. "It's not a problem. I'm only sad I missed you slapping the daylights out of Sawyer. I know Finn is the one who deserved it, but Sawyer can be a smug little jerk when he wants to be, too."

"Come on," Jade said. "Let's get you settled in and introduced to everyone. I think you're the last to arrive, so we should be departing soon. Morgan's husband, River, is here, and my fiancé, Harley, is around somewhere. Probably hiding from my parents. And Grandma is here, of course. She's excited to get to spend more time with you. We're hoping this time she shares. No one was able to get a word in with you or her at the party Saturday."

"What about Sawyer?" Kat asked, as they climbed a set of stairs to a higher deck.

"He's here. He was chatting up River about construction last I saw them."

That didn't surprise Kat. He probably had drywall and electrical conduits on his brain, with less than two weeks to closing the District.

The women led her through the luxurious interior of the yacht to the elevator. Looking around, Kat had a hard time believing she wasn't in a hotel. There was art on the walls, marble on the floors and polished wood everywhere. Everything was shiny and expensive, with inlaid gold, onyx and mother of pearl, making her feel incredibly out of place and wondering if she still had sawdust in her hair from working at the studio that morning.

They stepped out of the elevator onto one of the higher decks, where the rest of the family was gathered under shade sails around a hot tub and lounging area. Everyone cheered as she made her entrance, and the girls introduced her to the people she hadn't met yet. They mingled and nibbled on canapés while sipping cocktails and enjoying the sea breeze. Kat chose her seltzer and a seat far from Sawyer where she could protect her fair skin from the sun.

The rest of the afternoon was a blur. Once they set sail, the family moved inside, to where a "casual" buffet dinner of shrimp kabobs, baby back ribs, fire-roasted corn and twice-baked potatoes had been set up for them. The family seemed much more at ease without a bunch of guests around. They laughed, sipped their drinks, told Kat embarrassing stories about Finn and pumped her for information about the baby. When she finally told them it was a girl, there were more cheers of excitement.

After a few hours, Kat found herself really enjoying this time with the Steeles. She was having more fun with them than she'd ever expected to. They were remarkably down to earth once you set aside the luxurious surroundings. After eating, some people played cards on the top deck, while others went to a lower lounge to watch the water from shaded sofas. Kat was included in every conversation and game. They didn't look at her with suspicion the way she'd thought they might, nor did anyone pin her in a corner to grill her. Aside from Sawyer generally avoiding her, everyone was friendly and welcoming. Just the way she imagined a family was supposed to be.

She had no idea how things were going to go with Finn when he returned. She had her fingers crossed about that. But if she liked him half as much as she did the rest of this family, they might have a chance. Kat hadn't intended to start a family this way, but it seemed as if her daughter would at least get some decent aunts and uncles out of it.

"You guys need to come outside to the top deck if you're going to watch the fireworks the city is setting off over the harbor. We've got a surprise, too," Morgan said.

Kat had been watching Sawyer and Harley battle each other at chess when they heard the call from above. She was surprised to notice the sun had gone down while they were playing. When she reached the top deck, she noticed the whole boat was lit with pink light.

"Surprise!" Jade and Morgan said, as she stepped out.

"How did you turn the yacht pink?" she asked in amazement.

"All the lights are remote controlled fluorescents and can change to over two hundred thousand color combinations. Tonight, in honor of Baby Girl Steele, it's going to be pink. I don't care if it's the Fourth of July," Morgan declared.

"We've got a few minutes before the fireworks start," Jade said. "Come with us to get some drinks."

Kat followed the girls to the bar, where a gentleman in a polo shirt embroidered with the name of the yacht was waiting to make them a drink. She took her club soda and cranberry juice back with her, enjoying the view from the deck now that the sun had set. Charleston lit up, with the bridge stretching across the waterway and the Yorktown in the distance, was a stunning sight.

The three of them settled in a private area of clustered couches, away from the rest of the crowd on the third deck.

"Okay, so without everyone else around to hear, I'm curious about what's going on with you and Finn," Jade pressed.

Kat placed her drink on the table and settled back in her seat. "Not much, yet. But I'm hopeful for more than what his lawyers offered."

"Was he being cheap?" Morgan asked, an appalled look on her face.

"No, not at all. He was extremely generous, actually. But I guess I'm looking for something different from him. To be honest, what I want is a family for my child. For us both. I grew up with busy parents who were always working, and then they were gone and I was all alone in the world. I want to do this differently. I don't just want money from Finn, I want his time. Real, quality time."

"Do you want to get married?" Jade asked. "It seems like a big leap after a single date, especially for Finn, but I'm sure that's what Dad is going to be pushing for."

"Yes," Kat admitted. "I know it seems silly in this day and age, but I do want to get married to my baby's father. I know I don't love Finn and he doesn't love me, but this is about more than that. It's about creating a supportive and loving environment for the baby to grow up in. Maybe love will come in time. I don't know. I can only hope that Finn will step up and do the right thing, and that everything works out."

"Well, Finn is always surprising people," Morgan said. "I hope for your sake that he takes this seriously and you get everything you're hoping for. Then you can name the baby after her sweet and supportive Aunt Morgan."

Nine

Sawyer didn't pay much attention to the fireworks, the patriotic music or the impressive desserts the yacht's chef brought out when they were over. No, his mind was someplace else, thanks to overhearing Kat's discussion with his sisters.

After she'd walked out on him at lunch the other day, he couldn't decide if he was irritated or grateful. She'd pushed him away and he'd pushed back twice as hard on reflex. Maybe it was for the best, after everything he'd overheard tonight, but he couldn't help but feel like crap since it happened. He wanted to apologize for the ugly things he'd said. He'd almost pulled her aside twice today to do just that. The first time he'd been stopped by a text from Steele security about District protesters outside their corporate offices. Even with

Kat on the boat with him, he knew she was behind it. He'd stewed about it for a while and then went to find her again after his chess game. He found her with his sisters and hesitated. Now that he'd heard what she'd said to Jade and Morgan, he was glad he hadn't spoken to her alone. He needed to butt out of the whole situation.

Kat wanted to marry Finn and live happily ever after with their daughter. She knew the odds were stacked against her, and yet she wanted the best for her baby, and he could tell she wouldn't rest until she had it. Before Finn even knew what hit him, he'd be swept away in a tide of domesticity. He'd own a nice house in a good school district, drive a minivan and be celebrating his fifth wedding anniversary with Kat. Somehow, he did everything wrong and was going to be rewarded with a woman and a life he didn't deserve.

For the third time in recent memory, Sawyer was practically green with jealously of Finn. He hated that feeling.

And so he'd started smothering it with alcohol. Or trying to. The Scotch had unfortunately kicked in right about the time the yacht returned to port and everyone was unloading to go home.

Sawyer ordered a coffee and chugged it so hot he burned his tongue, but he wasn't sure it was going to be enough. He stumbled a bit heading down the stairs, but was lucky enough for Harley to be there and keep him from hitting the deck with his face.

"Whoa, there. Do we need to call you a car, Sawyer?" Harley asked. "I'd give you a ride, but you live the wrong way."

"Shh," Sawyer slurred, and looked around for Trevor and Patricia. "Don't make a fuss about it or my folks will make me ride home with them and stay at the house. I do not want to sober up with our housekeeper's homemade hangover juice."

"Ugh," Morgan groaned. "I think Lena just made us drink that as a punishment for partying as teenagers. It doesn't help the hangover at all."

"Well, you can't drive. Can you just sleep over on the boat tonight?"

"I'll take him home. I'm pretty sure it's on my way. Pregnant women are nature's designated drivers, anyway."

Sawyer turned around to see Kat standing nearby. She was the last person he needed to be alone with while his filter was down and his tongue was loose. "You don't have to do that. I'll talk to the captain about crashing here."

"No, you won't. You drove me home when my Jeep wouldn't start. I owe you one. Just promise me you won't throw up in the Lexus. You can't regift a car that smells like puke."

She smiled at her joke and his heart started racing in his chest. Kat had a light sweater pulled over her bare shoulders to protect from the chill of the sea air, but earlier, she'd worn only the strapless navy blue sundress. Her hair was pulled back into a high ponytail and it swung back and forth when she walked. He'd wanted to tell her how beautiful she looked today, casual and elegant, but it had seemed like a bad idea. Lately, all his ideas were bad ones.

"I promise," he said instead. Perhaps some time alone would be what he needed to apologize, and then both of them could move on.

Harley and River helped Sawyer walk off the boat, and loaded him into her passenger seat while Morgan put Sawyer's address into the GPS. "Are you sure you can handle him?" Harley asked with concerned eyes.

Kat nodded and climbed into the car beside him. "I'll be fine. I'll just slap him when we get to his place and he'll wake right up."

Harley's and River's laughter was muted by the slamming of the car door. As she started the engine, Sawyer pushed himself up in the seat and put on his seat belt for the ride.

"Thank you for driving me home even though you hate me."

"It's not a problem, and I don't hate you. You might be a jerk sometimes, but I don't want you driving if it isn't safe."

"I'm sorry," he said, after an extended silence.

Kat turned to him for a moment before merging into the traffic and heading to his place. "You're sorry for what?"

"For everything I said to you the other day. I was upset when you said we were over, and I lashed out at you. That wasn't the right thing to do. I know now that you just want what's best for your daughter and that's to be with her father. I shouldn't be angry or try to stand in the way of that. I only want what's best for you and the baby, too."

She seemed stunned by his apology, letting the words sink in before she finally responded. "Thank you, Sawyer. I'm sorry, too. I guess we both could've handled it better. I never should've entertained something with you when I knew what I wanted with Finn. I should've told you."

With the air clear, they drove in silence across the peninsula until they closed in on his place. "You have reached your destination," the GPS announced, disrupting the quiet inside the car as she pulled up in front of his house.

"You can turn into the drive just there." Sawyer pointed and hit a button on his key chain to open the gate to his private driveway.

She turned in and came to a stop, shutting off the engine. "Let's get you inside."

Sawyer looked at her with confusion. "You're coming in?"

Her pointed expression shot down any thoughts he might entertain about her inside his house. "I'm going to help you up the stairs and get you in the house. If you behave, I might make you some coffee and toast."

Sawyer nodded and opened the car door. He was feeling pretty steady on his feet now, but as they moved toward the stairs, he felt less sure. Kat was quick to move to his side. She wrapped his arm around her shoulders and put hers around his waist.

"Grab the rail and help me," she said, so he did.

It took three times fumbling with his keys and dropping them, but they finally made it inside his place. He stumbled in, shrugging out of his blazer and tossing it onto a wingback chair like he did every night. His keys went into a bowl by the door as he flipped on the overhead light.

He paused as Kat gasped, and figured the original rose medallion in the ceiling, along with the restored crystal chandelier, had caught her eye. Instead, when he turned, she was running her hand over the ornately carved wood of the staircase just to their right.

"The woodwork is beautiful."

Sawyer looked around his living room and nodded. "I forget you're a wood carver. You'll find a lot you'll like here. Much of the house had already been redone when I bought it, but thankfully, they left most of the original woodwork intact. The decorator I hired did a good job incorporating the existing historical details into my modern aesthetic."

"I'm surprised you got all those words past your tongue," Kat said with a smile.

"Very funny. The kitchen is this way."

Kat followed him through the living room and into the kitchen at the rear of the house. He'd had it done in all white, with black hardware and dark antique fixtures for a stark, clean look. It seemed to go well with the original white shiplap that ran through the home and the tiny white octagon tiles on the floor.

She strolled through the kitchen, touching the quartz countertop and the faucet before bending over to look at the wood cabinetry of the island. He'd had that piece done by a local carpenter who carved the details by hand. Kat noticed immediately, running her fingers over the scrollwork.

"You don't even cook in here, do you?" she asked, as she stood back up.

He shook his head, making himself dizzy, so he sat on a bar stool on the other side of the kitchen island. "I like things with clean lines, and designs that look tidy. I also like features that will help with resale down the road. This seemed like a good mix, whether I use it or not. And I have used the microwave," he said, pointing out the stainless-steel machine mounted into the side of the island. "And the coffee maker."

Kat nodded thoughtfully. "Well, speaking of coffee makers, you have been a good boy so far. I believe I promised you coffee and toast."

"Coffee is in that jar, and bread is in the pantry over there."

She followed his guidance, moving around the kitchen to prepare a late-night drunk man's snack. A few minutes later, she presented him with a steaming mug of black coffee and a plate with two dry pieces of toast on it.

"It's not haute cuisine, but it's what you need. When you're done, we'll follow it up with a big glass of water and some ibuprofen. You'll wake up feeling like a champ."

"You know a lot about being drunk."

Kat shrugged. "I went to college, same as you. Late-night parties followed by early morning lectures mean you learn how to cope, and quickly. I also lost my parents when I was in school. There are a few weekends

I don't remember after that happened. Water, Advil, toast and coffee are a combination that never fails."

"I think I would've failed the semester if I lost my parents."

"Well, fortunately, I went to an art school. They encouraged me to funnel my pain into my work, and my grades actually improved. Except for chemistry. I got a D in that," she said with a smile.

Sawyer chuckled and finished his requisite meal quickly. As she put his dishes into the sink, he went over to the refrigerator and pulled out two bottles of water. "Here you go," he said, handing her one.

"Thanks. How are you feeling?"

"Better. It all seemed to hit at once tonight. Drinking that late was foolish," he admitted. "But it got you here. I can't complain about that."

Kat set her water on the counter and looked at him with amusement crinkling her eyes. "Did you set all this up to get me to your house?"

"No," he said, with a dismissive shake of his head. "Lately nothing I plan works out as well as I want it to, so I've decided to give that up. Sometimes it's better to just go with the flow and see what happens. It always works for Finn, so why not me?"

She narrowed her gaze at him. "You're not Finn. You're Sawyer."

He shrugged and finished off his water. "Fat lot of good that does me. Finn is the one who reaps all the rewards. He has all the fun, gets all the girls, lives life to the fullest. He always gets what I want," Sawyer said, looking pointedly at Kat.

She dismissed his inebriated tirade, stretching out her hand and gently grasping his wrist. "You may look alike, but the world needs only one Finn. And it needs you to be yourself, because there's only one you."

Sawyer looked down at her hand and followed the line of her arm until he was gazing into her eyes. "Stay with me tonight."

Kat froze for a moment before dropping her hand from his wrist. He could tell by the line between her brows that she was conflicted. She wanted to stay. She wanted him. But she kept putting this fantasy of a future with Finn in front of her own needs and desires.

"Just one night. One last time."

She backed up until she hit the quartz countertop of the island. "You've been drinking. You don't mean it. We both agreed it was a mistake the last time."

He took a step forward and shook his head. "I know exactly what I'm saying, Kat. I'm not that drunk."

"I don't know, Sawyer. I—"

He took another step, but she didn't move away. "Finn will be home soon. And if you get what you want, everything that happened between us will be a deeply buried secret once you move on with your life. I will become your brother-in-law or the baby's uncle Sawyer. Nothing more. And I'll be okay with that, because it's what you want. But give me one last night to keep with me. A night to remember you by."

Sawyer reached out to capture the ever-present strand of auburn hair that fell along her cheek, and pushed it behind her ear. He let his knuckles graze her skin and felt her press into his touch.

* * *

"Please, Kat."

There was something in his voice. In the way he looked at her. Something that told Kat she wasn't going to be able to walk away from him. Not tonight.

She closed her eyes and leaned into the warm fingers brushing against her face. She longed to have those same warm hands on her body and his lips pressed to hers. These last few days, she'd missed Sawyer. Whether he was aggravating her or making love to her, she missed it. And she knew she would miss it for the days and weeks to come.

Why not indulge one last time? Give them both something to remember?

Opening her eyes, she closed the gap between them, cradled his face in her hands and pulled his mouth to hers. The rough stubble of his evening beard prickled against her hands in sharp contrast to her own soft skin.

The moment he realized she wasn't just kissing him, but saying yes to his proposition, the intensity increased tenfold. His arms wrapped around her, pulling her tight against him with the hunger of a man who'd long denied himself sustenance. He pressed her back against the island, his hands roaming across her body just as his tongue explored her mouth.

Kat met his intensity. With everything she had, she wanted him. And if it was the last time, she wanted to remember every moment in his arms.

Her breathing quickened when his lips traveled along her jaw and down her throat. He licked and nibbled at her skin, causing Kat to gasp and writhe as the pleasurable tingles vibrated through her nervous system. Her neck was her weakness and Sawyer instinctively seemed to know it. As her knees softened beneath her from the sensations, he tightened his grip, holding her upright.

And then, when she needed him more than ever, he retreated. She opened her eyes to see him looking down at her with desire blazing in his dark gaze. He seemed pensive, and it scared her. He wasn't changing his mind, was he? Then he took a step back, helping her regain her footing, and reached for her hand. "Come on."

"Where are we going?" she asked.

"I'm taking you upstairs," he said. "If this is the last time we'll be together, I'm going to do it properly, not some quick tumble on the closest hard surface."

She followed him back to the staircase she'd admired earlier, and they went up to the second floor. There, he opened a pair of French doors to the master suite, which took up the majority of that level. In the center of the room was the showpiece—a grand four-poster bed that was carved to look like ivy was wrapped around its massive columns and across the headboard.

Kat couldn't stop herself from walking up to it and touching one of the columns. It was an old piece. Better than her own work, she had to admit. It was beautiful. Perhaps the most beautiful bed she'd ever seen. She had the sudden burning urge to go to her shop and make a headboard at her first opportunity.

"I found this in the attic when I bought the house,"

Sawyer said, as he came up behind her and ran his own hand over the smooth, polished wood. "I had it restored and refinished. I must've known you would be here to see it one day."

Kat turned to face him, looking up at the dark eyes that watched her so carefully. He reached out to brush the hair from her face again and then softly ran his thumb over her bottom lip. Even as he teetered on the edge of being tipsy, he was more thoughtful and loving than any man she'd ever been with.

His attention to detail continued as they moved around to the side of the bed. They slowly removed each other's clothing, caressing and kissing the bare skin as they exposed it. Then he picked her up around the waist and lifted her onto the high mattress. She scooted back as he advanced, covering her body with his until his warm skin chased away the cool conditioned air being circulated by the ceiling fan overhead.

Sawyer propped himself on his elbows, looking down at her. Kat wished she knew what he was thinking, but she was too afraid to ask. Knowing the truth would only make things harder.

He slipped between her thighs, rubbing his hands over the outside of her legs and hips until she nearly purred from the caress. He dipped his head, drawing one of her nipples into his mouth. Sawyer teased it, tugging hard on her flesh until her back arched up off the bed.

Kat dug her heels into the mattress, lifting her hips and seeking him out. He didn't disappoint, moving forward into her without much effort. She was ready for him, welcoming him inside with a hiss of satisfaction.

From there, he took his time. He wanted a night to remember and they would have it. Every inch of her skin was caressed and kissed. Every sound she made he seemed to memorize. When he moved inside her with more urgency, Kat fought to keep her eyes open so she, too, could remember every moment.

Eventually, she lost that battle. Her release exploded inside her just as his mouth clamped down onto hers. He swallowed her cries, taking them into himself for safekeeping and mingling them with his own low groans as he poured himself into her.

It was a leisurely, but emotionally exhausting, love-making session. And when Sawyer collapsed at her side, he was curled up next to her with his hand protectively resting on her belly.

Kat knew it then. If she was being honest with herself, she'd known it before. She'd known it the first night they spent together, but she'd been too stubborn to believe it. It wasn't a part of her plan. It wasn't the way she wanted things to turn out. But that didn't make it any less true.

Kat was in love with Sawyer.

She could tell herself that she wanted to marry Finn, but that was just her own head getting in the way of what her heart wanted. She hardly knew Finn. But what she did know was that there was no way he could compete with Sawyer. His twin had already taken his place in her heart and no matter how hard she tried to push him out, Sawyer was still there.

She closed her eyes tightly and cursed herself. She was an idiot. She'd gone and fallen in love with the wrong Steele twin.

Turning her head, she looked over at him. His eyes were closed, his golden lashes resting on his cheeks. He'd already fallen fast asleep, thanks to the combined sedative effects of good sex and strong whiskey. She wanted to tell him how she felt, but seeing him asleep was enough to give her pause.

Sawyer was a good man. He was as stubborn as she was, for sure, but he had a very strong compass when it came to right and wrong. That he'd given in to his desire for her, even knowing it wasn't right, had to mean something. It meant he cared for her, too, no matter if he knew or understood that himself.

But that moral compass wasn't going anywhere. He'd asked her for one last night and that's all he would take. Once Finn was back in Charleston, he would step aside just as he'd said he would. Even if it hurt him. Even if it broke his heart to do it. And telling him that she loved him wouldn't help. It would only make it harder on both of them. She knew he would put the baby's needs first, just like she had.

And nothing short of a time machine would change the fact that Finn was her baby's father.

Ten

"Nǐ hǎo. Wǒ huíláile!"

Sawyer looked up from his computer and inwardly cringed at the sound of his brother's voice and his massacred attempt at speaking Mandarin as he came down the hallway.

Finn stopped in Sawyer's doorway. He was wearing his usual suit, but instead of a tie, his shirt collar was unbuttoned to show a gold necklace with a jade medallion he'd picked up overseas. "I have returned, twin of mine. Did you miss me?"

"Not particularly," Sawyer said flatly.

Finn smiled and continued down the hall without missing a beat. Sawyer didn't really want to follow, but he wanted to know how things had gone in China, and his father would probably be demanding a full report immediately.

Pushing up from his chair, he went out and followed Finn to the big corner office where Trevor Steele held court. His brother was already in there by the time he reached the assistant's desk.

"Sawyer, come in and shut the door," Trevor said.

Finn was grinning from ear to ear in one of the two guest chairs across from their father. Things must have gone well in Beijing. Or his brother was too busy doing other things to notice that it hadn't.

"The manufacturing plant is complete and operational. I returned home for a few weeks while the staffing team works on hiring from the local area and getting the team trained. I think we will have them punching out hammers and sockets within a month, conservatively."

Both brothers turned to Trevor for his reaction and Sawyer wasn't disappointed.

"Thanks for the update," Trevor retorted, "but I know exactly what's going on over there. Do you really think I'd send you halfway across the world to manage a multi-million-dollar operation and not know what was going on every second of the day?"

Finn's smile faded. "Of course you would keep abreast. You're the president of the company. I just wanted to share the good news with you and Sawyer."

Trevor sat back in his chair and crossed his hands over his chest. "You did fine, son. Better than I expected, really. But it's hard for me to focus on that considering the mess you left behind at home."

"Mess?"

Sawyer's hands curled into fists on the arms of his chair. Completely oblivious as usual. "He's talking about Kat and the baby, you idiot."

"That's not a mess," Finn argued, looking between his father and his brother. "My attorneys have it all handled. I'm going to meet with her this week to negotiate a settlement and get her to sign off. It's fine."

Trevor studied his sons for a moment and then pinched the bridge of his nose. "I don't know how the two of you could look so similar and be so different. You are a damn fool, Finn. It's not fine. You got a stranger pregnant."

"It was an accident! I assure you I did, and always have done, everything in my power to keep that from happening."

"Everything short of keeping it in your pants," Trevor snapped.

While Sawyer did enjoy Finn getting his comeuppance on some level, he was growing uncomfortable being in the room. "Do I really need to be in here for this? I thought we were out-briefing on the new facility."

He started to push up from his chair, but Trevor's sharp gaze caused him to sit back down immediately. "You stay," he said. "You've been the one handling things with Kat while he's been gone. You know her better than anyone."

"I don't see what the problem is," Finn argued. "I plan to take care of Kat and the baby."

"That's not enough. Writing a check and walking

away from your responsibilities is not enough. You've forgotten that I've met this woman. Your mother met her. Your grandmother and sisters have met her. And they like her. *I* like her. She's not your usual weekend delight that you can give a check to and send on her way. She's more your brother's speed, to be honest, but she had the misfortune of meeting the wrong Steele twin. She is smart and kind, and the best damn thing to ever happen to you. She could be the thing that turns your life around. And accident or no accident, she deserves better than what you're offering."

"You don't even know what I'm offering."

"I know what you're *not* offering," their father said sharply. "You know, I sent you to China in the hopes you would grow up. You're almost thirty-four years old and you've been causing problems for the family since you found that pecker between your legs. Now it looks like I'm going to have to make you man up once and for all."

Finn was pressed back so far in his chair, Sawyer thought he might tumble backward. He was smart enough not to say anything else at this point. Even Finn knew when to shut up and just listen.

"That is your child, and you're going to marry its mother. Steeles don't walk away from their mistakes."

"Only when we can't erase them and pretend like they never happened," Finn said.

Sawyer's eyes widened as he looked at his brother in shock. Maybe Finn wasn't as smart as he thought.

"What did you say?" Trevor asked in a biting, sarcastic tone.

"I'm talking about Morgan and how your *guiding hand* completely destroyed her life. You paid off River and just swept her marriage and her baby under the rug, but you can't do that with me, so you're bullying me into doing what you want instead."

Sawyer was afraid to take a breath. He sat still, waiting for the blowback. He'd never heard Finn—or anyone for that matter—speak to their father that way. He could see the anger twitching the muscles in his father's jaw as he considered his words.

"You're right," Trevor said at last, in a cold, calm voice. "I thought at nineteen that Morgan was too young and immature to make her own decisions and I was wrong. But this time, I'm right, and you've just proved you're still too immature to make your own decisions."

Finn didn't have anything to say to that. Neither did Sawyer. What could he say? This was what Kat wanted, although she probably would've preferred it not be a shotgun wedding.

"Tomorrow night, we'll have a nice family dinner to welcome you home. We will invite Kat. And there, in front of everyone, you're going to present her with an engagement ring and ask her to be your wife. Do you understand me?"

Finn swallowed hard and nodded.

"Very good. Now give your travel paperwork and receipts to your assistant to file and go get some rest. You're dismissed." Both brothers stood up, but Trevor's gaze shot to Sawyer. "Not you."

Finn basically ran from the office, leaving Sawyer

behind. He sighed and sat back in the chair, awaiting whatever tongue-lashing he'd earned lately. His father probably knew about him sneaking around with Kat. The man seemed to know everything that happened in this family.

"What am I going to do with him?" Trevor asked with a heavy sigh.

"If you make him marry her, he's going to be miserable. And he'll make everyone else miserable, including Kat."

"I know. But at some point, he needs to take responsibility."

"Let me marry her instead." The words slipped from Sawyer's lips before he'd fully thought them through. He didn't regret them, though.

Trevor snapped his gaze over to his son. "That's a generous offer. Would you care to tell me why you'd like to marry Kat in your brother's place?"

"It's the best solution," Sawyer argued. "Finn doesn't want to do it, but I will, and the problem will be solved. Genetically, legally, it will be my child as much as Finn's. She will look just like me. No one ever needs to know the truth."

His father considered his words for a moment and shook his head. "That's very pragmatic of you. I can always count on you to do what needs to be done, although I'm sure in this case there's more to your motivations than I really want to know. But I can't let you do that."

"Why not?"

"Because this isn't about you. If you want to help,

then I need you to back off and let Finn step up. Let things play out between the two of them. If he proposes and Kat turns him down to choose you instead, let that be *her* choice. If she has any damn sense, she would laugh in his face, but Finn has to make the effort or he never will."

Sawyer sighed. His father was right. This was Kat's decision. They could sit in this office and make all the plans in the world, but in the end, only what she wanted mattered. And as far as Sawyer knew, she wanted Finn. "Is there anything else?"

"Yes. That protest over the holiday. It was all over the news this weekend. That's blowback from your real estate deal, isn't it?"

Sawyer had hoped maybe word hadn't gotten to his father about that yet, but clearly he wasn't that lucky. "Yes."

"It's one thing to try to make money on a property deal, but I'll not have you dragging the family or the company through the mud to do it. Find out a way to make those people happy. Sometimes compromise is key, in business and in romance."

Oddly, this was a little bit of both for Sawyer. But his father was right. There had to be a middle ground that would keep protests off the front pages. The new building could be amazing, but it wouldn't matter if no one was willing to cross a picket line to see it. "Yes, sir."

"One last thing and you can go. Take your brother to the jewelry store. Make sure he picks something nice. Nothing gaudy or cheap. I don't want her turning him down just because he got her the Tuesday cubic zirconia special from Big Eddie on King Street."

Sawyer stood up and nodded. Helping his brother pick out an engagement ring for Kat was one of the last things he wanted to do, but he would to make sure she got something she would love. She deserved that much.

After stepping out into the hall, he headed back toward his office. There, he found Finn sitting on the edge of their assistant's desk, flirting mercilessly as though that wasn't a lawsuit waiting to happen.

"Come on, Finn, we need to go engagement ring shopping so you can propose tomorrow night."

Their assistant, Melody May, sat up at attention and pulled back from Finn. The smile faded from her face and she snatched the travel receipts from his hand without another word.

Finn matched her frown and followed Sawyer into his office. "You really think I should do this? Are you as crazy as Dad?"

"Shut the door," Sawyer said as he leaned against his desk. "And sit down."

"I just got one ass chewing. You don't get to boss me around, too."

"I'm older by two minutes. Now shut the damn door," he barked, pointing to the entrance, "and listen to me."

Finn reluctantly complied and flopped down into the guest chair. "What?"

"A lot has happened while you've been gone. We've all gotten to know Kat very well. Better than you know her. And like Dad said, we like her. The only thing wrong with her is that for some crazy reason, she seems to think that marrying you is the right thing to do. Personally, I think she could do better, but she hasn't asked my opinion."

"What's your point?" Finn said, crossing his arms defiantly over his chest.

Sawyer leaned in to his brother with his stoniest gaze. "My point is that Katherine McIntyre is the single greatest woman to ever walk into your life. She is smart, funny, talented, beautiful…and she's having your child. You don't deserve her in your bed and you don't deserve her as your wife. Not even close. But right now she's there for the taking. And if you let her walk out of your life, you're an even bigger fool than I thought."

"Good evening, Miss McIntyre," Lena said, as she opened the door to the Steele mansion. "Please come in. The family is in the library."

Kat stepped in cautiously and waited for Lena to close the door behind her before she started making her way toward the voices in the east wing of the house.

"Kat!" A woman's voice boomed across the entry-way.

She turned to see Morgan rushing over to her from the stairs. "Hey."

Without a word, she grabbed Kat's hand and dragged her away from the library toward the powder room. She tugged her inside and shut the door.

"What is going on?" Kat asked, awkwardly pressed against the pedestal sink.

"Finn is proposing to you at dinner tonight," Morgan blurted in excitement.

Kat's jaw dropped. "Are you serious? I haven't even seen him since he got back from China. We've spoken a handful of times on the phone. Proposing tonight? Really?"

Morgan nodded, a conspiratorial look on her face. "I've seen the ring. Sawyer took him shopping yesterday and it's ah-mazing."

She was stunned. This was just supposed to be a welcome-home dinner with the family. Her chance to see and talk to Finn in person for the first time since the night they'd gotten themselves into this mess. And he was proposing? In the moment, she wasn't sure what to say. Thank goodness Morgan had given her a heads-up or she might've appeared like a very ungrateful recipient when Finn popped the question. After all, this was what she wanted.

Right?

"Anyway, I thought you should know. It ruins the surprise, but personally, I'd rather be prepared. If he does it in front of the whole family, it could be nerve-racking. Plus, I wanted to squeal a little with you about it ahead of time. This is just what you said you wanted the other night on the ship! I'm so happy for you!"

Morgan scooped Kat into a hug and she returned the embrace. Why was her future sister-in-law more excited about this than she was? She pinched her eyes shut and tried to push the image of Sawyer out of her mind. That was over and done. He was stepping aside so Kat could have the family she wanted. It was all coming together.

"Okay, I'd better get back before someone wonders where I've been. See you in there in a minute." Morgan opened the door and dashed out of the bathroom.

Kat took a moment to compose herself. She checked her makeup and smoothed her hair. She wanted to look perfect for the moment. Finn should be proud of his bride, whether he'd intended for this to happen or not. After stepping out of the room, she turned and very nearly collided with Sawyer as he hung his coat in the nearby closet.

"Kat? I didn't know you were here already. Are you hiding in the bathroom?"

"Of course not. I was just putting on some fresh lipstick."

He nodded, trying and failing to look disinterested in her appearance tonight. "Have you seen Finn yet?"

"No. I saw Morgan briefly, but that's it so far."

He nodded again. There was a stiffness about Sawyer tonight. If he took Finn shopping, then he knew what was about to happen. He didn't seem to like the idea very much. Lately, neither did she. It made her want to ask the hard questions while she still had the chance.

"Can I ask you something before we go in there with your family?"

"Sure," he said, pasting on a polite smile.

Kat tried to think of how best to ask the question. "Can you give me any reason why I shouldn't marry Finn?"

She wanted to give him his chance. His moment. Not to do the honorable thing, but to tell the truth about how he felt about her, even if it turned the whole night upside down. Her eyes searched his face, pleading with him to be honest. Marrying Finn had seemed like a good idea until Sawyer showed up in her life. Now, she wasn't sure what she wanted, but knowing if he loved her the way she loved him would help her decide.

"I'm sorry, I can't," he said, looking away. Without making additional eye contact, Sawyer turned and walked across the hall, leaving her there alone and brokenhearted.

The rest of the evening was a bit of a blur, like she was walking through a dream. Kat was distracted and wallowing in her emotional turmoil. They gathered in the library for drinks and mingling before moving into the dining room.

As they migrated down the hall, Finn pulled Kat aside to chat in person at last. It was weird seeing him again after all this time, knowing he was her baby's father, looking so much like the man she loved but not like him at all. Later, as they were eating, she realized she couldn't really remember anything about their conversation. It had mostly been about himself and his work in China. Not once had he asked about her, the pregnancy or the baby. It made the news of his pending return to Beijing in a few weeks a little easier to swallow.

Besides that, it was hard to focus with Sawyer scowling at them. In the library, he'd pretended to be listening to what Grandma Ingrid had to say, but every time Kat glanced in his direction, he'd been looking at her as if he regretted not taking his chance when he had it.

Dinner wasn't much better. She was seated beside Finn, of course, but somehow ended up across from Sawyer. While she tried to engage Finn and River, to her right, in conversation as they ate, she could feel Sawyer's gaze on her.

She wasn't sure how she was going to get through tonight. When the moment came, and Finn got down on one knee, how could she say yes with Sawyer watching? It seemed the thing she'd once hoped for had become an impossible feat.

As Lena cleared the dinner dishes in preparation for dessert, Finn pushed back his chair to make a toast. Kat froze in her seat, finally forcing herself to reach out and raise her glass of sparkling water.

"I'd like to thank everyone for coming tonight and welcoming me home from China. It was an amazing trip and I look forward to returning and continuing to assist in Steele Tools' new venture there. It's such a fast-paced and colorful culture in some aspects, and then so peaceful and quiet in other areas. I was able to find something for each one of you on my trip. The bag of goodies is in the library and I'll hand them out after dessert. But right now, I have one special gift for Kat. I—"

Sawyer abruptly pushed his chair back from the dinner table. "You'll have to excuse me," he said, as he rounded the long table and practically ran into the hall.

Everyone sat in stunned silence for a moment before Finn recovered. "I hope he's feeling okay. Anyway, I wanted to thank all of you for welcoming Kat so warmly into the family while I was gone. I have heard nothing but glowing stories about what a talented and lovely woman she is. And although we haven't known each other for long, I look forward to having the opportunity to know her very well in the upcoming years."

As Finn reached into his suit coat pocket, Kat's heart started pounding in her chest. For a moment, all she could hear was its deep bass rhythm and the rushing of blood in her ears. She thought she might even faint. She closed her eyes, hoping the swimming in her head would pass before she made a fool of herself in front of these lovely people who had welcomed her into their family.

When she opened her eyes, she realized that Finn was down on his knee beside her. He had a small jewelry box in one hand, opened to display one of the most beautiful rings she'd ever seen in her life. The diamond in the center was a large and colorless oval stone, but what really caught her eye was the platinum band itself. The diamond was in a bezel setting with a knife edge designed band. There were three diamonds on each side that tapered in size to a double milgrain design. She could tell the intricate filigree etching had been hand done by an artisan who loved to work with metal and jewelry design as much as she enjoyed working with wood.

"Katherine McIntyre, I know that we are only at the start of our journey together. Tonight I offer you this ring in the hopes that it will be a long, happy one. Will you marry me?"

She didn't know what to say.

It was the moment she'd been waiting for. This might have started off by accident, but Finn was stepping up and helping her achieve her dream of having a real family for her daughter. Mother, wife, father, husband, child, family…it was all coming together. There was only one thing missing from the picture.

Love.

Kat had told herself she didn't need it. What the baby needed was more important. She'd told herself that if Finn would marry her, she would make a good life with him and maybe love would come in time.

The moment was right. The ring was perfect. The proposal was heartfelt and well-spoken. She was surrounded by her new family, who were nearly bursting at the seams, waiting for her to say yes so they could spend the rest of the evening celebrating the new couple. It was everything she'd thought she wanted.

It was just the wrong brother down on one knee.

Eleven

Sawyer could step aside because his father told him to. He could even take his brother shopping to pick out the ring he knew she would love. But he just couldn't sit at that table and watch Finn propose to the woman Sawyer loved.

Realizing that he loved Kat mere seconds before his brother stood up to make his big speech was Sawyer's typical poor timing. Before that, he'd known he cared about Kat and the baby. He liked spending time with her. If marrying her made her feel better about raising her daughter, he was willing to do it, and spare Finn from a fate he saw as worse than death. Sawyer knew he didn't like the idea of his brother with Kat. But until that moment, none of it had added up in his mind to love.

When he realized the truth, it was too much for him to take. He'd been in love before, so he should've realized it sooner. But he was stubborn. He knew Kat was never meant to be his, so he hadn't recognized the signs. How stupid could he be, to fall in love with the woman having his brother's child? Even after he knew she wanted to marry Finn for the child's sake, he couldn't stay away. The whole situation was doomed from their first kiss that day at the District.

So he left. Simple as that. His parents would probably be annoyed. He'd have to explain that he realized he'd forgotten an appointment or something. Left the iron on at home. He certainly couldn't tell them he was in love with Kat and didn't want to watch her get engaged to Finn.

His phone rang several times on his drive home that night, but he didn't answer. He put it on Silent and shoved it into the glove box of his Audi. He didn't want to hear about how it went. He didn't want to see a picture of the blissful couple. He just wanted to go home, drink a beer and reevaluate his damn life.

What he certainly didn't expect was to find his brother sitting in his office the next morning. When he opened the door, Finn was reclining casually on the leather sofa he kept near the window for visits and late afternoon naps.

"Good morning, brother," Finn said in a chipper tone.

Too chipper, to tell the truth. Sawyer looked at him with mistrust, going past the couch to toss his laptop bag onto the desk. "It's too early for you to be up."

"I'm still on Beijing time. I figure since I'm just going back in a few weeks, I shouldn't bother fighting the time difference and the jet lag."

"I figured you were out all night celebrating your pending nuptials."

Finn's brow furrowed in confusion. "Nuptials? You mean you haven't heard?"

Sawyer sighed and leaned against his desk. "Haven't heard what, Finn? It's too early for guessing games."

"You haven't looked at your phone!" Finn got up from the couch and walked over to him. "Hold out your hand," he said.

When Sawyer complied, Finn dropped the ring box into his palm. He opened it, expecting it to be empty, with the ring on Kat's finger, but it was still safely nestled in its velvet bed. "Tell me you didn't chicken out on her!" he said, gripping the ring box in his fist and slamming the lid shut. He would punch Finn in the face right now if he'd changed his mind and broken Kat's heart.

"No way!" Finn said, as he ducked out of arm's reach. "I did my part. Pretty well, too. I didn't want to hear about it from Dad later, so I had a very nice, heart-felt proposal prepared. But she turned me down. Flat."

Sawyer froze for a moment. A part of him was waiting for Finn to say he was joking, but the relieved smile on his face said it all. Kat hadn't accepted his proposal and Finn was thrilled, because there was nothing their father could do about it.

"She said no?"

"She said *no*. With Dad and everyone else there

to witness it. And while I'm relieved... I also have to say that I'm a bit concerned about why she changed her mind."

"Concerned?"

"Yes. Concerned that while I was out of the country, my twin brother may have swooped in and snatched Kat right out from under me."

"What are you talking about?"

"Come on, man. I saw you two looking at each other all evening. I asked you to handle the situation until I got back. I didn't mean sleep with her. What if I'd wanted to marry her? What if I'd really liked the idea of us starting our family together? You would've screwed it all up for everyone."

"Like that would've ever happened. You were only proposing because Dad was making you. And besides that, you never would've been in this situation if you hadn't gone to that party pretending to be me. She went there looking for me, not you. So don't try to act all innocent and put out. If anyone swooped in and stole anything, *you* tried to snatch Kat away from *me*."

"Yeah, well, now you have your shot. I'm off the hook with Dad and she's all yours."

Sawyer narrowed his gaze at his brother with contempt. "No matter what you do, you always seem to get away with it."

"What is that supposed to mean?"

"It means that I've never met someone so reckless, so irresponsible, and yet you never get what's coming to you. You never pay the price for your actions. Somehow you always get off the hook. You don't have to

marry the mother of your child. You didn't have to pay
when you wrecked Tom's motorcycle. Dad smoothed
things over when you got in trouble in school. No matter what happens, you never have to clean up your
messes. You always get one of us to handle everything
for you, and then you have the audacity to get irritable
with me because I happened to fall in love with the girl
you're supposed to be with?"

Finn opened his mouth, but stopped short of answering. His angry retort seemed to deflate inside him. He
looked at his brother for a moment and shook his head.
"Are you serious? You're in love with her?"

Sawyer clenched his jaw in irritation with himself
for letting that slip. He and Finn didn't have the kind
of relationship many twins had. They didn't share intimate details of their lives. Sawyer didn't want to hear
about Finn's shenanigans and Finn was bored by most
of what Sawyer did with his time. So this was a big
moment for them both. An awkward one, too.

"Yes, I am," he said, turning away and putting the
engagement ring box on the edge of his desk.

"And what the hell were you going to do if she accepted my proposal? Mope until the end of time?"

"I'm sure your marriage wouldn't have lasted that
long," Sawyer quipped.

"Very funny," Finn said. "I'm being serious."

Sawyer shrugged. He hadn't really thought that far
ahead. "Maybe moping. Maybe working myself into
a bout of middle-aged hypertension. If she accepted
your proposal, maybe I would've asked to take over
in Beijing, and disappeared for a while. I thought she

wanted to marry you. I wasn't going to interfere, no matter how I felt."

"Why not? You're always interfering in my life when you think I'm doing the wrong thing."

"*Because*...nothing was going to change the reality of the situation, and that was that Kat is having *your* child. Whether I loved her, whether she hated you. That's still *your* baby and I couldn't get in the way of that."

Finn dropped down into the guest chair and considered his brother's confession for a few minutes. "Does she love you?" he asked.

"I don't know." Sawyer followed suit and flopped down into his own desk chair with a heavy sigh. "We never really talked about it."

"But you said that she did want to marry me."

"I thought so. That's what she told Jade and Morgan on the Fourth of July."

"And yet, just a few short days later, she turned me down and made me look like an idiot in front of the whole family. I'd say she did some hard thinking since then. She's got to be in love with you. That's the only reason I could fathom."

"Because there's no way a woman wouldn't want to marry you otherwise?"

"I'm a catch, damn it. And so are you. I say she's in love with you."

Sawyer sat forward and rested his elbows on his knees. "Even if she is...what about your daughter?"

Finn paused and looked at his brother with surprise. His mouth dropped open as he scrambled for words. "She's... Kat's... *We're* having a girl?"

"Oh." Sawyer sat up straight, alarmed at letting that slip. "I didn't realize she hadn't told you yet. I'm sorry. The whole family knows. Morgan turned the yacht pink when we sailed on the Fourth."

Finn shook his head. "We didn't really get to chat about much, with everyone there. A daughter…wow. A daughter is exciting news. Perhaps a little bit of karma for me."

"Perhaps."

"And despite what you might think, I plan to be a part of my daughter's life. I might be a shameless flirt with commitment issues, but I'm not a deadbeat dad. Kat and I can work out the details, but I'll be involved with the baby. As for the mother…" His voice trailed off. "She obviously wants you. She should be with you."

Finn cupped the ring box on the edge of the desk and slid it across the smooth wood to Sawyer, who reached out and caught it before it could fall to the floor. "Take that," Finn said. "Give it to her. Hell, you're the one that picked it out, anyway. You knew what she would like. I'm sure she'd appreciate it a lot more coming from you."

"No, you should return it."

"Nah," Finn said. "There's no way I can walk back in there with a ring that expensive and tell the man at the counter that the woman said no. You take it or I'll stash it in a drawer somewhere and forget about it until some girl staying over finds it hidden away and thinks I'm about to propose. No thanks."

"It was expensive."

"So was that Jet Ski," Finn admitted. "And since I made you give it to me to go to that party for you, like a jerk, why don't we call it an even trade?"

Sawyer couldn't believe his ears. He'd dropped nearly twenty grand on that Jet Ski and yet it didn't come close to the price of Kat's ring. But he realized this was Finn's way of saying he was sorry. His pride wouldn't let him voice the words, not even to Sawyer. But he meant it in his way.

Getting up from his chair, Sawyer walked around the desk and stood in front of his brother with the velvet box in his hand. "You're sure?"

"Take it. Give it to her. Live happily ever after with the mother of my child," Finn said, as he rose to his feet. "Yes, you'll be my daughter's stepdad/uncle and I'll be her dad/uncle, but who cares about labels? We'll all raise our daughter together in whatever weird way makes sense for us, and it's nobody's damn business but ours."

Sawyer looked at Finn with amazement, and for the first time in a long time, felt the urge to give him a hug. He actually couldn't remember the last time he'd hugged his brother. But before he could do so, Finn surprised him and reached out to him instead. He wrapped his arms around Sawyer and patted him firmly on the back.

"Be good to them," he said. Then he turned and walked out of Sawyer's office without another word.

Kat had a million things to do before the District shut down in a few days. She hadn't done a single thing in preparation for the baby. She needed to clean house and buy groceries. So naturally, she was sitting on her piazza drinking tea and reading a book. It was a best-selling self-help title she'd picked up from the library. The author promised to help her identify her own self-sabotaging habits and live her best life.

So far it was stupid. But it was easier to read than think about what kind of disaster her life had turned into lately.

Some people would say things weren't that bad. She'd chosen not to marry a man who was all wrong for her. She supposed that was for the best, even if she did have to turn down Finn in front of his family. Despite that hurdle, her relationship with Finn may have actually become better for the rejection. He'd obviously been pressured to make the proposal and seemed relieved when she turned him down.

They'd had lunch together a few days later and finally got the opportunity to talk without anyone else around. Without interfering fathers and overprotective attorneys, they'd hammered out a plan to co-raise their daughter that made them both happy. Finn agreed to pay for private schools, and would be buying a place closer to Kat, with a bedroom for nights he had custody. Kat hadn't really wanted or needed his money, but would accept the child support payments he insisted on, given that he reduce the monthly amount in favor of setting up a trust fund for the baby that she would get when she turned twenty-one.

It was all very civilized.

And if Kat had heard from Sawyer since he'd walked

out of that family dinner, she might feel better about how it was all turning out. But she hadn't.

Perhaps she had read the whole situation wrong. Sawyer had told her he didn't have any reason why she shouldn't marry Finn. Maybe he'd been telling the truth. Maybe he wanted her only because he knew he couldn't have her. She was a forbidden temptation. And now she was just a single, pregnant lady. Not very tempting at all.

The sound of the doorbell caused Kat to sit up and set the book aside. Glancing out, she noticed a black Rolls Royce parked on the street. She went to the door and opened it, finding none other than Ingrid Steele standing on her stoop.

"Mrs. Steele? I mean, Ingrid?" She corrected herself. "What are you doing here?"

"I'm paying a call on my future granddaughter-in-law," she said. "May I come in?"

Startled, Kat took a step back and welcomed the older woman inside. "Would you like to sit on the piazza or in the house? I'll get us both a glass of tea."

"The piazza and tea sound lovely."

Kat rushed into the house to get some tea and returned to find Ingrid sitting patiently on one of her patio chairs. She handed her the glass and wished she had some kind of cookies or treats in the house to offer. Unfortunately, all she'd bothered to get at the grocery store of late were saltine crackers, cereal and granola bars. She wasn't sure if it was morning sickness carrying into the second trimester or if she was just nauseated by how awful things had become. Either way, chopped-up chocolate chip granola bars on a platter wouldn't quite cut it for the Steele matriarch.

"I didn't expect to see you today," Kat began. "Or for a while, considering how dinner ended the other night."

"Pish posh. You're family now, dear. The other night doesn't change that."

All things considered, Kat appreciated the sentiment. The Steeles weren't the average American family, but they were the closest thing she had. "She will be your great-granddaughter, of course," Kat said, rubbing her belly. It seemed to be growing a bit more every morning of late. "But I'm just…me."

"Well, maybe I'm old and sentimental, but I still think you'll be my granddaughter-in-law someday."

"You know that Finn and I aren't going to marry, right? He never really wanted to marry me. I think he only proposed because Trevor put him up to it."

Ingrid chuckled and shook her head. "Of course Trevor made him do it. But I'm not talking about Finn, dear. I'm talking about you and Sawyer."

Kat looked up from her tea in surprise. As far as she was aware, no one knew about what had happened between her and Sawyer. She forced the mouthful of tea down her throat without choking and asked, "What would make you say that?"

"I may be old, but I'm not blind, dear. There's been something simmering between you two this whole time. I saw that much at my garden party and during the Fourth of July gathering. It didn't matter that you rarely spoke and never touched. You were always stealing glances at each other when the other wasn't looking. I could feel the sexual tension in the air. If you were trying to hide how you feel, you were doing a terrible job, both of you."

Kat didn't bother to argue with her. There was no sense in lying about it now that things with Finn were settled. "Well, I honestly don't know how Sawyer feels about me. He never said anything."

"That doesn't mean much. Men are always stubborn about their feelings, especially in this family. I shouldn't say so, but Sawyer is my favorite grandchild. Even as a baby he was more serious and thoughtful. He would quietly sit in the grass and study a butterfly, while his brother ran through the yard, terrorizing everything in his path. He is my quiet grandchild, but still waters run deep in him. Just because he doesn't say it doesn't mean he doesn't feel it. How did he treat you?"

"When we weren't arguing…like gold."

"That sounds about right. Did you ever tell him how you felt?"

She gave a guilty shake of her head. "No. I was afraid to. And I kept telling myself that I should be with Finn, even though I knew it felt wrong. I thought it was best for the baby."

"What's best for the baby is what will make you happy, dear. Babies don't know anything about DNA or legitimacy. They just want to be surrounded by love and warmth. Don't you think Sawyer could give her that?"

"Absolutely. But he's not here. I haven't seen him since he ran out on dinner that night."

"I'm sure he's sitting at home wrestling with the situation, just like you are. He didn't bolt from the room in the middle of your brother's proposal because he had food poisoning. He couldn't bear to sit there and watch the woman he loved get engaged to someone else. I guarantee it."

"Yes, well, it's been days and I'm sure he's heard how it turned out by now. If he was trying to be a gentleman and let Finn have his chance first, it's done. He hasn't even texted to ask how I am."

Ingrid sipped her tea and then set it aside. "Sawyer is a lot like his grandfather in many ways. Maybe that's why I've always had such a soft spot in my heart for him. They're both perfectionists. Strategists. The two of them would play a single chess match for hours in the library. They didn't like to make a decision or move on a project until everything was just so. That might make them seem like they're slow to act, but once they've made a decision, they're absolutely certain they're making the right choice."

"So he's sitting at home trying to decide if he really wants me?"

"No, no. More than likely, he's plotting and planning how to woo you properly."

Kat wasn't sure she'd ever been wooed. But whatever he was planning—if anything—she wished he would go ahead and do it. She didn't like being in limbo.

"I wish I were as confident as you are," she said. "I asked him if he could tell me a reason why I shouldn't marry Finn, and he said he couldn't."

"Of course he couldn't. He wouldn't interfere if he thought that was what you wanted. It doesn't mean he didn't want to give you a reason. He probably could've named five reasons why you shouldn't marry Finn, without trying very hard. But he didn't believe it was the right thing to do."

"You think so?"

"I've seen my grandchildren grow from headstrong toddlers to corporate leaders and entrepreneurs. I know how they think. And I know," Ingrid said, as she reached out to cup Kat's cheek, "that he cares for you. Just give him time. I have faith that if you want to be a Steele, you will be before too long."

Ingrid looked down at her watch. "Well, dear, this was a lovely visit, but I've got to get going. I have an appointment to see my jeweler." She got up and slipped her purse over her arm.

Kat stood and followed her to the door. "Thank you for stopping by. I feel better about everything."

"I'm glad, dear. I'll be awaiting news."

Kat watched Ingrid go down her walkway and over to where a man was waiting to open the door to the Rolls. Once she'd settled inside, he shut the door and got in to drive her to her jeweler, or wherever her agenda was taking her next.

As the car disappeared around the next block, Kat let the piazza door close and returned to her spot on the sofa. She shoved the book to the other side of the cushions and thought over everything Ingrid had told her.

Perhaps Sawyer *was* sitting in his house, trying to decide on the perfect way to woo her. But she had no guarantees of that, just a confident grandmother. He could just as easily be working on his renovation plans for the District. That was right around the corner, and despite her best efforts, Kat was unable to stop it from happening. She was right back where she'd started, although now she had a baby on the way and a broken heart to complicate things.

That said, Kat wasn't the kind to sit around and wait on a man to decide what he wanted. She had a studio to relocate and a baby to plan for, so she would focus on what she could control. And if he ever showed up with his heart in his hands, maybe she wouldn't stomp on it the way he'd stomped on hers.

Twelve

It was the last day for the District as Kat knew it and loved it. By five today, everyone had to be gone, for renovations to begin. Most of the tenants had already moved out, leaving the old warehouse hollow and empty sounding, when it had once been filled with life and art.

She did love Sawyer, but a part of her would never forgive him for turning this place into some high-end mini-mall for people who liked to be seen as art savvy. Even if he just made repairs and reopened, it wouldn't be the same. Most of the people she knew wouldn't be returning, because they couldn't afford the rent. With each artist who had packed up and gone forever, the District lost a little bit of its soul.

Kat wasn't sure what she was going to do. She was

one of the few who could afford the new rent. She just wasn't certain she wanted to come back. It wouldn't be the same without Hilda and Zeke arguing, or the little chocolate shop owner coming around to test a new recipe on willing volunteers.

Kat's place had an old outbuilding at the head of the driveway that had once been the kitchen. It got so hot in Charleston during the summer that the early homes had been built with the kitchen separate from the rest. Kat's had been converted years later into a storage room when a new kitchen was added to the house, but it wouldn't take much to put her equipment out there. That would be more convenient, especially with the baby, but it wouldn't be the same.

As she opened the door to her studio, even it felt like its soul was gone. All her work and most of her tools were already packed up and gone. The movers had come the day before to take her bigger pieces of equipment and the giant owl that was too heavy for her to move. Today, she was taking a few last items off the walls and closing up shop.

The final thing, the most important thing, was for her to remove the sign above the shop door. The wooden plaque had been one of the first pieces she'd made when her father gifted her with some basic wood-working tools on her sixteenth birthday. The hand-carved sign had a crescent moon and stars etched around the edges, with a textured background that looked like cumulous clouds once she'd applied the dark oak stain and sealant. In the center were the words *Wooden Dreams*.

She had made the sign long before the idea of having her own studio developed. Her father had hung it proudly in the house, where it had stayed until after they'd passed and Kat sold her parents' home. After college, when she'd heard about spaces available at the District, she'd gone down to pick a location and knew exactly where the sign needed to be. It wasn't her best work, but it was one of her favorites, and Wooden Dreams became the name of her shop.

Looking up at it hanging there now, Kat felt the tears start to come.

Just one more item in the list of things she'd lost over the last few weeks. She'd lost her shop, her artist community, her chance at a family and, apparently, she'd lost her heart to a man too honorable to admit how he felt about her. Altogether, it was almost enough to send her back to the dark place she'd lived in after her parents died. Her little girl was the only thing keeping her going. And a little bit of hope. Hope that Sawyer might change his mind.

At least, if Grandma Ingrid was right to begin with. If she was wrong, then Kat had just given away her heart to someone who had no desire to take it. Either way, she hadn't heard a peep from Sawyer. Finn had called to let her know he was heading back to China, and Jade had texted her about setting up a date for a baby shower, but other than that, it was like before the baby, when there were no Steeles in her life.

She had to admit life was simpler then. And lonelier. But she loved her daughter's new family. So at least she had that.

In the empty cavern of the warehouse, the grind of the freight elevator was audible even on the far side where Kat's studio was located. She didn't pay much attention to it, though. It was probably another tenant here to load up their dreams and memories into cardboard boxes.

Instead, Kat unfolded her stepladder to take down her sign. On the second step, she couldn't quite grasp it, so she climbed to the third, which she hated because she felt so unsteady. Thankfully, she was able to hold on to the door frame as she reached up with her other hand to get the sign.

"Whoa," she said aloud, when the unexpected weight of the freed wooden panel threw off her balance. Her center of gravity was all out of whack because of the baby.

"Easy now," someone said, and she felt strong hands at her lower back and hip steadying her.

Kat tucked the sign under her arm and looked around to see who was there. To her surprise, it was Sawyer.

"Hand it to me," he said. "It will make it easier for you to get down."

She reluctantly passed him the sign and climbed down to the wood plank floors. Once she was on firm ground again, she snatched the sign from Sawyer and turned her back on him to return to her shop. While a part of her was happy to see him after all this time, he was the reason she was packing up today, hovering on the verge of tears.

"Kat?" Sawyer called after her in confusion.

"I appreciate your help in keeping me from falling, but why are you here?" she asked. "I haven't heard from you since the dinner party for your brother and then you show up out of the blue. It can't be just to see me or you wouldn't have waited so long. It must be because of the building. Are you here to make sure I don't chain myself to the front doors or something?"

Sawyer appeared contrite. He tucked his hands into his pants pockets and looked down at the ground the way he always did when he was thinking. "I'm sorry, Kat."

She put the sign into the last box she had left in the studio, and then turned around to face him. "Sorry about what? About closing this place down and uprooting everyone and everything I care about? About refusing to tell me how you felt for me, at the critical moment when I had to decide if I wanted to marry your brother? About disappearing off the face of the earth after I turned Finn down, making me wonder if I was crazy or just plain stupid for falling for you?"

He stood there and took every angry word she had to level at him. And when she was done, he reached into his breast coat pocket and pulled out an envelope addressed to her. "I'm sorry for all of it," he said.

Sawyer held out the envelope until Kat reluctantly took it from him. In the corner the address was imprinted for the District Arts Center. But it wasn't her District. This was his, with a fancy new logo to go with the new vision. She tore through the logo as she opened the envelope and pulled out the single-page notice inside.

Her eyes quickly scanned what was written, but she kept having to stop and go back because it didn't make any sense. She couldn't be reading the words she was reading. Starting back at the top, she went through it word by word, hoping this time she could believe what she saw.

It was an official letter from Sawyer's development company about the closure today. It stated that they expected to complete the necessary renovations in three months. At that time, any previous tenants who wanted to return to their studio would be grandfathered in to rent it at their current rate. Any new tenants would pay the higher rates.

Kat's hand began to tremble as she reached the end of the letter, making it hard to read. Especially while her eyes were overflowing with tears. Sawyer was going to fix the place up so it was safe, and let them return. Hilda and Zeke could reopen their studios. They could all do so if they chose to.

It was an incredible compromise and it made her angry that she hadn't thought of that first. But of course, Sawyer the Strategist had.

"Oh no," Sawyer said, whipping a pressed handkerchief from his pocket. "You're crying. I'm sorry. Please don't cry, Kat. I thought you would be happy."

She accepted the hankie, pressing it to her eyes and dabbing the tears from her cheeks. "I am happy. It's just, I don't know, pregnancy hormones combined with everything else. Ignore the tears."

Sawyer reached out to wipe a fresh one from her

cheek with his thumb. "That's hard for me to do. I don't like seeing you cry."

Kat shook her head. "I can't help it. What changed your mind about all this?"

"Once I realized how I felt about you, and that I wanted to be with you, I knew something had to be done about the situation here. You are more important to me than the bottom line. It may take a while to make back my investment in the renovations, but it isn't a rush. I think what I have planned will allow the community here to continue safely, but also bring in more foot traffic. It's a win-win, as long as you're happy." Sawyer reached out to take her hand.

"I'm happy," she said, as he squeezed it gently. "Thank you. On behalf of everyone here, thank you."

"I was just thinking, what would be the greatest gift I could give Kat for an engagement present?"

She froze in place, her hand still in his. She was almost uncertain she'd heard what he'd said, since he continued talking as though he hadn't dropped a bomb in the conversation.

"A ring is traditional, of course, and I have one of those, too, but I really wanted to give you something that would have meaning for you. This place is what brought us together, in a way, so it seemed sort of poetic that it would be what would bring us back together...for as long as we both shall live. I love you, Kat. More than anything."

"You love me?" Kat asked, the letter slipping from her fingers to the ground.

"I do. And I hope that you feel the same way. I

wasn't sure, so I'm taking a gamble here." Sawyer reached into the same pocket, this time pulling out a small velvet box. "Finn gave me the ring he proposed with. I knew you would like it, but it felt wrong to give you the same ring. I was going to buy a different one and then an opportunity came along that I couldn't pass up."

He opened the lid on the box, which looked a great deal older than the one Finn had presented to her. This ring was vintage, she presumed, without even looking at it. Once the box was fully open, Kat gasped at the sight.

The diamond ring was unlike anything she'd seen in the jewelry cases at the mall. It actually looked like a daisy. In the center was a large, round, canary-yellow diamond, surrounded by six smaller diamonds that were at least a third of a karat each. The flower was set in platinum, with leaves and vines engraved into the band. It was unique. Beautiful. And yet oddly familiar.

"This was the ring that my grandfather Edward gave Grandma Ingrid when he proposed. She wore it every day after that, even after he passed away, until a few days ago, when she gave it to me."

That's where she had seen it before. Ingrid had worn it every time she'd seen her. Except the last time, when she'd come by her house. Kat thought back to Ingrid's visit and her next stop, at the jeweler. Perhaps she'd been making plans then, having it cleaned or resized for Sawyer to give her.

"My grandparents were together for nearly sixty

years. I don't know how many I have to offer you, but I will happily give you any that I have left. If you'll have me."

"Will you marry me, Katherine?"

Sawyer dropped to one knee as he said the words and then held his breath. He wasn't certain what the answer was going to be. He'd thought for sure she would accept Finn's proposal, but she didn't. She hadn't said that she loved him, either. She'd just gotten weepy when he said the words, making him nervously talk far more than he'd intended to. But now he'd asked the question, and all he could do was await the answer.

After an extended moment of silence, he was getting more and more nervous.

"Kat?" he asked.

She was looking down at him with tears in her eyes and her hand covering her mouth.

"Are you okay?"

She nodded before wiping at her tears and taking a deep breath. "Sawyer, are you sure you want to marry me?"

He flinched at the question. "I'm absolutely sure. At the moment, I'm concerned about you, though. It doesn't sound like you want to marry me."

"I do," she said quickly, then crouched down until her eyes were level with his. "But what about the baby?"

Sawyer frowned. "What about her?"

Kat swallowed hard and bit her bottom lip. "Are you going to be okay with raising another man's child? Your brother's child at that. It's not the ideal way to start out a relationship, much less a marriage."

"You're pregnant?" Sawyer asked, with mock dismay and surprise.

Kat punched him in the shoulder. "I'm serious. It's a lot to ask of you, to help me raise Finn's baby. You and I both know how he can be. I have no idea how involved he's really going to be in her life. I'm not going to pretend it isn't a big deal."

Sawyer understood her concerns. He'd spent the last week thinking all this through. He made sure every eventuality was thought through, every *t* crossed and every *i* dotted. He no longer had any doubts about what he wanted to do, so he had to make sure the next words he spoke were enough to convince her that it wasn't the issue she believed it to be.

"Kat, I love you. And I love that baby. I have since the first moment I saw her on the screen and heard her heartbeat echo through the examination room. Yes, she's my brother's child. But that's as close as she could possibly be without being my own. As far as I'm concerned, she's as much mine as she is Finn's daughter, and that's how I'm going to treat her.

"I want to be there for every doctor's appointment. I'm going to be there when she's born and I'll fight Finn to hold her first. I want to be there when she takes her first steps and says her first words. That baby is a part of you, and a part of Finn. And as much as he makes me crazy sometimes, you two are the most important people in my life. So that means this baby is going to be an amazing combination of the two of you. She's already the love of my life. The apple of my eye. And I'll love her just as much as I'll love any children that you and I may have together someday."

"Stop now, or I'm going to get jealous," Kat said through her tears.

Sawyer smiled and reached out to caress her cheek. "There's nothing to be jealous about. There's not going to be another woman in South Carolina who is as loved and adored as my wife will be. But first, she's got to accept my proposal." He slipped the ring out of the box and held it up to Kat. "So what do you say? Do you want to marry me and become Mrs. Sawyer Steele?"

Kat looked at him and nodded through her tears. "I do. Yes!" She held out her hand and let him slip the family heirloom onto her finger. "It fits perfectly," she said, before leaning in and giving Sawyer a kiss.

"I know this isn't how you wanted things to turn out, or the family you envisioned when you came looking for Finn that day—" Sawyer began.

"It's not," Kat interrupted. "It's so much better." She kissed him again and he knew that she was right.

Their future together would be perfectly imperfect.

Epilogue

"And with the cutting of this ribbon, I'm happy to declare that the District Art Center is now officially reopened!"

Sawyer gave the nod to Kat and she, along with several of her fellow artisans, used the ridiculously large scissors to cut the ribbon. The audience cheered and the media happily filmed the crowds as they pushed through the front door to see the new and improved District.

Kat was bursting with pride as Sawyer sidled up beside her and wrapped his arm around her ever expanding waist. She was just a week into her third trimester now and she was starting to feel like an overfilled balloon. She couldn't imagine getting bigger and yet she had nearly three months left to go. Beatrice Astrid Steele, or Sweet Bea, as Sawyer referred to her, would be arriving sometime around Christmas. It was the best present she could ever expect.

The renovation of the District was a close second. Sawyer and his team had done amazing work on the building. It was basically a gut job, by necessity, but now there were sound floors covered in ceramic tile, ceilings that weren't on the verge of falling onto anyone's head, electrical and plumbing systems that worked and a new, blessed addition—air-conditioning and insulation. The open space around the warehouse was redone, too, with benches and fountains, trees, and an outdoor amphitheater for musical and theatrical performances. Later tonight, one of the local bands was going to be playing a concert to celebrate the reopening.

Kat and Sawyer followed the crowd inside. Most of the former artisans had returned, but in the unrented studios and newly developed spaces, there were some additions. Not only did they gain new painters, jewelry makers and other crafters, but they got some food vendors, too. A Mediterranean falafel place opened up near the entrance, an artisan Popsicle shop was on the third floor and a cupcake bakery—Kat's favorite stop—was on the ground floor.

There were no commercial chains, something Sawyer had promised her, but there was definitely a nice, upscale feel about the place now. Yes, there were artists at work, but it didn't feel like they were squatters in an abandoned warehouse any longer. It felt like they belonged, and their art was something worth coming to the District to see and, hopefully, to buy.

As they reached Kat's studio, with her Wooden Dreams sign in place, she was surprised to see there were already a few people eyeing her work. She kissed Sawyer on the cheek and went over to chat with her potential new customers.

A few minutes and a sale later, she turned back to find Sawyer on the phone. His face was as white as it had been the day he'd found out she was pregnant with Finn's child. Something was wrong.

She waited on eggshells until he ended the call and then turned to her. "What is it?" she asked.

"There's been an accident. Finn's private jet back from Beijing lost radio contact somewhere near the West Coast. They think the plane went down near Portland, Oregon."

Kat brought her hand to her mouth in shock. "Oh my God. Do they know if anyone survived?"

Sawyer shook his head. "They don't know. Rescue crews are searching for the plane in the woods and out at sea, but without a good idea of where it might've gone down, it might be a while before we know for sure if Finn is dead or alive."

* * * * *

THE TWIN SWITCH

BARBARA DUNLOP

For Susie Ross:
Thanks for the inspiration!

One

If I could choose my own sister, it would be Brooklyn.

She made me laugh.

Better still, she made me think. And when things went bad, which they often did, she'd lie down beside me on my blue silk comforter and listen for hours. She knew when the fix was ice cream and when it was tequila.

She was smart, too. She got straight A's right from elementary school.

Me, I was more of a B-plus person. But I was a pretty good listener. And I could twist a mean French braid, which Brooklyn liked.

She had long blond hair and beautiful blue eyes. She tanned, too. We both tanned.

Since we were little kids, we'd spent our summers at the beach on Lake Washington. First it was the swings and the jungle gym. A little older, we'd race to the floater in the middle of the swimming area, dive off, then dry on our towels in the sun. Older still, we hung out at the snack bar, batting our lashes at cute boys and getting them to buy us milkshakes.

I didn't get to choose my own sister. But it was happening, anyway.

In just two weeks, Brooklyn was marrying my big brother, James.

"I can see the Golden Gate Bridge," Sophie Crush said from the front seat of the cab.

I was in the middle of the back seat squished between Brooklyn and Nat Remington. That's what happened when you insisted on taking a hybrid from the airport.

"Do you think we'll have views from our rooms?" Nat asked.

"I want a view of the spa," Brooklyn said. "From inside the spa, I mean."

"You heard the bride," I said.

I flexed my shoulders in anticipation of a deep stone massage. I'd had one once before. It had been a little slice of Heaven that I was dying to repeat.

"Pedicures," Sophie said.

"Facials," Nat said.

"I want to sit in the sauna," Brooklyn said.

"I feel my pores opening up already," I said.

The sauna sounded like a great idea. So did a facial. I was the maid of honor, and I was determined to look my best.

Unlike some brides—more selfish brides—Brooklyn had chosen gorgeous bridesmaid dresses. They were airy and knee length with strapless sweetheart necklines and fitted bodices of azure-blue chiffon that faded to pale sky at the hemline.

My auburn hair was tricky but, happily, the colors worked. Because for a single twenty-six-year-old, a wedding was a really good place to meet new guys.

I was at a disadvantage this time since half the guests would be my own relatives. Plus I'd met nearly all of Brooklyn's friends and family over the years. Still, she might have an undiscovered hot second cousin or two in the right age range. A woman could never discount an opportunity.

The cab pulled to a halt beside a rotating glass door and miles of windows that looked into the lobby. Stylized gold lettering spelled out The Archway Hotel and Spa on a marble pillar.

Three men in crisp steel-gray short-sleeved jackets simultaneously opened our doors.

"Welcome to the Archway," one of them said to Brooklyn, his gaze lingering on her sea-breeze eyes before moving past her to me.

His smile was friendly. He was cute, but I wasn't about to get interested.

Not that I have anything against valets. He could be putting himself through grad school for all I knew. Or maybe he liked living near the beach and having flexible hours.

Brooklyn moved past him, and he held out his hand to me. I took it.

It was strong, slightly calloused, definitely tanned. Maybe he was a surfer.

I'm not a snob about professions. I'm a high school math teacher, and that isn't the most prestigious job. I'm open to meeting people from all walks of life.

He did have really gorgeous hazel eyes, and a strong chin, and a bright white smile.

I came to my feet and he let go of my hand, taking a step back.

"We'll take care of the bags," he said, his gaze holding mine a little longer than normal.

It took me a second to realize he was waiting for a tip.

I almost laughed at myself. He wasn't flirting with me—at least not with any romantic intent. He did this with everyone who arrived at the hotel. It was probably how he paid for his surfboard.

I rustled through my purse for a five and handed it over.

It was a splurging kind of a weekend, I reminded myself. You only got the perfect sister-in-law once in your life.

Two bellhops wheeled our luggage into the lobby and we followed.

"We could go see some male exotic dancers," Nat said.

Brooklyn winced. "Pass."

I smiled. I knew Nat was joking. If Sophie had suggested it, I might have taken her seriously.

"Don't be too hasty," Sophie said. "After all, what do you think James is doing with the guys right now?"

"You think James is watching male exotic dancers?" Brooklyn asked as we made our way past the fountain to the check-in desk.

"Female," Sophie said.

There was no lineup. In fact, there were three attendants available. Nice.

Brooklyn swung her tote bag onto her shoulder. "The guys are watching a doubleheader."

"Afterward," Sophie said.

I couldn't imagine James going to a strip show. He was absolutely not the type.

But Brooklyn got a funny expression on her face, like she thought maybe it was a possibility, even though the idea was ridiculous.

"Are you checking in today?" the woman behind the counter asked us in a chipper voice that said she was delighted to be here to help us.

"We're the Christie party," Nat answered, deftly pulling a copy of the reservation from her bag.

Hanging back, I spoke to Brooklyn in an undertone. "You're not worried about James, are you?"

Brooklyn frowned and gave a noncommittal shrug. Then she moved toward the counter, digging into her bag. "Do you need my credit card?"

"I just need one for check-in," the woman said. "When you check out, you can split the charges if you like."

I repositioned myself so that I was beside Brooklyn.

"He's not going to see a stripper," I whispered, wondering how she could possibly be worried about James's behavior.

James, with a master's degree in economics, who'd landed a job at one of the most conservative consulting firms in Seattle, who only spoke in complete sentences and who guarded his social media accounts as if he had the nuclear launch codes, would not be hanging out at a strip club.

I couldn't imagine him risking someone snapping his picture in a strip club—even if he did want to see naked women. Which he did not, because there wasn't a woman in the country more beautiful than Brooklyn.

Brooklyn was a fashion buyer for a chain of Seattle boutiques. But she could have been a movie star or a supermodel. There was nowhere for James to go but down in the looks department.

"What's wrong?" I asked her.

She turned her head and smiled. "What could possibly be wrong?"

There was something in her eyes. I couldn't quite put my finger on it.

"Did James do something?" I asked her.

"No."

"Are you mad at him?"

"No."

"Then what…?"

"Nothing." Brooklyn smiled again. "He's perfect. James is perfect. And I'm going to book a spa appointment." She reached for the brochure on the countertop.

"I can help with that," the check-in woman said as she handed Nat's credit card back to her.

"Something with aromatherapy," Brooklyn said.

I wasn't one hundred percent convinced by Brooklyn's nonchalance, but I thought about hot stones pressed slowly across my oiled back and decided anything else could wait.

Massaged and steamed and showered and dressed, I spotted Sophie sitting at the bar in the lounge. A jazz trio was playing in the corner while candles flickered on the mottled glass tables. The chairs were white leather, and a glass mosaic decorated the wall behind the bar.

I was wearing three-inch heels with my silver cocktail dress, so I was happy to rest my feet by perching next to Sophie.

"What are you drinking?" I asked.

"Vodka martini."

The bartender arrived, another cute guy. "Can I get you something?"

His smile was friendly, definitely flirtatious. And he was classically handsome, probably thirty or so, with intelligent gray eyes.

I certainly had nothing against bartenders, except when you met them at their work. There they flirted with everybody. Like the valets out front, their shift was made or broken by their tips.

"I'll take one of those," I said, pointing to Sophie's glass.

I smiled at him, but made it brief. I didn't want to spend the evening chatting with the bartender. I wanted to spend it with my girlfriends.

Across the lounge, a very handsome profile came into my view, distracting me.

Okay, this guy wasn't a bartender, or a valet, or a public school teacher of any kind—that was for sure.

His perfectly cut suit was draped over a perfectly sculpted body. His haircut was shaggy-neat, that kind where you paid the earth to look like you'd rolled out of bed and had every hair fall naturally into place.

Even as I mentally mocked the style, I liked it.

He turned, and I caught his handsome face full-on. He could have just walked off a magazine cover. He should have walked off a magazine cover with that chiseled chin and those startlingly bright blue eyes.

He caught me staring, but he didn't smile. I felt heat hit my cheeks, anyway.

And then it was over. He turned and kept walking like our eyes meeting had never happened. And maybe it hadn't. Maybe he hadn't been staring at me at all. Maybe it was just the fevered musing that took flight in my head when I saw a good-looking guy lately.

I'd read a statistic last month that said sixty-seven percent of women met their husbands before they graduated from college. So I was already in the bottom thirty-three percent.

When you added that to the twenty-one percent of women who never married at all, my odds looked grim. I had a twelve percent chance of meeting Mr. Right.

Don't get me started on the fifty percent divorce rate because that left me at six percent. And six percent was truly demoralizing.

"Earth to Layla," Sophie said.

I gave myself a mental shake. This was a girlfriends' weekend.

"Did Brooklyn come down already?" I asked, focusing on the here and now.

Brooklyn and I were sharing a room, while Sophie and Nat were staying together one floor up. We had ended up with a view of the bridge, while they looked into the building next door. We'd offered to trade, but nobody seemed to care about the view.

The rooms had enormous soaker tubs, steam showers and beds that felt like you were floating on a cloud. Nothing else much mattered.

"I haven't seen her yet," Sophie said.

I glanced around but didn't see her, either. "I have eight pillows," I said to Sophie.

"You counted?"

"I counted."

"Did you take the square root?" she asked, grinning as she bit the olive off her blue plastic skewer.

"If I include the gold throw pillow, the square root is three. I considered applying the quadratic formula, but—"

"Layla." It was Brooklyn's happy voice in my ear and I felt her arm go around my shoulders. "I thought you'd never get out of the shower."

"It's a great shower." There was something sensual and indulgent about endless hot water.

"What are you drinking?" Brooklyn sounded overly cheerful.

"Vodka martini," Sophie said. "You?"

"I had a Sunburst Bramble across the lobby there. I wouldn't recommend it."

She wore a short, mauve halter dress with a full skirt that swirled around her toned thighs. Her ankle-high gladiator heels were mottled purple and silver. As always, she looked trendy and stylish.

The bartender seemed to magically appear. "The Sunburst Bramble wasn't to your taste?" he asked Brooklyn, obviously having overheard her comment. "Would you like me to replace it with something else?"

"Would you?" Brooklyn responded. "That's so sweet of you."

He slid a slim, leather-bound cocktail menu in front of her.

"Why don't you pick," she said, sliding it back with a swish of her shoulder-length blond hair. "Something sweeter, maybe with strawberries or a little Irish Mist?"

I did a mental eye roll. This was the Brooklyn who'd gotten us free milkshakes at the beach all summer long. Only that Brooklyn hadn't been engaged to be married.

"How many drinks have you had?" I asked her, wondering if she'd hit the minibar while I was in the shower.

"Just the one. But I'm about to have another."

I told myself to quit worrying. She was in a good mood, and that was great. This was her weekend, after all. I didn't know why I was borrowing trouble.

The bartender brought me my drink.

"I'm off to the ladies'," Brooklyn said. "When my drink comes save it for me."

I turned my head to call after her. "Will do."

I saw three different men follow Brooklyn's progress as she walked to the lobby. It was always that way with her. I wasn't sure she even noticed anymore.

"I think Nat really wants to see exotic dancers," Sophie said to me.

I refocused my attention on Sophie. "No way."

Nat was the most straitlaced of the four of us. She was James, only in female form. She was literally a librarian.

"I think she might be ready to burst out of that shell."

"That would be entertaining," I said, thinking it really would.

Nat's long-term boyfriend had split with her a few months back. I knew she hadn't dated anyone since. I also knew Henry had been hard on her self-esteem.

Sure, Nat wore glasses. But they were cute glasses, and she had the sweetest spray of freckles across her cheeks. Her brown hair might not be the most exotic of shades, and she wasn't glam like Brooklyn, but she had the most beautiful smile that lit up her pale blue eyes.

"She's chatting up a guy right now." Sophie inclined her head.

I turned to surreptitiously follow Sophie's gaze.

Sure enough, Nat was at a corner table, head leaned in talking to a guy in a nicely cut suit jacket and an open-collared white shirt. He looked urbane attractive, but more fine-featured than appealed to me. But then I wasn't Nat.

Something banged above us.

I reflexively ducked as my adrenaline surged.

The room suddenly turned black, garnering audible gasps and a few high-pitched shrieks from the crowd.

It went quiet.

"Whoa." I blinked to focus.

"What was that?" Sophie asked into the darkness.

"Something broke."

"It sure did."

My eyes adjusted, and I could see the candles now, little dots of light on the tables illuminating the faces closest to them. They reflected off the windows. Beyond, across the bay, I could see the lights of ships and sailboats in the distance.

"Nothing but a power failure, folks." It was the bartender's hearty voice. "It happens sometimes. Please sit tight and enjoy the ambience. I'm sure the lights will come back on soon."

"At least we're not waiting on our drinks," Sophie said, lifting her glass to take another sip.

"I wonder if Brooklyn will be able to find us." I looked around, but I couldn't see much of anything beyond the candlelight.

"Hey, guys." Nat appeared and hopped up on the stool next to Sophie.

"What happened to your man?" Sophie asked.

"When the lights went out, he squealed like a little girl."

"That's disappointing," I said.

Sometimes I wondered if there were any good men left in the world. I had a list of qualities. I mean, it wasn't a long list, mostly to do with integrity and temperament. But squealing like a little girl was definitely not on it.

"So not the type to rescue you from a bear," Sophie said to Nat. She sounded disappointed.

There was laughter in Nat's voice. "Who needs rescuing from a bear?"

"I might go camping," Sophie said.

"You?" Nat asked.

Five-star restaurant manager, downtown high-rise-dwelling Sophie was definitely not the outdoor type.

"Well, maybe you," Sophie said.

Nat had been known to spend time outside—at least in her rooftop garden.

"Then that's *definitely* not my guy." Nat took a two-second gaze back over her shoulder.

I realized then, that after a mere five minutes I'd wondered if Nat's guy would be *the* guy. It could have been a really romantic story—Nat meeting the love of her life while spending a girls' weekend in San Francisco celebrating Brooklyn's wedding.

We were all single. Well, Brooklyn wouldn't be single for long. But Sophie, Nat and me hadn't had a lot of luck meeting men.

Good guys were hard to find. I could list the flaws in each of my dates from the past six months: too loud, too nerdy, too intellectual, too moody.

I knew how it sounded. And I realized perfectly well what I was doing with that list. If I focused on the guys, I didn't have to explore the possibility that it was me—which, of course, deep down, I knew it was.

I'd love to live in denial. And I would if I could figure out a way that I didn't know denial was denial.

So far, I hadn't been able to make that work.

"Where's Brooklyn?" Nat asked.

"Ladies' room," I said.

Sophie craned her neck to gaze across the dim room. "She should be back by now. I hope she's not stuck in an elevator."

"I'm going to go look for her." I slid off my bar stool.

"You'll get lost, too," Nat said. "Or you'll trip and break your ankle."

I remembered my black-and-gold sling-back stilettos. They were stylish, but not the most stable footwear in my closet. Nat made a good point.

Instead, I retrieved my phone from my purse and shot Brooklyn a text.

I climbed back up and took a sip of my drink.

We all stared at my phone for a few minutes, but Brooklyn didn't text back.

"Stuck on an elevator," Nat said in conclusion.

"Or in an ambulance," Sophie said. "I bet she was rushing to get back to us in the dark, and it all went bad."

"Don't even joke about that," I said. "There are five hundred people coming to her wedding."

"And it's a long way up the aisle at St. Fidelis's," Nat said. "What if she broke her leg?"

"She didn't break her leg," I said and then realized I was tempting fate. "I mean, I *hope* she didn't break her leg."

Brooklyn with a broken leg would be an unmitigated disaster.

It was thirty minutes before the lights came on. When they did, conversation around us spiked for a moment, and there was a smattering of applause.

The bartender went back to work, and the waitresses began circulating around the room. Brooklyn still hadn't returned from the ladies' room, and I looked at the lobby entrance, trying to spot her.

"There she is," Sophie said.

"Where?" I asked, disappointed in my powers of observation.

"Left side of the lobby. Talking to a guy."

I leaned in for a better angle, but I still couldn't see her.

"It looks like she got more support from random men than I did," Nat said.

"He's hot," Sophie said.

I got down from the bar stool so I could see more of the lobby.

"Whoa," both Sophie and Nat said in unison.

"What?"

I saw a broad hand on Brooklyn's shoulder, and I could almost feel the touch myself. The rest of the man was blocked from view by the lounge wall.

She smiled, and then the hand disappeared.

I surged forward, but whoever he was walked away too fast.

"Seriously?" Sophie said. "The three of us are all single, and *she* ends up with him in the blackout?"

"Fate is cruel," Nat said.

"What did he look like?" I asked.

"Hot," Sophie said.

"Tall," Nat said.

"Tall and hot," Sophie said.

"Thanks for that specific detail," I said.

Brooklyn was coming toward us.

"Who was that?" Nat called to her.

"Can I meet him?" Sophie asked.

"You don't get to call dibs," Nat said.

"Dibs," Sophie said.

Brooklyn was smiling and shaking her head as she drew closer. Her cheeks were flushed, and there was an odd brightness to her eyes.

"What happened?" I asked.

"The power went off," she said.

"Did you get his name?" Sophie asked.

Brooklyn shook her head. "Can't help you with that."

"He squeezed your shoulder," I said.

From my vantage point, the touch seemed intimate. That tanned, strong hand squeezing down on Brooklyn's shoulder had sent a shiver up my own spine.

I tried to imagine how James would feel about someone touching Brooklyn that way. He wouldn't like it. Of that, I was sure.

"He was saying goodbye," Brooklyn said.

"What's wrong with you?" Sophie asked me.

"Who squeezes a strange woman's shoulder?" I asked.

"Who doesn't?" Sophie returned.

"It's not like he kissed me," Brooklyn said.

For some reason, her words didn't make me feel any better.

"He can kiss me," Sophie said.

It suddenly occurred to me that Brooklyn might already know the man. That would explain the touch.

But if that was true, why wasn't she saying so? Was the guy an old boyfriend? Not that she could have an old boyfriend without me knowing. It was impossible.

"We're going to be late for our dinner reservation," Nat said.

"Was my drink ever served?" Brooklyn asked.

"I think it got lost in the excitement," Sophie said.

As if on cue, the bartender arrived. "I think you'll like this one. I call it an icy wave."

The drink was in a tall glass, blue green in color, with lots of crushed ice and a strawberry garnish.

"Thank you," Brooklyn said to him.

He waited while she took a sip.

I waited impatiently to ask her another question.

"It's good," she said.

The bartender beamed.

Before I could speak up, shaggy-neat-hair guy walked back into the lounge. The sight of him sent a jolt of electricity across my chest. I sucked in a breath.

He seemed to hear me, or maybe he just felt me staring, because he turned, and we locked gazes. This time there was no mistaking it.

His mouth crooked into a half smile. I couldn't tell if he was greeting me or mocking me. It could be that my lust was obvious to him even at this distance.

No, not lust, I told myself. Lust made my reaction sound salacious.

This was interest, no more, no less. And there was nothing wrong with being interested in a good-looking guy across the bar.

"We have a reservation in the Moonside Room," Nat said, interrupting my musings.

I forced myself to break the gaze.

And I was absurdly proud of breaking off the look first this time. I found myself smiling in satisfaction. I had to resist the urge to check shaggy-neat-hair guy's reaction to my shift in attention.

"I can have your drink brought up to the restaurant for you," the bartender said to Brooklyn.

No mention of my drink, or Sophie's. But then that was the way of the world.

"Thank you so much." Brooklyn flashed her friendly blue eyes.

"Not a problem."

I could tell the bartender thought he had a shot—despite the big diamond ring on Brooklyn's left hand. She had a knack for that—for doing nothing in a way that ever so subtly led men on.

Sophie was very pretty. Nat was girl-next-door cute. But none of us could hold a candle to Brooklyn's allure. Men tripped over their own feet when she was in the room. She invariably got us great tables and great service from earnest waiters and maître d's.

Mostly I just took the perks without bothering to be jealous of Brooklyn.

"Through the lobby?" she asked the bartender.

"Straight across to the gold elevator. It will take you to the fifty-eighth floor. Mandy can show you." He beckoned one of the waitresses.

"Just in case we can't read the sign," Nat whispered to me.

"Just in case he misunderstood the diamond ring," I whispered back.

"Men have no consciences."

"Luckily for James, Brooklyn does."

My best friend, and an only child with two distant, busy parents, Brooklyn had spent countless weekends and holidays with my big extended family. She'd had a crush on James since we were old enough to know what a crush was. He'd finally invited her to the junior prom, and there'd been no going back.

Their relationship made such perfect sense for everyone, including me. I'd been testing the term *sister-in-law* inside my head for months now. I couldn't wait to use it in real life.

As we walked to the elevator, I looked around for shaggy-neat-hair guy.

He wasn't in the bar, and he wasn't in the lobby.

Ah, well. There was always tomorrow.

The sauna and spa lounge were coed. He could be a spa guy.

Or maybe I'd check out the exercise room. He definitely looked like the weight-training type. And I could see him on an elliptical machine...or rowing.

I could definitely picture him rowing.

Two

I wasn't a morning person at the best of times.

It was doubly hard to wake up with the daylight filtered by an opaque blind, the air in the room cool on my face and cozy in a bed that was softer than a cloud.

Reluctantly giving up my state of sleep, I reached for the last wispy threads of my dream. There'd been a blue-eyed man on a surfboard off the beach of a tropical island. A dog was playing in the sand while the palm-frond room of a nearby hut rustled in the floral breeze.

I'd felt safe and warm inside the hut, but I couldn't remember why. I struggled to find the details, but the synaptic connections evaporated, locking me out of my subconscious.

It was morning.

I opened my eyes to see the bathroom light on, the door partially closed.

I listened, hoping Brooklyn would be done soon so I could take a turn.

I looked to the bedside clock and found it was nearly nine.

I'd slept a long time.

I was hungry.

As I waited for Brooklyn, I weighted the cost-benefit of eggs Benedict. It was my all-time favorite breakfast. But the béarnaise sauce meant extra crunches next week and maybe some extra laps in the pool.

My bridesmaid dress was exactly the right size, and too much indulgence this weekend would blow the lines. A custom-fit dress deserved the flattest stomach I could muster.

Still, one breakfast of eggs Benedict—how much would that hurt?

"Brooklyn?" I called out. "Are you almost done?"

My bladder capacity wasn't unlimited.

She didn't answer, and I got up out of bed.

We'd come back to the room together after dinner last night.

While we ate, she'd been alternately chipper and chatty, and then suddenly lost in thought. She was the first of my close friends to get married, so I couldn't tell if this was normal. It could easily be normal, but something seemed off.

I'd planned to talk to her once we got in bed. There was nothing like girl talk in the dark to get to the heart of a matter.

But I'd gone out like a light while she was still in the bathroom.

Now, I found it empty.

I was both surprised and relieved. I wouldn't have to wait any longer, but I did wonder why she didn't wake me up for breakfast.

I hoped they all hadn't eaten without me. I'd be more willing to dive into a plate of eggs Benedict if I had coconspirators in the indulgence. Hey, if the bride was going all out, I wasn't going to be a wet blanket.

I changed quickly, ignoring my makeup bag, and threw my hair into a ponytail. I climbed into a pair of jeans and a casual blue blouse along with a pair of ankle boots and some earrings. I was good enough for breakfast.

I headed for the Sunriser dining room on the main floor.

There I found Sophie and Nat. Like me, they'd decided it was a day to go for it with plates of gooey Belgian waffles and steaming mugs of hot chocolate.

"Where's Brooklyn?" I asked as I sat down on a cushioned seat at the table for four.

The room was West Coast elegant, with gleaming wood beams soaring above us and a high wall of windows looking onto the bay. Sunlight streamed in across leafy plants and navy-colored tablecloths, glinting off the glassware and silver.

"We thought she was with you," Sophie said.

"She wasn't in the room when I woke up."

The waitress offered me coffee, and I gratefully accepted, finding the cream in a little silver pitcher in the middle of the table.

"Did you check the spa?" Nat asked.

"No. Don't you think it's too early?"

"She's probably working out," Nat said. "Her wedding dress doesn't leave any room for error."

I found myself rethinking my eggs Benedict.

Nat cut into her waffle, releasing a wave of the delicious aroma.

"Are you ready to order?" the waitress asked me.

"Eggs Benedict," my mouth said before my brain could mount a decent argument against it.

Once made, I was happy with the decision. I could work out at the hotel gym sometime today. It was going to be worth it.

"The woman has willpower," Sophie said of Brooklyn.

I smiled at that as I sipped my sweetened coffee. It was true.

Thanks to Brooklyn's insistence, we swam to the far floater and back every time we drank a milkshake at the Lake Washington Beach. I didn't gain an ounce over summer breaks. To this day, I used swimming to stay in shape.

I should thank her for that.

I'd have plenty of time in the future.

She and James were shopping for houses in Wallingford. The area was close to my apartment in Fremont. After the wedding, we'd be able to see each other even more often than we did now.

While I waited for my breakfast, I shot her a text.

"At least we know she's not stuck in an elevator this time," Nat said.

"Are we shopping this morning?" Sophie asked.

"Do you need something?" I glanced at my phone, but there was no symbol to indicate Brooklyn was answering.

"Clothes," Sophie said. "Maybe some throw pillows or shelves. I could use some shelves for that little corner by the patio door. I bought those two blown-glass sculptures at the pier last month, and I have nowhere to put them."

"I don't need anything," Nat said.

"I respectfully disagree," Sophie said. "Your studio needs a complete makeover."

"It's functional," Nat said with a sniff.

"It's criminal," Sophie said. "All that glorious potential, and you haven't done a thing with it."

"I hung some pictures."

"That *I* gave you. On hooks that were on the wall from the last tenant. The arrangement doesn't even make sense." Sophie turned to me. "We should go on a shopping spree for Nat's place."

"We should probably ask Brooklyn," I said, thinking the weekend was supposed to be all about her. And I'd make it all about her, too, if I could only track her down.

My eggs Benedict arrived, looking outstandingly delicious.

"Brooklyn will go for it. She loves shopping," Sophie said.

I took a first bite. It was to die for.

I'd be happy to shop or sightsee or hit the pool deck. I'd even go for another massage. I'd always go for another massage.

"In that case, we can shop for Brooklyn," Nat said. "I don't want to clutter my place up with knickknacks and dust collectors."

"Another word for them is art." Sophie smirked as she went for her phone. "If the bride says we're redecorating your studio, we're redecorating your studio."

"That's not how it works," Nat said.

"It's exactly how it works." Sophie held her phone to her ear.

"I'm counting on you," Nat said to me. "Talk some sense into her."

"I can't see redecorating your apartment being Brooklyn's first choice," I said honestly.

My money was on Fisherman's Wharf or Golden Gate Park.

"She's not answering," Sophie said.

I hoped that meant Brooklyn was in a shower at the gym. She should really get over here and try some of these eggs.

"What the heck?" Sophie said, surprise in her tone.

I looked up.

She put her phone under my nose with a friend-finding app open. I squinted, but it was too close for me to see the little map.

When she spoke again, she sounded completely baffled. "What's Brooklyn doing back at the airport?"

My first thought was Brooklyn had been kidnapped.

It was the only thing that made sense.

She had no reason to leave the hotel voluntarily. We had spa appointments, and there were Belgian waffles and hot chocolate on the menu. What more could a woman ask for?

I wanted to call the police right away, but Nat convinced me they'd need more evidence before they opened a missing-person case. Brooklyn was an adult, and she hadn't been gone very long by law-enforcement standards.

Nat was right.

I was letting emotion overrule reason. That wasn't like me at all.

Instead, we checked the hotel room and discovered Brooklyn's suitcase was gone.

I took heart from that. I took that to mean she'd left willingly. Our best guess was that there'd been an emergency in the middle of the night—maybe a medical emergency, presumably one of her family members, maybe her mom or dad.

If something had happened to James, they would definitely have called me, too. Still, it made no sense that she wouldn't wake me up. I'd have gone with her.

While I was pondering the mystery, I came across her note.

I opened my mouth to alert Sophie and Nat. But then I read it and my heart sank to my toes.

I didn't say a thing. Instead, I hid the damning words in my jeans pocket.

"She's off-line," Sophie said, holding out her phone on the friend-finding app.

Brooklyn's icon had disappeared.

"Did she get on a plane to Seattle?" Nat asked.

"Possibly," I said.

"Should we go after her?" Sophie asked.

We should. We would. At least I would.

But I was going by myself. I didn't know much, but I knew Brooklyn hadn't gone back to Seattle.

"We don't know for sure where she went," I said. "Let's not all rush off." There, that sure sounded more like rational me.

It took me a few precious minutes, but I convinced Sophie and Nat to sit tight at the hotel, promising to track down Brooklyn and bring her back to San Francisco to finish off the weekend.

As I made my way to the airport, the note weighed heavy in my pocket.

Layla, it had said. *I'm more sorry than you can know. I've tried so hard, but I can't marry James. I've met my soul mate. Please forgive me.*

Her soul mate? What was she talking about, her soul mate?

James was her soul mate. He was the love of her life. They were fantastic together.

Sitting on a hard, plastic chair in the airport, staring at the departure board, I hunted through my phone and looked up the airspeeds of commuter jets, considering the radius of the distance Brooklyn could have traveled by now, and mapping out the cities in the circle: Sacramento, Reno, Los Angeles.

I rehearsed the many ways I could talk some sense into her.

It had to be temporary insanity—the stress of a five-hundred-guest wedding, or her mother fussing over the dresses and the flowers and the dinner. Or maybe it was James wanting children right away.

I knew Brooklyn wanted to wait a couple of years before they had kids. I didn't think the disagreement had been a deal breaker. But what did I know?

I knew I was going to find out.

I knew that much.

I thought about phoning James. But I couldn't exactly call him out of the blue and ask about his future kids. Plus, he'd want to talk to Brooklyn. I'd have to say she wasn't with me.

He'd try to call her, and who knew where that would lead. Nowhere good, that was for sure.

The marker for Brooklyn's phone suddenly appeared on my screen.

My heart jumped. I'd found her!

She was in Las Vegas.

I was on my feet and heading for the bank of check-in counters while I scrolled to see which airline had the next flight to McCarran Airport.

A few more searches on my phone, a plane ride and an Uber ride later, and I was in the lobby of the Canterbury Sands Hotel.

Brooklyn's phone told me she was here. Since I wasn't with NASA or the CIA, the accuracy of the app was spotty, and I couldn't pinpoint her, but she was definitely here somewhere.

I glanced around. The hotel lobby was posh luxury as far as the eye could see: marble columns, carved woodwork, potted palms, discrete lighting and leather armchairs set into corners and alcoves.

Since she wasn't conveniently hanging around in the lobby, I tried the front desk. Brooklyn wasn't registered. Or maybe she *was* registered, but the professional staff knew better than to reveal personal information about their guests.

I tried explaining I was Brooklyn's maid of honor and we were getting ready for a wedding. But the female desk clerk seemed unimpressed.

I supposed a wedding in Vegas was hardly a monumental event. I'd seen a bride in a limo as my Uber had turned into the hotel drive and another was visible right now posing for photos outside in the garden.

This bride looked gorgeous, and her groom looked happy, as he joked and jostled with his friends. I loved weddings. Who didn't love weddings?

When the bridal party moved on, and Brooklyn still wasn't anywhere in sight, I found an empty table in a lounge at the side of the lobby. I was going to wait it out. Odds were she'd pass by this central point sometime.

I'd tried calling her again, but she hadn't answered. I wasn't about to let her know I was in Vegas. I didn't think she'd run from me again, but it was possible.

I decided it was better to confront her in person. I wanted to see her expression when I asked what I had to ask—which was what *the heck* did she think she was doing?

It was hot, and I was thirsty, so I ordered a five-dollar cola. I was hungry, too, since I hadn't had a chance to finish my divine eggs Benedict. But I couldn't bring myself to order a twenty-five-dollar snack.

This might be a weekend of indulgence, but I had limits. I'd seen the waiter pass by with the order for another table. They served designer food here. Three shrimps and a swirl of greenery weren't going to impact my hunger in any meaningful way. So why waste the money?

I'd texted Nat before the plane took off, so they knew I was on Brooklyn's trail. I kept the soul mate thing—which struck me as a temporary thing—to myself for now. Instead, I let them assume Brooklyn was blowing off steam in the run-up to the wedding.

She was, in a way. Just not in a good way.

Halfway through my glass of cola, my attention caught on a man on the other side of the lounge. He rose and was moving in my general direction. He stopped at one table and chatted, then he stopped at another, and then he waved to a third.

I'm admittedly not the best at facial recognition. Every September I have to make a seating chart for each class and then work really hard to memorize the students' faces. But even with my limited skill, and at this distance, I could swear this was shaggy-neat-hair guy from San Francisco.

I squinted in the dim lounge light, watching him walk and talk and smile.

Then he looked me straight in the eyes, and my chest jolted with that same electricity. Either this was him, or I was a huge sucker for a particular type.

He was coming straight toward me now. Then again, I was sitting near the exit. I told myself not to get too excited. But when it came to good-looking, possibly eligible men, myself didn't listen much.

My brain started to hum. I should keep eye contact. I should smile. I should say something.

"Hello," he said, slowing to a halt next to my table.

"Hi."

A beat went past in silence.

I started to break it. "Were you by any chance—"

I stopped, distrusting my own memory and not wanting to look foolish. Then I told myself to speak up. That was what I told my students. If you have a question, speak up. There are no stupid questions.

"Were you by any chance just in San Francisco?" It did sound foolish when I said it out loud. Worse, it sounded like a line. I might as well have said: "Do you come here often?"

Sweat instantly gathered at my hairline.

"The Archway?" he asked.

Relief rushed through me. I wasn't imagining things. "Yes."

"I thought I recognized you."

My embarrassment disappeared, but my hormones zipped off like a rocket ship. Up close, he was a hunk, superbuff, great-looking, oozing sensuality.

"Business or pleasure?" he asked in a gravelly voice that seemed to come straight from his deep chest.

It was neither, but I wasn't about to go into detail.

"Pleasure," I said.

He swung his gaze around the lounge. "Are you here alone?"

"Yes." I hadn't found Brooklyn yet, so I was currently alone.

He smiled at that. "I'm Max Kendrick." He looked at my drink. "Would you like something more interesting than cola?"

I almost said no. I wasn't here to get picked up in a bar. Then again, this was far from a honky-tonk. It was a fancy hotel lobby. And hadn't I been fantasizing about this very thing just yesterday—meeting a great guy on my gals' weekend?

This one seemed pretty seriously great, and he was dropping right into my lap, and I was sitting here tongue-tied and questioning every breath I sucked into my lungs. I had to get a grip.

"Have you seen the price list?" I don't know why that silly question popped into my head. If he was staying here, and if he was offering, he must be able to afford the prices.

His smile broadened. "A time or two."

"Sure," I said, before I could come up with anything more senseless to blurt out.

"Great." He sat down at the table. "What's your pleasure?"

I considered pulling a Brooklyn by asking him to choose something for me, maybe batting my eyelashes and pretending to be überfeminine.

But überfeminine wasn't me. Neither was batting my eyelashes, or pretending I didn't know my own mind.

"A chardonnay."

"Any preference on the label?"

"No preference." Whatever the house served was going to be fine with me. Given what I'd seen so far of *the house*, I was betting their wine would be spectacular.

He gave the waitress a glance, and she came straight over.

"Can you bring us a bottle of the Crepe Falls Reserve?"

"Right away," she said.

"A bottle?" I asked, wondering if he was less of a gentleman than I'd guessed. Was he expecting me to knock back a few this early in the afternoon?

"Better value that way."

"So you're not trying to get me drunk?"

"Do you have a reason to get drunk? Is everything okay?"

"Everything's fine." The answer was automatic—even though *fine* was quite the stretch at this particular moment.

"Okay," he said, looking suspiciously at my expression. His gaze seemed perceptive.

I had to tell myself he couldn't read my thoughts. "It's all very fine."

"If you say so."

"I do." I took another sweep around the lobby looking for Brooklyn. I couldn't let her slip past me because I was distracted by Max Kendrick.

"You sure you're not with someone?" he asked.

I gave him a look of reproach. "I'm sure."

"You're jumpy," he said.

"You're suspicious."

He shrugged without denying it.

Fair enough, I supposed. We'd only just met.

"I'm watching for someone," I said.

"Who?"

"A friend. A girlfriend. I'm meeting her here and I don't want to miss her."

"That's not exactly alone."

"It is until she gets here."

"You lied."

"I didn't lie."

"You omitted. You're hiding something."

I wasn't about to touch that one. "You thought I was a cheater."

"Maybe."

"Is that a takes-one-to-know-one statement? Do you have a girlfriend? Are you a cheater?"

"Nope."

"How do I know you're not lying? Cheaters probably lie."

His smile said he got that I was joking. I felt warm about that. Not everyone caught on to my sense of humor.

The waitress returned with our wine, and we both fell silent as she poured.

When she left, he held up his glass for a toast. "To honesty and integrity."

"Faith and loyalty." I thought about Brooklyn as I touched my glass to his.

I took a sip. The wine was outstanding—crisp, buttery and light on my tongue.

"Now that we know we're on the same wavelength," he said. "Tell me something about you. Maybe start with your name."

I realized then that he'd introduced himself, but I hadn't.

"It's Layla—Layla Gillen."

"Nice to meet you, Layla Gillen. Will you be in Vegas for long?"

"I certainly hope not."

He quirked an eyebrow. "You have something against Vegas?"

"No, nothing. It's the first time I've been here." I scanned for Brooklyn again. I spotted a blonde woman in the distance, but she turned and I saw her profile—not Brooklyn.

"Where are you from?" Max asked.

I turned my attention back to him. "Seattle. You?"

"I have a place in New York, but I travel quite a bit. What do you do in Seattle?"

I didn't want to sound nerdy. Then again, I sure wasn't about to lie.

"I'm a teacher."

"What grade?"

"High school."

"What subject."

"Math."

His smile said he'd discovered an embarrassing secret.

My pride kicked in. "You have something against mathematics?"

"You don't look like any math teacher I ever had."

"I'm fully qualified."

"I'm not questioning that."

"It sounded like you were."

"No." He cocked his head and his gaze grew warm. "I was thinking if my math teachers looked like you, I'd have enjoyed the subject a whole lot more."

My heart fluttered. It seriously, embarrassingly, fluttered there for a second.

My cheeks grew warm, and I told myself to get a grip, covering the reaction with another sip of wine.

This was obviously a crush-at-first-sight, and I'd never felt anything like it.

I didn't want to check into a 700-dollar-a-night hotel room when I had a perfectly wonderful prepaid room waiting for me back in San Francisco. But evening was falling, and there was still no sign of Brooklyn.

Max had said goodbye after lunch, and I'd left the table pretending I had somewhere to go. I didn't, of course. But I'd found a comfortable seat at the opposite end of the lobby with a good view of the main entrances and exits.

The vibe of the lobby was beginning to change from daytime to evening. I knew if I wanted to continue blending with the crowd, I had to get out of my jeans.

There were shops dotted around the periphery of the lobby. The clothes were very high-end, but I managed to find a little black dress on a sales rack.

I wasn't about to interrupt my surveillance by heading into the fitting room. Luckily, the dress had simple lines and enough stretch that I was confident it would fit. My black ankle boots weren't exactly perfect for the occasion, but I was wearing a silver necklace and dangling earrings, and I could pull my hair up in a messy bun.

I'd do for the evening crowd.

I hated to interrupt my surveillance, but eventually, the need for a restroom break became urgent. In the ladies' room, I changed in a flash and was back out in the lobby again with my jeans and blouse folded into the boutique shopping bag.

"I take it you don't have a room?" It was Max's voice beside me.

I was embarrassed, like I'd been caught freeloading.

I worked to erase my guilty expression before facing him. I wasn't freeloading. I was genuinely waiting for a hotel guest. And, anyway, the lobby was a public space.

"My girlfriend has a—" I turned and my words dried up.

This afternoon Max had looked good in a dusty blue shirt under a steel-gray suit. Now he looked fantastic. His shirt was crisp white. His suit was black, and his tie was dark burgundy scattered with black flecks.

"A room?" he prompted.

"Are you going to a party?"

"I wouldn't exactly call it a party." He took in my dress. "What about you? Big plans?"

I didn't have any plans at all beyond staking out the lobby until Brooklyn arrived. I refused to let myself think she and her faux soul mate were holed up in a hotel room together for the night, ordering room service and lounging in a whirlpool tub.

The image was too much for me to wrap my head around, so I shook it out of my mind.

"You haven't found her," Max stated. He didn't give me time to answer. "What's really going on, Layla?"

"Nothing."

"Are you a private investigator?"

"No."

As I denied it, I wondered if Max wanted me to be a private investigator. Private investigator sounded like an exciting job, better than math teacher. Maybe I should consider switching careers.

"A stalker?" he asked.

"I'm not a stalker." I wasn't—at least not usually. Today, well, I supposed it was debatable.

"Have you tried calling her?"

"What a *great* idea." I wasn't annoyed with Max. I was just generally annoyed, and that put the sarcasm in my voice. "I don't know why I didn't think of it myself."

He didn't seem to take offense. "I'll take that as a yes."

"That's a yes."

He peered at my expression. "Did you have a fight?"

"No."

"Is she with a guy?"

I was trying not to think about that. I wanted to deny it. But I didn't feel like lying outright to Max. I didn't even feel like omitting anymore.

Other patrons milled around us, dressed to the nines, talking and laughing, coming together in groups and lining up at the on-site restaurants.

"I think she might be," I admitted.

"So she ditched you for a man." Max's words weren't a question.

It wasn't what he was thinking. But I couldn't explain the situation without giving away private information, so I just stood there looking like a pathetic fifth wheel abandoned in the hotel lobby.

"Join me for dinner," he said.

It was a mercy date if I'd ever heard of one. No thank you. "I have no intention of crashing your party."

"There's no party. There's just me."

I didn't believe that for a second. "Then why are you dressed like the top of a wedding cake?"

"Because this is a nice hotel, and it's after six."

"I don't believe you."

"You don't have to believe me. Just join me for dinner."

"So you're saying you have *nothing* to do tonight."

A man like that, in a suit like his, in a place like this? Not a chance.

"I'm saying there's nothing I *have* to do tonight."

"But you have options?"

"We all have options. All the time. Right now, you're my first choice."

"Why?"

"I swear, Layla, I have never had this much trouble getting a woman to have dinner with me."

"I can't," I said, even though I wanted to say yes.

A guy like this didn't come along every day—at least not in my life. In my life, a guy like this didn't come along *any* day.

"Why not?"

"I can't risk missing my girlfriend. She'll be through here anytime."

He gave me a look that said I was borderline delusional. "I'm no expert. But it seems like she doesn't want to be found."

Brooklyn might not want to be found, but for everyone's sake, I needed to find her.

"Maybe you should leave it until tomorrow," Max said.

"No." That would be bad. It would be very bad to leave

Brooklyn and her faux soul mate alone for the night. I had to find her as soon as possible.

"I'm assuming she's over twenty-one."

"She's twenty-six."

"There you go. She's perfectly capable of making her own decisions."

Technically that was true. But I knew Brooklyn wasn't thinking straight. Something was wrong, and I had to get to the bottom of it before she made a life-altering mistake.

"We can eat in the Grill Room," he said. "See that curved booth right there, the one facing the lobby? I'll get the hostess to seat us in it."

I gauged the view from the table. It was probably better than the view I had from here. And I was truly starving at this point.

"It's probably reserved." It looked like a prime spot.

"I'm sure they'll fit us in." He sounded confident in his ability to get preferential treatment.

"Do you come here often?" I asked. Then I laughed at myself. "I didn't mean that the way it sounded."

"You weren't going for a cheesy pickup line?"

"No."

"Too bad."

I ignored the flirtatious lilt to his words, refusing to let myself meet his gaze. It would be all too easy to let my imagination run away with me. And the last thing I needed was a further distraction right now.

"I'm a fairly frequent guest," he said.

"My lucky day."

"I was going to say it was mine."

This time I did look at him. I'm not made of stone. His smile was warm, and his eyes had an inner glow, and my heart fluttered again.

Before I could sigh or swoon or do anything else ridiculously humiliating, he started across the lobby to the restaurant entrance.

"Mr. Kendrick." The hostess's greeting was friendly as we approached.

"Hi, Samantha. Can you put us at the front booth?"

"Of course, sir."

She extracted two leather-bound, gold-embossed menus from below the counter. "Bernard will seat you."

"Hello, Mr. Kendrick," Bernard said. "It's great to have you with us tonight."

Max waited while I slid in one side of the booth, going partway around. I set my purse and shopping bag beside me.

I felt outclassed by the surroundings, and I was grateful to have ditched the jeans.

Max slid in the other side of the booth and matched my position. It was cozy with the high-backed plush seats, a flickering candle, the two of us sitting only a couple of feet apart.

I had an expansive view of the lobby, but the table still felt intimate.

"Can I have the waiter bring you your usual?" Bernard asked Max.

"Please," Max said to Bernard.

To me, he said, "It's a classic martini with a lemon twist."

"Sounds good." It did.

I hoped the drink would take the edge off my worry. Fretting over Brooklyn wasn't going to help me find her any faster. When she showed up, she showed up.

"The drinks will be out right away," Bernard said. "Please let me know if there's anything else you need."

"They really do know you," I said to Max as I took yet another scan of the lobby.

"They do. But they treat all their customers well."

That had certainly been my experience so far.

"This isn't the kind of place where I usually eat," I said.

He moved the glass-encased candle so we had an unobstructed view of each other. "What's the kind of a place where you usually eat?"

"The Rock a Beach," I said. "It's a funky little seafood place on Moiler Bay. They have picnic tables on a covered deck. There's great local beer on tap. You can get fish and chips served on newspaper or a wooden hammer to crack your crab. In the winter, they close it in with plastic sheeting and light a central fireplace. My family loves it."

"It sounds great."

"You wouldn't need a suit."

"It sounds like I'd need a bib."

"Recommended."

We both smiled.

"I'd like to take you there sometime," he said.

I could see it. I could picture that. And it was great. The image was so compelling that it took me a second to realize what he was doing.

He was *good*. And I was a fool for following along like a little puppy dog.

I wasn't usually swayed by emotion like this. I'm usually nothing but rational. I pride myself on it. I drew back, forcibly pulling myself from his spell. "Wow."

"Wow what?"

"That was fast, and not particularly believable."

"I—"

"You're a smooth talker, Max Kendrick. But here's a heads-up for you—what you're after is not what's going to happen."

"That's not where I was going."

"Sure it wasn't." Logic and reason told me that much.

"You're a skeptic, Layla Gillen. I'm simply enjoying our conversation."

I wasn't about to believe that. Guys often took a shot and backed off when you called them out on it.

Then again, he'd vaguely mentioned a second date. He hadn't suggested skinny-dipping in his hot tub or checking out his hotel suite. Maybe I was too quick to judge.

"Okay," I said. "My mistake."

"No. It was my mistake for letting it come out wrong. Can I back up a couple of minutes and take a do-over?"

He could. I wasn't about to say no when he put it so reasonably. But just in case I really did have his number, I was keeping up my guard.

Three

Just as the chocolate soufflé arrived with Devonshire cream and a whole lot of pomp and circumstance, I spotted Brooklyn. She was crossing the lobby, her long blond hair swinging in a high ponytail. I couldn't see her face, but I recognized her walk, the slant of her shoulders and the oversize green-and-gold earrings she'd bought from a funky little stand at Pier 54.

The soufflé looked magnificent—a molten center, topped with the Devonshire cream, powdered sugar and plump raspberries. I'd gone with a seafood salad for dinner, saving space for an indulgent dessert. But I couldn't let Brooklyn get away.

"I'm sorry," I said to Max, grabbing my purse and shopping bag as I slid from the booth.

The pastry chef and the waitress looked baffled.

"Is something wrong?" Max asked.

I kept my gaze on Brooklyn. She disappeared behind a pillar.

"I'll settle up later," I called back to him, tossing the words over my shoulder as I hurried away.

I felt terrible sticking Max with the bill. I told myself I could drop off some cash at the front desk. They might be sticky about confirming someone was a guest, but surely they'd take an envelope for them.

I also hated to waste the chef's hard work. He'd clearly taken pride in the chocolate soufflé. I also selfishly hated to miss eating it.

That was twice today.

Indulgence karma was not on my side.

I could see now that Brooklyn was alone. Perfect.

The lobby was octagonal with four passageways leading off the four corners. She headed down one of them. I thought it led to the pool, an outdoor restaurant and an atrium garden.

I wanted to call out, but I didn't think she'd hear me. And

I was half-afraid she might try to escape. She'd gone to a lot of trouble to stay away from me.

I knew why she'd done that.

I knew that she knew that I knew she didn't really want to do this. And she knew I'd talk her out of it without half trying.

I saw the paradox in my thinking. If she knew all that, she wouldn't be hiding from me. She'd simply admit she was wrong, and I was right, and she'd made a big mistake. But I was always the rational one between us. Brooklyn was emotional, and she could talk herself into peculiar things.

She was still a hundred feet ahead of me when she turned again, disappearing from my sight.

I broke into a trot, then discovered she'd taken a doorway that led to the garden.

I followed on polished brick pathway that wound through lighted shrubbery and towering palm trees. I hurried, but I couldn't see her in front of me. Then the pathway forked.

I stopped to consider my next move.

I could hear voices in one direction, and music and laughter. I could see the lights of a restaurant or a patio lounge.

The other way was quiet, no sound but a burbling brook beneath an arched footbridge.

Brooklyn liked to be where the action was, so I followed the music.

I came to a café called the Triple Palm. It was fresh and lively, with a breeze blowing through. Beech-wood tables and chairs were surrounded by greenery and decorated with lights and candles. A trio of musicians played in one corner, and a few couples danced on the raised floor. This was Brooklyn's kind of place.

I did a methodical search of the tables. Then I checked the bar area. Then I repositioned to see the entire dance floor.

No Brooklyn.

I couldn't believe I'd guessed wrong.

I didn't have any time to waste.

I trotted again. It was hard to trot in the heeled boots, but they were better than pumps or spiked heels. That was for sure.

I made it to the fork and over the footbridge. Things got quieter around me. The music faded into the distance. The lights were fewer and farther between.

I listened hard, but I didn't hear anything. My best guess was that Brooklyn was meeting her new soul mate in a secluded corner to talk or cuddle or kiss.

I couldn't see her having sex in a hotel garden, not when just anybody could happen by and catch her. That wasn't like Brooklyn.

Then again, *this* wasn't like Brooklyn. I realized there was a chance that she'd been having risky outdoor sex with James all this time without telling me.

I groaned out loud and quickly scrubbed that image from my mind.

"Layla?" It was Max.

I heard his footsteps before he appeared around a corner.

I was more than surprised to see him. "How did you find me?"

"I looked."

I gave him an eye roll.

"I saw you turn toward the atrium. There are only so many places you can go at this end of the hotel."

My guilt over cutting out on him came back. "I was going to drop some cash off at the front desk."

"What for?"

"To pay for dinner, of course."

He waved a dismissive hand. "Don't be ridiculous. I invited you."

"That doesn't mean you should get stuck with the bill. I didn't mean to cut out on you."

"You saw her, didn't you?"

I nodded. "But then I lost her."

"Did you check the Triple Palm?"

"She's not there. And she doesn't seem to be here." I glanced around. "Unless she's found a secret corner to hide."

"You did say she was with a guy."

I shook my head. "I know what you're thinking." I refused to let myself think that. "She's not like that."

"You don't know what I'm thinking. And not like what?"

"She's not having sex in a public garden, that's what."

He grinned in a way that said I was amusing him.

"There are other things for men and women to do in a quiet corner of the garden than have sex."

"I know that."

He shifted a little bit closer to me. "This is a very romantic garden."

Lighted mesquite trees towered above us. Small cactuses lined the path, with pink and yellow flowers adding color. The air was sultry sweet along the smooth, winding red-toned path, heavy with moisture and soft on my skin.

"That's not really what I want to hear," I said.

"Why not?"

His gaze captured mine. It was as sultry as the air, dark and deep.

I forgot what I was saying. "What?"

He shifted closer still. "You know, you are incredibly beautiful."

I couldn't help it—my heart warmed at the compliment. It beat more deeply, slowly, thudding inside my chest and echoing in my ears.

I told myself to hang on to reality. But myself didn't want to do that right now.

Max touched my arm. The touch was simple. It was light. His thumb brushed slowly across my skin, and I lit up like one of the mesquite trees. Logic and reason flew into the night.

"Max," I whispered.

"Layla," he whispered back.

The breezed cocooned us as he stepped in. One hand slid to my bare shoulder. His other touched the small of my back.

I put my palms on his chest, thinking to stop him, thinking they'd be a barrier between us that would pull me out of this spell.

But it didn't work out that way.

I touched the crisp fabric of his shirt. I could feel his heat beneath it. His chest was firm, his pecs defined.

I'm not shallow. I know there's more to a man than the shape of his body. But the particular shape of this particular man's body was doing very strange things to my brain waves.

I lowered my hands, feeling the ridges of his abs. A sudden vision of him naked bloomed in my mind, my fingertips trailing across his glorious frame.

I wanted that. I wanted it more than I'd wanted anything in a very long time.

He enfolded me in an embrace, the solid, strong, definitive hug of a man who'd decided exactly what he wanted. And what he wanted was me. I was torn between amazement and arousal.

I tipped my chin, and his lips touched mine, and my amazement fled. There was no room for anything inside of me except arousal.

His lips were hot, firm, moist, with the perfect amount of pressure.

He tasted like fine wine and smoky dreams.

My lips softened, they parted. I invited him in and his tongue swept mine in an encompassing kiss that sent waves of pleasure all the way to my toes.

My hands started to move. They unbuttoned his shirt. They touched his skin, and he gave a guttural groan.

"This way," he said.

I didn't know what he meant. I didn't care what he meant, just so long as his kisses didn't stop and he let me keep feeling my way to his shoulders.

I figured out what he meant, and it was a good thing.

I couldn't believe his room was this close. But there we were, down a narrow pathway, across a patio and through some French doors.

You really couldn't call it a room.

It was a suite—a presidential suite or a royal suite, or something with its very own name. I could feel how big it was even in the dim light.

Then Max pulled off his jacket and ripped his way out of his dress shirt. And everything around me disappeared. He was hot with a capital *H*.

Before I could look my fill, he pushed down the strap of my dress. He kissed his way across my bared shoulder. Every brush of his lips sent new tingles deep into my skin.

I breathed deeply—such a fresh crisp scent. My fingertips traced their way from his abs, to his pecs, up the breadth of his shoulders that went on and on. My lips followed suit, and I felt his warm breath on my hair.

I knew I should stop. My left brain told me I couldn't careen off on a wave of feeling. I had things to do. I had Brooklyn to find.

Finally, my right brain told me. Finally, after so very many disappointments today, an indulgence was mine for the taking.

The debate was very short.

Indulgence won with a capital *I*.

I didn't want to make Max guess, so I stripped off the little dress. I stood there in my panties, making myself perfectly clear.

I was in his arms in a flash, his embrace warm and engulfing. My breasts pressed against his bare chest, sending my arousal to new heights.

Then he lifted me like I weighed nothing. He started walking.

"Bedroom," he said.

My right brain cheered. It was probably the sexiest thing that had ever happened to me.

He carried me through a door to a second big room. Light filtered through an opaque blind, and I could make out a king-size bed, a padded headboard and a huge mound of pillows.

We collapsed together onto the soft bed, Max on top, propping himself with his elbows.

The quilt was smooth silk against my body. It was cool. A fan stirred the air overhead.

His hands clasped mine, and he moved in slow motion to kiss my lips.

I simultaneously moaned and sighed, melting against his mouth, then his thighs, then his chest as we pressed closer and tighter together.

His weight felt good. It felt sexy. It pushed me deep into the soft mattress.

His kisses were long and thorough, expertly sending messages to my breasts and inner thighs, making them tighten and buzz with desire.

His lips were magic. His hands did nothing but caress my palms, yet I was writhing and stretching and lifting my hips.

My panties were thin. So were his boxers. My thighs spread apart, and our touch through the whisper of fabric was a prelude to lovemaking.

I wanted him. I wanted him very badly.

I slipped my hands from his, wrapped my arms around him. He was steady and strong, like an anchor in a growing storm of desire.

He slipped off my panties and stripped off his boxers.

He produced a condom, then drew back to gaze into my eyes.

His were midnight blue, deep and dark in the weak light. Lashes framed their richness, their sensitivity, their intense passion.

"You okay?" he asked.

"I'm fantastic," I said.

He smiled then as he tore open the package. "You are all of that."

In seconds, his hips flexed and we were locked together.

"Still good?" he rasped.

"Oh, yeah."

His kisses began all over again.

His hands roamed my body, and mine roamed his.

He found all the points, and the spots—all the zones.

I indulged myself, tracing his iron biceps, bulging shoulders and the contours of his back. His hands were strong and broad, blunt and certain.

His rhythm was steady, teasing and building. I shifted my hips, tipping upward.

He rolled us together, slightly to one side, bringing a pillow beneath me before rocking back.

Pleasure rushed through me, leaving heat in its wake. Then again, and again.

"Oh, my." I gasped.

"Oh, yes," he said.

He wrapped me tight in his arms.

I clung to his shoulders, my fingertips gripping onto him tighter and tighter, hanging on as the world broke free.

I fell from the planet, throbbing, and I felt him follow.

The air was hot, perfumed and heavy. The sound of the fan whooshed loud above us. I could feel his deep breathing, the rise and fall of his chest, his heart beating hard, his sweat mingling with mine, and finally, the sweet weight of his limbs holding me fast.

Max spoke first. "That was…"

The fan circled a few more times.

"It was," I said.

He smoothed back my hair and lifted his head to meet my gaze.

"Layla," he whispered.

Then he tenderly kissed my mouth.

"Max," I said in return. I couldn't help but smile.

This was hands down the most amazing sex I'd ever had. I didn't know his secret, but I loved benefitting from it.

I was so satisfied.

I mean, sort of satisfied.

I mean, I was done…but I wasn't finished—not with Max, not with sex. It was a revelation. In this moment, I felt like I might never get enough of him.

He kissed me again, and I kissed him right back.

He kissed deeper and longer, and my arms went around him.

His hand covered my breast, and a quiver rolled through me.

His caress sharpened, and his kisses turned deliberate.

My energy roared to life, and arousal took serious root. Wherever he was going with this, I sure planned to follow.

In Max's bathroom, I was getting a sense of the opulence of the suite. The soaker tub was big enough for three. The multi-nozzle shower could host a party. And there were enough luxury bath products and plush towels to keep me happy...well, forever really.

I'd taken a quick shower and wrapped myself in one of the soft, white robes hanging in the bathroom closet. I hadn't yet gathered up my own clothes from the living room.

I wasn't so much looking forward to that part of the evening. Then again, I wasn't dreading it the way I ought to be dreading it, either.

I pulled down my hair, dried off the shower dampness with another of the towels. Then I used a little comb wrapped in a cellophane wrapper to tame the tangles. There was some nice-smelling lotion on the big marble counter, so I used a bit on my face and hands.

My mind began wandering to Max and how he could afford a hotel suite like this. Clearly he had means. He seemed intelligent, and he was definitely classy. How could it be that a great-looking guy like him was still single?

My brain paused for a minute, as single women's brains do. Was he married? He hadn't worn a ring—not that that meant anything. Lots of married guys didn't wear their rings when they traveled. I would imagine that went doubly for Vegas.

Then again, he might not be married.

I gazed at myself in the mirror and my brain insisted on going over the what-ifs. What if he wasn't married? What if he was everything he seemed? What if we fell madly in love, he wooed me around the world from London to Paris to Rome...?

Then I chuckled at myself in the mirror.

I was ridiculous.

This was a one-night stand. It might have been the greatest one-night stand in the history of one-night stands. But it was over. I was going to find Brooklyn and convince her to come back to San Francisco—or at this point maybe straight to Seattle. But I was going to find her and force her to come to her senses.

I was walking away from Max, and that was that.

I had to admit, I was glad we'd gone twice. It seemed more worthwhile that way.

I laughed at my reflection one more time before I left the dream bathroom.

Max was in the living room dressed in an identical robe. His hair was damp, and I could only conclude there was another bathroom somewhere in the rambling hotel suite.

I noticed my dress was neatly folded on an armchair. Since I hadn't seen my panties on the bedroom floor, I was guessing they were with the dress.

I gave a happy sigh inside. Guys like this sure *didn't* come along every day.

I headed for the dress. "I have to get going."

My guess was he wouldn't be disappointed to hear I was clearing out.

"You sure?" he asked.

My back was to him, but I strained to read his tone. Was that disappointment or relief I was hearing?

I shimmied into the panties. "I still have to find her."

My back to him, I dropped the robe and pulled the dress over my head.

There was a knock on the door.

It startled me, and I was weirdly embarrassed at being in Max's hotel room. I reminded myself that he might be married.

"Are you—"

"Can you hang on for just a second?" he asked.

"You want me to go in the bedroom?"

He gave me an odd look. "Not unless you want to."

My *married* odds moved from 50/50 to 25/75 in a good way. I stayed put.

Max opened the door, and a waiter wheeled in a cart. I could see a champagne bottle and two glasses, and a big silver plate cover.

"Shall I set it up for you, Mr. Kendrick?"

"No thank you," Max said, handing something to the man. I presumed it was a tip.

Max closed the door behind the waiter. "I thought you might be hungry."

"You didn't have to do that," I said, thinking his considerate gestures were getting a little out of hand.

"Come and look," he said with a self-satisfied smile.

I moved.

He lifted the plate cover.

The aroma hit me first. Chocolate soufflé.

"Are you serious?" I asked, even though I was staring right at it.

"I was sorry you had to miss it."

"You *replaced* our dessert?" After I'd so unceremoniously rushed away?

A teasing glint came into his eyes. "I hope you worked up an appetite."

For the first time, I felt self-conscious about our vigorous lovemaking. I wrapped my arms around myself.

His eyes dimmed a shade. "I'm sorry, Layla."

"No, no." I shook my head. "This was very thoughtful."

"I didn't mean to embarrass you."

"I'm not embarrassed."

"You look embarrassed."

"Well, now that we're making such a big deal of it. I guess I am. I'm standing here in the hotel room of a man I only just met who may or may not be married."

He drew back. "Whoa? *What?* I'm not married. What makes you think I'm married?"

I wasn't exactly sure how to phrase it—since now that he'd denied it, my suspicions seemed less rational.

"You didn't say you weren't," I said.

"I told you I wasn't a cheater."

I remembered our earlier conversation. "That was about a girlfriend."

"Seriously? A wife trumps a girlfriend, don't you think?"

I didn't have an answer for that. I mean, there was an obvious answer for that, so I didn't bother to say it out loud.

"Why didn't you just ask?"

He had me there. "I, uh, didn't think of it 'til later."

He looked thoughtful. "I guess I didn't, either. You're not married, are you?"

For a split second, I was offended. Then I realized it was a ridiculous reaction. He couldn't know it about me any more than I could have known it about him.

My embarrassment disappeared, replaced by self-deprecating humor. "Why didn't you just ask?"

"I was too intent on making love with you."

"I'm not married," I said.

He heaved an exaggerated sigh of relief. "Now that we have that out of the way." He then glanced to the soufflé. "Are you going to let this get cold?"

"No." I wasn't giving up the decadent dessert a second time.

Max took the soufflé and the bottle of champagne, and I brought along the glasses and plates. We settled cornerwise from each other on the padded chairs of a big dining room table.

"So are you some überwealthy—" I glanced around the place "—like prince or something?"

He laughed as he popped the champagne cork.

"This is just business," he said.

"What does that mean?"

Max nodded. "It means the corporation gets a really big discount. So don't be too impressed."

"What kind of business."

He filled my glass with the bubbling champagne. "Do we really have to talk business?"

I was curious, but I wasn't going to be annoying about it. "I suppose not."

"I want to pretend I'm on vacation."

"I wish I was on vacation."

He raised his glass.

I did as well.

"To vacations."

"I will definitely drink to that."

Once this was all over, and James and Brooklyn were safely married, I was seriously considering going on a vacation. I figured I was going to deserve it.

The champagne was crisp, smooth and ridiculously delicious. And I ate every bite of my soufflé while Max talked about his kayak trip to Angel Island.

So he did row…well, paddle, I guess. But he stayed in shape. He definitely stayed in shape.

Too soon the champagne bottle was empty.

"I have to go," I said again.

Brooklyn was still out there.

He took my hand lightly in his. "Stay here. With me."

I shook my head. As comfortable as I felt with him, we had only just met and spending the night in his hotel room seemed way too intimate, even if a part of me desperately wanted to sleep in his arms.

"Why?"

"You and I just met."

He thought for a moment before nodding. "Too soon?"

"Too soon."

I couldn't stop myself from liking the implication that there might be a *later*, an *again*, possibly a *future*. It didn't matter that I was getting way ahead of myself again. Max was one great guy, and if only for this moment, it felt like this could be the start of something.

He was quiet, thinking again. Maybe he'd try to change my mind. Maybe my mind could be changed. Maybe I was being too hasty in turning down his offer.

"What if you don't find her?" he asked.

"I'll have to…eventually."

"You're planning to wander the lobby all night long?"

I had to admit, I hadn't thought through past midnight or so. All of my plans ended with me finding Brooklyn. There were night flights back to San Francisco. We'd take one.

"Let me get you a room," Max said.

I didn't understand what he meant.

"At the corporate discount," he said, moving to pick up a hotel phone.

"You can't—"

"Sure I can. If you find her, no harm, no foul. If you don't, there'll be a room waiting when you decide you have to sleep."

I opened my mouth to protest again. But then I stopped myself. He was right, and I was going to be logical about it. If I didn't find Brooklyn tonight, my best bet was to try again tomorrow. I'd rather sleep in a discounted room than in a lobby armchair.

Unless I stayed with Max... Which I couldn't. I wouldn't. I had to trust my left brain on that.

"This is Max Kendrick," he said into the phone. "Can you book a tentative reservation under the name of Layla Gillen?" He paused. "One night. Is there anything available on thirty-five?"

He covered the mouthpiece and whispered, "Might as well have a view of the Strip."

I didn't need a view of the Strip. I'd rather take a bargain room overlooking the mechanical wing. Even at a corporate discount, this was going to hurt.

"Perfect," he said into the phone. "Thanks." He hung up and returned to his chair. "The key will be waiting at the front desk if you need it."

"What's the damage?" I asked, bracing myself. Maybe I would sleep in the lobby.

"Seventy-six thirty-two."

The figure wasn't computing inside my head. Surely to goodness, Max wouldn't have booked me a seven-thousand-dollar hotel room. "How much did you say?" My voice squeaked embarrassingly.

"Seventy-six dollars and thirty-two cents."

Wait, what? "That doesn't even make sense."

"I told you we had a good discount. You're basically just paying the tax."

Something didn't seem right to me. "They're giving me a free room."

"No, they're giving a good corporate client a free room. It's empty. Nobody's going to sleep in it if you don't."

"Let me point out the flaws in that logic," I said.

"Please don't."

"You can't operate at a loss and make it up in volume."

He smiled and reached out to cradle my cheek. "I'm pretty sure the Canterbury Sands isn't operating at a loss."

"They will be if they keep doing things like this." I leaned my face into his palm.

I wanted to stay. I really, desperately wanted to stay.

"You want help finding your friend?" Max asked.

"I'll be fine."

I told myself to stand up, but my legs didn't move. Then I ordered myself to stand up. Unfortunately, myself wasn't co-operating very well tonight.

"I have to go now," I said to myself as much as to Max.

"Okay," he said.

"Thank you for…" I wasn't exactly sure how to phrase it.

"Dessert?" he asked with a lift of one eyebrow.

"Dessert," I agreed with a smile. "It was a really lovely dessert."

I managed to force myself to stand.

He stood with me. "If it gets late, pick up the key." Then he gave me a tender kiss on the lips. The tingle told me mine were bruised—in a good way, a very good way.

I wanted to melt against him. But I knew that would be the end of my Brooklyn search. I owed it to my brother and to Brooklyn to stay strong.

"Goodbye, Max Kendrick. It was nice to meet you."

"It was nice to meet you, Layla Gillen."

Four

I set my alarm, and it's a good thing I did, because I was sound asleep when "Viva la Vida" came up on my phone.

My room was nowhere near the size of Max's. But it was beautiful and comfortable, and the view was off the charts. I was seriously thinking of applying for a job with whatever corporation he worked for. The vacation perks alone would be worth it.

I wondered again what he did for a living—also if there was a chance they needed a mathematician.

I wished I could luxuriate in the shower or maybe take a long bath in the jet tub. But I wasn't here for pleasure. I had to get back on Brooklyn's trail. So I pushed myself through a quick morning routine and headed for the lobby again.

In the Sweet Garden Restaurant, I found her. There was no mistake this time. I was looking at her head-on. And she was in the middle of the room with no quick exit.

I had her.

Intent on Brooklyn, I was almost to the table before I looked at her companion.

I stopped, froze really. Everything inside me turned ice-cold, and a roar came up inside my brain.

"You!" I called out, almost shouting.

The tables nearby went quiet, and I thought to move closer.

"You!" I rasped this time in a whisper.

Max stared at me in abject shock, all but dropping his fork into his scrambled eggs.

"Layla," Brooklyn said, guilt and astonishment ringing clear in her tone. "What are you doing here?"

I turned my head, frustrated with her but purely incensed with Max. "I'm here for you. I came to talk to you. I came to bring you to your senses. Why wouldn't you answer your phone?"

I struggled to make sense of the situation.

Had Max known who I was all along? Was he psychologically deranged?

"I didn't know what to tell you," Brooklyn said.

I turned back to Max. "What is this? Are you sick? Are you a pervert?"

He looked baffled by the question.

I kept talking. "Why would you do such a horrible, horrible thing?"

"Layla," Brooklyn cried out. "It's not his fault."

My focus remained glued on Max. "How is it not his fault? *How* is it not your fault?"

He'd slept with me. He was wooing Brooklyn by day and sleeping with her best friend by night?

"It's just happened," Brooklyn said. "We didn't plan it."

Max sat there silently.

Max, who'd kissed me so passionately, who'd held me tenderly in his arms, who'd taken me to heights of pleasure and then ordered chocolate soufflé.

"Tell her what you did," I said to Max. *"Tell her!"*

"Layla?" Now Brooklyn sounded worried.

"She doesn't know, does she?" I said to Max. "Do you feel the least bit guilty? Are you twisted?"

"Layla!" Brooklyn came to her feet. "I know this has to be hard for you."

Max stood, as well.

"He's a lying scumbag," I said to Brooklyn. "Let's go. Let's go right now and forget any of this ever happened."

I was having second thoughts about telling Brooklyn the whole truth about Max. Maybe she didn't need to know. Maybe this was a secret I should take to my grave.

The important thing here was that she came back to James. She could choose James over Max without ever knowing the depths of Max's depravity.

"You must be Layla," Max said to me.

I felt like my head might explode. "That's how you're going to play it?"

"Play what?"

I glared at him.

He stared back. His acting was superb.

"Layla?" A voice behind me joined the conversation.

It was weird.

It was stereo.

I turned to see Max standing behind me. The loud noise came up in my ears again, and my knees went wobbly.

"Layla?" Brooklyn asked from what seemed like a long distance away.

"Whoa." Max reached for my arm and took hold of me.

"Who?" I managed to ask.

I gaped at the Max behind me.

"I see you've met my brother, Colton," Max said.

"Are you kidding me?" Colton said to Max.

"Me kidding you?" Max asked. "What on earth's going on?"

"You met Brooklyn," Colton said to Max.

"*This* is the guy?" I said to Brooklyn.

"This is Colton Kendrick," Brooklyn said.

Her face was flushed. Well, she should be embarrassed.

"Brooklyn is engaged," I told Colton flatly.

"I'm aware of that," Colton said.

"So, what—"

"What are you doing?" Max's question rolled right over mine.

"It's complicated," Colton said to Max.

"It's simple," I said, my gaze taking in both Colton and Brooklyn. "Brooklyn is marrying my brother, James, in thirteen days at St. Fidelis's Cathedral. It's been planned for over a year, and there are five hundred guests coming."

Colton looked to Brooklyn and raised his brow. "Five hundred?"

"That's relevant?" she asked him.

"It's unsettling."

"Get over it—"

"Hey," I interrupted. "Can we take a reality check here?"

"Your brother?" Max asked me.

"They've been in love for years," I said.

"That *is* complicated," Max said.

"Not you, too."

Max gestured to Brooklyn and Colton. "It looks complicated to me."

"It's fleeting," I said, knowing it had to be true. "It's a phase, nothing more."

"Why don't we ask them about that?"

It occurred to me that I should be having this conversation with Brooklyn. It had nothing to do with Max. Max and I were done.

All night long and through the morning I'd hoped I would see him one more time. Now I never wanted to see him again. My memories of last night would always be tainted by these horrible circumstances.

"Can we go somewhere and talk?" I asked Brooklyn. The best thing I could do in this moment was to get her out of Colton's clutches.

She looked to Colton before answering.

That reaction was not encouraging.

"Go," he said gently. "You can't hide anymore."

The reluctance on Brooklyn's face hit me square in the stomach.

She was my best friend. We shared everything. I couldn't remember a single time, a single event, a single moment when she hadn't wanted to pour out her heart to me, and me to her. This man was coming between more than James and Brooklyn. He was coming between me and my best friend.

He had to be stopped.

Brooklyn headed down the hallway that I'd learned led to the hotel garden.

We didn't talk as we wound our way through the morning crowds.

She took a different route, but we ended up at the Triple Palm Café. It was quiet this morning, and we easily found a table by the rail overlooking the gardens.

As soon as the waitress finished pouring coffee and orange juice, I launched into the speech I'd been mentally rehearsing for hours.

"What is going on?" I demanded, but I didn't stop for an answer or even a breath. "You sneak out of the hotel room, leave me this stupid note, ignore your phone and shack up with some guy—"

"He's not just some guy, and we didn't shack up."

"Do you know him? Had you met him before Friday night?"

I could tell by Brooklyn's expression that the answer was no.

"Then he's just some guy," I said. "You've known James for years. You've *loved* James for years."

"I didn't plan this." Brooklyn's voice cracked ever so slightly, evoking an unwanted swell of sympathy inside me.

I didn't want to be sympathetic. I wasn't anywhere near ready to consider her side of the story. I was in full-on defense mode of my brother.

"I didn't want this," she said.

I kept my voice hard. "Then why did you do it?"

She scanned the garden as if she was framing her answer.

"Why?" I repeated.

"It's Colton," she said. "He's... We're... It's..."

"Do you have a brain tumor?" I asked. For the first time it occurred to me that this situation might not be Brooklyn's fault.

She rolled her eyes and lifted her coffee cup to take a sip. "I do not have a brain tumor."

"I've heard that people's personalities can totally change when they have a brain tumor. Do you need a CAT scan?"

"No."

"We can get you a CAT scan. I bet we can get one right here in Vegas, today. If there's something wrong with your brain—"

"There's nothing wrong with my brain. My brain is perfectly fine, thank you very much."

"How would you know?"

Now that I'd come up with the theory, I realized it had merit. This was a complete and sudden departure from the woman

I'd known my whole life. Something like this didn't happen, all of a sudden, out of the blue, with no warning whatsoever, if there was nothing physically wrong with a person's brain.

"Maybe it was a stroke," I said.

"Will you stop?"

"A ministroke. You remember my Aunt Sandy had one that time. You'd never have known it happened if she didn't develop the sudden poker addiction. She had all of her friends playing five-card stud for quarters. Before we figured it out, she won two hundred bucks and made Rachel Simms cry."

"A stroke?" Brooklyn asked. "Seriously?"

"It could happen."

"I'm twenty-six years old."

"I know that."

"Then you know I didn't have a stroke."

"Then *what on earth is wrong with you*?"

Brooklyn took another sip of her coffee.

This time I joined her. It was hard to carry on a decent argument in the morning without a shot of caffeine.

The waitress reappeared before Brooklyn could answer.

"Can I get you something from the menu?" she asked.

"An oatmeal muffin for me," Brooklyn said.

"A waffle," I said. "Make it with strawberries, whipped cream and chocolate topping." I figured it was the least I deserved given the stress of the circumstances.

Brooklyn looked surprised.

"It's not like I have to fit into my bridesmaid dress." I hoped the pithy comment shook her back to reality.

"I guess," she said, sounding hesitant.

I took in the nuances of her expression. "So you haven't completely made up your mind."

"I…"

I reached out and touched her hand. "Brooklyn, hon, shut this down before it's too late."

Remorse crossed her face. "Do Sophie and Nat know?"

I was reminded that I should text Sophie and Nat. "I didn't show them the note. Nobody but me knows about this."

Brooklyn gave a small, sad smile. "Thanks."

I pulled out my phone to text Sophie.

"What are you doing?" Brooklyn looked worried.

"I'm telling them I found you. I'll say you needed a night alone. I'll tell them we're coming back today."

"No."

I met her gaze, telling myself to be calm and patient. Brooklyn was rattled and confused, and I had to bring her back down to earth. "We have to go back," I said.

"I can't go back."

"Well, you can't stay here." I looked around at the meticulous, sculpted trees, the perfect gardens, the lights, the fountains. "This is a fantasy, Brooklyn. *He's* a fantasy."

"He's not."

"You don't even know him."

"Maybe not, not completely yet, but he's... There's something about him, Layla, something big, something huge, something I've never felt before, not even with—"

"James. Your fiancé. The man you love."

Her eyes took on a sheen of tears. "I do love James."

Now we were getting somewhere. I felt myself relax for the first time in two days.

"Thing is—" she traced the condensation on her orange-juice glass "—I'm not *in* love with James."

"That doesn't even make sense." My momentary optimism shifted. It turned to a block of cement in my stomach. "You're not making sense, Brooklyn."

"I wanted to be your sister."

This time I squeezed her hand. "You *are* my sister."

"I love your family."

"We love you. We all love you. It's going to be great. The future is going to be wonderful."

All she had to do was get up from this table, get into a cab with me and head for the airport. There were flights back to San Francisco all day long. We'd take one and forget this ever happened.

My mind flashed to Max.

Okay, so maybe I wouldn't forget every little thing about this ever happened. Even though I wanted to, my night with Max wasn't something I'd ever forget.

"You're not listening," Brooklyn said.

"That's because you don't know what you're saying."

She shook her head. "No. It's because you can't let go of the fantasy we spun, that I spun, that I let everyone believe in for so long. I am sorry, you know."

"Stop." I couldn't hear this.

Our breakfasts arrived, and we both took a breath.

The waffle looked fantastic, but I wasn't sure I could eat anything right now.

"I convinced myself I was in love with James."

"No." I'd seen them together. I'd watched them for years. It wasn't an act. "You've convinced yourself you're not."

"I just found out there's a world of difference."

"You've known that man—"

"Colton."

"Fine. Colton." His name felt like acid on my tongue. "You've known *Colton* for two days—*two days*."

"It's not like I'm going to up and marry him at an Elvis chapel."

"This isn't funny."

"It's a little bit funny."

"Brooklyn!" I didn't know what was wrong with her, but it was something profound.

"If we don't laugh, we're going to have to cry."

"You're destroying your life, and James's life, and my life." It made perfect sense that we should cry.

She split her muffin in two. "I'm changing our lives."

"Not for the better."

"You don't know that."

I picked up my fork and stared at the whipped cream melting over my waffle. The warm chocolate syrup was pooling on the plate. I suddenly felt tired. "Let's go home, Brooklyn."

"Stay," she said, her gaze turning warm, open and cajoling. She finally looked like regular Brooklyn again—the way she looked when she wanted something—free milkshakes for example.

"Make an excuse to Sophie and Nat, and stay here with me a couple of days."

"You want me to watch you date Colton?"

"I want you to meet him. You've met Max." Suddenly, her expression turned calculating.

I felt like I'd been slid under a microscope. I didn't like it.

"You've met Max," she repeated. It was clear the wheels were turning inside her head. "How did that happen? When did that happen? What happened?"

"We had dinner," I said. "And he helped me get a discount hotel room."

I was going to tell her the whole story. I wouldn't keep it from her forever. I just couldn't tell her right now, not right this minute. She'd latch onto it, and the discussion of my sex life would distract from the central problem—which was that she had gotten confused.

Then the wheels took a turn inside my head. "Wait. *You'd* already met Max?"

I couldn't help but wonder what Colton had told Max about Brooklyn. Was it possible Max had known or suspected I was Brooklyn's friend? Could he have been keeping me away from Brooklyn to help his brother?

That was a particularly mortifying thought. I'd hopped into his bed when maybe all he was doing was keeping me occupied for a few hours. We might just as well have done karaoke.

"I only met Max in passing," Brooklyn said. "Just for a minute when we first got here."

"Does Max know about James?"

"I don't see how. I've been with Colton the whole time, and Max only knew I was Colton's date. I got the impression Colton and Max have a lot of dates."

Well, there was another unsettling revelation. There was a reason Max was so suave and sophisticated during a one-night stand. He was good at it because he'd had practice.

My brain kept trailing its way to Max. But I knew I had to stay focused.

"So Colton knows about James." I was deciding how drastically to loathe Colton Kendrick.

Before she answered, Brooklyn cracked a soft, intimate smile.

I didn't like the looks of that, not at all.

"Colton knows all about James," she said.

I instantly made my decision. I completely loathed Colton.

Brooklyn wouldn't leave Vegas, and I wasn't going back without her.

It was all Colton's fault that I was maxing out my credit card at the Canterbury Sands Hotel. Sure, Max had bought me dinner last night and Brooklyn had signed breakfast to her room—not that I'd even tasted my waffle. But my free ride was now over.

Brooklyn had gone to meet Colton, and I was in the check-in line wondering if I dared ask about getting a corporate rate. If I'd known the name of the company where Max worked, I might have given it a try. But without that piece of information, I didn't think there was any way I'd pull off the ruse.

I wondered if Max and Colton might work for the same company. That would explain why they'd both been at the Archway at the same time, and why they were here in Vegas at the same time. Brothers could go on vacation together, of course. But Max had said they were on business. So them being in the same business made the most sense to me.

It seemed weird, being a twin, growing up together and then working together. That was a lot of togetherness. Don't get me wrong, I love my family. But I can't see spending every weekday with any of them.

There were three people left in front of me when Max appeared.

"How did it go?" he asked.

"Did you know?" I asked outright. Brooklyn might not have

told Max the whole story, but that didn't mean Colton hadn't found a way to share it with his twin brother.

"Know what?" Max asked.

I judged the space between us and the couple in front, then lowered my voice. "That Brooklyn was engaged to my brother."

"How would I know that?"

"From Colton. *Your* brother."

"I didn't. And, anyway, you never told me Brooklyn's name. How would I have put the two things together?"

He made a fair point.

I wasn't one hundred percent convinced, but I'd say I was ninety-five.

"I'm taking her back," I told him. "Colton can't have her."

Max obviously fought a smirk. "Don't you think that's up to Brooklyn?"

"She's not thinking straight. She'll come around."

"So you're staying for a while."

It wasn't a question, since there was no other reason for me to be in the check-in line.

"I'm not staying long. She'll come to her senses. Hopefully today."

I'd texted Sophie and Nat and told them they should head back to Seattle without us. I'd also sent a message to James telling him Brooklyn and I were taking an extra day to chill out before the wedding.

It was mostly true. We were taking an extra day on vacation. And I told myself *chilling* was a matter of degree. We were chilling a little bit.

My turn came and Max walked up to the counter with me.

"You can check Ms. Gillen in under an *H* rate," he said to the female clerk.

"Of course, Mr. Kendrick." She gave me a warm smile.

"Do you know *everybody*?" I asked him.

The woman glanced my way with a puzzled expression.

"I'm a friendly guy," Max said to me.

"Any preference on the room?" the woman asked, her gaze going from Max to me and back again.

"Did you like your room last night?" Max asked me.

"The view was off-the-charts." I'd easily admit that for seventy-six dollars a night, I'd take that room all week long.

"She was on the thirty-fifth floor," Max said to the clerk.

"I really appreciate this," I said to Max. And I did. Whatever else was going on here, he was saving me a fortune.

"No problem."

"Do you have a preference for a north or south view?" the woman asked me this time.

"Either is fine." Even if I did know the difference, I wasn't going to act like a princess.

"Thirty-five-oh-seven or fourteen?" Max asked.

The woman hit a couple of keys. "Thirty-five-oh-seven is available."

"Make it for three nights," Max said.

"I'm not going to be—"

"You can always cancel."

"It's not going to take anywhere near that long."

"Better to have a backup plan," he said.

"Oh, I have a backup plan all right."

The clerk handed me a key card.

"Do tell," Max said as we walked away.

I knew my way to the elevators. "Give my plan to an agent of the enemy? I don't think so."

"I'm not the enemy."

"Colton is the enemy."

"Colton is a very principled guy."

"He's seducing an engaged woman. How is that a principled guy?"

We came to the elevator bank and Max pressed the button. "Is that how you see it?"

It occurred to me that there was little point in going up to the room. It wasn't like I had anything to unpack. I was going to have to pick up a few things today, underwear for one.

I'd washed my panties in the sink last night and dried them

with the hair dryer. But it would be a whole lot easier if I had an extra pair.

The hotel had provided the basics, like a toothbrush and toothpaste. It would also be nice to change my clothes. My best vacation clothes were going home to Seattle with Sophie and Nat.

The hotel shops were superexpensive, but I didn't want to leave Brooklyn alone with Colton any longer than absolutely necessary. She'd promised to answer her phone when I called from now on. And I planned to call her very soon and meet up.

I stepped into the elevator and Max followed. We were the only two in the car.

"I can take it from here," I said.

The thought of him in my room gave me a little thrill. I thought if we were alone again, he might kiss me. Or I might kiss him. I didn't want to want him all over again, but there wasn't a whole lot I could do about my attraction.

"Room service can deliver anything from the hotel shops," Max said. "If you need clothes or cosmetics."

"You think I need makeup?" I asked.

I usually wore a little bit, but it was another thing that stayed back in San Francisco when I left in a hurry.

"I didn't say that."

"You don't think I'm pretty enough?"

I didn't want to be fishing for a compliment, but it turned out I wanted one. I found myself questioning his motivations again. It wasn't like I'd looked my best, either yesterday or today. And I had a feeling Max looked his best 24/7. At least he looked that way to me. I'd truly never met a more attractive man.

"You have a mirror," he said.

It wasn't exactly the flattering remark I'd been hoping for. Then again, it ought to be a lesson to me.

The elevator accelerated smoothly upward.

"What's your deal?" I asked.

"My deal?"

"Is this a favor for your brother?"

"Is what a favor for my brother?"

"Hanging out with me, keeping me busy, keeping the field clear with Brooklyn."

"No."

"I don't believe you."

It made perfect sense. Colton wanted Brooklyn, and he knew I wanted to take her away. I didn't yet have a bead on Colton's motives. I didn't buy for a second that he was as delusional as Brooklyn over their soul-mate-ness. So probably he just thought she was gorgeous and fun and friendly and smart.

She was all of those things. It was why James loved her.

"You seem extraordinarily devoted to your brother," Max said.

"I'm completely ordinarily devoted to my brother and to all the other members of my family."

"Well, I'm not."

"You don't even know my family." It came as a bit of a surprise to me that I'd crack a joke.

"Ha, ha. I mean Colton's on his own when it comes to his relationships. He doesn't need me as a wingman."

"Sure." Skepticism colored my tone.

Friends were always wingmen. Brothers were even better wingmen. I could only imagine twin brothers were the top of the heap. How could a person not be loyally devoted to their twin brother?

"You're a skeptical woman, Layla Gillen."

"I think you mean astute."

We arrived at the thirty-fifth floor and exited the elevator. I held the card to the lock and heard the tumblers click.

"I don't know why I even came up here," I said.

I had nothing to drop off or pick up. Okay. I should call Brooklyn and get her to meet me somewhere. Hopefully, she'd had a chance to think about all the things I'd said.

Liking my plan, I entered the hotel room and was immediately struck by the view.

The room was slightly bigger than last night's. It was on a corner with two walls of glass and a small sitting area overlooking feature hotels, fountains and the giant Ferris wheel just off the Strip.

I didn't want to love it, but I did.

I found myself drawn to the glass wall. "This one costs more, doesn't it?"

"A little," Max said.

The door banged shut behind him.

"What are we talking, eighty dollars, eighty-two fifty?"

"Something like that."

"Do you live like this all the time?"

I loved my job, I really did. Teaching was rewarding, and I loved the kids, and I dearly loved living close to my family. But there was something exotic and exciting about fine hotel rooms in iconic cities, where you didn't have to cook, run errands or make a bed.

They'd deliver new clothes if I asked. Who wouldn't love that? At least for a while. I'd like to fantasize about living that way for at least a little while.

"It can get old," Max said, and I realized he'd moved closer.

"Go ahead, burst my bubble."

He animated his voice. "But the perks can be great."

"No dishes."

"Somebody washes your sheets and cleans your shower."

"It could make a person feel lazy."

"I suppose." He brushed his hand lightly across my shoulder.

A sigh of contentment rolled all the way through me. His touch had been magic last night, and I could feel the arousal start all over again. It was like my hormones remembered. They remembered Max and they craved him now.

"Layla." His voice was deep.

I felt it in my chest and in the pit of my abdomen.

I wanted so badly to lean back into him, to feel his arms around me, his kiss on my neck, his hands...well, everywhere.

Shut up, right brain.

I squeezed my hands hard against the urge, and I felt the rectangle of my phone against my palm.

I summoned my strength. "I have to call Brooklyn."

Max's sigh was audible.

"She needs me," I said.

There was an edge of impatience to his tone. "If you say so."

"This isn't a game."

"Nobody said it was a game."

I turned to face him. It was a risk. My desire for him was acute and insistent. But I needed him to understand. "I'm not going to do this," I said.

"Do what?"

"Don't play dumb. I'm not going to muddle things up by kissing you…or worse."

"I wouldn't call it worse. I'd call it better." He grinned.

"Worse. It would be worse. I'm disgusted by your brother."

Something flinched in Max's expression.

I found it admirable that he'd want to defend Colton. It was admirable, but it didn't change my mind in the least.

Brooklyn was mine and she was James's. Colton would just have to accept that. And that I was going to win her back.

"We're adversaries in this." I figured we might as well have it out on the table.

"It's none of our business."

I coughed out a laugh at that. "It's entirely my business. And he's your brother. So keep your distance." I took a step back to emphasize my point.

"And what if I can't?"

I didn't believe that for a second. "Summon your strength."

"For you, I will try."

I rolled my eyes. "For me. Right. I'm calling Brooklyn now." I touched her contact name and put the phone to my ear.

"Let me know how it goes," he said.

I was about to point out that we wouldn't be having any future conversations during which I would tell him anything at all. But true to her word, Brooklyn answered her phone on the first ring.

Max gave me a mock salute and headed for the door.

"Layla?" Brooklyn asked into the silence. "Are you there?"

Five

"I'm here," I said to Brooklyn.

"Where's here?"

"My hotel room. I have a room now."

"That's good." She went silent for a moment. "Colton says he can get you a rate."

"Max already did."

"Max is there?" Brooklyn sounded intrigued.

The door clicked shut behind him.

"No, he's not. I met him in the lobby."

I really didn't like this new me who told Brooklyn half truths. Normally, I'd dish the dirt, however bad it was.

If this was a normal time, I'd be telling Brooklyn all about my confusing feelings for Max, how he turned me on and made me laugh, and how I had to fight those feelings for James's benefit. But these weren't normal times, and I sure couldn't tell those things to Brooklyn.

"Well, good on the rate," she said. "I saw the rack rates posted on the back of the door. That'll cut into the 401K."

"What company do they work for?" I asked.

"What? Who?"

"Max and... Never mind. Where are you?"

"In the car."

My heart sank a little. "You're leaving?"

"No, we're coming back. We did some shopping."

"For what?"

Brooklyn had brought her suitcase with her from San Francisco. Surely she didn't need any new clothes. I suspected Colton was trying to woo her with expensive gifts, perfume and jewelry.

For some reason I pictured a fancy engagement ring. Well, she already had one of those.

Then I thought back to this morning and wondered if she'd been wearing it. I wasn't sure. I hadn't thought to check.

"For you," she said.

I'd lost the train of our conversation. "Huh?"

"I bought you some clothes, something for the pool. Want to meet me there?"

"You bought me clothes."

"Yes."

"You and Colton bought me clothes."

"What is wrong with you? I'm not explaining Fermat's Last Theorem."

"You don't understand Fermat's Last Theorem."

"I know."

"*I*, on the other hand, do understand it. Because I have a master's degree in mathematics, and I had to study that kind of thing." I had no idea why I was going off on a tangent. Maybe I was unsettled by the idea of Colton doing such an ordinary thing with Brooklyn as buying a bathing suit. It was one thing to woo her with extravagance, but this was everyday life.

She and I were the same size. We bought each other clothes and borrowed each other's clothes all the time.

"It's a yellow-and-black two-piece, with this cute crocheted cover-up."

I did need a new swimsuit. Brooklyn knew that. She'd teased me about packing my old aqua-blue standby.

"We can get tall, frozen margaritas on the pool deck."

I was gazing out at the sunshine and blue skies. With all I'd been through the past couple of days, a deck chair and a margarita sounded pretty good.

"Will I have to mortgage the condo to buy one?" I asked.

"They're on Colton."

"Colton is *not* bribing me."

"What bribing? He's trying to liquor you up so you'll be happy."

"I'm not happy. I'm never going to be happy until you come to your senses."

"Fine. But in the meantime, let's mellow you out with tequila."

"Okay," I reluctantly said. There was really nothing for me to do alone in the hotel room.

If I was lucky, Brooklyn would come to the pool by herself. If I wasn't, I might be able to separate her from Colton by suggesting a swim. I was determined to get her away from him as much as possible.

"The Vista pool on the twenty-sixth floor. We'll be there in ten."

I ended the call and headed for the bathroom to put my hair up out of the way.

I found a hotel tote bag and a small bottle of suntan lotion.

I dropped my key card and the lotion into the tote bag, locked my purse in the little safe and took the elevator down to twenty-six.

Brooklyn and Colton were already there.

Colton looked so much like Max that I did a double take. But then he smiled, and I knew it wasn't Max. Colton looked buttoned-down and professional, a little unapproachable. Max came across as open and warm, even when you didn't know him. I thought his irises might be a shade darker than Colton's, his lips a little fuller and his eyebrows slightly heavier.

Brooklyn waved a purple shopping bag. "I bought you some new sandals, too."

"Thanks," I said as I approached.

"Hello, Layla," Colton said.

Brooklyn handed me the bag.

"Hello, Colton." I wouldn't be friendly. But I wouldn't be nasty, either. "Thank you for this."

"No problem."

"Oh, I can see this is going to be fun," Brooklyn said. "Both of you, lighten up."

"I'm not feeling light," I said.

"I can be light," Colton said.

He didn't look light. He looked wary.

I couldn't really blame him for that. I was his girlfriend's fiancé's sister after all. I hoped he felt wary…and guilty. I hoped he felt both wary and guilty. He deserved to feel that way.

"You should put on your suit," Brooklyn said to me.

She looked around the pool deck, then pointed. "We'll go over there, under the striped blue umbrella, the one that's open."

"Okay," I said.

It did look like a great spot, in front of a couple of palm trees, beside a Plexiglas railing.

"I'll get the drinks," Colton said. "Lime margarita okay with you?" he asked me.

"Sure." I didn't like myself for accepting his hospitality while being so cold to him. "Charge it to my room."

"Don't be ridiculous," he said, moving on to Brooklyn. "Lime?" he asked her.

"Mango," she said.

He smiled.

His eyes grew warmer, softer, when he looked at Brooklyn. I could see why she thought he was in love.

I turned and shook the image out of my head. Colton wasn't in love with Brooklyn. Colton barely knew Brooklyn. Whatever he was feeling was superficial and likely to disappear at any moment.

I was puzzled as to why Brooklyn was buying into his infatuation. Guys had been falling for her at first sight since we'd turned fourteen. She always brushed it off, laughed it off, took the free milkshake or martini and went on her way.

I wondered what was different this time as I let myself into the richly appointed changing room off the pool deck. The walls were a warm peach, with a matching marble floor. The decor was accented with polished cedar benches and cubical doors.

The countertops were decorated with baskets of the same high-end toiletries I'd found in my room. I hadn't needed to bring my own suntan lotion. There were five choices, all different strengths, here for the taking.

I changed into the suit and cover-up. It fit perfectly, and

looked terrific. Brooklyn always did have great taste in clothes. I tucked my jeans, blouse and underwear into the tote bag, helped myself to a striped beach towel from the shelf by the door and headed back out to the pool deck.

I decided that if I could find a way to ignore Colton, this could be a perfectly pleasant afternoon.

The deck loungers looked cushy and comfy. The buzz of conversation on the deck was just right. There was music in the background, but it was low and flowing, keeping with the laid-back mood of the pool deck.

I saw a waiter carrying a tray of frosty, garnished margaritas. They looked good. In fact, they looked delicious.

As I walked, the waiter stayed ahead of me, then he set down the drinks on the table next to Brooklyn.

Colton had settled on the opposite side of her, so I took the lounger across the table. It had been set up with plush fitted toweling with a folded towel waiting for me at the foot. I realized, again, I hadn't needed to bring my own supplies.

"You look great," Brooklyn said as she handed one of the lime margaritas across to Colton.

"Thanks for this," I said. "I love it."

"I knew it was you the second I saw it."

"She did," Colton said.

I wished I didn't have to acknowledge him, but that would be unforgivably rude.

I settled for making the oblique point that I had known Brooklyn her whole life. "Brooklyn's always had great taste in clothes. Even when we were kids."

Colton's smile said he knew exactly what I was doing.

Well, that was annoying.

"I'm learning all kinds of great things about Brooklyn," he said.

"Are you two going to be snotty?" Brooklyn asked.

"I think so," I said.

Colton grinned.

"Well, get it out of your system, I guess." She stripped off her gauzy bikini cover-up, plopped her sunglasses over her eyes and settled back on the lounger.

I looked at Colton, and he looked back at me.

"She's in love with my brother," I said.

"I respect that."

His answer was preposterous.

"No, you don't."

"I respect that she gets to make up her own mind."

I didn't have a ready answer for that. I couldn't disagree with it. But Brooklyn wasn't currently in her right mind, so it didn't really count.

I took a drink of my margarita, stalling for time.

"You disagree?" he asked, clearly sensing his advantage in the conversation.

"I think you've only just met each other."

"True." He nodded. "But there's enough that we know we need to give it a shot."

"Damn the torpedoes?" I asked. "Just test it out and see where it leads, no matter what kind of destruction you leave in your wake?"

"Layla," Brooklyn said.

"It's okay," Colton said. "She's entitled to her opinion."

I summoned my best sarcastic tone. "Thank you so much."

To my annoyance, Colton grinned again. "Brooklyn told me you were feisty."

"I'm not feisty."

Brooklyn lifted her glasses and opened one eye to look at me. "Are you kidding me?"

"Well, of course, I'm *feisty*. But my feistiness is not the reason for my reaction to this preposterous situation. I'm also logical and reasonable. I'm a mathematician, and this is completely illogical."

"I don't think love follows a mathematical formula," Brooklyn said.

"It obeys the laws of statistics and probability. Everything does."

"There are outliers," Colton said. He reached for Brooklyn's hand.

"We're outliers," she said.

I wanted to yank them apart, but I couldn't reach from here. Coming to my feet and marching around Brooklyn's lounger to pull their hands apart seemed ridiculously dramatic, not to mention futile.

I needed a better plan than that.

I took another long drink of the margarita, sitting back and moving my attention to the water polo game at the far end of the pool. I knew full well that tequila didn't improve a person's decision-making capabilities. But the drink was delicious, and lowering my stress level would at least help me cope with the problem—even if I couldn't fix it right at this moment.

One of the teams scored, and a cheer came up.

Behind them, a movement caught my eye.

Max.

He was wearing black swim trunks and nothing else, strolling across the deck as if he owned the place. The light was better here than it had been in his hotel suite that first night. His six-pack abs were rigid below his sculpted pecs. His shoulders were broad, his biceps defined, and I saw he had an abstract blackwork tattoo on his left shoulder.

I wondered why I hadn't noticed it last night.

Our gazes locked, and my stress level spiked.

I rocked to my feet.

"Let's swim," I said to Brooklyn.

"In the water?" she asked, frowning as she looked my way from behind her sunglasses.

"Yes, in the water."

"It's cold in there."

"I'm hot."

"I'm not."

"Come on." I took her hand and pulled her to her feet.

"Whoa—"

"We need some exercise."

"Hey," Max greeted us all as he walked up.

"We're going swimming," I said to no one in particular.

"It looks that way," Colton said on a laugh.

I tossed my cover-up onto the lounger, catching Max's appreciative gaze as he took in my new swimsuit.

"Hi, Layla," he said.

"Hi." I gave him the shortest possible answer, then I headed for the pool, Brooklyn in tow.

"What is wrong with you?" she asked.

I sat down on the edge and dangled my feet in the water. It did feel cold, but I wasn't about to let that stop me. I slipped into the shallow end, the water coming to my waist.

"We need to talk," I said.

"We can't do that on dry land?" But she came into the water with me.

My gaze drifted to Max for a second, and I found him staring.

I dunked down to my neck to cover up a little.

"You're stuck to Colton like glue," I said.

"He's worth sticking to."

"James," I said. "Remember James."

Brooklyn's expression sobered. "I do."

I pushed backward, partly to get into the deeper water and partly to get farther away from Colton and Max. My body was starting to get used to the water temperature, and it felt rather good.

"You need to look at the big picture," I said.

"I'm looking at the long picture, the rest-of-my-life long picture."

"You only just met this guy." I had to admit, Colton didn't seem awful.

He hadn't done anything to justify my dislike of him. I hated what he was doing, but I didn't hate who he was. He was likely a decent guy, but Brooklyn was taken. She and James had a history and plans and a deep, abiding respect.

"I told you how I feel," she said, looking disappointed in me.

I felt a sliver of guilt. How she felt was wrong, but I couldn't figure out how to make her see that.

I moved a little closer to her. "I'm afraid you'll wake up one morning and realize this has all been a fantasy. This—" I gestured around the lavish pool deck and the hotel behind us "—isn't real. It's *Vegas*, for goodness sake."

"My feelings have nothing to do with Vegas."

I didn't believe her. But my wandering gaze landed on Max again. A man in a business suit had stopped by their loungers to talk.

"Exactly how often do they stay here?" I asked Brooklyn.

"Colton?" Brooklyn said.

"And Max. I'm assuming they must work together. They seem to know everyone."

"Everyone here?" she asked.

"Yes, here." Where else would I mean?

"I think they know most of the staff. They think it's important to pay attention to the people."

She had me confused. Max and Colton paid attention to the staff members of a hotel where they did business?

"Why?" I asked.

"Why what?"

"Why would they make such a big deal about getting to know the hotel staff?"

"It's good management."

"What do they manage?"

Brooklyn's brow furrowed in a way that told me I was talking nonsense.

"The hotel," she said.

Reality dawned on me. It had been staring me in the face. My attention shot back to Max. "They manage the hotel? *This* hotel?"

"They own this hotel. And they own the Archway Hotel. Well, their family does. And about eight others across the country."

I blinked. Then I blinked again. "Wait...what?"

"Why did you think your room rate was so low?"

"I don't know. Max said it was a corporate thing."

"It is a corporate thing. In this case, it's a family corporate thing."

I felt like a fool. Who gave out a rate more than ninety percent off? Nobody, that was who.

Then I thought about James. How was James going to compete with this? He had a good job. And as far as I knew he'd made some decent investments. He was well on his way, but he wasn't a multimillionaire, or a billionaire, or whatever it was that Colton was.

James couldn't offer Brooklyn free, unlimited room service, spa privileges or clothes-shopping sprees in iconic cities around the country. I didn't think Brooklyn was a gold digger—far from it. She had an authentic system of values that she lived by.

Still...

I took another moment to look around.

This was pretty heady stuff.

"I'm not interested in Colton's money," Brooklyn said, sounding annoyed.

"I didn't say—"

"I can see what you're thinking."

"That's *not* what I'm thinking."

"Then what are you thinking?"

I struggled to mentally compose a response.

"If you're editing your words, you're not being honest," Brooklyn said.

She was right. I owed it to her and to James to be bluntly honest. "You're breaking my brother's heart."

She looked like she might tear up. "I'm going to break his heart either way."

"Not if you change your mind."

If she would only come to her senses, we could fix this, it could all go away, and she and James would be happy, like they were meant to be.

"I won't change my mind," she said.

"You don't know that. That's the thing about changing your

mind, you think something new. You think something different than you think right now, even if you're not expecting it. That's why they call it change."

She gave a sad shake of her head.

I took her hands in mine. "At least try. For me. Please. At least try."

"Okay," she said. "I won't get locked into a decision. I'll think about it a bit more."

"Good." I felt way better. At least this was the first step.

I woke up suddenly at 7:00 a.m., sitting bolt upright in my bed.

Worry over Brooklyn had kept me tossing and turning last night. Plus, the worry had been interspersed with guilt.

I'd never slept with a man and not talked it over with Brooklyn—often before, always after. And there was one time when she'd texted me during the kissing.

It was before our clothes came off, so technically not during sex. But I had answered the text to tell her the date was going well. That was true friendship.

And now, when my sex life impacted her most, I wasn't even sharing. The guilt sucked. But what had me throwing back the covers this morning was fear.

Max could have talked to Colton last night. He might have talked about him and me. He might have told Colton he'd had a one-night stand with Brooklyn's best friend, Layla. It would be a logical thing to do. It was certainly an interesting twist to the situation. It would be weird if Max hadn't mentioned it to Colton.

And if Max had told Colton, then it followed that Colton would tell Brooklyn. Then Brooklyn would know I lied, or omitted, or whatever you technically called it when a friend kept a highly significant piece of information from another friend.

The first friend should feel terrible, and the second friend would be furious. And the first friend had better come up with a rational and sincere apology.

And I would.

But first I had to find out everything Max had told Colton.

My phone rang and I grabbed for it. It was a long shot, but I hoped it was Max.

It was James.

I shifted my weight back onto the bed and reluctantly answered.

"Hi, James."

"You need to shut this down." His words were a punch to my stomach.

I had no idea how he knew what was going on. My first fear was that I had somehow given away Brooklyn's secret.

"Uh…" I struggled to come up with a response.

"I know how much you love hanging out with Brooklyn."

"I do." My heart rate steadied just a little bit, and I told myself to breathe.

"But I need her back. I need her back now, Layla. So whatever fun you two have cooked up there in Vegas, it has to stop."

"We will be back," I said.

"When?"

"Soon. Really soon. Just a few more…" I wanted to say hours, but I feared it could be days.

"It's irresponsible," he said, sounding annoyed.

"I've met a guy," I blurted out. It was the first excuse that popped into my mind. "And, well… I just need a bit of time."

"And Brooklyn to hold your hand?" James didn't sound any happier about that.

"You know I trust her."

"You lean on her too much."

"I know." I shook my head at the irony.

"Is she there?" he asked. "I tried her phone, but she must have let the battery run out again."

"Service is spotty in the hotel," I lied. "She's probably in the gym. She wants her wedding dress to fit. I mean, I know you haven't seen it or anything, but it's—"

"Don't tell me anything about the wedding dress! Brooklyn will flip out."

"Right. Yes. Of course. She's, uh, in the gym, I guess."

"You have to stop messing around, Layla."

"I will."

"I mean it. You might be her best friend, but I'm going to be her husband. And we've got a thousand details to take care of here."

"I know. I'll get her home. I promise."

He muttered something that might have been goodbye or a rare swear word. But at least he ended the call.

I breathed a sigh of relief.

It was short-lived when I remembered the problem I had with Max. I didn't have his phone number, but I knew his hotel suite.

Putting James out of my mind, I tossed on my jeans and a shirt, shoved my feet into my new sandals, finger-combed my hair and marched down the hall to the elevator.

It wasn't until I'd rapped at his door and was standing there waiting that I questioned my actions. What was he going to think of me showing up like this? He might not even be out of bed yet. I should have thought this through. Normally, I would have thought this through. But Max seemed to short-circuit the logical pathways of my left brain stem.

Reengaging them, I looked to the right and to the left, considering the option of abandoning my plan and rushing back down the hallway. But it was a long hallway. And if he opened the door and saw me running away, I'd feel even more mortified than I did just being here.

I stood my ground, hoping against hope that he hadn't heard the knock, hoping he was asleep, or maybe already at breakfast. He could be an early riser. He seemed like an early riser. Maybe he'd gone to the gym.

I pictured him at a rowing machine, shirt off, wearing black shorts like the black bathing trunks he'd worn at the pool yesterday. He'd looked hot, more than hot—cover-model hot. And not a cover model for a men's fashion magazine, a cover model for a magazine called *Muscle Monthly* or *Freak Fitness*.

The door opened.

It was obvious he was surprised to see me. His expression turned from surprised to curious, then to interested, then to sexy hopeful.

I was making the absolutely wrong impression. I wasn't here for an early morning roll in the sheets.

"Did you say anything?" I blurted out.

His face went back to puzzled again. "I'm going to need some context here, maybe a proper noun. Say anything about what?"

"About us, about you and me."

"What about you and me?"

I rolled my eyes. Aside from our one-night stand, was there anything else about us that was gossip worthy?

I was adept at sarcasm. "That we *ate a chocolate soufflé.*"

"No." Amusement came into his eyes, like he thought this was all good and funny. "Well, the waiter and the chef knew, maybe a few of the kitchen staff. Why? Are you counting calories?"

"Don't be a jerk."

"Are you in some kind of strict diet club?"

My pride took a reflexive hit. "Do I look like I should be in a diet club?"

"No. And I think we can trust the cooking staff to keep our deep dark secrets."

"I mean the sex, Max."

"No kidding."

"Did you tell anyone? Did you tell Colton we slept together?"

"No."

My shoulders slumped in relief.

"I take it you didn't tell Brooklyn," Max said.

"No. I mean not yet. It's not like it's a secret."

"Sure. I can tell that by the way you're acting right now."

"It's not that I'm not going to tell her. I'm just thinking about the timing. I want to get it right. And there was a lot going on yesterday."

"Do you want some coffee?"

I did. "No thanks."

He stood to one side. "Come in and have some coffee. We'll get our stories straight."

"There's no story to get straight. I'm not planning to lie to Brooklyn."

The coffee sure did smell good.

"How about you tell me what you want me to say and not to say, and I'll stick to that."

A door opened farther down the hallway, and I realized that I wasn't keen on standing outside Max's suite looking like I'd just rolled out of bed, which I had, just not his bed.

"Okay," I said, heading inside. "I'll take some coffee."

"Great." He shut the door behind me.

The drapes were open, letting the morning sun into the big living room. It was neat as a pin, with a fresh floral arrangement on the coffee table and a silver coffee service on the dining table. Two cream-colored sofas faced each other, with two taupe leather armchairs at one end, positioned toward the glass French doors.

I hadn't noticed these details the night I'd been here, but the pastel abstracts and mosaic-tile wall features and the huge gas fireplace made the room look far more homey than a regular hotel suite. And it looked like there was a second bedroom and bathroom down a short hallway. It was truly huge.

"Do you stay here a lot?" I asked.

"When I'm here in Vegas," he said. "A few days a month, usually, but sometimes longer."

I could hear him pouring me a cup of coffee. "It's nice," I said, continuing to gaze around the room and at the pretty garden outside.

"Cream or sugar?" he asked.

"Both, please."

"Sweet and smooth," he said. "More than just coffee."

I turned to frown at his insinuation.

He grinned unrepentantly.

I refused to buy in, putting on the judgmental schoolmarm

face that worked on my ninth graders. "Brooklyn told me you own the place."

He erased the grin. "My family owns a few hotels. It's not a chain, each is independently designed and run according to the market."

"You deliberately kept that from me."

He held the cup out to me. "Guilty."

"Why keep it secret?"

"I'm sure you can guess. It's the same reason I don't tell anyone right away. I didn't want to color your impression of me."

I moved closer to him and accepted the cup of coffee he was offering. "You think being überwealthy would make me like you less?"

"I'm not überwealthy."

I made a show of looking around the room. "Right. My mistake."

"*This* is why I didn't say anything."

"You do know with some women you're *more* not *less* likely to get lucky if they know you're rich."

"I wasn't thinking about getting lucky with you."

"Well, you did." I maybe should have been embarrassed about that. But I wasn't, not really.

Making love with Max had seemed so natural and wonderful at the time. Even looking back, I didn't regret it. I missed it.

He pulled out one of the dining chairs, the invitation implicit for me to sit down. It was the same spot where I'd sat while we ate the soufflé.

His coffee was now at the end of the rectangular table, the same spot he'd taken that night.

I sat.

"Muffin?" he asked, pointing to a basket as he took his seat.

They were plump and grainy, dotted with blueberries. On a tray beside the muffins were little pots of jam, cream cheese and butter.

I didn't see why I should try to resist.

I put one on a side plate and cut it in half, planning to smear it with cream cheese.

"I liked you," Max said. "I was thinking I wanted to get to know you better."

"You definitely did that."

"I don't want you to feel bad about it."

"I don't feel bad about it. And you don't have to dress it up. It was what it was." I spread some cream cheese on half of the muffin. "Plus, you bought me dinner, then a really great souf-flé, twice on the soufflé, and now these wonderful muffins."

"Are you obsessed with food?"

"Not normally. But I need to look good in a very fitted bridesmaid dress less than two weeks from now..." I pictured my dress and Brooklyn's dress, and James, and then Colton. "Well, you know, maybe."

I set down the muffin, untouched, wondering if I was stress eating and if I should stop.

"Eat," Max said. "You have to keep up your strength."

"I'm hardly wasting away." The food at the Canterbury Sands was arguably the best in the country.

"Taste," he said and took a bite of his own muffin.

He'd gone with the orange marmalade, which would have been my second choice.

I took a bite of mine.

The muffin was fantastic. I washed it down with a sip of equally fantastic coffee.

"When are you going to tell her?" Max asked.

I took it to mean he was itching to tell Colton about us.

"Today," I said. "I'll let you know when you're clear to talk."

He shrugged. "I'm not going to talk."

"I thought you wanted to tell Colton."

"Why would I tell Colton?"

"You're his brother. I assumed you shared that kind of thing."

Max gave a little smile. "Not since we were teenagers."

I didn't know why I found that surprising. I hadn't really considered what men shared about their sex lives. I guess I'd assumed they were pretty much the same as women. We shared all the time.

Sex was interesting, and confusing, and impactful. I couldn't imagine keeping it all to myself.

"Even under these—" I hesitated over my words "—unusual circumstances?"

"Do you *want* me to tell Colton?"

"No."

"Do you think it will help anything if he knows?"

"It won't help if either of them knows. It sure won't help if Brooklyn knows. It'll distract her. She'll figure I like you. And if I like you, she'll think there's a chance I might come to like Colton, too. And I'm not going to like Colton because that would be betraying my brother. Nothing is going to change that."

"Is she wrong?" Max asked with a funny expression on his face.

I was confused. I thought I'd been clear. "Wrong?"

"Do you *not* like me?"

I realized how my words had sounded. I felt bad about that. "I never would have slept with you if I didn't like you."

"So that's a yes." There was a vulnerability in the question.

I found my gaze trapped by his. "That's a yes, Max. I like you."

He put his hand over mine.

It felt like a switch had been flipped, a circuit completed, like what should have been two had become one. My blood rushed through my veins, upping my heart rate, flushing my skin to a tingle and clouding the logical resources of my brain.

"Layla," he whispered. His thumb stroked my palm.

"I don't…" I couldn't finish the sentence. I didn't want to lie. "We can't," I said instead.

"What would it hurt?"

"It's already too complicated." Even as I spoke, I was leaning toward him.

"I wish I could take that as a yes," he said.

"I wish I could say yes," I told him honestly.

He withdrew his hand, and I regretted my refusal. I could have said yes. I should have said yes. The world would hardly come to a screeching halt if I said yes to him…again.

But he stood up and drew back. He finished the last of his coffee and set the cup on the table with finality. It was obviously time for me to go.

"Thank you," I said.

I wasn't sure if I meant for the coffee, the muffin, for keeping quiet about our lovemaking, or for so easily accepting my refusal to repeat it. I supposed it applied to all of it. Each of those things was considerate.

"Thank you," I said again as I came to my feet.

"No problem." But his voice was tight.

I'd either disappointed him or upset him—maybe both, probably both. I hadn't meant to blow hot and cold, but that was what I'd done.

I headed for the door before I could make the situation any worse.

Six

Later that morning I convinced Brooklyn to take a walk with me on the Strip. I had to get out of the hotel for a while.

"We're going to sweat," she said as we cleared the hotel driveway and started along the crowded sidewalk.

I could already feel the intense heat of the sun on my head. I was glad I'd slathered some of the hotel's suntan lotion on my neck and arms.

"Look there," I said, pointing to a souvenir display in an open storefront. "Let's cover our heads."

The store was selling bright pink hats with glittering red letters that said Love Las Vegas. While I didn't completely agree with the sentiment, the colors were fun and I did want to avoid heatstroke.

We paid the inflated price and plopped them on our heads.

"Slushy?" she asked as we passed another stall.

"Absolutely." I was thirsty, and the drinks definitely looked refreshing.

She linked her arm with mine. "With tequila or without?"

"It's eleven o'clock in the morning."

"It's Vegas."

"It's still too early for tequila."

"Vodka then." Brooklyn laughed.

"I was thinking watermelon and maybe some of the blueberry."

The slush dispensers displayed their bright-colored wares through the windows of the machines. It was self-serve, so a person could customize their own drink.

"Pineapple," Brooklyn said. "Or maybe cola. I could go for a little caffeine."

"Late night?" I asked. Then I regretted the question. I sure didn't want to hear the details of Brooklyn's night with Colton.

"We talked and talked," she said.

I was grateful for her discretion.

"What size do you want?" I chose a medium plastic cup for myself.

Brooklyn took the same.

She mixed cola with lemon then mocked me as I made a rainbow out of blueberry, watermelon and peach.

It felt like old times as we headed down the Strip sipping our drinks.

We came across a woman in a crocheted bathing suit with a brown python draped around her neck.

"Is that real?" I asked.

It moved, and I knew it was. I jumped to the opposite side of Brooklyn, who laughed at me.

"Why is she doing that?" I squeaked.

Then I noticed other people wearing various snakes around their necks. Revulsion crept up my spine. Yuck.

"People pay for the pictures," Brooklyn said.

"Why?"

"It's Vegas," she said with a bored nonchalance and dismissive wave, acting like a local.

"You've been here all of *two days*," I pointed out.

We made it past the snake people. I couldn't stop myself from glancing behind us to make sure none of the slithery creatures were sneaking up.

"I've had the tour," she said. "It's a really wild place."

"I'll say." I shuddered as I gave a final thought to the snakes.

The last thing in the world I wanted was to feel one of them around my neck. Never mind pay for the privilege, never mind capture my look of horror for posterity and possible internet posts.

If for no other reason, I was a high school teacher. I had a certain dignity to maintain.

Droplets of water were condensing on my slushy. I switched the cup to my left hand and shook my right one dry.

We passed families, couples and gaudily dressed actors, hawkers handing out flyers, and sellers of every imaginable tourist trinket.

It took me six blocks to work up my courage. "You asked me about Max yesterday," I said as we stopped for a light at an intersection.

The crowd surged around us.

"I like him," Brooklyn said. "I guess I'm predisposed to like him, since he's a lot like Colton." She gave a little laugh. "Then again, he's a lot not like Colton, too."

The light changed, and we started walking, propelled along with the crowd as I framed and discarded wording inside my head.

"It must be weird being a twin," she said.

"I slept with Max," I blurted out.

Brooklyn stopped dead in the middle of the intersection.

I stopped, too, and a woman with two little girls banged into the back of me. "Sorry," I said to the woman.

She frowned at me.

"Seriously?" Brooklyn asked.

"Keep walking," I said.

"When? Why? How?"

I grabbed her arm and tugged her along. "The usual way."

"Ha, ha. Very funny. *When* did this happen?"

"I couldn't find you the night I got here. I looked all over for you. I staked out the lobby for hours and hours. You ignored my texts. You wouldn't answer your phone."

"So your solution was to sleep with Max?"

"I wouldn't have even been with Max if I'd been able to find you."

"So you're saying it's my fault."

"Yes. No. It's not your fault. You were, however, a contributing factor."

"You slept with Max." There was a note of wonder in Brooklyn's voice, a note of happy wonder.

"Oh, no, you don't," I said.

"Don't what?"

"Start picturing… I don't know—double dates or something."

It was clear she was doing exactly what I would have done in her shoes.

"I wasn't picturing that," she said.

"I'm on *James's* side."

We stopped for another light.

"You like Max?" Brooklyn asked.

"Yes, I like Max." There was no point in denying it.

Brooklyn knew perfectly well that I wouldn't sleep with a guy unless I liked him a lot.

"He's also very hot," I said, feeling like I needed more justification for my actions. It wasn't like I slept with every guy I liked.

"So is Colton."

Her words gave me pause. I knew Colton was a good-looking man. He was identical to Max, after all. But he wasn't hot like Max, at least not to me. There were differences in their expressions and their mannerisms, and definitely in their perspectives.

I couldn't see Max dating an engaged woman.

I wasn't sure why I felt that way, but I did. Maybe it was the way he'd reacted when I'd asked him if he was married. He was clearly appalled by the thought of breaking his marriage vows.

An engagement might not be a vow. But it was a promise. It was a promise that deserved to be kept.

We started walking again. The crowds thinned as the quirky storefronts turned to higher-end businesses.

"Where is this all coming from?" I asked her. "You were so happy. You were both so excited to get married."

She sipped her drink through the straw.

I figured she was composing an answer. I have to admit, if I was her, I'd have had that answer all thought up by now.

"It wasn't one single thing," she said. "I was excited about the wedding, and I was happy about settling everything, becoming an official member of your family after all those years. But then we started talking about kids."

"I'm sure James will wait on the kids." I was positive he

would. "You must not have made it clear how much waiting meant to you."

Brooklyn shook her head.

She spotted a trash bin and dropped the remains of her drink.

I did the same.

"It's not just the kids," she said.

I had to admit, I didn't think that could be the only reason.

"I was living a fantasy," she said.

"That's not a bad thing. It's a good thing. What woman wouldn't want to live out her fantasy of marrying such a fantastic guy?"

"It's nothing against James, you know."

I found that pretty hard to believe. Brooklyn was trying to replace my brother with another man. How could that be anything *but* a slight against James?

"Prewedding jitters really are a thing," I said.

At least people sure talked about them a lot. And I could easily see how a guy like Colton might sweep an uncertain Brooklyn off her feet.

He was exotic, handsome and wealthy. It seemed like he could give her anything she wanted. James could come off as staid by comparison.

"I was thinking this before I even met Colton," she said.

"You weren't canceling the wedding before you met Colton."

"I was silently panicking."

"Jitters," I repeated. "I bet lots of brides feel that way."

Brooklyn gave a heavy sigh of what I took to be frustration with my attitude.

"You promised you wouldn't make a quick decision," I reminded her.

It was clear that if Brooklyn decided now, James would come out on the losing end of that decision.

"You don't want to do anything you'll regret," I said. "Don't do anything you can't take back." I could hear the pleading tone in my voice. I wasn't particularly proud of that, but at the same time, I couldn't help wondering if it would work.

"I know," she said.

"Maybe you should talk to James about this."

Her eyes got really big. "Are you kidding?"

Hearing the words out loud made me realize it wasn't one of my best ideas.

"Are you *kidding*?" she repeated. "How exactly do you see that conversation going?"

"I don't suppose it would go well," I admitted.

"Darn straight it wouldn't go well."

I watched her stricken expression, at how worried she looked. Reality seemed to be finally settling in. She was talking about leaving James, about tossing away their years together, their plans and dreams on a whim.

"Do you think it's a sign?" I asked.

"Do I think what's a sign?"

"How afraid you are to talk to James. It could be a sign you're not ready to leave him."

Brooklyn fell silent, obviously giving my words some thought.

I started to hope.

I couldn't imagine a world in which Brooklyn wasn't with James. The planet would be out of kilter, off its axis.

I already pictured my nieces and nephews with James's eyes or Brooklyn's hair. They might want to stop after two, but I was thinking three or four would be better. They were both terrific with kids. I could imagine summer picnics and Christmas mornings, ballet classes or Little League.

My future plans included James and Brooklyn's happy family. They did not include Brooklyn bopping from Las Vegas to San Francisco to New York City with some stranger.

I tried to pretend Brooklyn hadn't ditched me. I knew that was exactly what had happened, and it hurt my pride to think she'd rather spend time with Colton than me.

I hadn't felt that way about James. It never seemed lik

Brooklyn was giving up time with me to spend it with him.
She and I still had plenty of time together. If I had a boyfriend,
we'd double date. When we were teenagers, Brooklyn was usually at our house, so I was with them more often than not. And
when I wasn't in a relationship, which was pretty often, we'd
do more group activities than one-on-one dating.

Was it odd that James and Brooklyn hadn't spent all that
much time alone?

Under the circumstances, I didn't really want to ask myself
if that was normal. It could easily be normal. It wasn't a sign
of anything negative. I had to be reengineering the past, seeing problems where they didn't even exist.

I didn't want to spend any extra money while I was here,
so I'd decided the hotel's courtyard lagoon pool was a better
choice than an overpriced lunch. It cost me nothing to find a
lounger under a palm tree, help myself to the complimentary
towels and suntan lotion, and say yes to the offer of ice water
from a friendly pool attendant.

It was warm, and I was comfortable. I'd even found a
half-finished novel buried in an app on my phone. It was
a comedy sleuth story, lightweight enough that I picked up
the plot in a couple of pages. It was exactly what I needed
to distract me.

"Enjoying the sunshine?" Max's voice alerted me to his ap-
proach before I heard his footsteps above the laughter of the
children in the pool.

I looked up and was struck all over again by his great looks.
He was wearing a white dress shirt with the sleeves rolled up
over a pair of casual gray slacks. He didn't exactly look like
he was working. He didn't exactly look like he was relaxing,
either.

"What is it you do around here?" I asked as the question
popped into my mind.

"In what way?"

"What's your job? When you spend time at one of your ho-
els, what do you do? I'm assuming they each have a general
anager, since you and—" I caught myself.

"His name is Colton."

"I know that." I took a beat. Saying his name always seemed to implicitly acknowledge his relationship with Brooklyn. But I couldn't exactly use "he who shall not be named" when I was talking to his twin brother.

I tried again. "Since you and Colton don't seemed to be assigned to a specific hotel."

Max looked amused, his eyes lighting in a way that both attracted and annoyed me. I hated that he could so effortlessly evoke an emotional reaction in me. I wasn't an emotional person. I was a logical person. And it wasn't logical for me to indulge in this attraction.

He sat down sideways on the lounger next to mine.

"We do a bunch of things," he said.

"Inspect the troops?" It sounded silly after I said it.

But Max flashed a grin, like he thought it was funny. "And the equipment, and the building. We check in with the general manager and the department managers to see how things are running. We look at financial reports, guest response amalgamations, troubleshoot, that sort of thing."

"What kind of trouble do you find?"

"It's a constant fight to stay ahead of upgrading. Sometimes a restaurant has run its course, people's tastes and trends change and we need to refresh decor and menus. There are mechanical breakdowns, human-resources issues—we once found fraud."

"Someone was stealing from you?"

"They were."

My curiosity was piqued. It wasn't what I'd expected him to say, and I couldn't help but wonder about the details of the crime. "Interesting. I'm good when it comes to numbers."

"Meaning you could help discover fraud or help perpetrate fraud?"

"Depends on the circumstances. You have a fraud that needs perpetrating?"

"Not at the moment, you know, since I'd be stealing my ov money. But I'll keep you in mind in case anything comes ι

"I've always wanted to moonlight," I said.

He chuckled.

"So you caught them?" I asked on a more serious note.

"Two employees were in on it. One was cooking the books. The other was signing off on bogus expenses. Turned out they were having an affair and had cooked up a plan to take the money and move to the Caribbean." Max paused. "Instead they moved to Nevada State Prison."

His tone and expression made me smile.

I was about to express my surprise that his job involved fighting crime, when my phone rang.

I picked it up from the little rattan table, expecting Brooklyn. But it was James's number that showed on the screen.

I felt a lurch of guilt for joking around with Max. But I put on a cheerful tone as I answered. "Hey, how's it going in Seattle?"

"Are you with Brooklyn?" James asked straight away.

I hesitated for less than a second. "Yes. She's here."

She was here somewhere, I reasoned, either in the hotel or in the greater Las Vegas area.

"Please put her on the phone."

"Why? Is something wrong? Can I help?" I hoped James wouldn't catch on to my stalling.

"Nothing is wrong. I'd like to talk to my fiancée."

"Did you call her phone?"

"Of course I called her phone. Just like I did this morning. Ask her if it's even turned on."

"I, uh, can't." My mind scrambled for an answer to his inevitable next question.

"Why not?"

"She's not exactly right here, right now." Inspiration was right in front of me. "She's in the pool." And once I'd given over to outright lies, my mouth seemed to go for it. "Brooklyn," I called out in a loud voice.

Max gave me a look that said he knew exactly what I was ~ing. I ignored him. "James is on the phone," I called to the ~itious Brooklyn.

I waited a moment.

"Can she call you back?" I asked James.

"Tell her to get out of the pool."

"She's...playing volleyball. It's a close game. She doesn't want to let down her team." Okay, I was starting to amaze myself. Not only was I breaking my own moral code, but it also turned out I was pretty good at it.

"This is getting out of hand," James said with obvious frustration.

"We're just cutting loose," I said, telling myself it was closer to the truth. "We're having some extra girl time before the wedding. You had a bachelor party."

"The bachelor party lasted six hours."

"So we're less efficient. I'll get her to call you back."

"Don't bother."

My stomach sank, thinking James somehow knew what was going on.

"Why not?" I asked. I could hear the trepidation in my own tone.

"Because I'm not waiting. I'm getting the next plane."

"Don't do that," I said too fast.

I could feel James gathering himself across the phone line. "And why not?"

I avoided Max's gaze. "I met a guy."

"So you said this morning."

"I know. But it really is maybe a thing. And Brooklyn's being my wingman. You know how worried she's been about me being lonely now that you're getting married."

James was silent for a second. "That's true."

His answer took me back. Brooklyn wasn't worried about me. *Was* she worried about me? Why would she worry about me? I wasn't lonely. There absolutely was nothing for her to worry about.

Well, not when it came to her marrying James, anyway. When it came to Colton, the story was completely different. In that, she ought to be very worried about my reaction to that.

Max was peering at me.

James was silent.

I recovered my surprise and told myself to take the win.

"Great," I said to James. "Thanks. It'll only be a little bit longer."

"Hurry up," he said.

"I will," I promised.

He muttered something unintelligible again, then the line went dead.

I lowered my phone.

"That was interesting," Max said.

"You could have given me some privacy," I pointed out.

"I could have," he agreed. "I take it I'm the guy—the guy that's maybe a thing?"

"It's not you. It's not anybody. There is no guy. It was a story." I told myself it was for a good cause. In this particular scenario the end more than justified the means.

"I think the word you're looking for is *lie*," Max said.

I flashed him a glare. He barely knew me, and here he was judging away. He was the one in the wrong. Well, his brother was the one in the wrong.

Many people were in the wrong, and I was trying to make it right...by doing something underhanded. Yeah, I got that.

"Come out with me," Max said.

I didn't understand.

"Let's go on a date. That way your lie won't be as much of a lie, and you'll feel better about it."

"I don't feel bad about it," I said.

His grin went broad. "You should see your face. It's killing you."

"I'm perfectly fine."

He got to his feet. "You are the most painfully honest person. I should definitely offer you a job in our accounting division."

"I already have a job." For some reason I felt the need to remind him, though it was irrelevant to the conversation.

"Let's go," he said.

"To the accounting office?"

How far was he planning to carry the joke?

"On our date."

"Now?" Not that I had said yes. Not that I was planning to say yes. Going forward, I was keeping my distance from Max, not dating him.

"Yes, now. Let's make you honest. You'll feel better, I promise."

"You have no idea what will make me feel better."

"A bottle of Crepe Falls Reserve says I will." He held his hand out to me.

I wanted to take it, and I had to stop myself from reaching up. And it had nothing to do with my competitive instincts or with a newfound weakness for Crepe Falls Reserve.

"There's a hot-air balloon tour this afternoon. It's really great. It takes you to the rim of the Grand Canyon," Max said.

I found myself hesitating—a hot-air balloon tour instead of waiting around for Brooklyn?

Brooklyn pitied me. She was worried about me. She probably thought I was lonely without her.

I didn't like to think that I might be lonely without her.

I sure wouldn't be lonely while floating over the Grand Canyon. I had to admit, a tour like that sounded marvelous. It sounded downright bucket-list marvelous.

Max wiggled his hand. "Come on, Layla. What've you got to lose?"

"A bottle of Crepe Falls Reserve, apparently," I said.

"That's the spirit."

Brooklyn didn't need to worry about me. I could take care of myself.

In fact, maybe I'd back off on pressing her to make the right decision. The novelty of Colton could easily fade, would most likely fade. But they needed time together—all alone together, with no distractions and nothing else to do but stare at each other.

That's what it would take for Brooklyn to get over Colton. Taking the adventure of a lifetime with Max might just be the best way to help James. I wasn't even deluding myself. I truly believed it was worth a shot.

"I can't be gone too long," I said.

"I'll have you back by dinner."

Floating near the rim of the Grand Canyon, I was in awe. The view of the red-rock cliffs was outstanding. The sky was crisp blue, and the mottled scrub of green cacti went on and on.

I was also afraid—not of the height. What scared me was the fun. I was having a whole lot of fun with Max on this exotic, expensive date.

The hot-air balloon ride was exhilarating on its own. But it had started with a twenty-minute helicopter flight from Vegas over Lake Mead to the balloon-launch site. There we were greeted by a professional tour guide dressed in a suit and tie, and an obviously knowledgeable balloon pilot named Rick, who briefed us on safety.

They gave us jackets in case we got cold, showed us how to work on the oxygen masks in case we went over 10,000 feet and then we had a toast with champagne before we left the ground.

The champagne was chilled, and it was high-end, and it wasn't served in plastic cups like you might expect at a picnic site. Oh, no, nothing that tacky. We were handed crystal flutes to ensure nothing marred the opulence of our experience.

With the colorful balloon above us, we soared past red-rock cliffs.

Max and I gazed out at the gnarled trees, the towering saguaro cactuses and the flashes of delicate, colored flowers that grew in bunches on the desert floor. A hawk glided above us and a coyote trotted below.

Rick, the pilot, was behind us, controlling the burner.

"Tell me about your brother," Max said.

The question put me on my guard. "Why?"

"I've been thinking about him since your phone call."

I really didn't want to think about that phone call. I didn't want to think about my dishonesty. I wanted to think about the beautiful desert rolling out in front of us.

"It's easy for me to see Colton's side in this," Max said, either not noticing my silence or not caring. "He and Brooklyn seem good together, and—"

"James and Brooklyn are *way* better together."

"I'm not saying they're not."

I pressed my point. "What they have is solid and real."

"It may well be."

I was determined to argue, but Max wasn't really arguing back. That annoyed me, but I wasn't exactly sure how to counter it. How did you complain about someone not fighting with you?

We both fell silent. The wind blew against our faces as we glided. The roar of the burner ebbed and flowed.

"About your brother," he said.

"What?" I asked, exasperated that he wouldn't just let it lie. "Are you scoping out the competition for Colton?"

"No. I'm trying to understand both sides."

"Why would you want to do that?"

"Because it's a reasonable thing to do when there are two perspectives."

"You're hardly a neutral party."

He was pulling for his own brother, plain and simple. Not that I blamed him. I was sure pulling for James. But I felt like I had a stronger claim. Which I know sounds ridiculous. Brooklyn's feelings were her own, not mine or Max's or Colton's, or even James's. Still...

"I'm considering the wisdom of helping you," Max said.

"Helping me do what?"

"I think you may have a point."

I'm not a suspicious person, but this sounded too good to be true. "About what?"

The balloon basket lurched. I fell against Max, and he wrapped his arm firmly around me, steadying me.

I didn't want to like the feeling. I wasn't a maiden in distress. I didn't need a strong handsome man to keep me out of harm's way. It wasn't like I was about to fall.

Still, I didn't pull back.

I wasn't sure why.

Okay, I was sure why.

The rocky basket was an excuse to hug Max again without admitting what I was doing. Then again, I'd just admitted what I was doing, so it wasn't like I was fooling myself.

"Colton and Brooklyn just met," Max said. "It's possible what they feel won't last."

"Exactly!" I blurted.

The basket lurched, more suddenly this time, and the floor seemed to drop from beneath us.

My stomach dropped along with it.

Max twisted his head to look back at the pilot.

I could imagine his question was the same as mine—something along the lines of "what the heck?"

"Wind shear," Rick called out. The roar of the burner became constant. "I'm fighting a pretty strong downdraft."

I was about to ask if we were going to fall, when the floor stabilized, our descent growing more constant.

"That was exciting," I said to Max. I almost, but not quite, kept the tremble from my voice.

"That's one word for it," he said.

"Were you scared?" I asked.

"Not so far."

The basket was rapidly descending.

The roar increased, and I saw the pilot was using both of the burners.

I found myself mesmerized by the rising earth. If I had to guess, I'd say we were a hundred feet above the sloped, tree-dotted hillside.

I wouldn't say we were plummeting, but we were falling faster than I wanted to hit the ground, that was for sure.

"There's a fifteen-second delay for the balloon to respond to the added heat," Rick told us.

"Are *you* scared?" I asked Rick.

He looked perfectly calm.

"We'll slow down in a moment," he told me. "We may make a hard landing."

"Is that a euphemism for *crash*?" I asked, not really sure that I wanted the answer.

"Landing," he assured me.

"Don't be scared," Max said.

"I'm not," I lied. I was getting scared now. The ground was only about fifty feet away.

"Feel that?" Rick asked.

Our rate of descent had definitely slowed down.

I heard him try his radio.

"Are you sending a Mayday?" I asked.

"I'm trying to raise a signal."

"There's no signal?" I was embarrassed at the little squeak at the end of my question. But I was starting to picture us stranded in the desert, injured by the fall, nobody knowing how to find us while we died of thirst or were attacked and eaten by coyotes.

Brooklyn tells me I get ahead of myself. She tells me that I love to play "worst-case scenario."

She's not wrong. I admit, I do do that. But in this case I figured I was playing "most likely case scenario." That was a completely different thing.

"We're being monitored on GPS," Max said, obviously guessing my worry. "They know where we are."

"I want to let them know we landed safely," Rick said.

I looked over the edge of the basket. There were trees directly beneath us, and we were closing in.

"We haven't landed safely," I pointed out.

"Once—"

A strong cross breeze gusted against us.

"Whoa," Rick said, shutting off the burners. "Hang on!"

Max plastered me to his stomach with one arm, gripping the edge of the basket with the other.

The basket caught on the branches of one of the trees. The branches snapped off and the balloon kept going.

Then we hit the next tree. This one had more strength and it held us in place. The wind buffeted the giant balloon, fighting with the tree for control of the basket.

"What is—" I began, but I didn't get to finish.

The basket tipped sideways. I cried out, but I was proud that I didn't actually scream.

My heart was pumping furiously as I grasped at the air, searching for something to hang on to.

Max's grip on me tightened as I almost slid out of the basket.

"Keep still. I've got you," he said.

Max kept us in place by holding on to the basket with one arm and me with the other.

I couldn't help but wonder how long he could do that.

Rick had been thrown, and he now hung from the lip of the basket, his feet kicking as he searched for a tree branch for support.

He seemed to find something. He breathed a sigh of relief and hoisted himself with his elbows, then his shoulders, farther into the basket.

"You okay?" Max asked him.

"Yes, you?" Rick asked.

"We're good," Max said.

"Sorry about the hard landing," he said.

I almost laughed. I assumed he was joking. "That felt like a crash."

"It's not a crash if you walk away," Rick said, keeping his tone light on purpose—no doubt.

"This is going to be interesting," Max said.

"Interesting?" I echoed with incredulity.

We were stuck in a tree with a ten-foot drop to the ground.

"We can do this," Max assured me.

I wanted to be brave. I wished with all my heart I could be brave. I didn't want to look like a coward in front of Max. But I didn't want to break my limbs, either.

The basket flexed beneath us, and my heart took a jump.

"Can you get your girlfriend down?" Rick asked.

I started to protest the title, but then I stopped. Under the circumstances, correcting Rick would be silly.

Max stretched out on his stomach, then he motioned to me. "Give me your hands."

I couldn't help glancing at the drop-off from the mouth of the basket. "What are you going to do?"

"If I hold you over the edge at arm's length, your feet will almost touch the ground."

"Almost?" I didn't really like the sound of that, never mind the idea of dangling in midair while Max lowered me.

What if he lost his grip? What if the basket tipped further and we both tumbled out? I'd break my legs and Max would break his neck.

Just then the wind gusted, catching the half-inflated balloon, lurching us against the tree.

"Do it now," Rick said.

"Take my hands," Max said.

I didn't hesitate anymore. Whatever courage I'd been looking for showed up in an instant. I skootched over and gave Max my hands.

He took me by the wrists.

"Hang on to me," he said.

I gripped his wrists the way he gripped mine.

"Slide backward," he told me. "Don't look down."

I decided that was very good advice. I settled my gaze on his.

He gave me a smile. "This is going to be easy."

"I don't believe you." But I was already inching back. Some primal part of my brain told me I had to act, I had to do exactly as he said to make sure we all got out of this without getting hurt.

"That's good," Max said as my feet dangled free.

I folded at the waist, then I wiggled back even more. As I reached the balance point, I took a breath and kept going.

Max's gaze remained locked with mine until I was dangling at his arm's length.

"It's about two feet to the ground," he told me. "Like jumping off a chair. Bend your knees when you land."

I was ready.

I nodded.

He let me drop.

Seven

We made it onto solid ground with nothing more than minor scrapes and bruises. Rick headed up the side of the hill with the radio to try to raise a signal. Meanwhile, Max sized up the trapped basket.

"It's not coming down," he said, coming over to where I was sitting on a smooth rock. "Not without help, anyway."

I was watching a moving shape on the horizon. "Is that a coyote?"

Max followed my gaze. "It is."

"Is it dangerous?"

"Only if you're a jackrabbit. It won't bother us."

"Are you sure?"

It was possible Max was lying to make me feel better. The animal had stopped now. It was staring right at us, and it looked hungry. There wasn't a lot of game out here in the desert. We probably looked delicious.

"What does your brother do for a living?" Max asked, sitting down next to me.

"He could have friends lurking out there."

"James?"

"The coyote."

I watched the nature channel. I knew coyotes traveled in packs. They might not be big, but a well-coordinated pack could take down a deer. I'd seen it happen, and it wasn't pretty.

"Is he a teacher like you?" Max asked. "Lawyer? Banker?"

"James is an economist."

The coyote put his nose to the ground and started toward us.

"Should we climb the tree?" I asked.

"Does he work for a government? A chamber of commerce? A Fortune 500?"

"A consulting firm."

Max seemed very calm. I decided to assume our lives weren't in imminent danger.

"I assume he's a good-looking man."

I took my gaze off the approaching coyote long enough to check Max's expression. That was an odd assumption.

"He's your brother," Max said. "The genetic odds seem to be in his favor."

The oblique compliment took me by surprise. I couldn't decide if I should thank him and seem conceited or let it slide and seem ungrateful.

Suddenly Max jumped to his feet and shouted, "Ha!"

The coyote startled about thirty feet away.

My insides froze with fear.

Max waved his arms. "Go on!"

The coyote twisted his body, turning away, but watched us over his shoulder as he trotted.

"Ha!" Max shouted again.

The coyote began to run.

"You said he wasn't dangerous." My voice had a definite shake to it.

"He's not."

"He was coming for us."

"He didn't know what we were. We're pretty far out in the desert right now. I doubt he sees a lot of people."

"He wanted to eat us." I was sure of that.

Coyotes were predators, and we were prey.

"He ran away," Max pointed out.

"You had to scare him away."

"I just let him know we were bigger than he is." Max sat back down and took my hand. "Relax. You're perfectly safe."

I gazed at the hill where the pilot had climbed. "What about Rick?"

"He'll be back soon."

"I hope he's okay." I wouldn't have wanted to be climbing around up that hill all by myself.

"What's the name of your brother's firm?"

"O'Neil Nybecker."

"That's a solid firm."

"He's a solid guy." I'd been bragging about my brother most of my life—except when I was really young, and except for those teenage years when he embarrassed me nearly to death. The rest of the time I accepted that he was an exceptional brother.

"Top of his class at UW," I said.

"Impressive," Max responded in an easy tone.

"His varsity four-man crew took silver in the nationals."

"Colton lettered in cross-country."

That wasn't exactly what I wanted to hear. "Is this a contest?"

"It's beginning to feel like one."

"You asked."

"I did," he agreed.

"What about you?" I found myself curious, thinking about what Max might have been like in college. "Did you run cross-country?"

"I played second base."

My interest was piqued. "I coach softball. Freshman and sophomore."

"Good for you."

"We all contribute to the extracurricular activities." I didn't want him to think I was bragging about some kind of extraordinary contribution to North Hill High. All the teachers were dedicated.

"Do you play?" he asked.

"I do. In a rec league. You?"

"Same."

There was something about his answer that projected a quiet confidence.

"You're really good, aren't you?"

"Lots of guys are better than me."

"No, they're not."

He smiled at that statement, but didn't answer.

"I knew it," I said.

"How long have James and Brooklyn been together?"

"Since high school. Even before that, really. Brooklyn's been my best friend forever."

"They have a lot in common?"

I thought about how to answer that. "Not everything. They're good foils for each other. James is solid and steady. Brooklyn is more impulsive, full of energy, great ideas and tons of fun. Together, they work."

"Do they fight?"

"Almost never."

"Do you find that odd?"

"I find it great. They've been around each other forever, and they've always gotten along."

"Do you think that could be the problem?"

I wasn't about to admit there was a problem.

I mean, I knew there was a problem. It was less than two weeks to the wedding.

Brooklyn was in Vegas hanging out with Colton instead of back in Seattle doing the final fitting of her wedding gown. But I wasn't ready to admit that to anyone but myself.

"There's no problem."

"Maybe they were too close. More like siblings than lovers."

"They're not siblings. They've been dating for years. Believe me, they know the difference." As I spoke, I couldn't help remembering Brooklyn saying she loved James, but she wasn't in love with James. At the time, it had struck me as a trivial distinction. I didn't even know what she meant.

"Okay," Max said with an air of finality.

"Okay what?"

"Okay, we'll do it your way."

"Do what? What are we doing?" I couldn't help but look around at the open desert and wonder if I'd missed something.

"We'll try to break them up. I'll help you."

I wasn't about to walk into that kind of a too-good-to-be-true offer. "Sure you will."

"I mean it. You could very well be right. The blush of their hormone high will wear off, and they could find that's all they ever really had."

"And Brooklyn's life would be ruined," I said, daring to consider Max might be serious. It would sure help for me to have him on my side. I'd rather it be an even battle than three on one. Plus, Max had the advantage of knowing Colton. That insider knowledge would definitely help me out.

If Max was serious.

I hoped he was serious.

I wasn't buying in without testing him. "Why would you help me?"

"I like you."

That seemed too simple. Also, it seemed unlikely. "You wouldn't betray your brother for some random woman."

"I don't consider you some random woman."

"I showed up randomly in your life two days ago."

"Three days ago, and it was more inevitable than random."

I guess I knew what he meant. First we saw each other in San Francisco. I wasn't about to ask if he'd felt something then, but I sure remembered the impact on me. Then there was the lobby lounge in Vegas, then dinner, then Brooklyn and Colton.

It did have an air of inevitability around it.

"It's still only three days," I said. "And he is your twin brother."

"And I don't want to see him make a mistake."

Now I had hope. "You think it's a mistake?"

"I give it fifty-fifty."

"I'd give it less than that."

"I've seen them together. They think it's real."

"They're wrong," I said.

"Do you want my help or not?"

"Yes. I do."

"Good. Rick's back."

I looked at the hillside and saw Rick coming our way. The sun was falling behind him, and the shadows were getting longer. We'd been away from the hotel for a long time. Brooklyn had to be wondering where I'd gone.

"Did you tell anyone we went up in the balloon?" I asked Max.

I hadn't texted Brooklyn. Mostly because I thought we'd be back before she and Colton returned. And also because I didn't want her getting the impression I'd gone on a date with Max.

It was a fake date.

If it was an actual date, there'd have been intimacy—flirting, kissing and hugging and things like that.

As I rationalized, I couldn't help but remember being in his arms when the balloon went down. But that didn't count. I'd feared for my life. Any strong man's arms around me would have felt good.

"I didn't tell anyone," Max said.

"So they don't know where we are?"

"We can tell them all about it when we get back. It'll make a really good story."

"That you saved my life." I guess if I was Max, I'd be bragging, too.

"I didn't save your life." He paused. "Maybe your ankle. I probably saved you from a broken ankle."

"Thank you," I said.

He chuckled. "I wasn't fishing for that."

Rick grew closer. "Help is on the way!"

The helicopter that flew us out of the desert brought us all the way to the hotel.

It was my first and only time using a rooftop landing pad. I had to admit, I found it incredibly efficient. I could see why the superrich liked to travel that way. It sure beat fighting traffic in my Honda on Route 99.

I called Brooklyn from the express elevator.

It took a few rings, and she sounded breathless when she picked up. "Layla!"

I didn't want to imagine what I'd interrupted, and I didn't ask. "Hi."

"What time is it?"

"Just after six."

"I was going to call you earlier." Her words were rushed.

I realized then that she hadn't even noticed I was gone. There was no way that was good.

"But I got distracted," Brooklyn continued.

"James called," I said, hoping to shake her up a little.

She paused, as I'd hoped she would. Her tone turned cautious. "What did he want?"

The question struck me as ridiculous. "He wanted you. He wanted to know what was taking so long. He wanted to come here to see you."

Her voice went up an octave, the sound of panic creeping into it. "He can't do that."

"In fact, he can."

"I need more time, more time to think. Seeing him is going to mess me up."

I took pity on her. I don't know why, but I did. "He's not coming. I talked him out of it."

"Good." Brooklyn seemed to calm down. "That's good. You're the best."

"No, I'm not." I felt like a traitor.

"Where are you right now?" she asked.

"I'm in the hotel."

"I'll come and meet you."

I could hear in the phone that she was walking now. I was encouraged that she wanted to meet me right away. We needed to find somewhere to talk—not that I was exactly sure what more I could say. But I had to keep trying. I had to keep trying for as long as it took.

"Do you have plans tonight?" she asked.

What a nonsensical question. No, I didn't have plans tonight. She was my plans for as long as we were stuck in Vegas.

"I'm free," I said.

"Because, well, Colton has tickets to the Twenties Tangle."

Colton, Colton, Colton. I wanted to bang my head against the elevator.

"He's had the tickets for months," she said.

I didn't care if he'd had the tickets for years. "Can he not go alone?" I caught Max's quizzical gaze.

"It's a dance," Brooklyn said.

"You're going to a dance?"

Her world was falling apart around her, and she was going to a dance?

"The Twenties Tangle," Max said to me.

I gave him a glare of frustration.

"We found this supercool flapper dress," Brooklyn said.

I covered my phone. "Your brother needs to stop."

"Stop what?"

"It's all silver and black," Brooklyn said into my ear. "With lace and tassels and sequins. There's a rhinestone headband, and you should see the shoes."

"Buying Brooklyn's affections," I said to Max.

He moved closer, keeping his voice low. "With what?"

"A dress."

"A dress?" He looked puzzled. "I thought maybe some diamonds or a car."

I gave him a shove with my shoulder.

He didn't even budge.

"We need to talk," I said to Brooklyn. "We need to have a really good talk."

"The dress is in my room. Do you want to see it?"

"No, I don't want to see your dress."

"I have tickets," Max said to me. "We can go with them."

I covered my phone again. "That's your big plan to break them up? A double date?"

"You want a dress?"

"No." I was insulted. "I will not be bought."

"It's a great party."

"I'm not here to party."

"Brooklyn seems like she's here to party. And we can't break them up if we're not with them."

I opened my mouth to shoot down the idea, but I realized he was making sense.

If I couldn't get Brooklyn to skip the dance—which seemed like a tall order, given her level of excitement—maybe the next best thing was to follow her there. It would be a whole lot harder for her to avoid me if we were in the same room.

"Fine," I said to Max.

"You'll take the dress?"

"I'll go to the dance."

"Then you will need a dress."

"Layla?" Brooklyn asked, clearly puzzled by my silence.

"I'm here," I answered her.

Brooklyn sounded fragile now, vulnerable as she spoke. "I really, really love the dress."

"Fine," I said. "I'll come and see the dress."

Max spoke up. "Colton's suite is next to mine."

Max's words gave me pause on a whole bunch of fronts.

I'd made passionate love with Max right next door to where Brooklyn was staying? We could have been caught that very night. They might have seen us on the patio, or out in the hallway, or—or...

The elevator doors slid open. We'd arrived at the lobby.

"I'll be there in three minutes," I said.

"I can't wait to show you." Brooklyn ended the call.

"How do you want to play this?" Max asked as we made our way through the main lobby.

"Good afternoon, Mr. Kendrick," a staff member greeted him in passing.

"Afternoon, Brian," Max responded.

I couldn't help but comment. "Of course, you know him, too."

"He's the events manager."

Other staff members watched our progress. I realized they were wondering who I was.

"Just another date, people," I muttered under my breath. "He does this all the time."

"Pardon me?" Max asked.

"Everyone's staring at me."

"They're staring at me. They're wondering when I'm going

to give them their next raise. So do we just up and admit we're going to the Twenties Tangle together? Or do you want me to casually bring it up? I can hang back and arrive after you, or we can tell them about the balloon trip."

"You mean the balloon crash."

"I wouldn't lead with that. It'll probably upset Brooklyn."

I knew there was wisdom in his advice.

"I'll go in first," I said. "You arrive casually in a few minutes and then mention you have an extra ticket—at an appropriate point."

"And the balloon adventure?"

"We'll play it by ear." It wasn't a secret, but if Brooklyn knew Max and I had spent virtually the entire day together, she'd start getting more ideas about us. I didn't need that, and neither did Max.

"If I don't buy you a dress, Colton will," Max said as we left Colton's suite. It was a mirror of Max's next door.

Brooklyn was thrilled when I'd agreed to come to the dance. I'd made them work to get my yes, and Max had played along quite brilliantly.

I figured Brooklyn would get all speculative on my feelings toward Max if I gave in too easily. Plus, I'd honestly held out hope that she'd change her mind and would spend the evening alone with me instead of going with Colton—wrong about that.

"You might as well pick it out for yourself," Max said.

I knew I didn't want to be indebted to Colton for a dress. And I knew Brooklyn would show up with something for me if she thought I had nothing to wear.

I decided Max was the lesser of two evils.

The other option was buying my own dress. A strong independent modern woman would likely insist on that.

But this strong independent modern woman had mortgage and car payments coming due, and she'd covered a whole lot of incidental expenses leading up to a wedding that might not even happen. Plus, I rationalized, it was Max's and Colton's fault I was in this mess, and this was no more than pocket change for Max.

I didn't really buy into that rationalization. But I did allow myself to be swayed by the mortgage payment and the fact that I'd only wear the dress once.

"Fine," I said to Max. "Buy me a stupid dress."

"You had to think a long time on that."

"I'm not thrilled about the idea of having a strange man buy me a dress."

"But…" he said.

"But what?"

"There has to be a *but*, since you said yes, anyway."

"But I have a mortgage payment coming up." I was going with blunt honesty from here on in. I didn't particularly care how embarrassing it got.

There was no point in pretending I had money. I was an ordinary schoolteacher with a nine-hundred-square-foot condo and a ten-year-old car.

He gave a low whistle. "Exactly how much are you planning to spend on this dress?"

I knew he was joking. At least I was pretty sure he was joking.

"A lot," I said. "I'm attending this dance under protest, and I have zero scruples about maxing out your credit card to look good doing it."

He grinned. "This I have got to see."

Before I knew it, we were out front of the hotel.

Max held up a hand, and a black SUV eased to a stop in front of us.

The driver jumped out, but Max was already opening the back door for me.

"Where to?" The driver asked.

"Crystal's."

"Yes, sir."

"Do they sell costumes?" I asked as I slid into the seat.

"They sell everything."

Max sat down beside me and the vehicle glided onto the Strip.

I watched the people on the crowded sidewalks while Max sent a text to someone.

I sent my own text, alerting Brooklyn to my dress-shopping expedition so she didn't get any strange ideas of her own.

A few blocks later we pulled up to a bank of glass doors set in a gleaming geometric building.

A man in a suit jacket opened Max's door.

"Mr. Kendrick," the man said. "I'm Dalton Leonard, an assistant manager here at the Crystal Shops."

"Hello, Dalton."

Max stood, then he turned to offer me his hand.

Feeling like I'd wandered into a fairy tale, I took his hand to steady myself.

"We're attending the Twenties Tangle," Max said.

Dalton turned his attention to me. "I'm happy to be of assistance, ma'am."

"Layla," I said to him and offered my hand.

He shook. "Of course, ma'am. Might I suggest Andante's on the second floor?"

"Sure." I wasn't about to argue. I was along for the ride on this one.

He gave a sharp nod. "Their selection of period dresses is wonderful. They also have modern ensembles with a nod to the past, if you'd like to go that route."

I wasn't at all sure what route I wanted to go.

"This way." Dalton gestured to the glass doors.

As we entered the opulent shopping mall, I was even less sure of what route I wanted to go—maybe straight back out the front door. I knew I'd joked about spending Max's money, but now that the reality of high-end Vegas shopping was staring me in the face, I didn't know if I had the nerve.

Don't get me wrong, I like designer brands. Brooklyn and I spent many happy hours haunting the outlet stores looking for good bargains. Brooklyn had a flair, and I had learned quite a lot over the years.

But paying full-blown retail in a place as fancy as this was enough to make my mouth go dry and double my pulse rate.

"You asked for it," Max whispered in my ear as we walked.

It was then that I realized I was still holding his hand.

"Are you testing me?"

"Maybe. If you want to back out, there's a used clothing store north off the Strip."

"There is?" I stopped.

I wished he'd said something sooner. I could afford to buy my own dress at a used clothing store. It was a perfect solution. Where else did a strong, independent, modern, *smart* woman go to buy a dress she'd only wear once?

Max tugged on my arm. "Oh, no you don't. We have a deal."

I peered at his smug expression. "You were testing me there, too, weren't you? There is no used clothing store."

"Not in your future. Dalton's getting away."

"Let him."

"That would be rude." Max kept tugging, and I started walking.

"I don't need a brand-new dress," I said.

"You may not need one, but you're getting one."

"I'll take the used option, thank you."

"That's way too much trouble, and not nearly as much fun."

I wasn't sure I was capable of having fun at this. It wasn't like I was going to enjoy the dance. This extravagant shopping trip was wasted on me, and Max should be spending his money on some other woman.

Wait a minute.

"Who were you planning on taking to the dance?" I asked.

"Nobody."

"You're lying."

"I'm not lying."

"The dance is tonight. You already had tickets. You must have had a date. Is that who you texted in the car? Please don't tell me you broke some poor girl's heart."

"I didn't break anyone's heart. I texted the Crystal Shops office to have someone meet us out front so we didn't have to

traipse all over the mall to find the right store. But thanks for
the vote of confidence."

"What vote of confidence?"

"That I had the power to break a heart by breaking a date."

"Well…" I didn't exactly know what to say to that. I could
deny it was what I meant. But I had absolutely no doubt he
could break a woman's heart by breaking a date.

"It's a charity thing," he said. "I always buy tickets, even
if I'm not in town. I wasn't planning to go."

Now I felt guilty instead of stupid. "I'm sorry I'm making you go."

"I offered. Here we are."

Dalton had stopped outside the doorway to a clothing store.

I could tell by the plush carpet, the gleaming racks and
the wide distances between the displays that the prices were
going to be sky-high.

"If this doesn't work for you," Dalton said, "try Silver's
across the way." He pointed to a dazzling sign. "Or one floor
directly up is Ace and Night. They also carry period clothing."

"Thank you, Dalton," Max said.

"Nancy Roth is the store manager here at Andante's. She'll
be happy to help if you have questions. Or call me if I can be
of any additional help." Dalton handed Max a business card,
nodding to both of us before he walked away.

"You live in a weird world," I said to Max.

"It's the same world you live in."

"Not really."

He put a hand lightly on my back and ushered me into the
store.

The gesture should have annoyed me, but it didn't. Strong,
independent, modern me had been left somewhere back on
the sidewalk. Fairy-tale princess me was about to buy a dress
for the ball.

A clerk immediately stepped up to offer help, and in no
time I had six dresses hanging inside my large dressing room.

One was opulent, with gold lamé fabric and black beading.
It all but screamed expensive. I tried on a pink one instead and

decided it wasn't my color. Then I tried one in a longer length, a pretty dove-gray tulle with a bow on the hip. I thought it made me look old.

"Are you coming out anytime soon?" Max called through the curtain.

"I don't love anything yet," I answered back.

"What about the blue?"

I took the blue dress from the hanger and slipped it over my head. It was satin on the sides with a long dark blue fringe at the midthigh hem, with nude fabric across the front covered in shimmering gold lace.

I'm not a prude by any means, but it made me look like a risqué pop-music star.

Still, I pulled open the curtain and stepped outside.

Max's jaw dropped. He didn't say a word, but his expression was comical.

"Maybe with the right shoes," I said.

"Definitely not in public."

"I'm not sure where exactly a person could wear this." Maybe in a stage show.

"My hotel suite," Max said under his breath.

I didn't think he meant for me to hear it. I pretended I hadn't, but my skin heated at the image his words brought to mind.

I felt sexy as he stared at me, and my mind wandered back to our lovemaking.

His blue gaze hung on to mine until I shook myself free.

"Next," I said and turned back to the changing room.

The final dress was a simple white sheath with jeweled spaghetti straps and traditional white-tassel fringe layers along its length. The final strands of tassel ended above my knee.

It didn't look like much on the hanger, but it was a perfect fit. It came with a matching jeweled headband, and my auburn hair set off the white.

It didn't strike me as the most expensive of the choices, and that made me happy. Despite my threat to spend Max's money,

I wasn't at all comfortable being extravagant. Though, judging by the store, nothing was going to be a bargain.

"Are you coming out?" he called.

I opened the curtain.

Max stared at me for a minute.

"Do you like it?" he asked.

"I do." I gave a turn so that he could see it from the back.

"You have good taste," he said.

I wasn't sure of his meaning. "I hope that doesn't mean it's expensive."

"It means it looks good."

The salesclerk reappeared. "Oh, that looks wonderful." Her tone was overly enthusiastic, which is what she got paid for. "I have just the right shoes," she said.

"Shoes?"

"You'll need shoes," Max said.

I knew that neither my boots nor my pool sandals were going to do it. But I didn't want Max buying me shoes on top of everything else.

"Don't even think about protesting," Max said. "The outfit comes with accessories. Got a purse?"

"I don't—"

"Purse," Max called out to the clerk, who was making her way across the store.

She gave him a wave to show she'd heard.

"This is ridiculous," I said.

"This is pretty fun," Max said.

"I don't see how it's fun for you." I moved to use a three-way mirror.

"You'd be surprised."

The clerk returned with a pair of silver high-heel T-strap shoes with teardrop cutouts. She brought three white-and-silver purses in various styles.

I took the chair next to Max and tried on the shoes. They fit.

"This one," Max said, holding up a small white pleated satin clutch with jeweled silver handles.

"Your boyfriend has good taste," the clerk quietly said to me.

It was a sure bet that coming from the clerk on commission, "good taste" meant expensive. But Max looked intent on buying the purse.

"He's not my boyfriend," I said back in the same undertone. "This isn't my life."

Her expression turned conspiratorial—one member of the sisterhood to another. "You should try to change that."

Max came to his feet. "It looks like we've got ourselves an outfit. Unless you need earrings?"

"I don't need earrings," I quickly said.

"Don't be too hasty," the clerk said.

She might have been supporting the sisterhood, or she could have been thinking about her own commission. Either way, I was standing firm.

Even a fairy-tale princess had to draw the line somewhere.

"No earrings."

Eight

"Your dress is gorgeous." Brooklyn took in my outfit, reaching out to strum her fingers through the fringe across my stomach.

She looked stunning in a fitted, lacy midnight blue, gold-trimmed dress with a fringe brushing her thighs. She wore jewel earrings and a matching necklace that sparkled with both clear and blue stones.

"Tell me those aren't real," I said.

She touched one of the earrings. "I didn't ask."

"How could you not ask?"

"I didn't want to know."

"Brooklyn." I was shocked by her attitude. "How can you accept—" I couldn't help myself. I reached out to touch the stones on the necklace. I was willing to bet a whole lot that they were real. "*This* from another man."

"Colton isn't another man." She got a determined look on her face. "Layla, I have to tell James."

Panic welled up inside me. "You can't."

"I know I promised I'd think about it. But this isn't fair to either of them. It's not right."

"You can't know yet," I said. "You can't be completely sure."

Her tone and expression were firm and a little angry. "I'm completely sure."

Colton appeared, and I glared at him.

He did a double take of my expression, but then looked to Brooklyn. "Dance?"

"I have to go to the ladies' room," she said.

"I'll come—"

"Don't," she said with her own glare at me.

I rocked back from her sharp tone.

And then she was gone, and I was standing there facing Colton.

"She's terrified of hurting you," Colton said.

I felt my hackles rise. I didn't need this stranger telling me about Brooklyn's emotional state. I knew Brooklyn's emotional state. I always knew her emotional state.

Right now her emotional state was terrifying me.

"We've been best friends our whole lives," I said to Colton.

"She told me. She loves you a lot."

"Why are you doing this?" I asked him.

"I offered to walk away," he said.

I found it impossible to believe that. "Sure you did."

"Did you?" a third voice asked.

I looked up to find Max beside me.

Colton shifted his attention to his brother.

"More than once," he said.

"Maybe you should insist," Max said.

I hadn't really expected Max to back me up when push came to shove. I felt good that he was on my side. I felt less alone in the fight.

"If I thought it was best for her, I would," Colton said.

"It is best for her," I said. I believed that with every fiber of my being.

"Are you going to marry her?" Max asked.

Colton's tone was incredulous. "We've known each other for four days."

"That's my point. You're taking away her happily-ever-after to offer what? A fling?"

"Don't insult Brooklyn. This is not a fling."

Max shifted a little closer to his brother. "What is it?"

"It's two people discovering each other and realizing they might not be able to live apart."

"That's ridiculous," I said.

It wasn't my most eloquent argument, but it had the advantage of being true.

"You're not being fair to her," Max said.

Brooklyn reappeared in time to hear Max's words. "You

know nothing about me," she told him tartly. To Colton she asked, "Can we please dance?"

"Yes, we can." Colton took her arm.

"Don't call James," I called out to Brooklyn.

"I'm going to dance," she replied, walking away.

"What do I do?" I asked myself as much as Max.

The image of James getting a breakup call from Brooklyn was too much to bear. I thought about rushing home so I would be there when it happened. But there was nothing I could say or do to soften the blow.

"They seem really sure," Max said.

"You're giving up already?"

"Not if you don't want me to."

"I don't want you to."

Max nodded. "Okay. I'll talk to Colton."

"Thank you."

"In the meantime." He glanced around the big ballroom. "We might as well dance."

I didn't much feel like dancing. Then again, I didn't much feel like standing here worrying, either.

"You look beautiful," Max said.

The soft glow of his gaze made me warm.

I felt beautiful. I felt guilty for feeling beautiful, but there it was.

I was at an amazing event, in a really fun outfit, with a su-perhot guy. And there was nothing I could do this exact moment to help either James or Brooklyn.

I knew enough to know that particular rationalization was true. But I couldn't decide if I was being logical or self-centered.

I was probably both. But it didn't change any of the facts.

"You look great yourself," I told him.

He looked genuinely pleased by the compliment, even though he had to already know he was the best-looking guy in a very crowded room.

It occurred to me then that he must always be the best-look-ing guy in the room. There wasn't much competition for him anywhere on the planet. Maybe Colton. But when you took in the subtleties, Max easily beat Colton.

"Let's dance," I said, and I linked my arm with his.

"Now you're talking."

The band was playing a slow song, and I nestled into Max's arms. It felt good to give in and accept that I'd done my best. I was tired now, and I had to take a breather.

My world shrank to Max, the warmth of his skin, the movement of his body and the beat of his heart.

He was a better dancer than I'd expected. He was tall, and he was sturdy and muscular. I was surprised he was also graceful.

"You're good at this," I said, gliding along, happy to follow where he led.

"You're very easy to dance with."

"It's more than just that. You've practiced, or maybe had lessons." I tipped my head to look up at him. "Did you take dance lessons?"

"Guilty. My parents insisted."

"Why? I mean, of all things, why would they insist you learn to dance." I indulged myself in tracing the contours of his bicep and shoulder. "You're not exactly built to do it professionally."

"My grandparents thought socializing was important for the business. Colton and I were constantly conscripted to entertain teenage girls."

"Boo-hoo. That must have been such a hardship."

"Most of them were a foot taller than us."

"Late bloomers?"

"A little bit."

"I find that hard to imagine." I couldn't picture Max as a short teenager.

"I was skinny, too," he said with a laugh.

"I thought you played second base."

"Not in junior high. What about you?"

"Skinny, yes. And I had braces. Plus with the red hair and freckles."

He smoothed a hand over my hair. His touch sent a warmth flowing down my spine.

"I like this color," he said.

"I like it now, too, but I sure didn't like it in high school."

"And I like your freckles," he said on a smile. "They're subtle, but interesting…pretty."

"They faded a lot."

"Well, you're perfect now."

I couldn't help a short chuckle at that. "You're the one who's perfect. I expect the girls couldn't get enough of you after you made it through puberty."

"Volume has never been a problem."

"A little full of ourselves, are we?"

"That's not the way I meant it. It's easy enough to get a date. The hard part is finding someone you want to spend more than an evening with."

"You must have had girlfriends."

"A few."

"When was the last one?"

"I'm not going to talk to you about my girlfriends."

"Come on. Dish."

"You tell me about your boyfriends."

"All imperfect. Every one of them had a fatal flaw." I was only half joking. "It turns out I'm very fussy."

"Yeah? How am I stacking up so far?"

I couldn't read his voice, so I looked up to see his expression. I couldn't read that, either.

"You're not my boyfriend."

"Not yet."

Now I knew he had to be joking.

"I'm gone tomorrow, next day at the latest," I reminded him.

I was reminded of Brooklyn, and that brought a wave of worry and sadness.

Max seemed to sense my mood, and he drew me closer.

"You really are going to have to give her space."

I knew it was my only choice. Brooklyn was angry with me right now. Anything I said was going to make it worse.

I pushed her from my mind.

Instead, I marveled at how perfectly I fit in Max's arms. I mean every curve, every nook, everything about me matched perfectly with him. I'd never felt such a huge, encompassing, incredible hug in all of my life.

I didn't want to move. I just wanted to stand here molded against him while I absorbed his essence.

I remembered being naked in his arms. I closed my eyes and inhaled his scent, taking myself back to those few hours in his hotel suite. Arousal pulsed through me, tickling my skin, heating my core. I wanted him all over again.

He kissed my neck, his hot tender lips sprinkling shivers of delight from the curve of my shoulder to the tip of my breasts.

I barely stopped myself from moaning out loud.

I wanted his kiss. I wanted his mouth. I wanted the deep soul-satisfying kisses that had guided me to paradise.

"Kiss me," I whispered.

"Yes, ma'am."

His lips unerringly found mine. They touched lightly at first, then firmer, then harder.

I squeezed my arms around his neck, and he pressed the small of my back, arching me against his hard thighs.

His tongue thrust into my mouth and I answered with enthusiasm. I knew where this was leading, and I couldn't wait to get there. Max was a fantastic lover. I wanted nothing more than to stop time and be swallowed all over again by his spell.

A warning ticked at my brain. I ignored it, but it became insistent.

Something was wrong. I was missing some vital piece of information.

The music swelled, and I remembered we were in a ballroom. We were in public, surrounded by other people.

My eyes flew open with my gasp.

"What?" he asked.

I looked frantically around us to see who might be watching. But Max had danced us into a dark corner. No one could see us. I didn't need to worry.

My fear disappeared. But Max still held me, so my arousal was strong as ever. I throbbed where we touched. My lips tingled from his kisses. I wanted everything we'd had that night—all over again.

Our gazes locked. Heat seemed to leap through the space between us.

It was odd the way it happened, like we had some kind of cosmic connection. Make that a solar connection, or microwaves or something. It was hot and magnetic and irresistible.

"Layla." His voice was strained.

"Can we go back?" I asked. My voice sounded breathless, like an Old Hollywood movie star posing provocatively in a long silhouette dress.

"You mean to the hotel?" he asked.

"Yes." That was exactly what I meant. "Your room. Now."

"Oh, yeah." He was moving for the exit before the words were out of his mouth.

There was a privacy screen in the limo, and I could only hope the intercom was turned off because Max pulled me straight into his lap. I willingly picked up the kisses right where we'd left off.

His jacket was stiff and boxy, so I reached underneath. I felt my way up his chest, over his pecs.

I felt his heartbeat. It was deep, strong and fast.

My heart was racing, too, pumping energy, sending hormonal messages to every corner of my body. I loved the feel of arousal, the heightened senses, the tingling waves of heat that left my body begging to be touched.

I found Max's hand. I set it on my bare thigh.

His touch was hot and sure.

He slipped his palm higher, which was what I wanted. It was exactly what I wanted.

I arched and moaned into our kiss. I teased his tongue with mine, clinging to his broad shoulders, shamelessly enjoying the stokes of his fingertips going higher and higher.

When he pushed aside my panties, I knew I should stop

him. I was willingly playing with fire, and we were in the back of a limo. It wasn't public, but it wasn't the privacy of a hotel room, either.

It wouldn't take more than a word or a movement to call a halt, to put this on hold until we were safely locked in his hotel suite.

In a minute, I told myself. Just one minute more.

But his touch grew more intimate, and I gripped his shoulders. Tension spiraled tighter and tighter within me. My brain started to hum, and a deep pulse grew to life.

I started to gasp, and my hips took on a life of their own pushing against Max's hand. I was past stopping, past slowing down. It was going to happen, and it was going to happen right now.

I bit my lip to keep quiet, but I moaned just the same.

I buried my face in the crook of Max's shoulder and shuddered as waves of pleasure crested over and over.

They finally slowed, then stopped, and I tried to catch my breath. "I'm…" I didn't exactly know what to say.

"Don't you dare feel bad about that," Max said in a low rumble.

I could feel his voice in his chest.

"And don't you dare feel embarrassed." He drew a deep breath himself. "You are amazing."

The limo slowed.

Max extracted his hand and smoothed down my dress as the limo came to a stop.

"Amazing," he repeated and gave me a tender kiss.

"How do I look?" I asked, aware that we were about to step into the bright lights of the portcullis and the lobby.

"Perfect," he said with a smile.

"You know what I mean."

"A little flushed. A little bright-eyed. It makes you even more beautiful."

The compliment made me happy. It was silly. I mean, what else was he going to say in a moment like this? Still, I liked it.

The driver opened the door.

"Ready?" Max asked me.

"I guess." It wasn't like I could get more ready by sitting here.

He stepped out first, then held his hand for me. He kept my hand in his as we walked to the door.

It was beginning to feel very natural, holding Max's hand while we walked.

Somewhere deep in my brain I knew that feeling was dangerous. But I wasn't using the rational parts of my brain, not right now, not tonight. Tonight I was letting emotion take over completely. Everything I had to analyze, rationalize and worry about would still be there tomorrow.

"Good evening, Mr. Kendrick," the doorman said.

"Good evening, Carlos."

"It still amazes me how you do that," I said to Max as we walked on.

"Practice," he said.

We turned toward his suite, silent as we made our way down the corridor.

He flashed the lock with his key card, and we were inside the darkened room.

"You need anything?" he asked me as the door swung shut.

"Do you?" I asked, turning to face him.

"Nothing but you."

"Same."

I was back in his arms. His kisses were more frantic this time. I could understand that. He was running behind me in the lovemaking, and I was feeling pretty frantic myself.

With one hand, he stripped off his jacket and shirt.

Then he pulled my dress up over my head. He jerked off my panties. I thought they might have torn, but I couldn't have cared less.

I pushed off his pants. A condom came from somewhere. And then he was lifting me, bracing me against the wall, kissing me deeper than ever and pushing inside me.

"Yes-s-s," I hissed, happily surprised by the strength of my arousal returning so quickly.

Usually the second time was milder for me, a muted echo of the first round. But not tonight. Tonight I simply couldn't get enough of Max.

His pace was firm and steady. His hands cradled my thighs. With every stroke, he brushed the tips of my sensitized breasts.

My every nerve ending was squealing with pleasure. My core was pulling tighter and tighter. I had to remind myself to breathe.

"Layla," Max called out on a gasp.

"Yes," I responded. "Oh, yes."

When I thought it couldn't get any better, it did. The earth paused and the room spun around me.

His pace increased, and he pressed me hard, dead center, and I cried out as pleasure cascaded higher and longer and deeper than ever before.

We pulsed together, slick and sliding, our chests pressing together as we dragged in deep breaths.

Max wrapped me tight. He kissed my neck, then my shoulder, then my lips.

"You look pretty content," he whispered.

It took me a second to form any words. "Actually, I'm pretty great."

He chuckled low. "I'm so glad to hear that. And I agree. You're pretty great."

I smiled. "Right back at you."

He kissed me again.

"Thirsty?" he asked. "Hungry?"

"I don't know what I am." I'd never felt quite this disembodied before.

I mean, I'd had sex in the past, with boyfriends I liked a lot. And they weren't bad at it. They were fine at it. But this was different. I couldn't put my finger on why or how, but it was a completely different experience with Max.

"Well, I've worked up an appetite," he said.

He slowly lowered me to the floor. "I can order something while we shower. Any preferences?"

"Something excessive," I said. "Something decadent and delicious, completely without redeeming qualities."

"Decadent and delicious coming up," he said. "Meet me in the shower?"

I woke up in Max's bed, in Max's arms.

It felt right. And that was worrisome—though it wasn't worrisome enough for me to move.

Okay, maybe it was worrisome enough for me to move.

I glanced at the bedside clock and discovered it was almost nine. Now that was enough to get me moving. My stolen night was over, and I needed to get back to Brooklyn.

I shifted the covers and moved my legs.

Max's arm snaked around me. "Don't go."

"I have to go."

"Why?"

"I need to find Brooklyn."

He heaved an exaggerated sigh. "Story of your life. Okay. I'm up." He sat up in the bed.

"You don't have to get up with me."

"I promised I'd help."

"That's true. You did." It wasn't something I intended to hold him to this morning.

I don't know why last night had changed that. But it had.

I wrapped myself in a plush robe and headed for the bathroom. There I washed my face and combed out my hair.

I often went without makeup, but I had to admit, I wasn't looking forward to taking the elevator back to my room in the flapper dress. Given how many people had attended the event last night, it was going to be pretty obvious that I'd made a last-minute decision to sleep in someone else's room—not my best look.

I made my way from the bathroom into the living room of the suite.

Max was pouring coffee from a room-service cart.

He turned and held out a cup for me. "Cream and sugar, right?"

"You just get better and better," I said, accepting the cup.

"I got you something else," he said.

"A blueberry bagel?" I asked hopefully.

We'd snacked on fancy pastries and liquor-laced hot choco-late last night. I knew the hotel bakery was out of this world.

"We can get those, too." He pointed to a shopping bag on the sofa.

I checked it to find a pair of black yoga pants and an over-size T-shirt. Beneath them were a pair of flat sandals.

"I figured you'd be overdressed for the lobby this morning."

"That was very thoughtful."

He gave a shrug. "You want me to order you a bagel?"

"I don't have time."

I took my coffee and the new clothes into the bedroom.

Max followed, then leaned against the doorjamb and watched me change.

"What are your plans?" he asked.

I stepped into the butter-soft yoga pants. "I'm going to stop in my room and then find Brooklyn."

"What do you want me to do?"

"Keep Colton occupied while I talk to her?"

I was thinking about tactics. I couldn't be confrontational anymore. It simply wasn't going to work. I supposed I could beg, but I didn't see that as a long-term strategy. I thought I might let her talk it through. Maybe when she heard it out loud she'd see the flaws in her judgment.

"I can do that," Max said.

"While you're at it..." I wasn't sure how far I should press him.

He didn't owe me anything. And I didn't want it to seem like I had expectations after the night we spent together.

"I could help him see the error of his ways?" Max asked.

I paused before pulling the T-shirt over my head. "I don't want you to think I expect that."

"You demanded it yesterday."

"Yesterday was yesterday."

He sauntered close to me. "Last night was one for the record books. But it doesn't change a thing between us."

"Okay," I agreed, liking yet not liking the sentiment.

"I'll still help you any way I can."

"I appreciate that."

"You go find Brooklyn. I'll make sure my brother has his head on straight."

I stuffed my feet into the sandals, took a final drink of the coffee and headed for the door.

Max took hold of my arm as I passed, stopping me, and pulled me in for a tender kiss.

"Bye," he whispered.

"Bye," I whispered back.

We both smiled, and I knew I had to get myself out of there quick.

Getting the elevator to my floor meant a trip back through the lobby.

As I wound my way through the morning crowd, I was enormously grateful for the change of clothes.

Max was a nice guy.

He was a great guy.

I felt light remembering our lovemaking, floating even, focusing on his smile, his laugh, our shower and the decadent pastries.

"Layla?" James's voice stopped me cold. "I tried your room," he continued from behind me. "But neither of you answered."

I turned. I had no choice. James was here. He was here in Vegas, and everything was about to fall apart.

"Where were you?" he asked.

"At breakfast," I said.

The coffee in Max's room didn't exactly qualify as breakfast, but short of lying to James's face it was the best I could do on such short notice.

"Why didn't you answer your phone?" he persisted.

"Battery." That part was true. It was low last night at the dance. But I had to turn the tables on the conversation before his questions got impossible. "Why are you here? I thought you said you'd wait?"

It was obvious he was annoyed. "I've waited long enough. I know you don't want Brooklyn to marry me."

His words rang nonsensically through my brain. "What?"

"You've been jealous—"

"Back up. *What?*"

"Of me and Brooklyn."

"Jealous of you and *Brooklyn*?" The idea was preposterous.

"You know it's true."

"It is absolutely not true." It couldn't be further from what was going on here.

"You've been that way all along," James said, looking more disgusted than I'd ever seen him.

He, too, had lost every ounce of reason. First Brooklyn and now James. Everyone around me was going absolutely batty.

"You're not making any sense at all," I said.

He shifted closer to me. His tone was laced with annoyance and accusation. "You know exactly what I'm talking about."

I stared him down. "I really don't."

I might not be perfect, but I sure wasn't envious. I'd been fighting tooth and nail here for James. I wasn't his rival. I was darn well his best friend!

James gave a flat chuckle. "The Fuzzy Lake trips. The club membership. Last Christmas. I tried to tell myself you'd get over it. I thought once we actually got married, you'd back off and give us some space. But *this*—" he gestured around the hotel lobby "—*this* nonsense is off-the-charts."

I stared at my brother in silence. I had nothing. I truly had nothing here.

"She's marrying *me*," he barked. "Not you. And this best-friend-and-intimate-companion-at-the-expense-of-everyone-else thing has got to stop, *now*."

I stepped backward from his growing anger.

A band was tightening around my chest. I wanted to fight back, but I told myself to calm down. Shouting at James wasn't going to change his mind.

I pretended I was in class, that I was confronting an unreasonable teenager. I dredged up a calm voice. "James, I don't want to come between you and Brooklyn."

He coughed out another laugh of disbelief. "Right."

"Seriously, James."

"Seriously, Layla."

We both stared at each other.

"I've been watching it for years," he said.

"Then you've been delusional for years."

I could never have guessed he felt this way. I thought he liked that me and Brooklyn were close. We were like sisters, better even, we were perfect sisters. There wasn't a reason in the world to be jealous of me.

"I don't think so," he said.

I moved in. "James, you are wrong."

He clamped his jaw. But I could see in his eyes that he was thinking.

"If I'm wrong," he finally said, "then prove it. Give her back."

"I haven't—"

He talked right over top of me. "Quit monopolizing Brooklyn's time. End this stupid trip so she can come home."

"I'm not—"

My breath stalled.

There was Brooklyn.

She was walking across the lobby with Colton. Arm in arm, they were talking and laughing. They looked for all the world like a couple in love.

"Not what?" James's annoyed voice sounded a long way off.

My expression must have given me away because he turned to see where I was looking.

Brooklyn spotted him and stopped dead.

"Who is *that*?" James asked.

My brain flatlined for a moment. I was honestly incapable of having a thought, never mind making a sound.

But then inspiration hit me.

"That's Max," I blurted out.

I started for them, walking as fast as I dared to the frozen Brooklyn with Colton standing beside her.

I could hear James following me.

"Max," I called out as soon as we were in range. "I'm over here. You remember I talked about my brother, James? James, I told you I'd met someone here. This is Max Kendrick."

My voice was way too high, and I was talking way too fast. I could only hope James would chalk my near panicked tone up to our fight.

I pointedly linked my arm with Colton's, pulling him to me, putting a few more inches between him and Brooklyn.

"Were you just at the gym?" I asked Brooklyn, broadly hinting that should be her story.

"Max Kendrick," Colton interjected smoothly, distracting James by offering to shake his hand.

It worked.

"James Gillen, Brooklyn's fiancé." James shook Colton's hand.

It was the first time I'd ever liked Colton.

Brooklyn finally found her voice. "I didn't expect you to come," she said to James.

"I got tired of waiting. And, frankly, I'm about done with the two of you."

The blood drained from Brooklyn's face.

"James thinks I'm monopolizing you," I blurted out. There was an edge of annoyance in my tone. But then I was still pretty annoyed by that accusation.

James faced Brooklyn and took her hands in his. "You two have had your fun. I've tried to be patient. But we've got responsibilities. There are dozens of things to do this week for the wedding."

Brooklyn looked my way.

James gave me a glare that seemed to say Brooklyn was making his point about my relationship with her.

I ignored him. I actually had bigger problems. I had to figure out what Brooklyn was trying to convey.

Her look said she didn't want me to take the heat. My look

told her to keep her big fat mouth shut. This was way too important to worry about me.

I'd talk to James later.

"Where's your ring?" James asked Brooklyn, frowning as he lifted her hands.

She looked at her fingers. "I..." The seconds ticked by, but I couldn't help her with this one.

She finally found her voice. "I took it off to go in the pool. It's a little loose. I've lost a bit of weight. You know, trying to make sure the wedding dress is perfect."

"I thought you were at the gym," James said.

"I'm going to the pool next."

James looked her up and down. It was obvious he felt like something wasn't right. "Where's your suit?"

"In our room," I quickly interjected. "She bought a new one. You're going to love it."

"Can we find somewhere to sit down?" James asked Brooklyn. Then he looked at me. "Alone?"

I knew that was what had to happen. And I knew that from here on in, it was up to James. This was his chance to tip the scales in his favor. I could only hope he didn't treat Brooklyn the way he'd treated me. If he did, the wedding would surely be canceled.

"We should get out of your way," I said to nobody in particular. But I gave a tug on Colton's arm, hoping he'd continue with my ruse.

And then I spotted Max.

He grinned as he sped up and strode toward us.

Then he frowned when he saw me on Colton's arm, confusion coming over his expression.

My heart was beating hard against my chest. If James turned around and saw Max...

Max slowed his steps, taking in all four of us.

His eyes widened ever so slightly, and I caught the moment where he figured out what was going on. He veered off into a women's clothing shop.

I nearly sagged with relief.

"Brooklyn?" James prompted.

"There's a lounge over there," I said and pointed in the opposite direction of the clothing shop. "It should be quiet this time of day."

I gave Brooklyn a quick hug. "Don't say a thing," I whispered in her ear. "We'll talk later."

"Tell—" she began.

"Shhh!" I cautioned.

She swallowed and gave me a slight nod.

"Can we hit the pool?" I asked Colton.

"Love to," he told me. He switched his gaze from Brooklyn to me and mustered up a smile. "Let's go buy you that new suit first." His nod to the clothing store told me he'd seen Max, just like I had.

"Perfect," I said. "See you two later."

I hated to leave Brooklyn on her own with James, but I had to get Colton out of there, and I had to trade him in for Max before things got any worse.

We found Max quickly.

"What happened?" he asked.

"James is here," I said.

"I got that," Max said. "Does he know anything?"

"No so far." So far, I was the bad guy. I was still miffed about that. More than miffed, really—talk about coming right out of the blue.

"What are you going to do?" Max asked Colton.

Colton glanced back over his shoulder, but Brooklyn and James had disappeared around the corner.

"This is more about what Brooklyn's going to do," Colton said.

"I told him you were Colton," I said to Max. Then I thought about the phraseology for a second. "Or that Colton was you. You know what I mean. I didn't know how else to explain him."

"Is Brooklyn going to tell him the truth?" Max asked.

"No," I said.

"Maybe," Colton said.

"No," I repeated. "Not yet. I told her to keep quiet for now."

"Of course you did," Colton said.

"She's not ready," I told him, hoping it was true.

"It has to be on her own time," Max said.

Colton looked like he wanted to argue. But then the fight seemed to go out of him. "In that case, Layla, we should get her stuff into your room."

I had to give him credit for a very good idea.

"There's only one bed in Layla's room," Max pointed out.

"We'll tell James there was a sale." I knew he wouldn't be overly shocked that Brooklyn and I would share a king-size bed. We'd done it before.

"You better slip her a key," Max said to me.

"I can do that."

"And then…" Max said.

"And then," Colton said with a sigh of resignation, "we wait. It's up to her."

"You bet it's up to her," I said.

"Layla." Colton sounded like he was summoning patience. "I want what's best for Brooklyn."

"No, *I* want what's best for Brooklyn," I countered.

Colton shook his head. "Difference is, I want Brooklyn to be happy. You want James to be happy."

"That's not fair."

Colton's feelings for Brooklyn couldn't hold a candle to mine.

For a second, my reaction gave me pause. I was forced to wonder about James's tirade. Was there a grain of truth in his accusations? Was it possible I'd hampered their relationship all this time?

Was it my fault she wasn't sure of her feelings?

"I love her," Colton said.

"You barely know her," I said.

"This isn't getting us anywhere," Max interjected.

Max was right, but I couldn't back off, especially if I was partly to blame.

"What happens in a year?" I asked Colton. "Or a month? Or a week? What happens when you lose interest in her?"

"That's not going to happen."

"It's impossible for you to know what's going to happen. Brooklyn isn't the woman you've met here. She's on vacation. She's going through a thing. The real Brooklyn is completely different. She has foibles. She has flaws."

"She squeezes the toothpaste in the middle?" Colton asked with sarcasm.

"She's addicted to pistachio nuts. She binge-watches fashion TV. She refuses to fill her car up with gas."

Both Colton and Max blinked at me as if I'd forgotten my own name.

"And a whole bunch of other things," I said. "Things that James knows about and accepts and loves."

"I'm not giving Brooklyn up," Colton said. "But if she wants to give me up, I'll step aside."

I didn't believe him.

"I'll step aside without a fight. In fact, I'll back off right now. I'll make myself scarce for the day or a couple days, whatever it takes." He started to nod. "She should spend some time with James. That's the only way she'll know for sure."

I agreed with him. What's more, the offer seemed too good to be true.

"Her engagement ring is in the safe in my room," Colton said. "Let's go get it, and move her things."

"You'd really do that?" I asked him.

I was primed to dislike him. I preferred not to like him. But even I had to admit this was an honorable thing to do.

"I'm doing it," he said.

Max gave me an I-told-you-so look.

I couldn't say I exactly blamed him. Colton was busy validating the arguments Max had been making all along—that Colton wasn't despicable.

He was still wrong for Brooklyn. But maybe, hopefully, he'd meet a nice woman in the future.

I could wish him well somewhere that was not with me and my friends and family. I could do that.

Nine

It was hours before I got Brooklyn alone.

We were at the Triple Palm Café in the hotel atrium and the sun was going down.

"How are you feeling?" I asked her, leaning in as James left the restaurant to talk to the front desk about a room.

He'd been terse with me since I'd joined them fifteen minutes ago. I knew he wanted me to leave them alone, but I couldn't stay completely away. There was way too much at risk.

Brooklyn's happy expression faded as James walked away. She looked completely miserable. "I'm more confused than ever."

I didn't know what to say to that. I didn't exactly know what she meant. I hoped it was a good thing. I hoped seeing James had reminded her of what they had together.

"Confused how?" I asked.

"James is...you know, he's James. He's sweet and patient, and he's always so good to me."

Sweet was debatable in my books after this morning. But I didn't disagree. I didn't want to interrupt her flow.

"I know what he wants, and I know where we're going, and I can still see our future together so clearly."

I nodded.

"But, Colton." She gave a sigh. "He's..."

I waited.

She seemed to be searching for the right word.

"New?" I prompted.

"Exciting, fun, exhilarating."

"He's got a lot of money to throw around," I said.

I still thought it was an uneven playing field tilted toward Colton.

Brooklyn looked like she was disappointed in me. Well, join the club. "You know it's not just that," she said.

"Can I ask…" I wasn't sure I was ready to take the plunge. But my gut told me it was all-or-nothing time.

Brooklyn waved a hand that said caution should go well and truly to the wind. "Ask away."

"Do you know how Colton feels about you? I mean do you really, honestly know? People aren't always what they seem."

I told myself I wasn't betraying Colton by questioning his motives and his morals. It was a legitimate question, a real concern. He trotted around the country, maybe around the globe for all I knew, romancing a huge variety of different women.

From what I'd seen of him online, he was active in city after city, at event after event. I'd counted no less than a dozen different women on his arm in the past couple of years. He didn't seem like the kind of guy who was in it for the long haul.

"I'm not looking for a guarantee from Colton," Brooklyn said.

"If it wasn't for Colton, would you be giving up on James?"

Brooklyn had to think about that one.

"Maybe," she said. "I don't know. Maybe not."

"So—at least in some ways—you're pinning your future on Colton."

"I'm not."

"Come on, Brooklyn. This is me."

"Okay, maybe I am, in some ways. I want to be with him. I really want to be with him."

"I'd so hate to see you make a mistake. After this first blush of lust—"

She looked genuinely insulted. "It's not lust."

"Okay. I'm sorry. Infatuation then. But after the first blush wears off, you could be left with nothing. You might spend the rest of your life regretting your choice. Can you tell me right here, right now, with one hundred percent certainty that you're positive you won't regret giving James up, giving up your life, your wonderful, incredible life together? Can you?"

Brooklyn sat back in her chair. "Nothing is one hundred percent."

"Lots of things are one hundred percent."

We both fell silent.

"What about tonight?" I asked.

"What about it?"

"James is getting a room."

Brooklyn didn't seem to comprehend.

"For the two of you," I said. "To sleep in. Together."

"We don't need to have sex."

I tried not to spend much time—any time at all, really—thinking about my brother's sex life. But this was a pretty obvious problem.

"You don't think he might expect it?" I asked.

Again, Brooklyn wasn't keeping up with the implications. She looked at me blankly.

"You can't—" I realized my voice was getting loud and I lowered it. "You can't jump from sleeping with Colton to sleeping with James like—" I snapped my fingers "—that. I mean, I don't mean to get all judgey or anything."

Brooklyn reared back. "I'm not sleeping with Colton."

I stilled. I mentally backtracked over the past few days. "What?"

"You thought I was sleeping with Colton?"

I didn't know what to say. I'd been sleeping with Max, and I'd just assumed that Brooklyn and Colton were also burning up the sheets.

"Thanks a ton," Brooklyn said.

"I'm sorry. I mean, you've clearly been…"

I wasn't exactly sure how to phrase it. They thought they were falling for each other, romantically obviously. And wouldn't that normally include sex?

Apparently not. My opinion of Colton went up another notch.

"I'm not cheating on James," Brooklyn said.

"I'm sorry," I repeated. There wasn't much more I could do but apologize.

"Would you cheat on your fiancé?" she asked.

"I've never had a fiancé."

"Well, you wouldn't. I know you wouldn't. And I wouldn't, either."

"I don't think I would."

For some reason I pictured Max. I knew there was no way in the world I'd ever cheat on Max, engaged or not.

Not that we'd ever be engaged. Not that we were even truly dating. But while I was sleeping with him, there's no way I'd have any interest whatsoever in another man.

I gave myself a moment to think that through.

"So you're deciding this without even sleeping with Colton?"

"There's no other way," Brooklyn said.

I almost asked her if she wanted to sleep with Colton, but then I realized that wouldn't do anything for James's side in this.

Brooklyn had to want to sleep with Colton. She had to be dying to sleep with Colton. That is, if she felt at all about Colton like I did about Max.

"You know James so much better," I said, instead.

"You're right."

I caught sight of James coming back down the path toward the café.

He had a glare for me that clearly said "Back off."

"Here he comes," I told Brooklyn.

She swallowed. "Can we order a drink?"

"Do you think it will help?"

"I don't think it will hurt."

"I better not stay," I said.

James pulled his chair back to sit down, his attention on Brooklyn to the exclusion of me. "These prices are outrageous."

"We're lucky we got a sale," I said, sticking with my story.

"There weren't any discounted rooms available today," he said, looking my way, then he looked irritated.

"Did you book something?" I asked, ignoring his attitude.

"Just for one night." He reached out and took Brooklyn's hand. "We need to go home tomorrow. Your mom's antsy about the dress and the cake, and there are still details to work out about the rehearsal dinner. I told them lobster and filet, but you need to look at the menu."

"Do they have the coconut-cream pie?" Brooklyn asked.

"I'm sure they'll make it available if that's what you want. I had to confirm the violet arrangement for the centerpieces."

Brooklyn smiled. "That was my favorite."

He gave her a kiss on the hand. "I know it was your favorite. I want everything to be your favorite. And for that, you need to come home."

James slid his gaze to me. "Layla can always stay a couple of days on her own if it's that important to her."

"It's not Layla's fault," Brooklyn said.

"You don't need to defend her."

Brooklyn looked confused. "I'm only telling—"

"There's no reason for me to stay," I interrupted.

Brooklyn gazed into James's eyes.

After a moment, she looked down at their clasped hands. His were strong and wide. Hers sparkled with the diamond ring.

She tipped up her chin.

She squared her shoulders.

A bird swooped and chirped from the tree above us, joined by three of its friends.

I found myself holding my breath.

"Okay," Brooklyn said in a hollow voice. "We can catch a flight in the morning."

James had his phone out in an instant to book with the airline.

I was filled with relief.

But a split second later, I thought of Max, and my relief turned to disappointment. I told myself to buck up. I'd gotten exactly what I'd wanted, what I'd been fighting for, for days now.

My fling with Max might have been pretty great. It might

have been fantastic. But it was always going to be temporary. It was always going to end exactly this way—with me leaving and him moving on to the next hotel in the next city with the next woman.

Self-pity wasn't going to change a thing.

"Congratulations on your success," Max said. His tone was considerably less than sincere.

"I'm not going to apologize for being right," I told him.

After leaving Brooklyn and James, I'd come straight to Max's suite, finding Colton there, as well.

I hadn't wanted to say anything to Colton about Brooklyn's decision. But my expression must have tipped him off.

He guessed, and I couldn't lie.

"You're not right," Colton said to me. "And neither is Brooklyn." His voice was laced with a steely determination that made me nervous.

I knew he'd promised to let her decide. But right now he didn't look like a guy who was about to give up the fight.

"You said it was Brooklyn's call," I reminded him, putting an edge into my own tone.

"Is she at least going to talk to me?" he asked.

"I don't know." I didn't.

When I'd walked into Max's suite, I was operating on the assumption that Brooklyn would talk to Colton directly. But thinking it through now, I wasn't sure how that could happen with James by her side. And my brother didn't show any signs of leaving his fiancée's side before he got her on that plane tomorrow morning.

I was torn. Part of me couldn't help but sympathize with Colton. In his shoes, I'd sure want a final conversation with Brooklyn. On the other hand, judging by the expression on his face, if he got the chance he might try to change her mind.

I couldn't imagine how hard that would be on Brooklyn. I didn't even want to speculate about whether it might work. It was better for everyone if Colton didn't get the chance.

"James got them a room," I said.

Colton's jaw went hard. He swore.

Max shook his head, looking disappointed.

Colton marched for the door.

I didn't like where this was going. "You won't—"

He shot me a hard look, and I closed my mouth.

"Break my word?" he asked. "No, Layla. I'm not going to break my word. This is Brooklyn's decision. I can't force her to give me a real shot."

"She did," I felt forced to point out.

Colton stopped with his hand on the doorknob. "Not really. She went back to him before we had a chance."

Max touched my arm, and I knew he wanted me to stop talking. It was obvious he didn't want to upset Colton any more than necessary.

"She has a deadline," I said.

Colton sneered at my logic. "Weddings can be postponed."

"There are five hundred guests."

"It's the rest of her life."

The way he said it, something about his expression got me worrying.

I wasn't worried he'd break his word. Oh, no, I was worried that he was right. We were standing here talking about the rest of Brooklyn's life.

Letting my mind follow his logic for a minute, I tried to imagine canceling the wedding. I pictured my parents' reactions. My dad would freak out about the cost. My mom would focus on the social embarrassment.

Then I pictured Brooklyn's parents. They'd be baffled. I'd had several days to mull the idea, and I was baffled. They thought James was the perfect man for Brooklyn. He was successful, professional, kind and smart, with two feet firmly planted on the ground.

They'd never forgive her for letting him get away.

Brooklyn's parents knew her well, just like I knew her well. If all of us, including Brooklyn, thought James was the right choice, he must be the right choice. Seeing James had obviously put everything in perspective and solidified her decision.

Colton wasn't even a fling. She hadn't even slept with him. How could they possibly understand their feelings for one another when their entire relationship had been platonic?

"She seems sure," I said, telling myself it was true.

Colton gave a cold, chopped laugh. "Well, as long as she's sure."

And then he was gone. The door banged hollowly behind him.

Max and I stared.

I thought I should apologize. Logically, I knew none of this was my fault. I'd done what any reasonable best friend would do. I'd tried to keep Brooklyn from getting swept up in short-term emotions, to make sure she considered all the ramifications of her decision.

"What about you?" Max said.

I didn't understand the question. Was he thinking the same thing I was thinking? Was he asking for an apology?

He pivoted to face me and took both of my hands in his. His touch was tender, and his gaze softened to azure. "What about us?"

Then I understood. "I can't stay." Even though, this exact moment, I was wishing with all my heart that I could.

He searched my expression for a minute. "Do you think this is something?"

I did. So help me, I did.

I'd never felt anything like this before. Max was exciting and funny, smart and thoughtful. Sex with him had been amazing with a capital A.

So I stood there wishing. I wished with all my heart. But I knew my weakness.

From minute one, I looked at men as potential life mates. I did it for myself and for all of my friends. In the presence of an eligible man, I went from logical mathematician to hopeless romantic.

Maybe it was my age. Anthropologically speaking, I was at a prime age to seek out a mate and have children. I took some comfort in having a logical basis for my illogical emotional reaction.

This was nothing more than anthropology.

"It's something," I said as disappointment slithered through my aching chest. "It was a wonderful weekend. Honestly, it was the best fling of my life."

He stared at me while my words hung there between us. I could only imagine he was wondering how many flings I'd had.

None was the answer. But I wasn't about to admit it. Let him think I flung, or flinged—or whatever the heck you called it—all the time. It was easier that way.

As the silent seconds ticked by, my words felt more and more like a lie.

I doubled down. "Let's not try to make it what it wasn't."

"What wasn't it?" There was a challenge in his deep, soft tone.

I was dying here. "Something serious. Something real. Something lasting."

"You're sure about that?"

I was sure. I had to be sure. I had no choice but to be sure.

I could estimate the mathematical odds of Max's and my vastly different lives meshing in any long-lasting way. Sadly for me, I could estimate them with extraordinary precision. Technically speaking, those were some very, very long odds.

Lightning hadn't struck here, even though I could swear I heard a sizzle somewhere in the middle of the night.

He reached out and tenderly stroked my hair. "Ah, Layla." He sounded sad.

I didn't exactly know what he meant. But my entire body sighed, and I only just stopped myself from leaning into his palm.

"I should go," I said.

"How long?" he asked.

My confusion must have been apparent.

"How long do we have before you go?"

"Really?" I had to admit, I was pretty startled by his re-

quest. Not unwilling, I'm embarrassed to say, but startled. "You want to hop in bed, sort of, for the road?"

Looking distinctly annoyed, he let his hand fall to his side. "Did I say that?"

"It's what you meant." I was positive on that.

He might try to walk it back, but that was exactly what he'd meant.

"I was going to suggest a chocolate soufflé." He paused. "For the road."

I tried to interpret his expression. It looked sincere. And if that was a lie, he'd thought it up awfully fast. Still...

"There's something wrong with you," he said, a trace of humor in his tone. "So skeptical."

"Are you denying you want to have sex with me?"

"I'll always want to have sex with you. But if we're talking a last memory here, I'd rather it be chocolate soufflé." He smiled. "Do you have any idea how cute you look eating chocolate soufflé?"

"I do not." I looked exactly the same eating chocolate soufflé as I did eating anything else.

"It's like you're having an orgasm right there in front of me."

"Shut up." I wasn't going to be embarrassed.

He was making this all up.

"Hot chocolate is a close second," he said. "But there's nothing like chocolate soufflé to get you going."

"You're impossible."

"You're beautiful." He gently touched beneath my chin.

"Now you're trying to distract me."

"I'm trying to change your mind. Don't go."

"Max."

"I'm serious. You don't have to leave."

"Don't do this."

It was bad enough that my brain took off on flights of fantasy about happily-ever-after. The last thing I needed was Max feeding into it.

"You know it's over," I said for both of us. "Don't pretend, not even for a little while."

I needed to stay strong. This talk of a possible future was making me even sadder than I already was.

"Why?" he asked. "Give me one good reason why we don't have a shot?"

"There's a wedding in eleven days. Brooklyn needs me. James needs me. My family is counting on me."

"This isn't about the wedding. The wedding is short-term. After—"

"No." I put my fingertips across his lips to stop him from talking.

I realized my mistake when pulses of energy shot desire into my palm and up my arm, heading for my heart.

"We're not going to recapture this," I said, much as I was thinking I would love to do that very thing. "You've got hotels to run and I've got students to teach. Brooklyn is a permanent part of my life, and Colton is a permanent part of yours."

"We can work around that."

"Listen to yourself." I was starting to feel desperate.

I took a step back.

He stared at me for a long minute.

I wanted to leave, but I couldn't seem to make my feet move.

"If you're not feeling it," he finally said.

"I'm not feeling it," I lied. I was feeling it all too strongly.

"We're not going to have that soufflé, are we?"

I shook my head. "Goodbye, Max."

His mouth tightened down to a thin line. "If that's the way you want it."

I stood my ground. "It's the way I want it."

After a moment, his eyes hardened, his gaze remote, and he took a step back—him and his perfect shaggy-neat hair and his perfect body and his perfect lovemaking.

He was writing me off, and it was physically painful.

I wanted to tell him I'd had a fantastic time, that he was an amazing man, that the reckless emotional side of me I barely knew had wanted to hang on to him and never let go.

But I'd never been one to give in to that side. And I wasn't about to start now. Right now, I had to get Brooklyn to Seattle and to the church. She'd made a brave and good decision, and I had to support her.

The sooner I turned Max into a memory, the better off I'd be.

Nat stood next to me in front of the mirrored wall in the bridal shop. It was our final bridesmaid dress fitting before the wedding on Saturday.

The dresses were light and breezy, azure-blue chiffon with knee-length hemlines. Their snug, fitted bodices with strapless sweetheart necklines were feminine and beautiful.

Nat was wearing a pretty pair of silver sandals with a satin band and two-inch heel.

I was feeling bold. I'd gone with a strappy, stylized pair with higher heels and a lot of jeweled flash.

I figured I could make it down the aisle and through the photo session without completely killing my feet. And, after that, there was a sit-down dinner that would give them a rest.

For the dancing, I'd tuck a pair of blue ballet flats into my purse. I'm not masochistic.

"You look great," I said to Nat.

It was true, but she seemed uncertain as she gazed into the mirror. Feature for feature, she was as pretty as any of us. But she never saw it, and was always doing everything she could to downplay her looks.

"You look tall," she said and put on a grin.

I was glad to see her mood shift. I knew she'd been fighting depression since Henry had dumped her. Not that Henry was a prize. Still, it was hard on a person's ego to be the one left behind.

That hadn't been the case with me and Max.

I'd been the one to make the decision that it was over.

And it was over, and it was the right decision, and I had to stop thinking about him when there were so many other things that needed my attention right now.

I put a foot forward in the reflection and turned my ankle back and forth to make the jewels sparkle. "I couldn't resist them," I said to Nat.

"Your funeral," she answered back.

"I'm not going to dance in them or anything."

"Even without any dancing, you're going to have to last at least two hours on your feet." Nat was practical, as always.

I was practical, too. But I wasn't obsessive about it. I knew there were times when impracticality was the most practical thing to do.

"I'll be fine," I said. It would be well worth sore feet and maybe a blister or two to be immortalized in these babies in the wedding photos.

Sophie came from behind us and stood on the other side of Nat.

"We're going to knock 'em dead," Sophie said.

"That's Brooklyn's job," I pointed out, glancing to the closed curtain of the cubical where Brooklyn was slipping into her wedding dress.

She'd seemed happy since we got back from Vegas. There were times when I thought she was a little too happy. I hadn't spent as much time as I would have liked with her these past days. James was sticking close to her, and he was still giving me the cold shoulder.

I hadn't brought up his outburst in Vegas. I knew we'd have to talk it through at some point. But I'd decided it wasn't urgent.

To be fair to him, I'd mulled over the amount of time I spent with Brooklyn, trying to see it from his perspective. I had to admit we did spend a lot of time together. But it had remained steady over the years, and James had never said it was a problem.

He'd gone off about the Fuzzy Lake trips. Sure, Brooklyn and I always shared a room at Fuzzy Lake. But my parents had always been with us on the trip. We'd started going to Fuzzy

Lake when we were kids. It wasn't like Brooklyn was about to sleep with James with our parents along with us.

I mean, maybe once they got into their twenties, or maybe last year when they got engaged. But nobody had suggested it. My mom had booked the rooms the same way she always did—me sharing with Brooklyn, and James sharing with our cousin Neil.

And we'd had a blast. There was no denying everyone had a blast at Fuzzy Lake.

Brooklyn and I had a standing date at a Seattle tennis club. There was that. Friday afternoons, after school was out and she left the store early, we'd play a match, then stop by the lounge for a drink. The drinks often turned into appetizers that substituted for dinner.

It wasn't like James would leave the office early. And Friday was the one day a week that Brooklyn and I truly got to touch base.

I couldn't figure out what James meant about last Christmas. Nothing out of the ordinary had happened last Christmas.

The more I thought about it, the more self-righteous I started feeling. Honestly, if James had a problem with me and Brooklyn, he should have spoken up before now. We could have talked it out. I could have given him my perspective instead of having it turn into some big thing.

Keeping it bottled up inside hadn't helped anyone.

I hadn't told Brooklyn about James's outburst, either. The wedding lead-up was running smoothly, and I didn't want to introduce a problem. Not that it was a real problem. It was just, well, weird.

I hadn't brought up Colton, either, even though I was dying to know how Brooklyn felt. If ever there was something we should be talking through, this was it. But she hadn't mentioned him at all. It was like we'd both agreed to pretend Vegas hadn't happened. It was a strategy... I supposed.

Deep down in my logical soul I knew that if mentioning Colton's name was going to mess up the wedding, the wed-

ding should probably be messed up. But I couldn't bring myself to test it.

"Brooklyn will knock them double-dead," Sophie said,
bringing me back to the present.

We all smiled at our reflections, knowing it was true. It
didn't matter how much we dressed up, or what kind of shoes
we wore, Brooklyn would be the most dazzling woman in the
church, hands down.

Brooklyn's dressing-room curtain opened, and we all
turned to look.

Her bodice was pure white lace with a V-neck and cap
sleeves. It was fitted snugly to her impossibly slim waist. The
silk underskirt was full and flared out, covered with a wispy
sheer net that was dotted with hand-stitched lace appliqués.

Her hair was gathered at the back with a jeweled comb, a
few blond wisps framing her face and fanning over the dangling white sapphire earrings that matched her elegant choker.
She was upscale enough for a fashion runway.

"You're a knockout," Sophie said, stepping to one side.
"Come here. Stand with us."

Nat and I moved, too, making more room for Brooklyn.

"Do you have the shoes?" I asked.

Brooklyn looked tall and elegant. And the dress looked to
be exactly the right length, barely brushing the floor in a circle of lace and fanning out just a few extra inches at the back
in a nod to a bridal train.

She stuck out one of her feet to show off her wedding shoe.

"Perfect," I said.

"Ouch," Nat said.

"Wimp," I said to Nat.

"You'll all be envious of me during the ceremony," Nat said.

"I don't think she'll be worried about her feet while she's
saying her vows," Sophie put in.

I had to agree with Sophie on that.

If I was the one getting married, the last thing I'd be thinking about was my feet.

Max popped into my mind, fully decked out in a black tux,

with a white shirt and a bow tie. He looked sexy and mascu-
line. I could see his great hair, his smile and the crinkle of
his blue eyes.

As if he was right there in front of me, he took my hand,
and I could feel the wedding ring slide onto my finger, cool
and smooth, a circle of gold. I lifted my face for his kiss.

Man, did I miss his kiss.

I gave myself a firm mental shake.

Marrying Max. Talk about letting my imagination run away
with me again.

Max was a memory now.

"My feet," Brooklyn said, and she met my gaze in the mirror, "will be the last thing I'm thinking about."

For a second, there was something in her eyes, a brittle-
edged determination that caught me off guard. But then it was
gone, and I wondered if I'd imagined it.

Then I wondered if I should gather up some courage and
talk to her, have a heart-to-heart, bring everything out in the
open in all its ugly glory before she said her final "I do." A
best friend would do that.

"Still, they'll look really great," Brooklyn continued with
a grin, giving Nat a one-armed hug. "And that's what really
matters, isn't it? My feet?"

Brooklyn seemed relaxed again. She seemed genuinely
happy.

Again, I felt like I was looking for problems that weren't
there. I did that sometimes. I really did.

"I'll never understand that attitude," Nat said to all of us.
"Sacrificing comfort for beauty."

"Beauty's fun," Sophie said.

I glanced at myself in the mirror. I was vain enough to like
the way I looked, vain enough to hope any eligible men at the
wedding would find me attractive.

I mean, that was what I always wanted.

But my heart really wasn't into finding a long-lost second
cousin of Brooklyn's that was my age. I wasn't ready to meet

another man. What I really wanted was for Max to see me in this dress, and for Max to find me attractive.

I'd tried to deny it. But denial had never been my best weapon. Reality was my best weapon. I had to confront and embrace reality and find a way to make it work for me.

The seamstress joined us, checking the fit of our dresses. She was unhappy with Nat's waistline and Sophie's neck. So the two of them followed her across the shop for alterations.

"Do you miss him?" Brooklyn asked me, meeting my gaze in the mirror again.

"Who?"

"Max."

I was surprised that she'd asked. I was a little worried that she'd asked. Vegas truly was better left in the dust.

"No." I was determined. Fake it 'til you make it and all that.

"Liar," Brooklyn said.

I gave my bare shoulders a shrug. "There's nothing to miss. It was a thing, and then it wasn't. It ran its course."

"Is that how you remember it?"

"It's like missing a chocolate milkshake after you drank it. It was good, but it was never going to last forever." I tried for a lighter tone. "For one thing, they melt."

"Guys like Max don't melt."

"They don't last, either."

Brooklyn nodded, and then she got a faraway look in her eyes.

I couldn't stay silent anymore. "What about Colton?"

She didn't respond.

"Brooklyn?"

"Hmm?"

"Colton?"

She blinked her way back. "I made the decision to leave Colton. It was final."

I accepted that. "I made a final decision to leave Max."

"My final and your final are not the same thing."

"They're both final."

She seemed to think about that. "You know, you were right all along."

"That's what I like to hear." I kept the jokes running, afraid of letting the conversation get completely serious.

"Colton was a fantasy," Brooklyn said. "I got cold feet. But right is right, and marrying James is right."

I took heart. "That's good."

She linked her arm with mine. "But you're still allowed to miss Max. You know, in the middle of the night when you're thinking about his cut bod and the way he made you moan."

"He didn't…" I didn't know why I would deny it to Brooklyn.

I needed to be honest with her at least. It was the way to get our relationship back on an even keel. And I desperately wanted our relationship back on an even keel.

"Fine," I said. "He was off-the-charts—as a lover, I mean."

"I knew what you meant. Nobody can take away your memories."

"That's right."

The memories were mine to keep.

"And it gives you a benchmark," Brooklyn said. "Like James gives me a benchmark."

"He does?" I was beyond heartened to hear that.

"You know he does, for honesty, integrity, kindness and hard work."

I wanted to ask about sex. Then I wanted to ask if she was madly in love with James. I opened my mouth, but chickened out.

She loved him. She definitely loved him. She always had and she always would, and that was the foundation of a good marriage, a great marriage. She and James had all the ingredients of a great marriage.

"He's funny, too," I said, instead.

"A dry wit," she agreed.

"Did you tell him…?" I struggled with the nerve to finish the question. "Anything at all?"

"I told him I'd gotten nervous."

Since Brooklyn hadn't slept with Colton, I supposed that was probably enough.

"What did he say?" I asked.

"That he was grateful I was back."

"I know he is."

"Thank you for doing it."

"For lying to James?" I realized this might be the right time to bring up his outburst.

Then again, this was probably exactly the wrong time to bring up his outburst.

"For coming after me," she said.

I liked that we were being honest again. I wanted the heart-to-heart to keep going.

"If I hadn't...would you have come back?"

"I don't know." She got the faraway look again. "I was in pretty deep. It was fun and frivolous and overwhelming. I wanted to stay in the whirlwind forever."

"That's how I felt, too. Max was a whirlwind of exhilaration. But twisters are exhausting, and they can kill you in the end."

"They are. They do," Brooklyn said. Her gaze held mine for a moment. Then she turned and took my hands. "Thank you, Layla. You kept me from making a very big mistake."

I felt a welling behind my eyes. "I'm glad. You're welcome. You can always count on me."

"I know."

Ten

Organ music rose through the church rafters and the perfume of white moonstone roses wafted through the foyer where the bridal party was gathered. The stretch limousine that had dropped us off now waited at the bottom of the sweeping concrete stairway to take the bride and groom to Briarfield Park for photos after the ceremony.

James and Brooklyn had picked the park's west gardens as a backdrop. The mottled browns and deep green would highlight Brooklyn's white dress and our pale azure.

The July weather had cooperated. If anything, it was too hot for the groomsmen in their formal suits. But the garden was shaded, which the photographer told us was perfect for the pictures.

So we had that going for us.

Brooklyn's dad, Patrick, took a stealthy peep through the doorway.

"It looks like they're ready for us," he said.

Nat, who was to be first down the aisle, moved to the edge of the doorway, still out of sight from the congregation but ready to walk as soon as she got the musical cue.

Brooklyn had chosen "A Thousand Years." I thought it was perfect. Everything about the ceremony was going to be perfect—from the music to the flowers to the vows.

We were all ready.

I gave my skirt a final swish to make sure it wasn't developing static. Then I straightened my bouquet in front of me. My sandals felt good so far, and I knew my hair was in place.

I suddenly felt Brooklyn's hand on my arm.

She squeezed hard, and I turned sharply to see what was wrong.

Her eyes were huge, and her cheeks were flushed against her pale skin.

"What?" I asked, worried the heat might be getting to her.

"Layla." There was apprehension in her voice.

"What's wrong? Are you dizzy? Do you feel faint?"

It was really hot here in the church, over eighty-five degrees outside. And I knew Brooklyn hadn't eaten anything today. I tried to remember the last time she'd even had a drink of water. As her maid of honor, I should have paid more attention.

"I can't," she said in a breathless voice.

"You can't what?"

She shook her head.

My heart started sinking fast.

She couldn't be talking about the wedding. Not now. Not *right now*.

"I'm scared," she said.

"Of what?"

Patrick arrived beside us. "Here we go. You look stunning, Brooklyn." He placed her hand on his crooked elbow.

Brooklyn looked at me for help, but I didn't know what to do. Should I say something? Should I take her aside?

"You should go, Layla," her father prompted, directing with a meaningful glance to where Nat and Sophie had moved into the open doorway.

The organist started playing "A Thousand Years."

"Brooklyn?" I asked.

This was real. This was forever. As much as I longed for her to marry James, I couldn't ignore the stark expression on her face.

Then, behind us, one of the outer church doors swung open. The double doors were wide and heavy, made of thick polished oak with black iron hinges that groaned with the effort.

A hot breeze blew in as I turned.

My heart thudded hard when I saw Max silhouetted by the sun. But it stopped abruptly when I saw it wasn't Max.

It was Colton. Colton was standing in the church doorway.

He was dressed in blue jeans and a soft blue button-down shirt. His hair was messy, and a sheen of sweat covered his forehead.

I don't know why those details seemed important. But in my brain, time had slowed—every second was an eternity.

He spotted Brooklyn and froze.

She froze, too. She grabbed my arm again. This time her grip was even tighter than before.

Patrick frowned at Colton. "Excuse me. We're about to start a wedding ceremony."

Colton broke from his pose and marched toward us.

"Brooklyn," he said.

"No," I said. "No, no." This couldn't be happening. Everything was perfect. Everything!

Brooklyn sucked in a breath. It was both a gasp and a whimper.

"What's the meaning of this?" Patrick demanded of Colton.

Colton focused on Brooklyn. "Can we talk?"

I reflexively wrapped an arm around Brooklyn.

"You can't do this," I said to Colton.

But then I saw Max.

This time it really was Max in the doorway. My heart staggered to a temporary stop.

"Please," Colton said, although his voice seemed to be far away from me now.

My arm slowly dropped to my side.

I drank in the sight of Max—the blue of his eyes, the rakish stubble of his chin, the muss of his hair and the breadth of his shoulders straining against an olive-green T-shirt. He was my every dream come to life.

"What *is this*?" Patrick bellowed. "*Who* is this?"

"Brooklyn, please." Colton was in front of her now, barely inches away.

"Don't you dare touch my daughter," Patrick said.

Max moved my way.

"You can't be here," I told him.

"I couldn't stop him," Max said, slowing in front of me. His gaze held mine. "Truth is, I wouldn't stop him. I didn't want to stop him."

Nat and Sophie were staring, openmouthed, their bouquets now dangling by their sides.

It occurred to me that the congregation could see them. The minister could see them. James could see them.

Everyone in the church would know something was wrong back here.

"This is Colton," Brooklyn said to her father.

"Who is Colton? What's he doing here? Was he invited?"

My eyes begged Max to do something. I wasn't honestly sure what I wanted him to do.

Brooklyn had been freaking out a few moments ago. She was calm now. She was focused on Colton. She was gazing up at him as if the rest of the world didn't exist.

There was no way to pretend she wanted to marry James.

It was an utter disaster, but marrying James would be an even bigger disaster.

Colton was her soul mate. Any fool could see that.

"Oh, no," I whispered under my breath.

Max was the only person who heard. "There's nothing we can do to change it."

I wished there was. I truly wished there was something I could do to fix this.

Max took my hand. "Don't even try."

"Dad—" Brooklyn said.

James burst through the doorway. "What's wrong? Is somebody hurt?"

Nat and Sophie stumbled over each other getting out of his way.

"What is *he* doing here?" James demanded.

"You know him, James?" Patrick asked.

"It's Max, Layla's..." James spotted Max holding my hand.

His gaze flew back to Colton. There was a snarl on his face and a challenging rumble in his deep tone. "Who, exactly, are you?"

"James, we have to talk," Brooklyn said.

But James's gaze didn't waver from Colton.

I squeezed Max's hand. I couldn't believe this nightmare

was unfolding in front of my eyes. I wanted to say something.
I wanted to do something. I wanted to help James and Brooklyn, but I had no idea how.

My parents appeared then, along with Brooklyn's mother.

"For goodness sake, *close the doors*," Patrick barked.

My dad shut the double doors behind him.

"Brooklyn," James said. "You better explain."

"Come with me," Colton said to Brooklyn.

Brooklyn didn't respond. She looked like she was in shock.
She was pale, and I thought she might actually faint.

I tugged my hand from Max's and elbowed Colton out of
the way. I took both of Brooklyn's hands in mine.

"Look at me," I told her. "Look at me."

She did.

"You can't decide like this."

"But—"

"You can't. Let's walk outside. Let's breathe for a minute."

She stared at me. Then the uncertainty vanished from her
face and she started to smile.

I suddenly saw the girl from the jungle gym, and the beach
and the floater—the one who got free milkshakes and raced
me until we were exhausted.

The old Brooklyn was back.

"I love you, Layla," she said.

"I know you do. I love you, too."

"You're my best and forever friend."

"I know that, too."

She looked to James. "I'm so sorry, James. I'm *so* incredibly sorry. This is all my fault." A tear then formed in her
eye. "And, Dad, please know I didn't plan for this to happen.
Please forgive me."

"What is this about?" Patrick asked.

"I have to go," she said. "I'm so…"

She looked at Colton, and he reached for her, taking her
arm, drawing her to him.

In seconds, his arm was protectively around her and he
was spiriting her out of the church foyer onto the sidewalk.

"Come with us," Max said into my ear.

I couldn't even process the request.

My attention was on James. He'd gone from ruddy anger to a face that was pale as a ghost.

Behind him, my parents looked like they'd been blind-sided, which they had. I hadn't seen that expression of confusion and disappointment on my mother's face since she caught Brooklyn and me dipping into the rum-punch bowl when we were sixteen.

I wanted to tell them Brooklyn hadn't cheated. I needed to tell them that much.

I also needed to apologize for my part in it all. I'd obviously made a mistake somewhere along the line—lots of mistakes, really.

Things would have been better if I'd left Brooklyn in Vegas. I shouldn't have tried so hard to bring her back. I should have listened to what she was trying to tell me. I shouldn't have been so selfish about wanting her for a sister-in-law.

"Let's go," Max said, taking my hand again.

I snapped it back, awash in guilt. "I can't leave."

My family was hurt. They'd been deeply wounded by Max's family. They were staring at him right now as if he was the enemy, which in many ways he was.

They felt betrayed. I'd feel betrayed if I was them. And I was the only person who could explain. Not that I had the first clue of what to say to make things better.

"It's not up to you to fix anything," Max said, seeming to read my mind.

"They're my parents. He's my brother."

"I have to go," Max said, putting a question, an invitation and a demand all into his expression at once.

"Then go," I said.

"Layla."

"Go!" I repeated.

He took a backward step, watching me as he went. Then he took another, and another, his expression hardening with each one.

My heart cried out too late.

He was already gone into the blinding sunlight.

"I know how James feels," Nat said to me.

We were on the porch at the back of my parents' house gazing at the lights in the garden.

It was Saturday, nearly a month after the debacle of the wedding. My parents had insisted James come out to the friends-and-family barbecue. They thought it was time for him to get back into circulation.

He'd kept to himself these past few weeks, angry with me, angry with the world.

"I think I do, too," I said to Nat.

I was sad and listless, as well.

I missed Max. I missed him more than I could have ever imagined. And with Brooklyn gone—off on the exotic and exciting life she'd chosen that I could barely imagine—I couldn't seem to figure out how to restart my own life here in Seattle.

I told myself it would be better in September once school started up again.

"You've never been dumped," Nat said.

"I…" I paused to think about it.

She was right.

I'd had breakups before, but I'd always been the one doing the leaving.

"It was bad with Henry," she said. "I thought he might be the one, and it sent me for a loop. But we weren't even engaged. James was left at the altar. And he was madly in love with Brooklyn. It doesn't get any worse than that."

I supposed it didn't.

I'd tried to be realistic with James, to talk him out of his funk, to tell him life would be good again. It would be great again.

But I wasn't selling it.

I wasn't even sure I was feeling it.

I knew he still blamed me. He blamed me for Vegas—

although I'd done my absolute best. And he blamed me for monopolizing Brooklyn for all those years. The one time I brought
up his outburst, he said he never had a chance. I'd never given
him a chance to be Brooklyn's soul mate.

I'd disagreed. I'd tried to explain. But he wasn't in the mood
to listen.

Looking back, I wondered if I should have tried harder to
see his side. After all, the breakup was about him. It wasn't
about me.

"Funny," I said to Nat.

"What could possibly be funny?"

"I made the same mistake with James as I did with Brooklyn. I spent all that time trying to talk her out of her emotions.
I was so focused on the logic of her marrying James that I ignored the fact that she wasn't in love with him."

"You're a math teacher," Nat said. "It's your job to be unemotional."

I supposed that was true. I mean, maybe it was true.

"I wonder if it's causation or correlation," I mused out loud.

"Huh?"

"Do you suppose being a math teacher makes me unemotional? Or did I end up being a math teacher because I was
already unemotional?"

"Does it matter?"

"I'm not sure. But I'm trying to understand myself."

"Why?"

"Because I'm making a lot of mistakes."

As I said the words, I realized they were true. They were
at the core of my funk.

I was making mistakes and losing confidence in myself.
I'd always been rock-solid in my convictions, convinced that
solid logic kept you on the right path, and that I had solid logic.
Emotions merely got in the way of good judgment.

"That doesn't sound like you."

My phone pinged with a text message for me.

I automatically glanced at it and was surprised to see
Brooklyn's name.

I'd felt too guilty to talk to her right after the canceled wedding, feeling like I owed loyalty to my family. She'd seemed to respect the difficult situation, keeping her distance.

I sure missed her.

"It's Brooklyn," I said to Nat.

Nat sat up straighter. "Has she been staying in contact?"

I shook my head. "No."

"Me, neither," Nat said. "It was a crappy thing she did. And I didn't really know what to say."

"Are you angry?" I hadn't thought about Nat or Sophie being angry at Brooklyn.

"A little. I mean, I still love Brooklyn, but she's always been this beautiful windstorm of a person, swirling through life with the world laid out in front of her, oblivious to the destruction she's left behind."

I blinked at Nat. I didn't know what to say.

I supposed it was true, at least on some level. But it wasn't Brooklyn's fault that the world treated her like a goddess. She could have taken way more advantage than she did. Considering the sycophantic men that sought her out, I always thought she stayed pretty grounded.

"I'm sorry," Nat said. "I sounded like a witch there."

"Don't be sorry," I said. "You're not completely wrong. I just think—at least on balance—she did the best she could."

Nat nodded to the phone. "You should check to see what she said."

I was dying of curiosity, so I picked up my phone from the low table in front of me.

Her message came as a shock.

"What?" Nat prompted.

"She wants me to come to San Francisco."

"To stay for free at her new boyfriend's opulent hotel?" There was a trace of sarcasm to Nat's tone.

"No. I mean, well, probably that, too. She wants me to stand up for her when she gets married to Colton."

James's voice startled me. "You have got to be joking."

Both Nat and I turned to see James walk onto the porch. "Just like that? That fast? She's going to take up with the jerk?"

"He's not—" I stopped myself.

"It does seem awfully fast," Nat said.

James plopped down in a chair across from us. "I dated her for eight years—*eight* years. We were engaged for more than a year. And she makes a decision this fast? How does that work?"

"I won't go," I said.

"Of course you won't go," Nat said.

"You should go," James said in an irritated tone.

"I'm not going to do that to you." Even as my left brain made that perfectly reasonable logical decision, my right brain zeroed in on Max.

If I went to Brooklyn's wedding, I'd see Max. I'd love to see Max. I'd honestly give almost anything to see Max—even if he was angry, which he most certainly was.

He hadn't tried to contact me at all since the wedding.

I wanted to be mad at him for that.

I wasn't mad.

I didn't know how I felt—which was the crux of my problem.

"She's your best friend," James said.

I didn't argue that point. It was empirically true.

He drummed his fingertips on the arm of the chair. "She's been your best friend since you were, what, six years old?"

"They met at my birthday party," Nat said. She looked at me, and there was a wistful look in her eyes. "I never knew why you didn't end up as my best friend."

I felt a lurch of guilt. The emotion was strong. I realized in that moment how pivotal emotion had been to the makeup of our friendships.

I'd never thought about it before. I'd never analyzed it. Brooklyn and I just clicked.

Nat was a perfectly wonderful friend, and I adored her. But there was some kind of inner magic with Brooklyn. I felt happy just being around her.

"If you don't go, you won't forgive yourself," James said to me.

"It doesn't feel right," I said.

Wow—another emotion pushing me to make a decision. I was losing it.

Logic told me I was Brooklyn's best friend. Best friends went to each other's weddings. James was hurt, but it wasn't Brooklyn's fault. If she wasn't in love with him, she wasn't in love with him. It was marrying him under those circumstances that would have been the worst wrong.

"You have to go," James said.

I looked to Nat.

She gave a shrug. "It's Brooklyn. And you're part of the world that falls in line for her."

James looked surprised by Nat's words.

But Nat didn't look annoyed. She looked accepting.

Nat was right. James was right. Logic was right.

"I'll go," I said.

I closed my eyes for a brief second and Max's image came up behind my eyelids.

He didn't enter into the equation. I was positive on that. I knew I'd never be selfish enough to use Brooklyn as an excuse to see Max.

But then the image sharpened inside my mind, along with a wave of scents and sounds and tactile memories. The thought of Max brought such a wave of joy and anticipation that I had to wonder if I'd finally mastered the art of denial.

Brooklyn met me at the San Francisco airport.

I'd worried on the plane that it would be awkward. But we hugged, and it felt perfectly natural.

When she drew back, her smile was as ordinary as ever.

"Good flight?" she asked.

It had been a fantastic flight. "You didn't have to fly me first class."

Between the first-class lounge, preboarding, the big comfy

seat and a mimosa with breakfast, I couldn't have been more spoiled.

"Colton insisted," she said.

"Quit trying to make me like him."

"Oh, you're going to like him all right. I can guarantee it."

"Bold," I said. "He can't buy my love."

Brooklyn flashed a really big diamond ring. "He bought mine."

"Yowza," I said. And I meant it.

I held her hand still and stared at the multicarat solitaire in a swirl of gold. The big stone was flanked on each side by two small emeralds. It was nontraditional, and it suited her.

"Let's go grab your bag," she said. "I've got a driver waiting."

"A driver? Like in a suit and a cap?"

She seemed to ponder that as we started walking. "I don't think he had a cap."

"Is that how you live now?" I fell into step in the crowded concourse. "Big diamonds and luxury sedans?"

"It's not like that."

I realized too late that I sounded judgmental. I didn't want to be judgmental. I wasn't judgmental. And I wasn't jealous.

At least I wasn't jealous of Brooklyn's new wealthy status. I might have been jealous of her happiness.

She looked really happy. And that made me think Colton must not be all that bad.

Brooklyn could have had James. And James was quite a catch. So if Colton was better than James, then he had to have something going for him.

If he was anything like his twin brother, he had quite a lot going for him.

I was going to see Max today.

I was going to see Max…

"Layla?" Brooklyn's voice sounded hesitant.

"What?" I gave her my full attention.

"I haven't changed."

"I know you haven't changed." I linked my arm with hers.

"Not really," she said. "Not how it counts."

"You quit your job?" I thought that was an easy assumption.

"I did."

"What will you do here, or in Vegas, or, you know, everywhere. You can't go to the spa every day."

"I'm not going to the spa every day. I might go every week. It's free for me now. Free for you this weekend, too."

"I don't think I'll be going to the spa." That wasn't where my head was at, at all.

"You can," she said.

"What are you going to do?" Now that we were talking about it, I was pretty curious about what rich people did all day.

"The Kendrick hotels have boutiques. I'm still going to be a fashion buyer, and maybe some other things, too."

"They had an opening?" I was willing to bet the owner's wife got a job whether there was an opening or not.

"I know what you're thinking."

"It's a valid thought."

"I expect they've created a special position for me for now. And everyone's going to think I'm a dilettante. And they'll probably hate me."

Her assessment seemed accurate. Although, I didn't think anyone had ever hated Brooklyn in her life. I wasn't sure how she'd cope with that.

"I'm going to have to prove myself. I'm prepared for that."

"You're prepared for people not to like you."

"I'll win them over," she said.

I believed her. And I was feeling proud of her for throwing herself into an uncomfortable situation. She could have simply gone to the spa and shopping every day. I doubted Colton would have minded.

We skirted a family pushing a huge luggage cart.

"Speaking of hating me…" she said.

"James?" I guessed.

"Is he doing okay?"

"He's getting there."

"Honestly?"

"Honestly, I think it's going to take a while. He is back to work. And he's playing tennis on Saturdays. And he did tell me to come here to be with you."

"I'm glad you came," she said.

"So am I."

Brooklyn pointed. "Carousel three. That guy there is our driver. He'll get your bag."

"It's blue and silver," I said.

"Like I won't recognize it."

Of course she'd recognize it. She was with me when I bought it. I felt silly having described it.

"I'm still me," Brooklyn said.

"I know that."

She sobered. "I didn't have a choice."

"I know that, too. I'm sorry, Brooklyn."

She looked puzzled.

"I'm sorry I pushed so hard for you to walk away from Colton. I was wrong to do that. You knew what you wanted, and I wouldn't let you tell me how sure you were."

"I wasn't sure," she said. "I got scared. I took the easy path. Marrying James was the easy path."

"It didn't end up as the easy path." I spotted my suitcase. "There it is."

Brooklyn signaled the driver and pointed to my bag.

"I try not to think about that day," she said.

I understood that. "All those guests, the flowers, the dresses. All that food."

Brooklyn looked puzzled again. "Oh, yeah."

"What were you thinking?" I asked.

"Nothing."

"Come on. Give."

She didn't answer.

"This is me," I said.

She pursed her lips, then her tone changed. "I was thinking I almost let Colton go. And that terrifies me."

Something shifted in my stomach—a burst of fear and regret.

I had let Max go that day. I sure didn't like to linger over that. When I thought about it, all I saw was the disappointment on his face, the disappointment that turned to anger as he had backed away.

Eleven

Colton's parents, David and Susan Kendrick, were gracious and welcoming. Colton was cordial, clearly giving me space. Brooklyn's parents seemed tense and uncomfortable. But they were there to support her. I admired that.

There wouldn't be a church or a walk down the aisle this time. The intimate ceremony was to take place in the Kendricks' private villa at the top of the Archway Hotel.

It was a magnificent suite with high ceilings, soaring windows and an expansive concrete patio where we'd all have a wedding dinner later on.

I was struck by the difference between this wedding and the one we'd spent a full year planning. Brooklyn had changed into a V-neck, tea-length ivory dress with a lace-covered bodice and see-through lace three-quarter-length sleeves with a full, flowing chiffon skirt. It was pretty, but hardly dramatic.

I had gone with an off-the-shoulder, teal-green satin. It had a beaded front and an asymmetrical hemline that dropped at the back. My hair was half-up, while Brooklyn's flowed in smooth waves over her shoulders.

It was clear I was more extravagantly dressed than the bride, but nobody seemed to care.

We were sipping champagne and making small talk while the hotel catering staff arranged a table and some flowers in front of the windows that overlooked the bay. A female reverend wearing a lovely cream-colored stole was lighting some candles on the small table.

The bell sounded in the villa, and what I guessed to be a butler opened the door.

I held my breath, waiting to see if it was Max.

It was, and energy rushed through me at the sight of him.

He was in a black suit, not a tux. But the effect was the same.

He looked sophisticated, handsome and confident, in his prime and at the helm of his world.

Then I saw there was a woman beside him—a beautiful blonde woman in a strapless burgundy cocktail dress. A wide band with ornate silver beading glittered beneath her bust. The two-layered skirt landed a few inches above her knees.

It was a perfect dress for dancing. And she was the perfect date for Max.

"Max, Ellen," Susan called out. "You're right on time. Come and say hello to Brooklyn's best friend, Layla."

Susan seemed to know Ellen. She seemed to know her quite well.

I felt like a fool. I'd been pining away for Max, assuming I'd angered him or hurt him, maybe even broke his heart by not leaving with him from the church that day.

Instead, here he was out on the circuit again. Or maybe she was an old girlfriend. Maybe they'd reunited. That would explain Susan's friendliness.

Whatever it was, I was totally in Max's rearview mirror.

I was never going to learn.

I took a long swig of my champagne, pulling my attention from Max and vowing not to look at him again until this was all over.

"Are we ready then?" asked the reverend.

"I'm more than ready," Colton said, and he took Brooklyn's hand.

She looked relaxed and happy—glowing like a bride should be glowing.

I took my place beside her.

Max or no Max, I was going to spend the rest of the evening being happy for Brooklyn. She deserved it.

The sun was dipping down as the reverend spoke of love, respect and commitment.

The clouds turned pink while Brooklyn and Colton said their vows.

I keep my attention firmly focused on the happy couple and the wonderful view.

Max might as well have not been there.

Except that he was there.

And I knew he was there.

I might not have been looking at him, but I was aware of his energy with every fiber of my being.

I wished my being wouldn't do that.

I wished with all my heart that I could ignore him standing there, and that I could ignore Ellen sitting behind him on the French provincial chair next to Susan and David.

Max had a girlfriend.

Short weeks ago in Vegas he'd asked me to see where our relationship might go.

I'd said no, and he'd bounced back in a heartbeat.

By the time Colton kissed the bride, I was angry with Max, and I wondered what I'd ever seen in a man so shallow.

I was mad at myself, too. I had a flawed gene or something. Eligible men made my brain turn to mush. And this eligible man had been the worst of the worst.

I glanced his way, and caught him looking back. I was mentally catapulted into his arms, into his bed, plastered against his slick naked body, which had taken me straight to Heaven.

My skin heated and my hormones rushed to life.

Then Colton whooped, and everybody clapped.

Brooklyn was married.

When Colton let her go, I gave her a warm hug. "Congratulations. I love you."

"Thanks," she said. "I'm so glad you came."

We separated. "So am I. *So* am I."

While the photographer worked with Brooklyn and Colton, and the hotel staff set up for dinner, I found my way to the powder room.

Like everything in the villa, like everything in the entire hotel, the powder room was posh and beautifully appointed.

I wasted as much time as I could fussing with my hair, washing my hands, rubbing on some wildflower-scented lotion. I had no desire to make small talk before dinner.

When I left the powder room, I found a door that led to the far end of the patio. The patio was a crescent shape, giving me privacy.

The sun had gone down, and the lights of the harbor were coming up.

It was a serene and beautiful sight. I tried to absorb the serenity, but my nerves didn't want to calm down. They were an insistent jangle of frustration and disappointment.

I heard footsteps.

I could tell it was a man.

I willed them to go away, to stay away, to let me wallow here all by myself.

I absolutely didn't want it to be Max.

It was Max.

"Don't make this harder," I said as he stopped next to me at the rail.

"Harder than what?"

"Harder than it has to be. We don't have to talk. We don't have to interact." I kept my gaze focused on the view in front of me.

"What if I want to interact?"

I gave a chopped laugh. "I can't see why you'd want to do that. I'm the one-night stand that was forced to attend your brother's wedding."

"Nobody forced you." He sounded annoyed.

"You're right. I'm here for Brooklyn. I'll always be there for Brooklyn."

"Layla."

"Go away."

"Look at me."

"No."

He angled his body to try to get in front of my face.

I kept my gaze fixed on the view.

"Why are you being like this?" he asked.

My nerves were stretched about as far as they could go.

Max had completely and unequivocally walked away from

me. He was indifferent and erratic, and all I could think was that I wanted him.

I wanted to hug him close. I wanted to kiss him. I wanted to make love with him over and over and over again.

I almost laughed. I was laughing at myself for being so out of control.

"What's funny?"

Nothing—nothing was remotely funny.

I sobered and looked him in the eyes. "What do you want from me, Max?"

"What I've always wanted from you."

"So, sex."

He frowned. "No, not sex. Why are you always talking about sex?"

"That's what we have together…" I caught myself. "I mean, that's what we had together."

"I don't want sex," he all but shouted.

Then he glanced over his shoulder toward the other end of the patio. He lowered his voice. "Of course I want sex. But I don't *only* want sex."

"Well, there is the chocolate soufflé, I suppose. But that's really only good with the sex. At least that's how I remember it. I mean, when I think about chocolate soufflé." I was babbling, but I couldn't seem to stop myself.

"Have you had too much to drink?" he asked.

"I don't believe so."

"You were there, right?"

I had no idea what he was talking about. "I was where, when?"

"In the church, at your brother's wedding, when I asked you to come away with me, to be with me, to *stay* with me."

"Did you mean for the weekend?" I asked, my own voice getting louder as I grew angry.

He opened his mouth to answer, but I didn't let him.

"How fast did you find her?" I asked. "Same day? Next day? Did you ask her to come away with you, too?"

"Who?" Max barked.

I didn't seem to care that others might be listening. I knew that was weird. But I didn't quite know how to stop it. "What do you mean, *who*?"

"It's a one-word question, Layla."

"Let me spell out a one-word answer—*E-L-L-E-N*." I thought about the spelling for a second. "At least I assume it's one *L*. That would be the normal spelling." I realized too late my dramatic answer would lose some of its oomph if I got the spelling wrong.

"Ellen?" Max asked.

"Give the man a prize."

"My cousin?"

I stilled.

My brain flatlined.

Ellen was his cousin?

"Layla," Max said, his voice echoing in my ears.

I was mortified. Now there was an emotion for you. I had absolutely no trouble feeling that one.

"I thought she was your girlfriend." There was no way I could talk myself out of this corner. The bald truth was my only option.

Max lowered his voice. "I don't have a girlfriend."

"How was I supposed to know that?"

"I was with you less than a month ago."

"You weren't exactly *with* me."

"What would you call it? And don't you dare say it was a one-night stand."

I struggled for the right words. "Well, we'd called it quits in Vegas."

"You walked away in Vegas. I came after you."

I shook my head. That wasn't exactly what had happened. "Colton came after Brooklyn. You were with him."

Max took my hand.

I knew I should pull away, but for the life of me, I didn't have the strength.

"Colton might have come after Brooklyn. But *I* came after *you*. My brother is perfectly capable of kidnapping a bride all on his own. He didn't need my help." Max paused. "I came after you, and you turned me down flat."

I remembered his expression all over again. "I..."

He waited. "You told me to go, in no uncertain terms."

He was right. I had done that.

"I didn't mean forever," I said.

This time it was Max who went still. He drew a deep breath. "It sounded like you meant forever."

"I couldn't leave my family then."

I realized I could leave them now.

It would be tough, and it would take them a while to get over it, and maybe it wasn't the smartest, most logical thing for me to do. After all, I hadn't known Max very long, and what we had might or might not last. I might be hurting my brother and my parents over something that wasn't even going to last.

But this was too important.

I was in love with Max.

It was another emotion that was perfectly clear to me. Two in one day, how about that?

"I love you," I said.

It was a stupid thing to say out loud, especially under the circumstances, and especially since he hadn't said it first, and because it laid me bare and vulnerable. But the odd thing was I didn't care.

"Not as much as I love you," he said.

My heart all but shouted with joy. I made a last-ditch fight for logic. "You can't know yours is more."

"I loved you first," he said. "That makes mine more."

"You can't know you were first."

He moved his mouth toward mine. "I don't care." He drew closer and closer.

It wasn't a contest. It wasn't—

He kissed me, and my world lit up with love and joy, excitement and hope.

It was a long time before we moved a few inches apart.

"Neither do I," I whispered to him.

"*There* you are." It was Brooklyn. "Quit ruining Layla's makeup and get in here for the pictures."

Max grinned.

"She doesn't seem surprised," I said.

"She's been with us for a month. She knows how I feel."

I gave Brooklyn a reproachful look.

She grinned like she didn't care.

Max put a hand on the small of my back, urging me toward the door.

"Some best friend you are," I said to Brooklyn.

"I didn't want to push," she said.

"*This time* you don't want to push?" Brooklyn had been talking me into outlandish things since grade school.

She turned serious. "You had to figure it out for yourself. I couldn't afford to be wrong."

I realized in that moment that she was smarter than me. I'd tried to push her in the wrong direction and nearly ruined everyone's lives.

She went ahead of us, joining Colton in the living room.

Max raised my hand to his lips and put a featherlight kiss on my knuckles.

"Now what?" I asked.

He gave a contented smile. "Now, we have dinner with my family, then wedding cake, then my suite and then chocolate soufflé."

My heart seemed to bloom inside my chest. "I do love chocolate soufflé."

When I pictured my wedding—and I'd pictured it a lot over the years—I imagined a long white dress, a flowing train, maybe a nod to a veil, nothing covering my face, but a bit of gauze and lace streaming from my hair. And the flowers, I loved a wildflower bouquet: daisies and primroses, violets and cornflowers. I pictured greens and colors in a messy bundle, maybe tied with ribbon instead of arranged into a plastic handle.

It would be at St. Fidelis's, our family church, which was big

enough to hold all the friends and relatives that would come
to celebrate. I wanted a rehearsal dinner at the tennis club—it
had a magnificent view of the harbor.

And the reception, ah, the reception. There were three possible hotels in the downtown area. I'd thought I'd tour them
and make my choice. There'd be a nice dinner, a band, dancing
and a huge cake, maybe five tiers, but not a fruitcake. I wanted
people to enjoy eating the cake. Vanilla pound cake, maybe,
or something layered with puff pastry, buttercream icing for
sure. I absolutely adored buttercream icing.

In all those years, in all my musings, I'd never once pictured myself getting married in Vegas.

Don't get me wrong, an Elvis chapel might be right for some
people, but it wasn't what I had pictured. We were set up in
a wonderful corner of the atrium at the Canterbury Sands. It
was tasteful and beautiful and, it turns out, everything I really
wanted in a wedding. Because all I really wanted was Max.

Brooklyn was here, but she was the only person from my
side.

I knew my eloping would upset my family. But I didn't
know how to do this without upsetting my family. A Seattle
wedding, even a small one, where I married Colton's brother
would be unthinkable. A big wedding was completely out of
the question.

September was coming fast, and Max and I were absolutely
sure about our future. I wasn't going back to teaching at North
Hill High, and I couldn't imagine telling my family I was quit-
ting my job and moving in with Max without marrying him.

So here we were.

I'd call them later tonight and give them the good news. At
least I'd act like it was good news. It was good news to me. I
couldn't be happier.

We were on a small patio, near the babbling brook, beneath
the palms and mesquites and amongst the cacti and wildflow-
ers blooming in the gardens.

I'd gone with a simple white dress, knee-length, with a
scooped neckline and wide shoulder straps, with just a hint

of eyelet in the breezy cotton fabric. But I had my wildflower bouquet and some really awesome shoes, white and jeweled with high, high heels. I only had to stand in them for thirty minutes or so.

"When you know, you know," Brooklyn whispered to me in an I-told-you-so tone.

I'd give her that one. She had told me so.

"I know," I said back.

"I know you know," she said with a grin. "Now, look." She nodded her head.

I looked down the pathway expecting to see Max and Colton. His parents were already here, as was the reverend who had married Brooklyn and Colton.

To my surprise, I saw Nat and Sophie.

I think I gave a gasp because Brooklyn laughed at me.

"How did you…?"

"Brooklyn told us," Nat called out. "There was no way we were missing this."

"I can't believe you're here," I said to both of them.

"I can't believe you weren't going to tell us," Sophie said.

"You know it's—" I spotted James—my brother, James—coming down the pathway.

Shock didn't begin to describe my reaction. Then my reaction turned to fear.

How was he here? Why was he here? *What* was he going to do?

"Hi, Layla," he said. He sounded calm, like the old James—the James-who-wasn't-so-angry-at-me-that-he'd-never-get-over-it James.

"I don't understand." I didn't.

"Brooklyn called me," he said.

I sought out Brooklyn again, not bothering to disguise my astonishment. "*Why* would you do that?"

"They're your family," Brooklyn said.

At that very second, I saw my parents.

They were smiling, and looked for all the world as if this were a perfectly normal wedding.

My mom pulled me into a hug. "It's not your fault," she said and held me tight.

My dad hugged me next.

Then I stepped back to take in everyone.

"We're all happy for you," James said.

I watched his expression closely, not quite trusting it, worried about what would happen when Colton arrived with Max.

"Are you okay?" I asked.

His gaze slid to Brooklyn. "This is weird," he said.

"I'll say it's weird." My brain was scrambling to take it all in.

"I'll manage," he said. "And I know it's not your fault. I'm sorry I said those things."

I had to ask. "Did you really feel that way?"

James shrugged. "Sometimes. But looking back… Clearly, as they say, it wasn't you. It was me."

"I'm so sorry."

He shook his head. "Don't be. I'm fine. I'll *be* fine."

My mom reached for my hand. "This is your day, honey. Don't you worry about anything else."

Max and Colton came around the corner from Max's suite patio.

They both stopped dead and stared at my family.

Colton saw James and a muscle ticked in his cheek.

"You didn't *tell* them?" I asked Brooklyn.

"I was worried they'd be worried."

A few seconds slipped past in silence.

It was my dad who stepped up, walking toward Max and Colton, holding out his hand to Max.

"We haven't been properly introduced," he said. "I'm Al Gillen."

"Max Kendrick." Max shook his hand. His expression remained wary.

"I understand you're marrying my daughter."

"Yes, sir."

My dad looked around the garden. "I can't say this was what I was expecting."

"In a wedding?" Max asked.

"In a Vegas wedding," my dad answered. "It's nice here. It's really nice."

Max caught my gaze. He looked as confused as I felt.

"Brooklyn invited everyone," I said.

Colton's eyebrows went up, and he quickly sought out Brooklyn.

Brooklyn gave her best sparkly, love-me smile. "Everyone is happy for Layla. And everyone is happy for Max." She took my hand. "Let's do this. We can finish the introductions later."

Max was already moving to my side.

"Are you okay?" he asked as we positioned ourselves in front of the white vine-entwined arch.

"I'm pretty stunned," I said.

"And your brother?"

I gave a glance to James. He was staying well away from Colton, but otherwise he looked like he was handling it.

"It must have been his decision to come."

Max squeezed my hand. "I'm glad. I'm really glad your family is here."

"So am I." For a second I had to fight a tear of joy.

"They love you," Max said. "And I love you."

"This is a good beginning," I said, facing the reverend, seeing my life with Max flowing out like a pathway in front of me.

Brooklyn would be in our lives, and Colton would be in our lives, and our families would be there to support us.

In time, James's broken heart would heal. This was the start of that, too.

"Family and friends," the reverend began. "We're gathered here to celebrate a day of happiness."

Max put an arm around me and pulled me to him.

I rested my head on his shoulder, feeling his steadiness and strength, knowing deep in my soul my decision was right. Our happiness was going to last forever.

* * * * *

COMING SOON!

We really hope you enjoyed reading this book. If you're looking for more romance, be sure to head to the shops when new books are available on

Thursday 9th January

To see which titles are coming soon, please visit

millsandboon.co.uk/nextmonth

MILLS & BOON

JOIN US ON SOCIAL MEDIA!

Stay up to date with our latest releases, author news and gossip, special offers and discounts, and all the behind-the-scenes action from Mills & Boon...

 millsandboon

 millsandboonuk

millsandboon

It might just be true love...

GET YOUR ROMANCE FIX!

Get the latest romance news, exclusive author interviews, story extracts and much more!

blog.millsandboon.co.uk

MILLS & BOON

THE HEART OF ROMANCE

A ROMANCE FOR EVERY KIND OF READER

MODERN

Prepare to be swept off your feet by sophisticated, sexy and seductive heroes, in some of the world's most glamourous and romantic locations, where power and passion collide.
8 stories per month.

HISTORICAL

Escape with historical heroes from time gone by. Whether your passion is for wicked Regency Rakes, muscled Vikings or rugged Highlanders, awaken the romance of the past.
6 stories per month.

MEDICAL

Set your pulse racing with dedicated, delectable doctors in the high-pressure world of medicine, where emotions run high and passion, comfort and love are the best medicine.
6 stories per month.

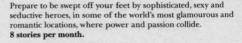

True Love

Celebrate true love with tender stories of heartfelt romance, from the rush of falling in love to the joy a new baby can bring, and a focus on the emotional heart of a relationship.
8 stories per month.

Desire

Indulge in secrets and scandal, intense drama and plenty of sizzling hot action with powerful and passionate heroes who have it all: wealth, status, good looks...everything but the right woman.
6 stories per month.

HEROES

Experience all the excitement of a gripping thriller, with an intense romance at its heart. Resourceful, true-to-life women and strong, fearless men face danger and desire - a killer combination!
8 stories per month.

DARE

Sensual love stories featuring smart, sassy heroines you'd want as a best friend, and compelling intense heroes who are worthy of them.
4 stories per month.

To see which titles are coming soon, please visit

millsandboon.co.uk/nextmonth

MILLS & BOON
MEDICAL
Pulse-Racing Passion

Set your pulse racing with dedicated, delectable doctors in the high-pressure world of medicine, where emotions run high and passion, comfort and love are the best medicine.

Eight Medical stories published every month, find them all at:

millsandboon.co.uk

MILLS & BOON
True Love

Romance from the Heart

Celebrate true love with tender stories of heartfelt romance, from the rush of falling in love to the joy a new baby can bring, and a focus on the emotional heart of a relationship.

Eight True Love stories published every month, find them all at:

millsandboon.co.uk/TrueLove

MILLS & BOON

HEROES

At Your Service

Experience all the excitement of a gripping thriller, with an intense romance at its heart. Resourceful, true-to-life women and strong, fearless men face danger and desire - a killer combination!

Eight Heroes stories published every month, find them all at:

millsandboon.co.uk/Heroes

MILLS & BOON

HISTORICAL

Awaken the romance of the past

Escape with historical heroes from time gone by. Whether your passion is for wicked Regency Rakes, muscled Viking warriors or rugged Highlanders, indulge your fantasies and awaken the romance of the past.

Six Historical stories published every month, find them all at:

millsandboon.co.uk/ Historical

WANT EVEN MORE
ROMANCE?
SUBSCRIBE AND SAVE TODAY!

'Mills & Boon books, the perfect way to escape for an hour or so.'

MISS W. DYER

'Excellent service, promptly delivered and very good subscription choices.'

MISS A. PEARSON

'You get fantastic special offers and the chance to get books before they hit the shops.'

MRS V. HALL

Visit millsandboon.co.uk/Subscribe
and save on brand new books.

MILLS & BOON
A ROMANCE FOR EVERY READER

- **FREE** delivery direct to your door

- **EXCLUSIVE** offers every month

- **SAVE** up to 25% on pre-paid subscriptions

SUBSCRIBE AND SAVE

millsandboon.co.uk/Subscribe

LET'S TALK

Romance

For exclusive extracts, competitions
and special offers, find us online:

 facebook.com/millsandboon

@MillsandBoon

@MillsandBoonUK

Get in touch on 01413 063232

For all the latest titles coming soon, visit
millsandboon.co.uk/nextmonth